KEL
+
VICTOR

Born in Liverpool in 1966, Niall Griffiths now lives in Wales. *Grits*, his first novel, is to be filmed for television. He is also the author of *Sheepshagger* and, most recently, *Stump*.

ALSO BY NIALL GRIFFITHS

Grits
Sheepshagger
Stump

Niall Griffiths

KELLY
+
VICTOR

V

VINTAGE

Published by Vintage 2003

2 4 6 8 10 9 7 5 3 1

First published in Great Britain in 2002 by
Jonathan Cape

Vintage
Random House, 20 Vauxhall Bridge Road,
London SW1V 2SA

Random House Australia (Pty) Limited
20 Alfred Street, Milsons Point, Sydney
New South Wales 2061, Australia

Random House New Zealand Limited
18 Poland Road, Glenfield,
Auckland 10, New Zealand

Random House (Pty) Limited
Endulini, 5A Jubilee Road, Parktown 2193,
South Africa

The Random House Group Limited Reg. No. 954009
www.randomhouse.co.uk

A CIP catalogue record for this book
is available from the British Library

ISBN 0 099 42205 0

Papers used by Random House are natural, recyclable products made from wood grown in sustainable forests. The manufacturing processes conform to the environmental regulations of the country of origin

Printed and bound in Great Britain by
Cox & Wyman Limited, Reading, Berkshire

TO DEBBO

VICTOR

I sleep, but my heart waketh; it is the voice of my beloved that knocketh, saying, Open to me, my sister, my love, my dove, my undefiled: For my head is filled with dew, and my locks with the drops of the night.

I have put off my coat; how shall I put it on? I have washed my feet; how shall I defile them?

My beloved put in his hand by the hole of the door, and my bowels were moved for him.

The Song of Solomon, 5: 2–4

Jesus Christ. She is fuckin gorgeous. I can't take me eyes off her. I haven't slept for three nights and me eyeballs are burning like I've been staring at the sun an all thee really wanner do is slam shut like the metal grille over the bar will do in a couple of hours but I can't stop lookin at her. She's fuckin amazing. I just can't stop lookin, altho gawping is probly a better word for what I'm doing, *gawping* – gob hangin open, encrusted eyes drooping, I must look a right fuckin state altho, it must be said, no different to everyone else here, downstairs in Magnet, seein that it's three days inter the new millennium and everyone here started partying last century. The whole bleedin place is coming down; a few brave souls are twitchin spastically across the dance floor in some parody of dancing, but most people are just sittin slumped, wasted, staring down at table tops or the glowin ends of ther cigarettes. There's not enough energy in this whole friggin place to power a light bulb. That girl over there, tho . . . she's like a torch in all this gloom. Glowing an putting everythin around her in the shade, even her mates, the one with the bleached crop and the other one with all the caked-on make-up an her hair standin up a full foot from the top of her head. She's not even that special to look at, the girl, no mad clothes or mad hairstyle or anythin, she's just . . . I dunno . . . somethin about her. Some big fuckin unusual something about her. Like a rare animal I've never seen before, or, no, like some *mythical* animal that I never believed existed until I laid eyes on it. The lights down here flashin across her face, red an then white, red an then white. Illuminated red, illuminated white. Curly strands of sweaty-lookin hair danglin in her eyes. Gemstone choker around her neck. Red an then white. She keeps glancing up at me, one quick glance then she looks away again. She knows I'm lookin at her. Jesus, I must look a right fuckin wasted mess; all's I wanner do right now, fuckin heaven to me now, would be to go to bed with her and curl up an go to sleep, just drift off to sleep with me face pressed against her back, breathin her in. I'm gunner go over an talk to her. Next time she's on her own up at the bar or wharrever, I mean I don't wanner look a twat in front of her, an my, mates if she knocks me back, now, do I? Too fuckin right I don't. Not in the delicate state I'm in. She's glancing up at me again. She's smiling. Is that smile for me? Is that an invitation? I can see her teeth. I can see dimples in her cheeks, red an then white. I can see nothing of her now cos suddenly Dermot's daft fat face is filling me entire field of vision.

—Dermot!

Craig an Quockie leap up an on him like lions wanting to greet a gazelle to death, knuckling his head, chucking his cheeks. He just grins an takes it all. A sloppy grin; he's still pissed by the looks. He was so out of it when he boarded the Dun Laoighaire ferry seven days ago that we had to help him up the gangplank an it doesn't look like he's sobered up yet, which, knowin Dermot, is no fuckin surprise in the slightest. Human friggin hoover, that's ar Derm.

Craig's hangin around his neck, yellin into his ear over the loud music: —Yer ahl twat, Dermot! Thought yer weren't coming back til tomorrer!

Dermot looks at his watch squinty-eyed. —It *is* tomorrow! Half past one in the morning! How was yeh New Year's!?

—Ask me when it's over, lar! We're still fuckin on it!

Quockie goes off to the bar to get bevvies.

—Y'alright there, Victor!?

I look up at Dermot. —Not bad, mate, yeh!

—Yeh dancing?!

Ah, the old routine. —Yis asking?!

—I'm asking!

—Well, fuck off!

He roars with laughter an sits down opposite me.

—Lookin a wee bit fucked, there, Victor! Worth it, was it?!

There's no need to think about that. —Yeh! Too fuckin right it was!

An it *was*, as well, from what I can remember of it all;

the party at Quockie's, the Creamfields down at the docks, the whole fuckin Mersey like a river of light . . . The big TV screens showin the celebrations crawlin across the planet towards us, Australia, India, Turkey, Russia . . . coming closer every hour. This immense happy thing moving across the globe towards us. Truly fuckin wonderful. I'd never seen so many people in tears. Apart from when the Scum put two past us in the final minute, of course. An after Hillsborough.

Dermot tells us about his New Year's party, a typical Dermot story, involving vast amounts of drink and drugs and dirty sex. Quockie returns from the bar, puts a pint of Guinness in front of me an ruffles me hair. I smile at him and say 'Ta' but I don't think I can drink that Guinness; me throat's beginning to close up all sore an swollen, me nose is stinging like I've snorted flame an I can feel me eyes shrinkin back into me skull, actually creeping back in there like snails into ther shells. Dermot's ramblin on an Craig an Quockie ar listenin an laughin loud an I'm craning me neck to look over Dermot's pumpkin shoulder at the girl, *the* girl, who's now talkin to her mate with the piled-up hair, ther faces close, serious-looking. I wish *I* was that close to her. I'd be able to smell her if I was, an she'd smell like lemons or something, mints. Still talkin into her friend's ear, she looks over at me an grins. Definitely a grin. At me. Unmistakable, a come-here-an-talk-to-me grin, that was. Deffo. An fuck it, I friggin well *will*. I'll go to the bog first to check me legs, see if ther still workin, like, see if thee can support me, an then I'll go over there an talk to her. So fuckin what if she knocks me back? It's happened before. No worries, I'll just crash back at Quockie's place or somewhere so I don't have to come down on me own. No big deal, being knocked back. Just one of those wanky things that this fuckin life's full of. One of those wanky little humiliating embarrassing shitty disgustin little things.

Dermot leans over the table an pokes me hard in the chest.

—Oi! I don't think you've been lissenin to a single fuckin word I've just said! Praps ye'd like to share with the whole group what it is that's so much more interestin than Dermot's millennium celebrations!

7

I nod over his shoulder an he spins in his seat to look, as do Quockie an Craig. Aw Christ, she saw that, the three of them spinning as one to gawp. That's pure fuckin embarrassin.

—Don't all fuckin stare at her, Jesus!

Dermot turns back, shaking his head. —Who, Victoria?! Yer one with the big hair?! Fuck no, my man, don't go anywhere near! That's Victoria Halligan! She's a whore! A what d'ye call it, a . . . thingio . . . a vixen . . .

—A VIXEN?! Craig looks flummoxed.

—Yeh, ye know! A thingio! Whips an chains an all that gear!

—Whips an chains . . . That's a dominatrix, Dermot, yer soft get!

—That's the one!

—Vixen me hole! That's a fuckin female fox!

—That's the one! Knew it had an 'x' in it somewhere, like! But don't ye go anywhere fuckin near that one, Victor! Not unless ye want to pay for the privilege of bein tied up an flogged with a big dildo up yeer arse!

Craig grins. —Voice of experience there, ey!

Dermot nods. —Yeh!

—Christ! I was only fuckin joking!

Dermot shakes his head an puffs out his cheeks. —Never again, tho, son! Never a–fuckin–gain!

He goes off into another story an then I'm standing, me legs surprisingly steady, then I'm walkin across the dance floor between the twitching people tryin not to stumble an at the same time tryin to sway me hips a bit, some feeble attempt at lookin sexy in case she's watching me. I feel self-conscious an awkward an completely fuckin wasted, it's like the act of walking just these few metres has finally exhausted the last shred of energy in me body an I'll collapse, here, I'll just any minute shut down an fall asleep here on the dance floor, curled up tightly into a ball. I stumble over the step leading up to the toilets an feel me face flush red. If she saw me do that, she'll be laughing now, fuckin laughing, or, what's even worse, feelin embarrassed for me. That's fucked it all, now. I've got no bleedin chance. That two fuckin inches of raised floor has blown wharrever chance I might've had with her. She won't want to know me now. Ridiculous pathetic wasted bastard tryin to look sexy walkin across the dance floor an trippin up over the step. She's probly sniggerin with her mates now, all of them waitin for me to come back out of the bogs so thee can watch me make a dickhead of meself again. Sniggering behind ther hands. Ther hands with filed an polished fingernails an rings an bracelets an maybe a small scar here an there which I'd want to know the history of, which would cause an ache in my heart to not know the history of.

Cool an quiet in the bogs, the clean water cascading down the urinal that covers one whole wall, you piss directly into the cascading curtain of clean water. Just the very act of doing that feels somehow cleansing, refreshin, altho I can feel spilled piss soaking into the soles of me trainies an me own piss is all thick an syrupy, orangey-yellow murky, a foul smell risin from it like detergent or somethin from all the chemicals I've ingested over the last few days. So many fuckin chemicals all leavin me body now an all I really wanner do is sleep, just drift away off into sleep and sleep for fuckin ever. Quockie an Craig'll probly be up for carryin on the party now that Dermot's back in the city but I might just go an crash somewhere. Or might not. Dermot an his irrepressible energy'll wake me up, no doubt. Craig's probly sacked the idea of a recovery trip, a chill-out holiday to Wales tomorrow cos he hasn't slept for ages either an he'll be in no fit state to drive, so I can spend all day tomorrow in bed. Just curl up under the covers an do nowt. I'll have another bevvy now an see how I feel after that; a vodka an orange or something, the orange for the dehydration and the vodka for the kick. I suppose that's what I'll do. Fuck, it's what I bleedin well *always* do, innit?

This piss is never-ending, all the toxins sluicing out through me knob, an it's nice to feel them go an just stare into the water falling in front of me eyes but three lads come into the bogs an two of them go off into a cubicle together an thee other stands guard at the door, leanin back against it, arms folded, face set. Out of the corner of me eye I see it's Darren Taylor, fuckin mad psycho stabber Darren Taylor, an I can feel him glaring at the back of me head an I know from past experience that soon it'll be a case of 'the fuck's *your* fuckin problem, lar?', so I squeeze out the last few drops an shake off an leave the toilets without washin me hands even tho I want to cos Darren'd probly see that as some evidence of effeminacy or something and a perfect excuse to administer a leathering. He's *that* bad; damaged fuckin goods. I saw him glass a Blackburn fan in the Grapes last season after a cup tie, for no other reason than Liverpool lost 1–0, and this bloke wasn't one of the travelling army, fuck no, he was just a family man with two small kids in tow. Darren left him under a table where he'd crawled for protection, his hands over his face and blood spurting like a fountain through his fingers, his two kids screaming for ther dad. A wrong one, Darren Taylor; bad, fuckin *rotten* inside, like. There's too fuckin many like him in this city. In this world. A fuckin sickness. No lie. Place's fuckin full of em.

Outside the toilets, into the corridor that leads to the dance floor, the music again in me head pounding, I take three steps into the noise an there's a tap on me shoulder. Just two quick taps like, fairly hard as if delivered with a rigid finger. Aw fuck, I'm thinkin, Darren's fuckin followed me outside. Keep walkin or turn to face? Keepin walkin would be ignorance, construed as a definite insult like, so heart beating I turn to face not Darren's sneering pockmarked dial but *her*, that girl, the one with the hair an the smile an the gemstone choker, the one I've been gawping at all fuckin night. All her clear skin an wayward tresses. Me heart begins to boom.

—Are you alright?!

I try to swallow but there's no spit. —What?!

—Are! You! Alright?!

—Yeh! Why?!

—I saw yer fall over the step an thought yer might be feelin unwell! Sick or something! So I came over to see if yer needed any help or anythin!

—No, I'm fine!

She leans in closer. —What?!

—I said, no, thanks! I'm fine! Just dead fuckin tired, like!

She nods. —I'm the fuckin same! It's been a good long

party! Haven't stopped for a week! No sleep, no food! I'm fuckin *knackered*!

—You *know* it!

—What?!

—I said, you *know* it!

She looks puzzled for a moment then yells: —Yeh!

She leans closer again. Very close. Me face burns at the proximity of her as if she's giving off heat or like I'm drawing, sucking heat out of her. She smells kind of musky, a sweatiness underneath her faint soapiness as if she hasn't washed for a few days an she's shoutin somethin in me ear but all I can see is her face in the lights, the red an the white, the bloodshot lace in the yellowed whites of her eyes an her thick lips all cracked an dry an scummy in the red an white flashing lights. How fuckin gorgeous she looks like this.

She's lookin intently at my face as if she's expecting an answer. God, she is so fuckin gorgeous. I've never seen such a face as this one here in me eyes.

—What?!

—I said! She puts a hand lightly on me shoulder an I almost involuntarily flinch away from that soft touch, so hot, so weighty. Her breath on me ear. —I said! Do yer wanner go upstairs! Where it's quieter! I'm sick of havin to shout at people!

—Yeh! Okay! I nod too vigorously an follow her across thee almost empty dance floor, just one gurning lad in a Carlsberg shirt, no one else. On the other side Quockie ambushes me an grabs me head in both his hands. I look at the girl an she points upwards an I nod an watch her climb the stairs, the band of bare back between her cropped top an jeans, the fall of her dirty hair almost obscuring the large black flower tattoo on her shoulder blade. Her small steps, the delicate movements of her small arse. It's like a huge hole has opened up in me chest an is slurping everything in.

—Victor!

Quockie swivels my head in his hands to face him.

—Victor! Have yer pulled, man?!

—Don't know! Maybe! We're just goin upstairs to talk like!

—Well, don't you forget! Tomorrer! We'll pick yer up! Two o'clock downstairs in thee Everyman!

—Alright!

—You'd berrer fuckin be there, lar! Tellin yer! No lyin in with the judy!

—Alright!

—I mean it! Don't fuckin lerrus down, Victor!

—I won't, man! I'll be there!

—Everyman bistro, two o'clock! No fuckin later!

—YEH!

Quockie puts a big sloppy kiss on me forehead an then lets go an I see Dermot grinning an givin me the thumbs-up, Craig bellowin something at me which I've got no chance whatso-fuckin-ever of hearing so I just flap me hands at them all an go up to the upstairs bar. Me gob's dry an me hands're tingling. I take the steps two at a time with an energy I never in a million years would've thought I had, shufflin sideways-on like a crab through that group of scallies who never seem to do anything else but stand here at the top of the Magnet stairs in a silent pimply huddle. Thee never give anyone any grief or anythin, they just stand here, mumbling, twitching, sipping alcopops. Probly bagheads. It's just as packed up here as it was downstairs but it's a fuck of a lot quieter, no music, just a babble of voices, and me heart starts to thump but in the wrong way when I can't see the girl but it rights itself again when I recognise the tangled back of her head at the bar talkin to Sadie, the pretty Manc barmaid (an City fan, fair do's) with the specs an the blonde hair, used to work in the Number 7 bistro with all thee other pretty waitresses, or most of them anyway. Nice to spend an afternoon in the Number 7, seeing the sights. One of Dermot's favourite cake-and-beer-on-a-comedown places, that is.

I make me way over to the bar an stand next to her. She smiles at me an hands me a pint of Guinness.

—I didn't know what you were drinking, so . . .

—Nah, this is fine.

—I saw yer drinking it downstairs see so I thought: safest bet.

—Ta.

I sip it; warm and manky. The Guinness is friggin hanging in
this upper bar but I'm gunner drink it anyway. God, I'd drink
piss if she handed it to me. I'd drink fuckin *strychnine* if she
handed it to me, the silver rings on her fingers an the cluster of
bracelets both leather and steel around her thin, white wrist.

—Eeyar, there's a space over there.

—Alright.

I follow her over to the big windows at the front of the
bar which look out on to Hardman Street, crammed traffic an
teeming people, big jostling groups of them, long strings of them
silent but colourful behind the glass, the party continuing.

—God, look at it, she says, looking over her shoulder through
the glass. —It's like the world'll never be the same again.

I look at her looking, see the strained muscles in her craned
neck, the prominent sinews bulging the material of her choker.
Sharp line of her jaw, the kohl caked into crumbs around her
eyes. A big bloke in the street pulls faces at her through the
window an she smiles at him then turns to me.

—I'm Kelly. What's yer name? Who are yer?

—Victor.

—Victor?

—Yeh.

She wrinkles her nose. —That's not a very common name.
Don't meet many people called Victor.

—I know. It's me dad. He used to love those epic gladiator
films in the sixties an seventies, like, an there was one actor
called Victor Mature. Me dad used to think he was ace, this
feller, so that's what he named his firstborn: Victor. Me. He
was gutted when he found out that the actor, this Victor
Mature bloke, in real life was a big puffy coward who used
to cry in his trailer an who refused to fight the lions an tigers
until thee were drugged an had ther teeth an claws pulled.
By then tho it was too late, so . . . I shrug. —I'm stuck with
it. Victor.

She looks me up an down, just once an quickly. —Nah, it's
good. Victor. It suits yis. Better than a borin old fuckin Dave
or Steve.

—Yeh.

She takes a pull at her bottle of Source. —So how was yer millennium? What did yer do?

—Loadser stuff. Did yer go the docks? The Creamfields, like?

—Seventy quid? Fuck that. There was a free party out at Otterspool, spent New Year's Eve there. You could see the lights an everythin from there, it was sound. Dead impressive, like. I was expectin some fartin little firework display but it was spectacular, really. Dead impressive.

—Even better close up, tho.

—Yeh, but was it worth seventy quid? The Pier Head do, like?

—Dunno. Never paid. Craig, that's one of the lads I was with downstairs, he has some connections with *Mixmag* or something so he got us free passes. Don't know whether I would've considered it seventy quid well spent like if I had've paid but for free it was great. Had to go somewhere, didn't I? Town was fuckin dead.

—I know, yeh. Most pubs closed at ten. Streets were completely fuckin deserted. An good on the punters for stayin away, I reckon; the landlords were too bleedin greedy. Twenny quid to get in, at least three quid a bevvy. People made ther own entertainment an sacked it all off. Good on em.

She grins and goes: —People power.

—Yeh.

I sip at the warm, sour Guinness and watch her over the rim of the glass. Is this it, then? Is it gunner be this easy? Five minutes or so of small talk an then back to her place? Maybe not, no; maybe she thinks I'm boring. Maybe she thinks I'm ugly close up. Maybe she prefers taller fellers. Or maybe she was just heartily sick of me gawping like a twat at her an wants someone to escort her home an we'll get to her door and she'll say 'Thanks, tara' an fuck off away an the only time I'll ever see her again is to gawp at her some more across a pub.

The way her lips bulge as she sucks at the bottle, bulging outwards so I can see the pinker, unadorned flesh closer to her teeth behind the maroon lipstick. When she swallows, her eyelids slide slowly down over her pale grey eyes.

She catches me looking an I cough an she smiles.

—Yer look exhausted.

—I am, aye. Absolutely fucked. Haven't slept since the twentieth century.

—Come on, then. She finishes the bottle an places it on the narrow window ledge behind her. —Let's go back to mine. Come back to my place.

Without waiting for an answer she turns an walks out an I leave the rest of me pint on the floor an follow her, out into the blast of cold air an the noise of the city like a slap on me face, once twice forehand backhand, as if it's challenging me to a duel. Pistols an wigs at dawn. The girl – Kelly, did she say? Kelly, aye – grabs hold of my hand an squeezes tight. There is ozone in thee air from the firework displays an faintly I can smell the sea. I can hear sitar music from somewhere, behind the people chanting and cars honking an engines revving. And the dance beat that's been a constant presence for the past ninety-six hours has now kicked off inside me chest: Dumfdumfdumfdumf.

—How far is it back to yours? I ask without looking at her. —Do we need a taxi?

—It's not too far. A cab would be nice like but we'd never get one here, we'd have to walk down to Chinatown an if we do that then we might as well walk back to mine. Same distance about. Are yer alright? Can yer manage it? Ten or fifteen minutes?

—Yeh. I smile at her an she smiles back an gives me hand a squeeze. Her skin is cold and smooth. —I'm fine.

We walk down Hope Street between the two cathedrals, colossal an illuminated in the night, blue mist around ther steeples. Party detritus is everywhere, burst balloons an streamers an broken glass, empty bags, bits of food. Clusters of people either trudge tiredly homewards or sway an sing on corners. Cackling laughter an whistles.

—I remember when I was little, Kelly says. —The year 2000 seemed like this massive mad date, this, like, magical friggin time in the far future when we'd all be driving around in floatin cars an livin on pills. We could have holidays on Mars an stuff. Everythin was gunner be, like, suddenly different, all fuckin science fiction, aliens livin in ar cities an us livin on other planets, that kinder stuff. But nothin's changed, tho, has it? An nothin *will* change, either. It's all gunner stay the same. Nowt'll ever be any different.

—Apart from the livin on pills bit. *That's* come true.

She laughs. —*Is* right. An that millennium bug; now what the fuck was all that about? Nowt went wrong at all. People were goin on about catastrophe, war, an look what's happened. Fuck all.

—You know it.

I want to tell her that the human forces that inform us about ar lives, that tell us what's happened to us and what's going to happen to us an how we should feel about such things know absolutely fuckin nothing about how we live and how we feel an that ther pontifications have the hidden agenda of shaping, of moulding us into easily manageable forms. And, too, I wanner tell her that this is an intolerable situation an that sometimes I think that I really can't stand it and that sometimes I think it will cause me to implode, shrivel up, die, but I don't. Instead I imagine how her skin will feel and wonder if I'll get to feel that skin. How her breath will taste.

—You alright?

She's lookin at me concerned, her head tipped to peer into my face.

—Yeh, just really fuckin tired, like, that's all. Comin down *hard* now, like.

I stroke the back of her hand with me thumb an she returns the gesture. Heat and tingles.

—Are yer always this quiet? Or is it just cos yer crashing?

—Erm . . .

—It's alright. Not a criticism. I noticed that in Magnet before, like, yer mates were bein all loud an gobby but you were just sittin there all thoughtful-lookin. Like an . . . oasis or something. A patch of calm.

—That's nice.

She squeezes me hand again. We turn off Faulkner Street on to Bedford Street South. A shadow scurries away from a stinking pile of bin-bags an she points at it.

16

—A rat, look. Bleedin size of im.

We watch it scarper down an alleyway. Hunched, low shape with trailing tail.

—Right bold bastards, thee are, she says. —Glad I live on the top floor cos people on the ground have been findin em in ther fridges an everythin. Christ knows how thee get in there, like, but thee do. Takin over the whole bleedin city. Remember when the binnies went on strike about ten years ago? Fuckin horrible that was. I was livin out in Kensington at the time, like, an the alleyways were just chocka with rubbish. The rats were friggin everywhere. Scurryin all over the walls. The council was payin people to kill them, fifty pee a tail. All these little scallies with cricket bats an carving knives wading through the shite. An the *stink*, Jesus. Whole flat was full of it. It *reeked*. You could even taste it, in the back of yer throat, like. Made me gip.

—Why were yis livin in Kensington? Rough fuckin part of the city, that.

She shrugs. —Cheap rents. I'd just started workin in a shop at that time an the wages were shite, so Kenny was all I could afford. Whores below, junkies above. But dead cheap.

—Yer workin now?

She nods. —Same shop, aye. Newsagent's off Parliament Street. Then her face suddenly goes all serious: —But not for long, tho. Not for fuckin long.

I think of her out in Kensington, between prozzies and bagheads. Think of her lying awake at night, kept from sleepin by the noises. Alone in her bed. Or living with someone an clinging to them, and them cradling her head an stroking her back an hair, them knowing her, knowing what she liked, what she hated. And humped shadows of rats cast huge on the walls of her bedroom.

—Eeyar.

She lets go of me hand an takes keys out of her pocket and leads me up the few stone steps to the doorway of a townhouse. We go in an she closes the door softly behind us an we climb the stairs in the darkness to the top of the house, ar footsteps echoin down the stairwell, hers short an rapid an mine scuffed and slow. There are party noises behind some of the flat doors and I watch Kelly move under a skylight, briefly crowned blue by the moon as if for a moment she wears a hood of light. She opens another door at the very top of the house, what would've been the roofspace when slave-owners or shipping magnates lived here, an she takes some time to do this as there are five locks an she drops the keys once whispering 'Shit'. Then I'm in her flat an it smells of incense and onions. There are clothes piled up on chairs, CDs in stacks on the floor and a small telly on a wooden stool in the corner an a spider plant on the window sill. Books piled horizontal against one wall and empty glasses and an ashtray on the coffee table containin some spent matches an the lipsticked roach end of a spliff.

—Sit down.

She tosses her bag on to the couch an I sit in a chair in the corner, by the window. She goes into the kitchen, through multicoloured plastic strips that serve as a door.

—Want a drink?

—Alright.

—What?

—Alright.

—No, I mean what d'yer want?

—Erm, what're you havin?

—Whiskey. Jameson's. That's all I've got to be honest unless yer fancy flat cider.

—Whiskey sounds good.

—On its own?

—Sound.

When she comes back in, I'm thinkin, I'll take full control of the sitch. None of this fiddlin an friggin an fartin about, I'll down me whiskey an grab her an pull her to me an kiss her, hard. I'll press her face to mine an rummage inside her gob with me tongue an from there on it'll all happen. It's not so much that I'm horny as that I really fuckin want this Kelly, really fuckin *want* her with an ache an a needing, my face in hers and her skin an everything she is, all the small-hipped an slim-waisted fuckin presence of her with her jewellery and make-up and her eyes an teeth, I want all that inside me

18

arms I want to crush it all an eat it, gulp it down. She's
fuckin amazing. Just the way she is, the way she moves. She's
all there. Not one fuckin thing out of place about her, she's
just all fuckin there. She's as much Kelly as a shark is a shark,
as a cat is a cat. I want her like I've never wanted anyone
before, it's like there's a screaming gulf inside me that only
she can fill. Or should that be bridge? Well, what the fuck,
she's coming around the couch towards me, her hips swaying
and she hands me a glass of whiskey an I thank her an go to
gulp it down but there's too much of it an the swallow I *do*
take sets off the gag reflex which I have to mask by covering
me gob with a hand an pretending to cough. But me eyes are
pissing water.

—Went down the wrong way, yeh?

—Nah, it's not that, it's . . .

I set the glass down on the window sill by the plant an
wipe me eyes with the cuff of me sleeve pulled down over
me knuckles. I should make the move now, I should just grab
her an pull her to me but she's sitting on thee end of the small
couch by me an her knee is touching mine an that is enough
to turn me to soup. I can't do fuckin anything. I want her so
desperately much that I am robbed of all will. Helpless before
the strength of this need. Nowt I can do but just sit here an
spectate, see what happens to me. Just observe meself as if I
am *not* meself, as if I'm just a member of an audience. Aw
fuck. This isn't working out. Maybe I should just go.

—Sure yer alright?

—Yeh, I . . . just took too big a swallow, yer know . . . it's
been one long bastard party . . .

I wipe me eyes again and look up at her smiling but I can't
see anything cos me eyes are closed and there is pressure on the
nape of me neck, she is pushing my face into hers and her tongue
is right down deep in my mouth. Whiskey taste an tobacco taste
an the old copper of chemicals. Her lips are so soft on my face
contrasting with the one meaty muscle of her tongue and me
heart flips an jumps and starts to thud wildly and I put me
arms around her an squeeze her tight, her small back in my
palms nobbles of her spine and the arch of her ribcage as I

crush her to me, crush her to me. Ar tongues are thrashing like eels, I run mine over her teeth an gums an wrinkled roof of her mouth, I worm the tip under her own leaping tongue to flick at the tautened string under there. Her breasts squash firm against me chest. I'm grunting, groaning, we're both grunting and groaning an the darkness of exhaustion inside me head is beginning to part down the middle like a curtain to let in nothin but light, pure white light shadowless an formless, just this creepin, spreadin whiteness. Only a crack at the moment but it's growing, it's beginning to sprawl an spill.

We part panting but she doesn't release the pressure on the back of me head, she slides her mouth across my cheek to me burning ear. She whispers in a voice gone thick: —Aw God . . . I'm gunner fuck you so *harrrrd* . . . yer goin to love fuckin me, you are . . . you'll never want another woman ever again . . .

We stand up. Me head's whirling, expandin slowly with light. We walk down the corridor, her leading, me following. We're in the bedroom. She's tearing at me clothes, draggin me fleece up over me head, pushing me back on the bed to yank me trainies an socks off an then wrench open me jeans. I'm aware of a smell, an unwashed smell rising up from me feet and armpits but she doesn't seem to mind an nor is it important. She throws me kex over her shoulder an I hear loose change scatter and roll and then she's tearing me shorts down me legs, me knees two white pointed humps in the semi-darkness and my knob already hard, straining, harder than it's ever been hot iron so stuffed with blood I fear it might explode an she opens my legs with two hard punches one blow with a closed fist on each inner thigh an she grabs my dick in that fist tight and pulls it down to point at her face her lovely face and I see her face rise between my legs, her eyes wild an open an her swollen lips pulled back from her teeth almost in a snarl and she descends as if feeding, as if fuckin *rending* and I am inside her wet, warm and all fuckin wonderful aw Jesus oh God oh fuck I am inside her my dick is in her mouth. Muffled groaning from her as she sucks hard, so powerful, it's like she's sucking all the sourness out from inside me body an all the darkness out from inside me head to make room for a blinding brightness that grows in intensity the longer she sucks. I close me eyes an all I can see is this growing white. I'm grasping, twistin the bedcovers in me clawed fists an I go to clutch her head but she disengages an stands upright an tears her tight top off over her head an pushes her jeans down over her hips with her thumbs, her eyes glaring at me like firepits in the moonlight.

—Johnnies, I manage to croak. —I've got none . . .

She shakes her head. —Fuck, *I'm* willin to take the risk. I can tell yer clean. An I had an AIDS test recently an it came up negative so don't worry.

The test, I'm thinking, she's had the test. Why? Dirty needles. Anal sex with some junkie bastard. Rape, maybe. Her at the centre of some grotesque gang bang, a foul image takin shape inside me head which spins apart an disintegrates when she straddles me on her knees an slips my dick roughly up into her, one grunt as she is penetrated an then she's rocking back and forth such heavenly fuckin friction. No pictures in me head now, nothing utterly but this breaking wave of light bone-white. Like fuckin heaven.

This isn't like a usual shag, this. There's something different, something much fuckin *better* about this one. It's never been like this before. It feels like this is where I was born to be, here under this panting thrusting Kelly, craning me neck upwards to kiss her me hands sliding up over her prominent ribcage to hold her hanging breasts perfect palm-sized. It feels like wherever I may find myself in the future, breathing in water or spinning through space, I'll always always be yearnin to be here again. Flat on me back an straddled by her for the first (and only?) time. Oh my good fuckin God yes.

She's clutchin me shoulders tight. Fingers diggin painfully into me. Her movements, her rocking is accelerating. She's leaning forwards close to me with her eyes closed and muttering things, hissing behind her teeth:

—God . . . you fuckin . . . cunt . . . aw fuckin God fuck me you bastard . . . fuck . . . you fuckin cunt . . . *fuck* me . . . *fffuucckkk* me . . .

I am so hard. I am *so* hard. It's never been anything like this before. Her movements are frantic and her hands are around my neck, tight around my neck and squeezing hard and I cannot fuckin breathe, me brain is whirling as it becomes starved of oxygen but all the time this bright white fuckin light growing an clotting an threatening to absorb an overwhelm. Her thumbs are pressin down on me windpipe an I'm wheezing, fuckin panting for breath an she is panting too and keening I think she's coming and precisely at the point when the light is blinding, is unbearable, is promising to burst an become black she relaxes her grip on me throat a bit and the light explodes, just fuckin booms out silently like a detonation in me head some lovely fuckin catastrophe an I am coming harder than I've ever come before, the muscles in me shoulders contracting as thee pump the spunk out of me lungs, me guts, me burning guts and right up into her. Like all me bones are pulverised. Like me skull is stuffed with cloud. Aw Christ aw Jesus I'm coming. I'm coming. I'm coming. I've come.

She releases me neck an flops bonelessly sideways, face up on the bed. Her panting subsides as does the ballooning of me chest an the thumping of my heart. Breath scalding me bruised throat. An I'll never be able to come again, I think; it's as if a lifetime's worth of semen was expelled in that one orgasm. Almost like some irreparable damage has been done; the human body cannot experience something of that intensity an come away unscathed. Fuck no.

—Is that . . . I say, not really sure of what I'm about to ask. It's just that *something* needs to be said, even tho it hurts like fuck to talk an me voice is little more than a squeak. —I mean . . . no protection like . . .

—I told you, she says, quietly. —I'm clean.

—No, I mean . . . babies . . .

I feel the mattress wobble underneath me as she shakes her head. —I've just come off the pill. I was in a long relationship. Should still be working.

Meanin what? *What* should still be working, the relationship or the pill? I turn me head to look at her an maybe ask her but she stands an leaves the room (God, the fuckin *shape* of her) an comes back in and holds her palm out, open, two little white pills in it. I sit up an shake me head.

—*More* E? Fuck *no*.

—No, ther just downers. Diazepam. Help yer get off to sleep, like.

—Okay.

She hands me one an a glass of water an I swallow it down, painfully past me sore throat. She swallows hers as well.

Diazzies? What the fuck's she on diazzies for? What's wrong there? Doctor only prescribes diazepam for unhappiness or debilitatingly manic energy. Altho I know fuckloads of people who buy downers illicitly to help them through comedowns. Yeh, that must be it. Just a purely practical supply an use. Pragmatic, like. Just functional. Not sadness or mania, just easing the comedowns.

Not sadness. *Not* mania.

She climbs into bed nearest the wall, facing me, an holds her arms out towards me, open. I roll into them an we lie like that for a while, holding each other, listenin to each other's heartbeats an all the city noises outside, barkin dogs an sirens an distant fireworks an raised human voices an the overhead clatter of the police helicopter. I remember something.

—D'yer have an alarm? I've got to meet some people tomorrer in the Everyman.

—What time?

—Two.

—That's alright. She yawns. —I'll be up well before then.

—Okay. We're off to Wales, see. It was arranged ages ago. Chill out for a day or two, like.

—Oh well. Have a good time.

She kisses me on the lips an rolls on to her side, her back to me, smooth back, shadowed on the spine an shoulder blades where the bones an muscles bulge the skin. And that big black flower tattoo. I shuffle up against her an press me face into that back but when I feel the diazepam begin to take effect, start to knock me out, I turn away from her again, roll away as if from a light too bright to bear.

And have a strange, blurred dream; I'm in a forest, hangin from a tree branch, a noose around me neck, only I'm hanging *upside down*, me feet skywards, an I'm stretching as if some power

23

in the sky is drawin me upwards towards it, tryin to tear me free from the gravity which in turn is pulling me back towards the earth. It's like I'm on a rack an I can hear me bones cracking an the rope creaking as it stretches an I know I'll die like this, torn in two by opposing forces but I don't care. I'm in pain an I'm about to die, horribly, ripped apart, but I really don't fuckin care.

I wake up an there's a wind moaning around the house an some weak grey light through the curtains and I'm facing Kelly's back again, that big black flower in me eyes. There's loneliness, even tho I'm sharing a bed with someone there's a kind of desolation as if I'm missing something, craving for a certain thing terribly altho what it is I have no clue. Just a painful sensation of bein incomplete. I knuckle the crusted ick out of me eyes an lie there listenin to the wind an watchin the gentle rise an fall of Kelly's back an rememberin the recurring nightmares I used to have as a kid, after me dad took me to a fair on the Wirral an bought me a helium-filled balloon an I let it go an watched it rise upwards, up an up until it was just a dot, a pinprick, then so high it was invisible. I would have bad dreams about being that balloon, the delirium of rising higher an higher an nothing could stop me, the planet shrinking below until I could see patchwork fields then distant cities then the sea an then the curve of the earth itself football-sized, tennis ball, marble, an the sky around me getting blacker an the higher I got the higher I wanted to be knowin that sometime I would pop so I wanted, *needed*, to get as high as I possibly could in the limited time before I burst an fell all the way back down to the ground, a limp shred of red rubber trailin a length of string. I'd always wake up before I burst cos I used to get panicky an afraid an I'd be in a hell of a state when I awoke, sweatin an hyperventilating, an rememberin that now sets off me heart thudding an me skin prickling so to counteract this I focus closely on Kelly's back, see the ink of her tattoo just beneath her skin, a Big Dipper of moles between her shoulder blades. The feel of her hands around me neck. Hurts me now to swallow. A small, headless zit an next to it a long, thick black hair on its own like a spider's leg probly from my head or chest an I reach to pluck it off but it's attached, ugh, not very nice. She sighs in her sleep an half turns towards me, her eyes opening so for some reason I pretend to be asleep an then I *am* asleep, or very nearly, feelin one of her hands around me upper arm, how comforting, how safe.

Music wakes me up, slow and sad; 'Green Eyes' by Nick Cave. I can hear kitchen noises, the clattering of cups and cutlery, the rumble of a boilin kettle. I rub me eyes an sit up an find meself touching me body, me torso an legs, as if I'm checkin for wounds or breakages. Fuck knows why. There's nowt wrong but a stinging, swollen sensation in me throat as if I've got an infection there an a horrible fuzzy thickness clotted in me head, some small aches in various joints probly from thee impurities the recent shedloads of chemicals were cut with. First sober morning of the New Year, the New Century. The New Millennium. An I greet it on the first relatively clear-headed occasion with a great big cheesy grin, rememberin the sex with Kelly, rememberin Kelly herself an listening to her hummin along with the song. Then the grin quickly fades. Always this worry, this sense of daftness. Feeling like, thinking: Oh yeh, maybe this is the *one*, an the girl coming in all offhand and diffident an sayin very little except to tell me to go an without the offer of her phone number, occasionally an empty, never-to-be-honoured promise to call *me*. I fuckin hate that, I do: No, yer can't have my phone number, give me yours instead. I fuckin *hate* that. Maybe Kelly'll be the same. Maybe I should just sod off right now. Get dressed an slip out, tell her I'll see her around. A pre-emptive strike; forestall the humiliation before it befalls me. It was great fuckin sex, the best I've ever fuckin had to be honest, so at least I've got *something* to take with me, some souvenir of this dalliance over an above feelin like a knobhead: the memory of her hands around my throat. All that light bursting inside.

—Oh yer awake. I was gunner give yis a nudge. It's gone twelve. I've made some tea.

She places a tray of tea things on the floor an sits on thee edge of the bed. Here she is. She's here.

—How d'yer have it?

25

—Just milk.

—Good, cos I've got no sugar anyway.

She hands me a LIVERPOOL CHAMPIONS OF EUROPE mug. She's wearing a tatty ahl floor-length stripy dressing gown an she smells completely clean, utterly incorrupt, apple shampoo an coal tar soap evidently fresh from the shower with this smell off her an the glow in her skin an her hair combed straight back wet over her head. She blows on an sips at her tea an smiles at me an I can still see the evidence of binge in her face, the eyes slightly bloodshot, lips cracked. But now I feel like an ahl fuckin jakey next to her cleanliness an am acutely aware of the smell, the stink, the ripe bleedin *stench* rising up from me crotch an armpits and waftin out from under the duvet pulled up to me chest an held in place there with me elbows. I sip at the tea. Me throat burns as I swallow but that's alright; lookin at Kelly here sittin by me now I'm fuckin *glad* of that pain. I *want* it. Tell me you would take it away from me an I'd tell yer to fuck off.

—D'yer want anythin to eat?

I shake me head.

—Good cos there's nowt in. Flat's bleedin empty, I haven't been shoppin for ages.

She drinks more tea an stares out the window at the huddled red-brick backs of terraces, the spire of the Anglican cathedral towerin over it all. —It's been one long friggin hooley, she says. —One *fuck* of a party. She looks back at me. —Did yer sleep alright?

—Sound, yeh.

—D'yis want some more? Another hour or so?

—Nah, I'm alright. Got to meet some mates in the Everyman in a couple of hours. Craig an Quockie? Thee were with me in Magnet last night. We're off to Wales for a couple of days. Chill out, like. Kip in Craig's van an come down among the mountains.

She nods. —Aye, yer said last night. D'yer not have work to get back to soon?

'Work': Christ, now *there's* a concept impossible to comprehend. Forgotten what the fucker feels like, an long may it friggin stay that way.

I shake me head. —Nah. Sacked it off. I was labourin on that new Urban Splash thingio, that warehouse development, like, yer know down by the Kingsway tunnel?

—Yeh.

—Signin on snide like as well. Saved up some money for this millennium do. Still some left in the bank as well, enough for a few weeks, like. I finish the tea an put the mug down on the floor. —So fuck work for as long as I can.

—Is right.

—Have a bit of a party, yer know. Just take it easy for a bit. Clubbin it, druggin it . . . it's a new fuckin millennium. Which probly means arse all in the wider scheme of things, like, but it seems a good time to make a change, dunnit?

God, listen to me. Bletherin on tryin to sound cool. But this small talk, this sittin on the bed drinkin tea an spoutin shite of no import; I could do it all fuckin day. I could do it for the rest of me friggin *life*, man. With the presence of her by me, the smell of her, the fuckin *flesh* of her . . .

—More tea?

—Nah.

—Is there anythin at all that yeh *do* want?

You on top of me. My dick inside you. Coming like a fuckin volcano with your hands squeezing my throat for ever an ever an ever. Falling into that swirling light as me fuckin heart explodes. I say: —Nah.

—There is, she nods. —Or there's somethin that yer *need*, anyway.

She's smiling at me, a kind of purse-lipped, semi-smirky smile.

—What's that?

—A shower. You fucking ming, lad.

I laugh. —Aye, I know. I can smell it meself. Not one drop of water has touched my body this century. Apart from rain.

I duck me nose underneath the duvet an sniff up. Rank. —Phyew, Christ. I tell yer what, tho, I'm not gunner have time to go out to Lark Lane an back before two. An besides

27

which, mad Irishman Dermot's back so the place'll be a fuckin pigsty. Can I grab one here?

—Yeh, no problem. I left the boiler on anyway so there'd be some hot water for yer.

—Nice one.

—Just help yerself. First on the right.

—Alright, ta.

She takes the tea stuff out an I slide out of the bed an bundle me clothes up in me arms an scoot into the bathroom. It's tiny an steamy with a plant on the cistern an a bath with a shower attachment rigged up above the taps, a surprising lack of oils an ointments an stuff – just two types of soap, some all-in-one shampoo an conditioner an some green bubble bath with a picture of a pine forest on the label. Not girly at all. I've seen girlier *lads'* bathrooms. I dump me gear on the deck an raise the bog seat for a wee an suddenly me stomach starts to cramp, probly from the baby laxative all the recent whizz was cut with so I pounce on the seat an reach behind me to pull the flush so Kelly won't hear the noises an let it all fall out into the rushing water, all the excesses of the past week or so, the sourness, the acid alcohol an the sulphurous chemicals curdled to poison inside, all of it out into the clean tumbling foam. Colossal fuckin relief. I'm on that bog for about ten minutes, making sure it's all out, all the toxins, all the badnesses. Horrible bleedin pong. But there's a can of air-freshener tucked beneath the U-bend so I give the place a liberal blast of that while the cistern refills an then I flush it all away out into the Mersey. I sniff the air a few times but I can't detect any lingerin niff beneath the lavender air-freshener. Wouldn't want Kelly smellin *that*. She might've had me knob in her gob recently an made me come buckets by asphyxiating me to within a centimetre of me life but I really don't want her smelling me poo.

Into the shower, hot water on full blast, stinging, blistering hot. Fuckin wonderful. Like a scouring. Like a shriving, almost, a casting-off of all exhaustion an muck an stickiness and badness, the water swirling grey down the plughole an only running clear after I've been under it for ten full minutes an soaped me entire body, from footsole to headcrown, three times. City life, see;

the dirt just clings to yis. An city *partying* life is even worse, all that standin in taxi ranks among exhaust or at bus stops, rubbing up against people, traversin streets through fumes an dirt-drifts an greasy drizzle. All manky. But worth it just to scrub it all off an feel clean again, reborn, see it all slough off you an yer skin bared, clean. An that's another thing; usually, it's a slightly discomfiting experience havin a shower or a bath, not to mention a shite, in another person's bathroom, largely because of the unfamiliarity of ther tap controls an soap-scents an towel textures an stuff, all the little differences, but here, in Kelly's flat, it feels entirely perfect. Proper. Correct. It's almost like I know where everything is; me eyes are closed against the soap suds but I know that if I lean a wee bit to the right I'll be able to reach the towel hangin to dry over the radiator. I'll be able to . . .

—Christ!

Another hand grabs mine an I scream, snatch it away in shock.

—Oh shit! Sorry! I didn't mean to scare yeh!

I instinctively cup me knob an balls in me hands all protective an open me eyes, blinking rapidly against the stinging. Kelly's there, her face in the steam. Smiling a little bit an staring into my blinking eyes. The light greyness of *her* eyes the colour of the soap I've just used. Thump thump thump.

—I . . . I must've forgot to lock the door . . .

She shakes her head. —There isn't a lock on the door. But I'm sorry I scared yeh. I thought yer knew I was here like an you were, like, *reaching* or somethin. I didn't mean to scare yis.

Her lips seem swollen, her pupils vast. High pink colour in her cheeks. God, she is so fuckin beautiful. *No*, I think, *scare me . . . put a fear on me . . . terrify me into a fuckin rapture . . .*

I take me hands away from me bits. She glances down at them, once, then looks smirking back up at me face.

—What d'yer want me to do with *them?*

Swallow.

—Ey? What d'yer think I should do with *this?*

She flicks, hard, the end of my stiffening knob and just that touch, that momentary contact is enough to rock me back groaning against the wet tiles. The thunk of me skull on the porcelain. My mouth is hangin open an the shower water is drilling on to me tongue, hot an sweet.

Kelly shrugs the dressing gown off her shoulders an lets it fall to her feet an she steps out of it, for a few seconds perched on one leg like a flamingo or a crane in the mist from the shower. Holy God, the fuckin *shape* of her . . . Muscles on her thighs bulging as if more than life is tryin to burst out of her an her hips curving around the dark triangle of hair curls an her coiled navel which I notice for the first time is pierced by a tiny barbell, her ribcage swellin like a shelf to support her out-thrust tits, aw Christ alfuckinmighty her *breasts*. I reach out for them two-handed, me arms stiff and swaying in front of me moronically like a zombie or a Frankenstein's monster in an old black-an-white film.

—No, no. Put yer arms down.

I do. Feelin fuckin stupid. Daft for obeying so automatically an yet so fuckin *horny* as well . . . I glance down an see only the eye at the end of my dick at the level of me belly button, *that's* how fuckin horny I am. It's upright. *That's* how horny I am; I can look down into it, into myself. Narrow an dark an about to burst.

Kelly steps in with me, one foot, two then sinks to sit on the edge of the bath, her back straight an her legs wide open. Wide open like a butterfly's wings, the sinews at her groin like cables straining, bulging.

—Lick my cunt, she says in a voice thick but expressionless. Flat an sexy as fuck.

I get down on my knees, the porcelain painful against the bone. Between her spread legs, her fanny, the lips a darker colour than her inner thighs an split slightly apart an gleaming inside where it's pinker, softer, more raw. It's absolutely beautiful. Every wee fold and curl.

She grabs the back of me head an draws me roughly down to her centre, repeating her demand more urgent, harder:

—*Eat – me – out.*

I do. Me arms go around her waist an I engulf her whole

sex with my gaping jaw, me lips curled down an back over me teeth, a straining at the root of me tongue as I plunge it up into her, the water drumming on me back, yearning I am, *stretching* to taste her uterus, her womb, all the fluids inside her an everything she is what powers her through tubes an bags upwards to lap at the place where she herself beats. Right fuckin inside her, I want to force me whole fuckin face inside her, rip my own face off with my bare hands an stuff it up inside her with my fists. Taste everything she is or was or ever will be. Lick up an up, deeper an deeper until it's like I'm lickin through her past, her girlhood, her infancy. I'm licking her breasts from the inside. I'm tonguing her kidneys. I'm gunner taste the backs of her eyeballs, run me tongue over every crease an ridge of her brain, me chin all slick I'm eating her cunt.

She's crushing me head in her thighs and clawin at me back. I can hear her moaning over the hiss of the shower. I clasp a hip in each hand and feel each ball-joint there rotating, spinnin in ther sockets. I'm gunner make her come like this, lick an lap an plunge until she bursts like a dam, until she gushes into me mouth an I'll gulp every last drop, lick up any spillage from the bottom of the bathtub an gnash up at her until she comes some more. I'll be fuckin filled with her fluid, *bloated*, I'll fuckin *burst* with it an flood the whole fuckin city.

No I won't, cos she's tearing me head away from her, forcin it up with her hands an I can feel me face all wet an glistening with her an she tastes of something sweet like jam or treacle. She holds my face an inch or two in front of hers her tunnel-pupils her lips so full an calls me names, a fuckin bastard, a cunt an then she slides her arse down the side of the bath an gropes under her and slips my engorged dick up into herself. The shower water on top of me head is running all cold but the rest of me is fuckin aflame, she's biting me shoulder, really frigging diggin her teeth in like an bouncing up an down on me an I'm jerkin me hips as fast as I can in this cramped position, me legs all twisted an screaming at the knee and ankle. Her hands around me back, ripping at lumps of skin as if seeking to pull it away an without even bein fuckin fully aware that

I'm gunner do it I find meself bendin me arms back at thee elbow awkwardly to reach back an up an take her hands in each of mine an bring them up towards my neck. Place them around my throat. She whines and growls in me ear an starts to apply pressure very quickly becomin harder, tighter, an I feel me knob surge inside her harder than I ever thought it could get so hard like fuckin steel an me skull throbs as me brain urgently tries to suck in oxygen me mouth is open gulping air only as far as me wisdom teeth, I can't breathe. Fuck, I'm dying. And again like a door swingin open in me head to let the light in, the bright burning light this wave of almost solid light so fuckin amazing there's a shadow, a shape seemingly in that light altho not one of darkness in fact one of even brighter whiteness if that could be possible but surely it can't be, some drifting golden form beckoning is it? Calling? I want that light to be brighter I *need* the fuckin light to be brighter an Kelly's bouncing madly in me lap her head turned back to face the ceiling offering me her throat, she's barking at the ceiling as she comes her elbows pressed hard into me chest to constrict my lungs all muscles in me body howling out for oxygen me chest labouring like a bellows for breath, a booming in me head and in me guts an the light bursts into a million glittering particles each one of which spins, spins away. Kelly's hands leave my throat an the oxygen torrents back into me body, every cell expands and glugs greedily and me hands shake uncontrollably on Kelly's shoulders as I come, come, Jesus Christ, I come from the centre of me like a fuckin volcano.

Everything spinning. Kelly leans an turns the shower off an in the new silence all there is is the sound of my own wheezing in me ears, me battered throat sucking in air, the sledgehammering in me head an breast subsiding, Kelly's head resting on me shoulder, her hand stroking softly the drenched back of me head. Waiting for things to still, return to calm. Or as calm as they ever could be. Which isn't very –

Good God. I've never experienced anything like this in my entire fuckin life. No drug, no view, no activity or taste or sensation fuckin *nowt* has ever come close to this fuck *no*. This is . . . this is . . .

—Kelly.

No answer.

—Oi, Kelly.

—Mm?

—Kelly, this is . . . this is erm, fuckin . . .

She kisses me once, on the lips, and is out of the bath an puttin her gown back on in two, three seconds.

—You'd better go, she says. A snailtrail of my come down her thigh quickly covered up by the gown. —It's not far off two.

This is not, like, a dismissal. Her tone is too gentle and her eyes are too soft. She's just tellin me the time an that I'm gunner be late for me appointment, that's all.

I take a deep breath which irritates me raw, scoured throat an sets me off into an abrupt an explosive coughing fit. Hacking an splutterin, I'm aware of meself skinny, white an folded side-on into the bath in an inch of cold water, clutching me throat an coughing me guts up. How pathetic. How just fuckin pitiful. But when I open me eyes again Kelly's not there, the bathroom's empty, so I climb out of the bath shivering an dry meself (knob rubbed red-raw, raggedy-lookin, exhausted, spent, useless) an get dressed and use her toothbrush an deodorant an go back into the bedroom and put me socks an trainies on (socks minging, smellin of friggin vinegar) an then go into the front room where Kelly is, dressed now in a baggy grey jumper and black jeans. She hands me a folded piece of paper, frilled at one edge as if torn from a spiral notebook.

—Eeyar. That's me number. Give us a ring when yer get back.

—Okay. I'll only be a couple of days.

—Whenever yer get back.

—Don't really wanner go any more, to be honest. But it was arranged ages ago, so I suppose I've got to really. Can't let people down.

Shut up, Victor. This is embarrassing.

—You'd better leg it. It's nearly quarter to.

—Ah, they'll be late anyway. Craig always fuckin is.

Shut the fuck *up*, Victor. Just shut it.

33

I slip her number into me hip pocket an she kisses me on the cheek an puts her hand on me shoulder an just that action, just the proximity of her hand to my neck is enough to make me heart flutter faster an blood begin to gush down to my knob all hot and eager. Whether she notices this or not I don't know because she shoos me to the door.

—Go on. Gerrout. Yer gunner be dead late. Have a great time an give me a bell when yer get back.

She opens the flat door an I'm out on the landing. I turn an smile at her and she smiles back an we say tara an I wave over me shoulder as I go down the stairs, hear her door click shut. I go down the dark stairwell an through the main hallway, red lights flashing on the alarm box an I open the big heavy wooden house door and step out into the drizzle. Head off towards the RC cathedral, massive an spiky.

I feel . . . erm, I feel . . . how the fuck *do* I feel? Terrified. Over the bleedin moon. Exhilarated. Like shite. In shreds. Brilliant. How the fuck would anyone feel after they've just had the best sex they've ever had during which they probly nearly died, were nearly strangled to fuckin death and they absolutely fuckin loved it? Wanted it more an more an more? It's impossible to assimilate that, to reduce it to one simple emotion or verdict. It's unprecedented. I've never known anything like it before. So I don't have the words for what I'm feeling, this new swimming in me head, me heart. This exciting tightness at the back of me throat an on my skin. Yet if I had to sum it up in one word, one idea, that one word would be: Powerful. *That's* how I feel, in one word, strangely powerful; and as if the brighter, sharper colours around me an the clearer noises of the world have been bettered, improved by me an my new strength. Like I now have the power to make the world around me a better place an that's pure fuckin lovely, that's ace an wonderful, but the worryin question here is where will all this end? How far is all this gunner go? End too soon an it'll be a disaster; go too far and it'll be the same. I may fuckin die in both cases. Previous girlfriends, like, with them I've always been able to tell how and when it might end, I've always been able to single out the element of incompatibility that will finish it, but with this one, this Kelly ... I can't see any of that. Nothing. I know I've only known her for a few hours, like, an all that but, still, there don't seem to be anything at all in her that one day might drive me away. The space between us is one I'd like to occupy for a long, long time. An that fuckin scares me, really; wonderin where it'll all end. Havin no clue. How long will her hands be around me neck.

Get a fuckin grip, Victor. Yer don't even know the girl. Be fuckin realistic, there could be any friggin number of things about her that you might not like. She could be a Nazi. Might support fox-hunting. Could be a fuckin Man U supporter for all you know. Soon have yer packin yer bags an leggin it, that last one, wouldn't it? Too fuckin right.

It's drizzling, so I pull the hood of me fleece up an duck into a phone box by the nurses' halls behind the new art college. The only coin in me pocket is a two-pound piece; I recall small change flyin all over Kelly's bedroom last night when she yanked me trews off. I put the coin in the machine and dial me mam's number. Elizabeth (after Elizabeth Taylor; imaginative feller, me dad) answers.

—Hello?

—Lizzie? It's Victor.

—Victor! Happy New Year!

—And you.

—Did yer have a good one?

—Sound, yeh. The best. The Pier Head was ace. Fuckin top.

—Did yer see Orbital?

—Yeh.

—Aw cool as.

—Yeh. I hope you behaved yerself?

—Oh aye yeh. *Still* half E'd up. Buzzin. Mam wants to know why I keep huggin her all the time.

I laugh. I can hear voices in the background. —Who else is there?

—Mam, Kirk, Jean. Curtis an Stevie went off to London the day before New Year's an thee haven't come back yet.

—How's ar Jean?

(Elder sister Jean, named after Jean Simmons in *Spartacus*: 'The more chains you put on her, the less she looks like a slave.' Top fuckin line.)

—Fine. Enormous.

—She's only five months gone.

—I know but yer should see the size of her. Like she's swallered a Spacehopper.

—Has she thought of a name yet?

—No. Dad wants Russell.

This makes me laugh. —Oh, now *there's* a fuckin surprise. Bleedin film's not even *out* yet.

—I know. He's glued to his PC, gettin every last scrap of info he can about it. Says he can't wait. Every single one of his bookmarks have the word 'gladiator' on em.

—He's friggin obsessed.

—Is right.

—What did ar Jean say?

—Wharrabout?

—About naming the babby Russell.

—Oh, she asked him why the fuck he thought he had any right to make any contribution whatsoever considerin he frigged off five years ago. An he's never even met the baby's father, his own fuckin son-in-law.

—Fair enough. Except ther not married, are thee? Jean an Jocky, like.

—No, but . . .

—So you've seen him recently, then?

—Who?

—That elusive, two-timin get we've got to call Dad.

—About a fortnight ago. He's still with that slag. Wants yer to phone him, Vic. Said he hasn't spoken to yis for a year nearly.

—Which is a fuckin lie. About six months it's been, that's all.

—Phone him anyway, tho.

—I will. I suppose. Listen, I've got to go an meet some people; can I speak to me mam?

36

—Yeh, I'll go an get her. Look after yerself. Don't do too many drugs.

—Nor you. Yer only fifteen friggin years old don't forget.

—Sixteen in a couple of months. An I'd like a Smarties tube full of eckers for me birthday.

She puts the phone down an I hear her voice, fainter, talkin to me mother. Footsteps move quickly.

—Victor?

—Hiya, Mam.

—How are yer, son? Have yer had a good time?

—Sound, yeh. Met a girl.

Why the eagerness here? Why can't I wait to tell me mother about Kelly? The little boy needs to be heard sometimes.

—Aw Christ.

—Why 'Aw Christ'?

—Cos if she's anythin like yer others yer in for a rough friggin ride. Again.

—Nah, she's not, Mam, she's lovely. She's cool. Name's Kelly. Only met her last night.

—Well, don't, yer know . . .

—Don't what?

—Just be careful.

—I will, yeh. Have yer seen me dad recently?

—Few weeks ago. Just for a cup of tea, like, in town. Phone him, Victor, he'll be glad to hear from yeh. Yer *know* yer his favourite.

—I will, yeh. I'll phone him in a minute. How're you an Frankie gettin on?

—Good. Really bloody well as a matter of fact. He's takin me to Spain in a month or two. Booked the villa an everything.

—Spain, yeh? Which part?

—Oh I don't know. Some foreign name. Corfu or some-where.

—That's in Greece, Mam.

—Oh is it?

—Yes.

—Well, maybe we're goin there then. I don't bloody know. Somewhere hot anyway.

37

—Well, don't let him get yer E'd up in Ibiza.

She laughs.

—Mam, I've got to go. Money's runnin out.

—Okay, Vic. Phone yer dad.

—I will. Be happy.

—Look after yerself. Will we see yer soon, do yer think?

—Soon, yeh. I'll ring an let yer know. Next week or something, yeh? We can meet up in town.

—Okay. Tara, son.

—Seeya.

I press the NEXT CALL button and key in me dad's number, having to rack my memory for it cos it's been such a long time since I last used it. There's only 46p left so I'll have to make it quick.

—Dad?

—Victor?

—Yeh.

—How the fuck are you, lad?

—Not bad, Dad. Not bad. Had a top New Year's.

—Good to hear it. New millennium, eh. Let's hope it's better than the last one. Altho I doubt it.

Aw Jeez. Grumpy ahl get never changes. —What did yer do? Anything special?

—Stayed in. Few mates an a bit of bevvy, yer know. Billy Evans got hammered an started on Connor. You remember Connor? Used to take yer fishin in Bala Lake when yer were little?

Vague memories of a gangly feller with a mad cackle laugh an sideburns like hairy lambchops. —Yeh.

—Knocked Billy out with one punch, stuck him under a cold shower to sober him up. Billy woke up an went after him with a frozen leg of lamb.

—Sounds a laugh.

—It was alright. What're yer up to?

—Just off to meet Craig an Quockie in thee Everyman so I'll have to be quick. Met a woman last night, Dad.

Here I fuckin go again. What's wrong with me? Like an excited little kid. Why do I do this?

38

—Oh aye?

—Yeh.

—Be hoped she's better than that last one yer brought round. Her with the baldy friggin head.

—Oh yeh, God, *miles* better. She's lovely.

—Is she?

—Yeh.

—Sure now?

—Yeh, course. Only met her last night, tho . . .

And when she makes me come she chokes me, strangles me with her delicate hands and it feels like she's draggin me up to fuckin heaven an I come enough to drown meself. I come so hard there's bits of brain in it. I nearly turn meself inside friggin out.

—Yeh, Dad. She's *dead* nice.

—Good. Gunner get to meet her then, are we?

—Maybe. Are yer still with thingio? What's-her-namey?

Just windin him up here. I am able to say her name, but it does stick in me throat like gristle in scouse.

—Christine, soft lad. Her name's Christine. Yer *know* it is. An yeh I'm still with her cos I'm friggin well fuckin *married* to her. Til death us do part is what thee say.

My fuckin hole. Those words didn't mean a great deal when he left me mam in the lurch, did thee? He goes on:

—An she'd love to see yer again, yer know. She's a good woman. Once you've met her, *once*. In near on three years. Bring yer new one – what's her name?

—Kelly.

—Bring Kelly round sometime. We'll go out for food or something. That new Mexican place. Or make a roastie.

Memories of the last time me an me dad met up come hauling themselves back; the row in the Italian restaurant down Dale Street: Get a proper job, son, a career, what the fuck are yer *doing* with yer life? Enjoying meself, Dad, like *you* weren't at my age cos you were stuck in a fuckin frozen-food factory with a mortgage and three kids. Fitter, son, machine fitter; learnin a trade I was. Skilled fuckin job. Aye, skilled in lettin yer life slip out of yer hands, yeh. In givin yerself up to someone else.

In pissin what's left of yer youth up the wall. An treatin the mother of yer kids like a fuckin skivvy.

That's how it went. All bleedin night. Ended up us pushing each other through the taxi rank, bellowin abuse, threatenin violence, assassinating each other's character in a way that sliced me mind an still does. I've got absolutely no fuckin desire to repeat that again. And as if readin me mind over the phoneline me dad says:

—That's all forgotten, son. Water under the bleedin bridge. New century an all that, we'll start from scratch. Yeh? What d'yer reckon?

07p.

—Sounds good to me, Dad.

—Good.

—I'll give yis a bell in a week or two an we'll arrange something, yeh?

06p.

—Bring the new one. What was her name again?

—Kelly, Dad.

—Kelly.

And just the fuckin feel of her name on me lips makes me pulse thud. Just telling her name to my father.

04p.

—Yeh. She's ace, Dad.

—I'm sure she is, Victor. Bring her round an I'll take youse both out to a fancy place. Feed yis both up.

—Alright. I will.

02p.

—Money's nearly gone, Dad, I've got to go. Phone yer again soon, yeh?

—Make sure yer do. Don't leave it as long this time.

—I won't.

—And phone yer mother.

—Okay. See yer soon.

I hang up with, it must be said, some small relief. Love me dad as I do, an close to him as I am, there's a tension between us and an awkwardness that's been there since before he split up with me mother, since I knew for sure that he was shaggin around. It doesn't undermine or in any way fuckin *jeopardise* the relationship I have with him, but it does, like, colour it a bit. An take Kelly to meet him? Jesus, that seems wrong, somehow. I don't know why, it just does. Like: Dad, meet Kelly, the girl who strangles me half to death when we screw. Or like: an image rising up in me head of a jaguar circling an old bear; both of them with claws an fangs, both dangerous, but one grumbling and growling in the corner an thee other slinking and spitting. That cat image morphs into a close-up of Kelly's body, her belly especially, the flatness of it, the colour of it, warm an smooth on me palm. The bolt through the navel. Good God, I would lie in the mud for Kelly. Fuckin abase meself. Fuckin *drown* meself in the mud for her if only I could press me face to that stomach one last time before doin it.

What the fuck's happening here? Never felt anythin like this before. What the fuck is happening?

Through the nurses' halls an thee RC cathedral swells like a mountain in the drizzle. Its size, its friggin vastness, seems to make thee air throb in front of me face. I see it every day but it's somethin I'll never grow accustomed to, never take for granted. Nor thee Anglican one, either; I'll never get used to the way thee bulge so big, to the sense of the aeons of air they contain. Monuments to the madness, the hysteria. The screamin an demandin that's been on us since we first crawled out of thee ooze. The uncontrollable force inside, see what it sometimes makes us do.

The street sweepers are out in force here, brushin up the thick layers of party rubbish into the gutters an then shovellin it up into the open backs of the idling bin wagons. Fuck of a job that must be today; the entire city's swamped in shite – cans an bottles an wrappers an clothes an banners an all sorts. Tons upon tons of garbage. The sweepers themselves are unshaven an hung-over-lookin, just generally unhappy. First day back at work. Two scally girls in tracky bottoms an scrunchied hair dance on thee edge of a raised flower bed, pointin at passers-by an chanting: —Ewe, jee, ell, why, you ain't got no alibi, you're UGLY!

Cheeky little shlappers. A street hawker by them is sellin

socks an underwear from an open suitcase positioned on the top of a bin so I get some money from the cash machine (balance surprisingly healthy) an buy from him a pair of woolly socks – white, but what can yer do? Only colour he's got – an a pair of navy blue boxers, both for £1.99. I dash out of the drizzle downstairs into thee Everyman bistro an go straight into the bogs an strip off (bruises an bite marks on me legs, me belly, aw Christ, Kelly, these marks I would retain for ever) an change into me new garments an stuff thee ahl ones in a whiffy bundle down the back of the cistern. Cleaner, fresher in new socks an undies. I swill me face at the sink an look at meself in the mirror. That fuckin face has been through things. The bloodshot eyes an the faint bruises on the neck tell stories that I would never tire of hearing, both horrific an wonderful at the same time. Hopeful an hopeless in turn an turn again. Never get used to hearing them, never ever grow bored.

I'm fuckin starvin. Me belly's rumbling. I haven't eaten since . . . fuck, I can't remember the last time I ate. About a friggin *week* ago. I leave the toilet an go up to the food counter, hearing some crappy poet declaiming in the third room ('I had me a jar in Flanagan's bar' is one cringy line) an fill a plate full of pasta salad an bean salad an two pieces of chicken pie an a big piece of bread, pay for it an take it to a table in the corner nearest the door an fetch a pint of lager from the bar. I just pick at the food initially, wary of how me body will react, but then I find meself cramming it in, stuffin it in, me cheeks bulging an me belly gaping open to receive it all. I can't eat it quick enough. I'm fillin me gob before each big swallow hits bottom. I want to eat fuckin everything. I'm fuckin ravenous. A plate of chips as high as meself, stinkin of vinegar. A bathtub full of scouse. A piece of cheese on toast as big as a mattress. A whole loaf of bread. A whole roast chicken, *two* whole roast chickens. With a thousand spuds. Chocolate cake the size of a tractor tyre. Eat an eat an eat an eat until me belly bulges tight as a bastard drum an I can't fuckin move. I'm fuckin ravenous.

Eat me out, Kelly said. *Eat my cunt*, that's what she said. An I did, didn't I? I slurped her in an swallowed her down. I did an I'll do it again.

Aw Kelly. Aw fuckin Kelly. Never anyone like you in all me life.

Craig an Quockie come in as I'm chewin the last bit of bread. Ther energetic, even healthy-lookin, exhibitin no signs of ravage which by all rights they fuckin well should be doing considerin the bender they've been on. We've *all* been on.

—Here he is. Netherley's premier fanny magnet.

Thee sit down.

—Didn't think yer'd be ere. Thought yer'd still be shacked up with that fanny. What happened? Chuck yer out? Said yer knob was too small an you were a shite shag an that she never wanted to see yis again as long as she lives?

I swallow, painfully, the last ball of dough an wash it down with lager. Quockie grins.

—Oho, the silent mysterious touch, ey? What's this, too cool to fill us in? Leave us guessin, yeh?

—Yer gettin nowt from me. Get yer wank fantasies from some place else. What happened between me and that woman was a moment of pure magic between a man and a lady and I will not sully its purity by turning it into a lascivious tale to entertain you both with. It was beautiful and it shall remain that way. Buy a copy of *Razzle* if yis want somethin to toss over.

Craig laughs. —Oh fuck off. Ponce.

—So it was good, then, yeh? Quockie says. —She seemed nice, like. Craig tried to tap her mate, yer know the one with the short bleached 'do? Wasn't havin any of it, tho, was she, lar?

—Weren't havin any of it at all. Craig shakes his head all serious. —Didn't wanner know. Would hardly even talk to me.

—I'm not fuckin surprised, I say. —When I left yer could hardly pronounce a bleedin word. Probly just fuckin slobbered all over her.

—Nah. I think she's a lezza, he grins.

—Tell yer what, tho, Quockie says. —Dermot pulled the *hugest* fuckin woman I've ever laid eyes on. No messin, as wide as she was tall. Yowge. Pure fuckin Spacehopper. With a muzzy.

Craig groans. —Aw God, yeh. Fuckin muzzy. An no soft downy stuff or anythin like, we're talkin pure fuckin

43

Tom Selleck. Long, black hairs, like. Like fuckin pubes. An yeller-headed zits all over her face. Should've seen it, man. Shockin.

—No bother on fuckin Dermot, tho, was there? Yer know ar Dermot; shag anythin. Stick it in a knothole if it had hairs round it.

Typical Dermot story, that; he's the most gleefully undiscerning feller I've ever met. I've seen him pick up women in leg braces, old grannies, sumo wrestlers. He's not arsed, an he's perfectly happy to be that way. Any woman is fair game to him, he seems totally devoid of any sense of attractiveness or compatible age or ability or anything like that at all. Normal rules don't apply where he's concerned. An he's probly one of the happiest, most centred people I know. Work *that* one out.

—So yer gunner see her again, then? Craig asks an I just nod an say yeh an then change the subject cos there's nowt I can say about Kelly that wouldn't be trivialised in the act of saying it. So instead I say:

—Is that what youse did, then, after I left? Just went home, like?

—Yeh. We were fucked. Went home an slept for about twelve fuckin hours.

—Bit of entertainment outside, tho, Craig says. —Darren Taylor bottled one of the bouncers for some soft-arsed fuckin reason known only to hisself an there was a runnin battle all down Hope Street. Doormen steamin out of the Phil an Blakey's, thee legged Darren an is psycho fuckin mates all the way up past Mountford Hall, bottles an glasses flyin an everythin. Fuckin mental. Free show, like, bit of entertainment.

—Why'd he kick off this time?

—Who?

—Darren.

—Ah fuck, does that cunt fuckin *need* a reason? Craig asks. —Fuckin psychopath, that knobhead. Damaged bleedin goods, like. I heard recently that he's workin for one of the Maguires now, which doesn't fuckin surprise me. Only a matter of time before that mad bastard drifted into their fuckin orbit. Get on well, they will, him an Tommy Maguire; two brainless violent fuckwits together. Jesus.

He shudders, genuinely, it seems, an turns to Quockie. —D'yer wanner get straight off, Quox, or should we have a bevvy first? Set us up for the journey, like?

—God, yeh. Don't wanner go into Wales sober, man.

Quockie takes orders an goes up to the bar an Craig tells me about his brother Eddie, how he's all dead excited cos his missus is expectin ther first kid. Eddie, an my sister Jean as well; babbies seem to be poppin out everywhere. Craig seems to be as pleased by the prospect of becoming an uncle as Eddie is of becoming a dad:

—Yeh, I can't fuckin wait. Take im rowin on Sevvy Park lake, take im to is first match. Pure lookin forward to it. It'll be sound.

—Might be a girl.

—Nah, she's had a scan, Michelle has. It's a wee lad.

Quockie comes back with the pints an I drink mine fast an fetch another one for meself along with a whiskey nip. I have a few of them an so does Craig, Quockie stickin to just a couple cos he's driving, an I'm fairly wellied by the time Quox stands up an rubs his hands together an says: —Right! Come ed. Arses in gear. Wales, here we come.

We leave the bistro an climb back up into daylight an get into Quockie's knackered old Bedford van, me clamberin into the back on to the musty ahl mattress in there cos Craig's already bagsied the shotgun seat. He chops up three thin lines on a cassette box an he an Quox snort one each an he holds the box over the back of the seat to me.

—Wee sniff for the road, Vic?

I shake me head.

—No? Why the fuck not?

The mattress is comfy. I wanner dream about something. Plus I'm pure fucked. —Just wanner get me head down for a bit, that's all. Recharge an that.

—What's the friggin matter with *you*? What's the cob on for? Not is usual chirpy self today, is he, Quox?

—Ah, it's that new judy. Soppy get's in love.

—Suit yerself, Victor. Craig snorts thee extra line an leans back sighing in his seat. —Aaaaahhhhh. Right then. Fuckin onwards. I wanner be among sheep an hills before teatime.

—Will be, boss.

Quockie puts a tape in an drives off into the city to the first Stone Roses album. I settle back against the wheel arch, a tartan blanket wrapped around me, an start to nod off as we approach the Mersey tunnel, by the warehouse development that I was working on back in the last century. Mixin cement. Carryin the bricks. Well-paid but shitty work an I'm glad to fuck it's over. I've got money in the bank to last me a few weeks, not much to worry about. A little bit of fuckin freedom. Tiny figures in yellow hard hats crawlin over the steel bones of the roof, a giant crane boom swingin a shadow over it all. Fuck work. The exhaustion. The coercion. *Fuck* work, the regimentation, the subservience. Never any light flashin in yer brain, only a never-endin greyness the colour of the million breeze blocks I helped to lift and cart an deposit in piles. Bollox to all that. The enemy of happiness. Put me at the point of death with my brains detonating in light, pumping into Kelly as she chokes me into the guts of the sun an nothing, no one will ever match or know my happiness. Fuck it all.

We enter the tunnel as 'This Is The One' starts to play. One of me all-time faves. I try an keep meself awake to hear it all but I'm asleep before we next hit daylight an when I wake up there are great big green things outside the van, coated in mist an rising up massive to touch the sky. They are mountains.

I stretch an yawn an Craig turns in his seat.

—Back with us, Vic mate, yeh?

—Sort of.

—We're in Wales, lar. Deep in Wales. Past Bala. Quockie's tryin to find a shop to get some beer but I've told him he'll be friggin lucky. Nowt here but sheep.

—We're comin up to a village, Quockie says. —Look on the map. It begins with two els.

—Oh does it? So does every other fuckin place around here, yer divvy. That narrows it down to about three bleedin thousand.

Quockie takes one hand off the wheel an stabs with a rigid finger at the road map spread out across Craig's knees.

—Well, look for the closest one to where we are, soft lad. We've just left a place beginnin with Dol an we're comin up to a place beginnin with Mach. Work it fuckin out.

—Where are we headed? I ask.

—Aberystyth, Craig says. —On the coast.

—Why there, specifically?

Craig shrugs. —Why not? Nice enough place. I went there on holiday once as a kid. Pier, pubs, all that seasidey shite. An Quockie's gorrer mate there as well. Some one-armed cunt.

—Ey?

—An old acquaintance, Quockie says. —Lost one of is arms to gangrene. He was a junkie. Haven't seen him for ages cos he did a bunk after rippin off Tommy Maguire but just before Christmas I got a postcard off him, a postcard of this place Aberystwyth, like. So that's where I assume he's livin.

—Bit daft, that, I say. —Sendin a fuckin postcard, like, if he's in hiding.

—No address on it or anythin like that, Quockie says. —Just 'Happy Chrimbo', yer know. He might not even be livin in Aberystwyth, he might've just been passin through. But don't tell any cunt about it, alright? Tommy Maguire finds out, he'll kill him, after sawin off is other arm first. So keep yer gob shut.

—Me lips are sealed, I say. —Anyone who screws Tommy Maguire's got my friggin admiration.

—Is right.

Craig holds up the map. —Next biggish place accordin to this is this one beginnin with Mach. Mach-in-leth or somethin. Might as well stop there. Yeh?

—Alright.

—Should be a bridge comin up on yer left, yer wanner turn on to that an the town should be just over it. Bound to be shops there, it looks quite big. Big enough to have a train station an stuff anyway. All these other places are just diddy little villages. Hamlets, like. No shops or nowt.

I stretch an yawn again and, thirsty, ask Craig to pass me a beer. He shakes his head.

—All out, lad. That's why we're tryin to find a shop, like. Supplies.

So I spark up a ciggie instead. We're drivin through a thick pine forest, a river glintin through the trees on the left. I've always loved these places, woods an mountains an rivers. Wild places, like. There's a bit of it on the Wirral but it's nowt compared to Wales; it reminds me of fishin in Bala Lake with me uncle Con when I was a kid, how I just used to stare across the lake at the mountains in the mist an the little whitewashed cottages on them, imagining what it'd be like to live in one of those houses an the first thing I'd see each morning would be the huge lake an thee other mountains on thee other side of it. That's what I always wanted to do, live in one of them cottages with dogs an cats. Maybe one day I still will. If I can break the pull of the city, tho, which is as strong as fuckin steel if you were born in it; petrol in yer blood. The Mersey in yer veins (is right, yeh, all manky, polluted). Maybe I can persuade Kelly to move with me into one of those little white cottages on the mountainside. Have ar own still, grow ar own weed. All life would be would be walkin through the mountains an the forests, sailin on an swimmin in the lake an mad sweaty dangerous sex in the cottage. Ah how pure fuckin lovely that would be. Perfect. Like a dream come true. My life would be fulfilled an I could want for nothing else.

We turn left over a bridge an enter a town, smallish but big enough to have a centre, like, a town hall an clock an rows of shops. Craig points to a supermarket an Quockie pulls into the car park behind it, finds a parkin space an turns thee engine off. Me ears start ringing in thee unaccustomed silence; we've been drivin for about three hours, the dashboard clock says 6:30 PM. It's dark outside.

Craig turns around in his seat. —Yis comin in, Vic?

—Nah. I'll wait here in the van.

—Has laughing boy still got his cob on? Quockie is grinnin at me in the rear-view mirror. —Woke up missin his girlie, has he? Dreamin about her? Ah. How sweet. Or it *would* be

48

if she wasn't at this very moment off porkin some scally in St Luke's Gardens. Six of his baghead mates waitin ther turn in a queue.

Craig laughs. —Yeh! Spit-roasted by two crack dealers for a rock! On her hands an knees in piss in the London Road cludgies!

—Fuck off, youse.

They laugh, I scowl at them an thee laugh some more. I *am* missin Kelly, course I fuckin am. Not that ther foul images struck a nerve or anything like that, fuck no, but I've woken up feelin empty an echoing an Kelly is a ghost inside me, several ghosts, the smell of her hair in me nostrils an the taste of her cunt deep, deep in me throat. She's here like an empty presence pressed against me chest. Which makes no bleedin sense at all but that's how I feel.

I delve in me pocket an give Craig some money. —Eeyar. Get us eight cans or so of some strong cider an somethin to eat. Pasty or butty or somethin. I'm Lee friggin Marvin.

—Alright.

Thee leave the van and slam the doors an I just sit there smokin an listenin to the ticking of the cooling engine. Craig's left his moby on the dash so I dig out the crumpled piece of paper with Kelly's number on it, me heart beatin at the sight of her handwriting an tap in the digits. Ring ring. No answer. I give up after nineteen rings an put the phone back on the dash. She'll be out with her mates: the prozzy an the one with the bleached crop. Dunno ther names. She'll be out bevvyin somewhere and thinkin about me. About how much she's missin me. About how much she wants to be with me. About how big a bleedin mistake it was an how she never wants to see me again. Worrying about whether I'll pester her on the telephone, regrettin the fact that I know her number and where she lives. There was a kind of coldness in her voice when I left, wasn't there? And after the second time we fucked, in the bath in the morning, like, an I had a coughing fit cos she'd bruised me throat an when I looked up again she wasn't there. I'd fuckin embarrassed her. I'm shite in bed compared to her previous boyfriends, one of whom she's with right now. Bein with me only made her realise how much she still wants to be with him. Me knob's too small. I'm too clingy, too demanding. She's embarrassed by the way I wanted her to strangle me, she doesn't like the feelings that uncovered in her. She never, ever, wants to see me again. When she thinks of me she mutters the word 'dickhead'.

I flick the butt out of the window. Street lights are on now, the light from them seeming brighter than I've ever seen it before. Colours seem crisper, clearer, all sounds seem sharper an louder. Like I've taken some mild acid or something. I'm acutely aware of me own heartbeat, me own breathing. How alive I am. What's going on here? My heart is fluttering like a bird.

I want to be with Kelly.

Kelly. She's where I want to be.

The other two get back in the van, carrying plastic bags out of which thee pass me eight cans of scrumpy an a Cornish pasty an a packet of Wotsits. I put the food to one side an crack open a can.

—Jesus. Not very fuckin friendly round here, are thee? Craig says, unscrewing a big placcy bottle of cheap beer. —See the friggin looks we were gettin in there? Like we were bleedin Martians or something. What was ther fuckin problem? He takes a swig from the bottle then answers his own question: —Cos we're Scousers, probly. Worried we're gunner rob em blind.

Quockie shakes his head. —Nah. I think it was probly me.

—Oh aye? An why d'yer reckon thee were all staring at you, then, Quockie? Fuckin irresistible, are yer?

He takes a bite of a sausage roll an swills it down with cider. —No, but I'm Chinese, in case you haven't fuckin noticed. Probly don't get many of us round here.

—Yer arse. What the fuckin ell d'yer call *that* then? Craig points at a nearby Chinese restaurant an takeaway under a street light. —Local family that, is it? Good old Welsh name that, innit, Kam Sing. Dai Kam Sing, hot meals to take away, look you.

—Could be.

—Don't be soft. The Chinese are everywhere, man, even

here in the Welsh mountains. Yer all over the fuckin globe, lar.

—Yeh, but we assimilate arselves into the local communities to such an extent that local people who aren't Chinese take ar names. Or the names of ar concerns, like, ar restaurants an stuff. I mean, just cos a place has a Chinese name don't mean it's Chinese-run. Probly hasn't been a Chinese person in that place since it was opened. The owners rent it out, like.

—Bollox, Quockie. Fuckin bollox.

Quockie drains his can. —Ah, what the fuck would *you* know about it, anyway. Bleedin WASP like yerself.

Craig splutters crisp crumbs against the windscreen. —WASP? Fuck off. White, yeh, you've got me there. Anglo-Saxon, well, more Celtic blood than anything. And Protestant? No fuckin way, man. More Coggy than the friggin Pope, me. Or I used to be, anyway. Catholic from the moment I was conceived, lad. So WASP, yer arse. Get fucked.

—Yeh, well. Yer still don't know what yer talkin about.

Craig stares at Quockie disbelievingly then shakes his head an looks away. We eat an drink in silence for a while. Quox finishes his sausage roll an stuffs the polythene wrapper in the ashtray an rubs his hands together.

—Right, then. What's the plan? Stay an find a boozer an get wrecked here or drive on to, where is it, Craig?

—Aberystwyth.

—Yeh, Aberthingio. How far is it on the map?

I butt in: —Thought yer wanted to find yer mate, Quox? That one-armed bloke.

—I told yis, Vic, I don't even know if he lives there. I got a postcard off him, that's all. Just thought I might bump into him if we went there, like, that's it. I haven't got a fuckin clue where he lives.

—Yes you have. The postcard. That's a clue.

Quockie just sighs an asks Craig again how far it is to Aberystwyth. Craig measures the distance on the map with his thumb.

—About twenny miles or so. Half an hour's drive. I say we go on to there. It's a much bigger place than here. An it's a student town, like, so the pubs'll be busier. More to do. More women. *And* there's a sea.

—Alright then, sept all the students are gunner be on holiday. Victor?

—Yeh, I say. —Press on to the other place. This town's a wee bit small really. Pub crawl around three bars or so an that'd be it.

—Alright then. Avverwristjob or whatever the fuck it's called, here we come. He starts thee engine an reverses out of the car park. Promenade an pier, Craig said; that means there'll be water. An ocean. I can sit by it an feel its pull an think about nothing. Except Kelly of course. I'll attempt to rid me mind of everything but the soothing suck of the waves but I know she'll walk in there, her hips all swaying an her hair in ringlets around her face an her tight tummy exposed. Smiling. Her hands curled into claws an reaching for me.

Quockie puts the tape back in an presses PLAY: 'I Am the Resurrection'. And I fuckin well *am*. The whole fuckin world will know. I am. An I want no one but Kelly to hammer nails through my bones.

We pass a sign: ABERYSTWYTH 18.

—Eighteen miles, Quockie says, lookin at Craig. —About half an hour's drive. You were right.

—Always am, lar, Craig grins at him. —Always fuckin am.

And sure enough about half an hour later we crest a big hill an a large town is spread out an lit up below us. At its farthest end the lights mirror themselves, watery flickering reflections; the sea, bouncing the lights back. Like a long string of pearls or diamonds. Like *two* long strings of pearls or diamonds.

—This is more like it, Quockie says. —This is a *town*, innit? This is, like, built up. We can have a proper jollier here.

—Told yer, didn't I, Craig says.

—Yer did, Craig, yeh, yer did. But stop bein so fuckin smug now, will yer, or yer can bleedin well *walk* back to Liverpool.

Craig grins. —Yer still not used to it, are yis? Still can't get used to me knowin everythin. Being the best. Yer not at all comfortable with that fact, are yer? Neither of yis.

—Have yer heard this twat, Vic? Heard the *shite* he's comin out with?

—I'm tryin to ignore him, I say, and in truth I am; I'm just lookin out the windows at the unfamiliar town, the steep hill we're descending an the big grey university on the left, the halls of residence an then the hospital an then the townhouse terraces, pubs an chippers all lit up an the streets full. It seems a busy enough little town, alright. Like a smaller version of Liverpool even; gangs of girls in short skirts an platform shoes, even tho it's freezing. Scallies in trackies on the prowl. Student-lookin types, either late away or early back, too fuckin loud an boisterous; that student loudness of attention-seekin an not just havin a good time. The place looks alright. Interesting.

We stop at a junction an Quockie points at a signpost.

—Where the fuck do we go now? Can't understand a bleedin word of that, look. It's all in bastard Welsh. What the fuck does 'traeth' mean?

—It means 'beach', soft lad, Craig says, also pointing. —See, there's English underneath. It's bilingual. Are yer thick? An you livin in a bilingual area of Liverpool. Your pictogram things above the English. How thick are yer?

—Not as thick as you. 'Pictograms'; ther called ideograms, Craig. Eye-dee-oh-grams. Fool.

We turn right an follow the road between terraces until another 'traeth' sign directs us left an we follow it an then we're on the prom. A long, curving promenade with a pier an ruined castle all lit up at one end an a mountain at the other. It's quite impressive. Music thuds from various illuminated pubs an there are lots of people an when Quockie turns thee engine off I can hear the crash of the waves an seagulls calling. Long time since I've heard that; Liverpool may be a coastal city but there's no waves on the Mersey. And the seagulls won't fly further inland than Chinatown.

—Well then. Here we are.

Quockie cranes his head to look back up the promenade.

—Where to now? Where d'yer reckon?

—First alehouse we see, Craig says. —Have a few scoops first, check things out. Move on later if we feel like it, go somewhere else. We're on ar jollies, we can go friggin anywhere.

—Vic? You're bein very quiet there in the back. That sound alright to you?

—Fine, I say an thee get out an Craig opens the back doors for me an I stand on the road and stretch, me joints cracking, the fresh cold air smellin of sea an I inhale it deeply in, great big gulpin lungfuls of it. It smells all dead clean and fresh and, what's the friggin word, invigorating; that's it, *invigorating*. Smells cleaner an richer an *better* than any sea air I've ever smelled before.

Craig nods over the road at a loud an lively pub, silhouettes of people pressed against the big bay windows. It's called the Glengower.

—Wharrabout that one?

—Knob off, Craig, listen to the bleedin music out of it, will yer. Fuckin Steps or some such fuckin God-awful toss.

—Looks lively enough, tho, Quox. Don't wanner dead place, do we? Just have a drink or two an then move on, like. Don't have to listen to the fuckin sounds, do yer?

—Can't help *but* listen to em. Friggin deafenin. Victor?

I shrug. —I just wanner few pints, to tell yer the truth. As soon as possible. Couldn't really give a shite what the musical accompaniment is.

—Come ed then.

Craig leads us over the road an I see a shop on the next block, tell them I'll see em in the pub cos I'm out of ciggies. Tell them to get me a pint in. As soon as is humanly possible I'll be pissed. I'd drink anythin put in front of me tonight, anyfrigginthing. As long as it's got an alcohol content. As soon as I can I'll be staggering an swimmin in thee head an Kelly might come up in front of me all eyes an hands, all slim an sexy. Drink might convince me that she likes me a lot an that she wants to do it all again, again an again an again. Over an over. That she, like me, cannot as yet envision any end an there's no limit to what we can do together, to the adventures we can have. It'll all make perfect fuckin sense when I'm drunk. I'll be able to work everythin out when I'm drunk. Altho probly not the fact that it's only twenty-four hours since I first met her an yet it feels like I've known her since I was born. An at the same time it feels like I've never met anyone like her. Like I've been asleep until now. Like to be with her is what I was born for.

Jesus, Victor, listen to yerself. Catch yerself on, yer knobhead, yer fuckin losing it. Becomin obsessed. Gerrer fuckin grip, lad.

The shop's a small newsagent/grocer/offy. There's a couple at the counter, a small blonde girl an a bigger bloke with short dark hair, streaks of grey in it. Ther both wearing weddin rings, I notice; a young husband-an-wife couple. That's nice. Ther talkin to each other in Welsh but thee talk to the shopkeeper in English when thee ask him for two bottles of red wine an a bottle of vodka.

—On the raz tonight then, the shoppy says in a mild Brummie accent. —Party, is it?

—Just off to a friend's house, the blonde woman says. —Up Cliff Terrace.

—Films an food, her husband says. —An booze, of course.

How nice that sounds; to be married in this seaside town, to be takin drink to a mate's house on a terrace on a cliff to eat an watch videos an get drunk. Drinkin with yer wife an mates in a terrace perched on a cliff. How fuckin lovely that sounds.

The couple leave the shop an I buy twenty Lamberts an a half-bottle of Vladivar. I swig deeply at the vodka on the way to the pub an stash it in thee inside pocket of me jacket, walk into the noise an crush of the hot, loud, bright pub. It's bleedin packed. People are shoulder-to-shoulder an three-deep at the bar an I can't see Craig or Quockie anywhere. Some students are singin in a corner, some big blokes in rugby shirts are playin pool. Pubs are the same wherever yer go; apart from the local accents, this could be any 'fun' pub in any town or city anywhere in the Isles. Altho I do like the sea there outside the windows, all black an immense. I squeeze through the crush of people down some steps into a lower bar, less full, an spy Craig an Quockie at the pinball machine talkin to a man in a Tommy Hilfiger coat an wearing a short ponytail. His face is flushed red. He falls silent an eyes me sideways as I approach an Craig hands me me bevvy an nods at the bloke an says: —Yer alright, mate. He's with us.

The man nods at me an continues talkin in an Irish accent: —So anyways, I said to meself, I said, *those* lads look like they could do with a wee bitty guidance, like, someone te point um in the right direction. Unfamiliar faces like, maybes on their hollyers, they might not know how the land lies around here. Might not know where to obtain certain, erm, *provisions*, kindy thing. Was I wrong?

Craig smiles an shakes his head. —We're alright, lad. Brought gear down with us like. An we're only in this town for the night anyway.

Quockie leans an whispers somethin in Craig's ear. Craig nods. —Draw. We could do with some draw.

—Oh could yez? The Irishman's face lights up. —Well, as it so happens . . .

Thee barter for a bit, Craig tryin to knock the price down, the Irishman lavishly praisin his own merchandise, before they come to some agreement an Quockie puts money on the glass of the pinball machine an thee Irishman swipes it off into his pocket an hands to Craig a small bag of what looks like some decent bush. Not that yer can really tell just from appearances, like, but . . . well, we certainly don't seem to've been burned.

—Good wee bit o' smoke, thee Irishman goes on. —Hydroponic, likes. I know they all say that, like, but believe me, lads, it's the real deal. Grew it meself. Ye'll enjoy yeerselves on it, sure ye fuckin will. An should ye need any more of it or in fact anythin else . . . He shakes ar hands one by one, just one single firm handshake each. —Just ask around fer me. Name's Liam.

—Alright, Liam. Nice one.

—Pleasure to meet yez. Enjoy yeer stay in sunny Aberystwyth. He walks away a couple of steps an then turns back. —Ey, yeer not here lookin for a mahn called Colm, are ye? From your neck of the woods, likes?

—How many arms has he got? Craig asks, an me an Quockie burst out laughin. Thee Irishman, the Liam feller, looks puzzled for a mo then realises it's some kind of private joke an grins along with us. He says: —Well, good luck te yis if yez are, an then walks off into the heave of the top bar.

—Pleasant enough feller, Quockie says. —Very approachable.

Craig snorts. —Fuckin Irish Ali G if yer ask me, lar. See his friggin Hilfiger gear? What the *fuck* does he think he looks like?

—Nah. Perfectly sound bloke, Quockie says an I have to agree. Stupid fuckin coat sure enough, like, but Liam was a perfectly okay geezer. Then Quockie suggests that we adjourn to the van to sample the chonga an again I have to agree, but Craig catches sight of two girls who come an stand with ther drinks at the edge of a table a few yards away from us an mutters: —No rush yet, lads, no rush yet . . .

The eyes on him. Fuckin focus in them like a cat in a window watchin a bird.

Quockie follows his line of sight an sees the girls an immediately he's standing upright, back stiff, chest thrust out, shoulders thrown back. Craig's the same. Ther like a pair of preenin fuckin pigeons or somethin. Pigeons wantin to be hawks.

—Aw no, I say. —This is meant to be a *comedown* trip, not a bleedin sharking one. I thought we were just gunner get nicely wrecked by the sea?

—It's alright for you, Craig says, not taking his eyes off the girls. —You got yer hole last night. I didn't.

—And this morning, I can't resist adding.

—And this fuckin morning then. Me an Quox haven't had a poke for friggin ages. In that right, Quockie?

Without looking anywhere but at the girls who have now noticed thee attention ther getting and are now beginnin to laugh louder, flick ther hair back, swish their legs together an stuff, Quockie solemnly nods an says: —Near six friggin months, lar. Got bollox like fuckin coconuts.

I remember something. —Wharrabout that Geordie girl in Modo? End of November after the Underworld gig at the Royal Court?

He shakes his head. —Nah, I'm talkin about a *proper* shag. That was a friggin disaster, that was, man. Pure fiasco. Couldn't get it up cos of that mental fuckin speed an she crashed out in the taxi back anyway. Friggin farce. She's lyin there dead to the fuckin world an I'm on top of her with an acorn knob. He shakes his head again. —Sooner forget about that one, man. Doesn't count. An in the morning, when she woke up like, know what she said?

—What?

—She looked down at me dick, like, an said she was surprised that me japper wasn't sideways. Yer know, horizontal.

—Aw fuck that, lar, Craig says. —Sack that shit.

—Well, I did. Whole thing was a fuckin disaster.

Throughout this conversation neither Quockie nor Craig have taken ther eyes off the two girls, who, if they stick ther knockers out any further might break ther own bloody backs. I realise the futility of attempting to distract Craig an Quockie's attention away from the women so I ask Craig for some of the weed he's just bought an he hands me the bag an I take some out an wrap it up in two Rizlas glued together an hand him the rest back.

—I'm gunner have a smoke in the van, I say. —If yis have no luck then comen give us a shout. Otherwise . . . I smile an shrug at them but ther already over there with the women, Quockie throwin the keys back to me.

Oh well. Good fuckin luck to them. I'm gunner get drunk an stoned an full of dreams. Craig an Quockie might get somewhere tonight but they'll never get to the places I went to with Kelly, no way. Fuckin never. No one will. I must be friggin blessed.

Kelly. Ah fuck, Kelly.

I leave the pub. There's a phone box on thee other side of the road. I walk over to it an go in an tap in Kelly's number. It starts to ring.

Me heart's goin like a fuckin jackhammer. Me stomach's in a vice an I think I'm gunner be sick. Aw Jesus Christ, I can't go through with this. Can't fuckin do this. I'm gunner throw up. I'm gunner *hang* up as well.

—Hello?

—Kelly?

—Victor?

—How are you?

—Where *are* you?

Boom boom boom boom.

—Wales. In the middle of Wales. Aberystwyth, it's called.
Lively enough little town, like. Just bought some chonga an
Craig an Quockie have tapped, it looks like. I'm just gunner
have a walk on the beach an a smoke. How are yer?

Boom boom boom boom.

—Alright.

Boom boom.

—What've yer done today?

—Not much. Went out with Victoria.

—Who's Victoria?

—A mate. One of the girls I was with in Magnet thee other
night. With all the piled-up hair?

—Oh yeh. I remember.

The whore. The one Dermot had a session with. The
professional dominatrix. What did Kelly do with her? Why
did she go out with *her*?

—Did yis, did yis have a good time?

She laughs. —Alright, yeh.

—Where'd yer go?

I'm not really listening to her answer. Her voice, saying
somethin about Wales, I think, is registering inside me as a
buzz somewhere at the bottom of me throat where all me
innards begin. My mouth is so dry.

—Kelly, I . . .

I miss you like fuck. I've only known you about twenty-four
hours but I can't get you out of my head, the thought of you, the
shape of you. The way yer move an talk. I don't fuckin know
what's happening to me. It feels like I might burst an die.

—What's up?

Her voice. I reply: —Nowt. Just a bit tired, that's all. At a
bit of a loose end, really. I'm on me own.

She doesn't say anything.

—Suppose I'll just have a walk on the beach an get wrecked. Kip in the van. The beach is nice here. Stones an shingle. With a big hill all lit up at one end of it.

Rambling divvy. Talkin shite.

She doesn't say anything.

—Kelly?

—Yeh?

—What's up? Are you alright?

I can almost hear her shaking her head. —Ah, just something that happened today. I saw Peter, remember the ex I told you about?

Peter? Who the fuck's Peter?

—No.

—Well, he's a knobend anyway. An arsehole. But just seein him, like, yer know, it was weird. When're yer back?

Peter? Who's this fuckin Peter? Knobend or no, who the fuckin hell is he an where, *how* did she see him today? —Tomorrow.

—What time?

—Dunno. Depends on Quockie, I suppose. He's driving.

—Early or late?

—Haven't got a clue. But probly early cos Quockie's gorrer get back handy to arrange something for Chinese New Year or something like that. Don't know what, like.

—Okay. Meet me somewhere.

—Yeh. Where?

She's silent for a few seconds then she says: —Natural History Museum.

—Alright. What time?

—Erm . . . two o'clock?

—Sound.

—If yer can't make it then give us a ring. Otherwise I'll see yer there.

—Okay. I . . .

I can't fuckin wait. I can't, fuckin, *wait*. Can't wait to smell the skin on yer neck, to see you moving across a room, see your hair in yer face. The little whirling tunnels in yer ears. The grey of yer eyes so close to mine as I start to fight for

60

breath, as light starts bursting behind me eyeballs. Breakin like a wave.

—Hurry back. An take care, she says and hangs up. I'm holdin a dead phone.

Museum, two tomorrow. Nowt, no illness no war no fuckin global catastrophe will prevent me from bein there. Should the millennium bug decide to kick in tomorrow an bring missiles down around me ears I'll be on the museum steps at two o'clock tomorrow. If the museum itself was to collapse I'll still be there standin among the rubble at two o'clock tomorrow. If I was to friggin *die* tonight my ghost will be there, the Natural History Museum at two o'clock tomorrow.

This is fuckin great. *I* am fuckin great.

I go back to the shop for more beer, eight cans, an drink a few of them an some of the vodka in Quockie's van, smoke a couple of weak spliffs. It's strong chonga; weak as the spliffs are made it still hits me like a hammer, makin both me mind and body sluggish an gooey. Not particularly pleasant. In fact a certain kind of paranoia creeps into me as I'm sittin here in the front seat with crowds of unfamiliar people walkin past, some of them peering in the windows at me, makin faces which look ugly or just simply curious. I feel like a friggin exhibit. As if I'm on show. As if all the women in scanty clothes walkin past know that I like to be choked when I'm coming. Know that I like to be hurt, pushed to thee extremes. Know that I'm sittin here thinkin about nothin but the tightening pressure of Kelly's hands around me neck and how I'd fuckin beg for that, how I'd do anything to feel that constriction. And the women here are tellin the men about me an the blokes are sneering through the glass at me, thinkin me abject, thinkin me soft. Excludin me from ther ranks. Labelling me as not one of them. Which is a sensation I've always had cos I've got to admit to meself that in a way I've always been a wee bit submissive, where women an sex are concerned, like; I've always liked them to assume control. Nothin like this, tho, this thing with Kelly; this is a further development. This desire, this fuckin *need* to feel her hurting me, to surrender meself up utterly to her an her mercy. To let her do wharrever the fuck she wants with me. It's strange.

It's frightening. It's takin me over. An I cannot tell a soul about it; I mean, all blokes, on sites an in pubs an stuff, they'll boast about anythin sexual, any perversion as long as it casts them in the dominant role; sex with underage girls, the handicapped, trannies, animals, old grannies, anythin goes as long as they, the men, are on top. But submission, like, that's fuckin taboo. It's just not talked about. It's just not fuckin *done*.

Jesus, what's happening to me? Where will I be in a year's time? An will the bruises left by Kelly's fingers still be visible on my flesh?

Ah Kelly. You lovely, mad bastard. Natural History Museum, two o'clock tomorrow.

In need of another human voice apart from the yelling an singing outside the van I turn the radio on an tune in to a local English-language station. And hear a news item about a woman, a mother, collectin door-to-door for Cancer Research an dragged into a house by two men an held captive there tied to the bed an raped an sexually tortured for two days. Somehow she managed to escape but a week later in her hospital bed she committed suicide by overdose. The men are in prison an will be there for a very long time. But she's dead an her children have no mam an her husband has no wife an the fuckin world is not as it was.

Jesus suffering Christ. This fuckin planet is truly uninhabit-able. It really fuckin is. We can't live here, *I* can't live here. It's impossible to live on this fuckin planet.

I turn the radio off an take the vodka an a couple of cans down on to the beach, down some concrete sea-eroded steps an on to the crunching shingle with the black sea crashin an hissing somewhere in front of me. Plenty of debris on this beach, spent fireworks an the blackened circles of old bonfires left over from the millennium hooley. When just for a fuckin moment it looked like anything was possible. When it looked, if only for one night, as if we might possibly realise ar mistakes an do something to rectify them. Staggering a bit, the booze an bush beginnin to really work on me now, I sit down on a rock with thee edge of the sea only a foot or two away an sip at the vodka an gulp at the lager. Pissed an self-pitying, feelin utterly alone an aching. Bright lights an activity behind me up on the promenade an in front of me the sea's endless blackness, always rolling in. Easy to understand suicide here, at night-time on a beach, the way the dark water pulls you, draws yer in. Sucking you towards something which seems to offer a promise deep inside you of a destination strangely like light. As if in the cold an slime under the waves with the crawling an flopping goggle-eyed creatures you'd find a place warm and well lit. Where you'd wanner stay for ever an where yer'd never rot.

Aw fuck's sakes, Victor, shut up yer morbid cunt. If yer really feel that way then walk into the waves. Go on, gerrup off yer arse an walk into the sea with yer gob open. Breathe in the salty ocean.

The Natural History Museum. Two o'clock tomorrow.

I suck at the vodka an the lager until almost all brain activity is pummelled into stillness. I throw up into the sea, only a bit of acidic bile. Then I'm back in the van, in the front seat again listening to the Stone Roses album again an then Craig an Quockie are leanin in thee open window with the two girls who thee introduce to me as Fran and Jane. I smile at them all, all four of them.

—We're off back to Fran's house, Craig's saying. —Few bevvies an a smoke, like. D'yer wanner come?

An I *do*, kind of, but I'll be a gooseberry an it'll make me yearn for Kelly more an besides I feel like I'll be asleep in a few minutes. Comatose, like. I'm really quite bleedin wasted. So I tell them no, that I'll just stay here in the van an get stoned an sleep.

—Ah, Craig says. —Yer missin that Kelly one.

—I think I'll just stay here in the van an get stoned an sleep, I repeat.

—Alright then. We'll be back early-ish cos Quockie's gorrer be back in Liverpool before twelve, haven't yer, Quox?

—Yeh.

They go an I finish the bevvy an curl up in the back of the van an crash out, very, very heavily. Like a friggin mountain fallin over. When I wake up I'm moving, the van's moving

63

through hills again an we're heading towards Kelly an the Liverpool Natural History Museum. Still a bit pissed I groan an sit up. The dashboard clock says 10:28 AM.

—Oh look, Quockie says. —It's awake.

Craig turns in his seat to look at me. —Good_ kip, Victor lad?

I shake me head. Feel like shite. —How'd youse get on with them women?

Quockie snorts an shakes his head vigorously. —Tell im, Craig.

—Fuckin madness lar, tellin yer. Pure madness.

—Why? What happened?

—Well, we gets back to ther gaff, gets stoned, ther both up for it. *Well* fuckin up for it. All over us weren't thee, Quox?

Quockie nods. Craig continues: —Then one of em starts on about how thee discovered these dead bodies in a disused mine last year an about how it turned out that one of ther fuckin mates had killed em. Couldn't really work out what thee were sayin, to be honest, thee were fuckin hysterical, like. Cryin an everythin. From what I could gather, like, thee found these dead bodies in a disused mine, worked out that one of ther fuckin *mates* was a fuckin murderer an then thee all fuckin murdered *him*. Beat the bastard to death. Somethin like that, wannit, Quox?

—Somethin like that, yeh. Couldn't really understand what thee were goin on about like. Thee were in hysterics. Fuckin put the shits up *me*, man, I'm tellin yer.

—Yeh. So we waited for em to calm down, like, an then fuckin legged it. *You* were flat out, Victor. We got ar heads down for a couple of hours an here we are. Whole bleedin thing was a dead loss, like. Be back in the 'Pool before twelve.

An we are. In a world of fuckin madness, of murders an rapists an people walkin into the sea an never comin back out again. In thee aftermath of a global party which has left me friggin shredded. An a woman, a woman who is growin to fill my entire head. My complete fuckin being with her hands an her face an her voice an her walk an her hands again.

I'm back in the flat off Lark Lane at ten to twelve. Dermot's not in but he's been here recently cos the place is a pit: pizza cartons, empty ale cans arranged in pyramids; a dirty vest on the mantelpiece above the leccy fire. Time for an hour's kip an a bath to complete the sobering-up process an in just over two hours I'll be with Kelly again.

The Natural History Museum, two o'clock. Two o'clock in thee afternoon at the Natural History Museum. Sober an spruced with me heart booming there's nowhere else I'll be. Slippin into hot soapy water I think of the Natural History Museum; bones of huge creatures that once thundered across thee earth. A magnificence that once was, never to be again. Fuck knows why, like.

Natural History Museum. One forty-five.

I'm early an nervous an leanin with me back against one of the big pillars at the top of the steps, under the roof out of the drizzle. I'm nervous as fuck. Shittin meself. The whole city, the whole bleedin *world* seems nervous in sympathy, all the cars disappearing into the hole of the Mersey tunnel as if they're tryin to hide from something. All of it, the buildings an traffic all slightly shaky an blurred as if everything's recoverin from a gigantic hangover, which I suppose in a way it is. Sounds of jackhammering from thee Urban Splash development across St George's Gardens grate in me sore skull an ears an again I remember workin there, using those very jackhammers, hoistin buckets of cement up the pulley, carryin hods of bricks up fifty foot of ladder. Fuck all that. I can see the workers, small at this distance, the shiny yellow of ther hard hats. Fuck all that. The money's good to have, like, but fuck work. *Fuck* work. I'd fuckin hate to be back on the site now, feelin sick an hung-over, wearin wet an mucky clothes an liftin heavy things. Horrible friggin way to spend yer days. Sooner be here with me heart in me gob thumpin nineteen-to-a-dozen waitin for Kelly to come.

Kelly. Where is she? I can't properly remember what she looks like, not in the details, like, I mean. I just remember dark brown hair. With a maroony henna tinge. Eyes grey-blue. Beautiful fuckin smile. Strong hands.

A skinny, spotty girl in a tracky gleamin with dirt an lank hair tied back in a ponytail picks her way slowly up the wide stone steps towards me. A baghead on the skank, without a fuckin doubt. Obvious, man. She might as well be wearin a sandwich board with those exact words on it: BAGHEAD ON THE SKANK.

She smiles without showing her teeth. —Got any odds, lar? she asks in a Dingle accent so it comes out like: *Gahrrny oddzzz, lahhhr?*

—Alright.

I dig into me pocket an pull out a handful of smash, count it – 32p – an give it to her. Her hand's tremblin like a jakey's reachin for his first pint of the day.

—Nice one.

She looks at my face. The skin around her eyes all bruised-lookin, yellowish, browny. If her eyes hadn't've been robbed of ther colour thee'd be a deep green, like mine. In fact I think she was probly quite pretty at one time like, good bone structure, before the skag took a hold. Before it sucked out of her all youth an energy an replaced them with nowt but need.

—Wharrer *you* friggin lookin at? she says.

—You.

—Why?

—Cos yer lookin at *me*.

She looks me up an down an then back up at me face.

—Wharrer yis doin here?

—Waitin for someone.

—Waitin for someone, yeh?

—Yeh.

—Girlfriend, yeh?

—Erm . . . I suppose so, yeh. Only been seein her for a couple of days, like.

—Ah. She nice, is she?

I open me gob to answer even tho I don't really know what I'm gunner say – probly just 'yeh' – but the girl's away, there's a group of suits comin up the steps an she's among them with her hand out an her faded, pleadin green eyes. Her arse in her tracky kex is almost all bone, two twin points of bone.

66

She puts me in mind of the crackwhore, *my* crackwhore, the crackwhore in my crackwhore story (an we've all got one, almost every bloke I know has got a crackwhore story): About two years ago I'd just split up with a girl from Garston called Michelle. Been seein her on an off for ages, nearly three years, but she'd had enough an had met someone else so that was it for me, dumped, jettisoned. Fucked. I got rat-arsed in Kavanagh's an went round to the Coronation buildings for a bottle an to see Jerry Gowan, the dealer who lives there, to score whatever he was sellin at that time but on the way round there I was approached by this prozzy. Young, mixed race, pretty face ravaged by years of poverty an childbirth an substance abuse, just general unhappiness. Usually I wave away or dead-head prozzies on the make, like, but there was somethin about this one. Somethin that demanded attention. She asked me if I was lookin for business, I said no but if she could score me some rock I'd share it with her (Jerry Gowan won't sell rock; anythin but that, cos of the risk in it. An I *really* wanted some rock at the time). She said okay, so went round to her dealer's, a place off Mount Street, scored the stones an we went back to her flat to smoke them. Scummy little studio place on Roscoe Street, bed an telly an fridge, nowt else. Anythin else in the way of appliance or furniture long since carted off to Cash Converters an never redeemed. So we starts doin the rocks in. Good gear. An without me even askin her to, or even in fact really *wanting* her to, she started goin down on me. I was tryin to tell her that it didn't matter, I didn't expect anythin in return for the crack we were smokin, like, we could just sit an smoke an talk if she wanted to like but –

Oh good fuck there's Kelly wavin at me. She's walkin towards me across St George's Gardens with a grin so big I can see it from here an she's wavin at me. Wearin a grey hoody an a long denim skirt frayed at the hem an Adidas trainies an lookin absolutely fuckin wonderful. Smiling at me, wavin at me, me an only me. Aw Jesus Christ, this is the fuckin one, man, this is it she's it this is all entirely the fuckin *one*. What I've been waitin for for so fuckin long it hurts to remember. Since the day I was born an took me first friggin breath.

I watch her stand at the kerb an look left an right. Green Cross Code as taught in school. Protection against mangling, maiming. The shattering an shredding of that beautiful face an body. Everythin around her seems to throb, glow with a brighter colour as if infused with something, some charge, some *force*. Just the sight of her rocks me back on me heels. Burning in me belly, in me balls. She's crossin the road now. Hands in her pockets an I can see her teeth cos she's smiling at me. She's comin up the steps towards me. Her hair's tied back an the drizzle has pasted a few dark curls on to each pale cheek. Dewdrops on her eyelashes. One tiny rivulet snaking down between the tiny pores of her nose, finding an following a furrow in the minute laughter-line at thee edge of her maroon lip.

—Hiya, you.

—Iya.

More real, more solid in me eyes. Christ alfrigginmighty, she's utterly fuckin beautiful. She just *does* it for me, just pushes my buttons. Sets me pulse racing. That face; it's like everythin I've ever looked for without knowin it. An now here it fuckin is in mine.

—How're you?

—Good. Ace, now.

Her smile widens. I don't know whether to hug her, whether it'd look kind of clingy, whether it'd fuckin *be* kind of clingy, an my arms make an involuntary pathetic little jerk upwards like the stunted wings of a flightless bird. A penguin or something. Which is embarrassing an I feel me face ignite. But then her face is right in mine, I mean *right* in mine, I can see the seashell spiral of her ear an smell her soap an shampoo an she pecks me just once on the cheek an squeezes me bicep once, just the once an quickly, quick squeeze an release, she asks me how I am again in a tone that implies she expects no answer an that is absolutely perfect, absolutely right. All her movements, this whole greeting thing, it's absolutely perfect an completely friggin *right*. Intimate an not intrusive. Close but not cloying. Just fuckin perfect. My God, she's like, *is*, a lovely fuckin *dream*.

The baghead girl is sittin on the stone balustrade an staring at me an Kelly, her expression unreadable. I give her a little

68

smile an turn to go into the museum with Kelly. The heat of her by me. Her presence, thee air she displaces as she moves. I can hear the swish an snap of her denim skirt against her legs as her thighs move within it.

—How was Wales?

—Good. Green an sheepy.

—Did yer have a good time?

I shrug. —Suppose so, yeh. Got wrecked. Stoned, drunk. That's about it, really.

She laughs. —Could've done that *here*, man.

—Yeh, but this was by the mountains an the sea. Made a change.

An there were cottages an a landscape that I want to live among with you. There was a certain natural loveliness that could only ever be enhanced by you, a mountain range in miniature in *your* shape only, a vastness and an edge-of-the-worldness that I think has both its beginning and end in you. In yer face. In yer words. In the wee pit of yer belly button an in yer hands, ferocious an delicate. Yer fuckin gorgeous.

I decide not to tell her about Craig an Quockie gettin off with those two mad girls because she might then think that I did the same. She might not believe that I just stayed in the van an crashed an thought an dreamed about her.

—So did it work, then?

—What?

—The trip to Wales. The recovery trip. Are yer recovered?

I smile. —Yeh.

—That's good.

I ask her what she did last night an she looks at me kind of shocked.

—What?

—You. Last night. What did yis do?

—Oh. She puts her hands back in her pockets. —Went out with Victoria.

—Where to?

She shrugs. A *big* shrug, as if she's pushin somethin off. —Just pubs an that, yer know. Jacaranda, Magnet. Usual places, like.

She shrugs again, seems to distance herself from something, some memory. I remember now, on the phone, her tellin me that she'd bumped into one of her exes, Peter was his name? She called him . . . what did she call him? 'A knobhead, an arsehole.' Somethin like that. I want to ask her about it but evidently she doesn't want to talk about it, her face almost stern, so I just follow her into the lift after we've shown ar passes at the desk.

The doors close an she presses a button.

—Which floor? I ask.

—Three.

I try to remember what's on floor three. Big skulls an teeth an claws. —Dinosaurs?

She nods an smiles. —Dinosaurs, yeh. Yer won't be scared? Yer won't run away?

I laugh. —Might do. Might shite me kex in terror.

The doors open an I stand back to let her leave the lift first. So I can look at her from behind. The nape of her neck. A tiny zit on her jaw. The glimpse of bare ankle between her skirt an trainies. Backs of her ears all pearly. When she dies they'll preserve her an put her in a glass case an display her in a building like this so the race will never be without her in some form even if it is only as a pickled exhibit, lifeless an embalmed. Because even in that state she will improve the world, make it better than it is. Because without her, completely without her, the planet would crumple in on itself around that space an implode an compress itself to the size of a pea. A wee green pea, spinning in space.

Except she *won't* die. Not before me, anyway. I'll make double fuckin certain of that.

She's standin in front of the allosaur, the bones of it, lookin up at its face caught in mid-roar or gnash. The picture of her like that, tiny before the beast of bones. Hands in her pockets gazing enraptured up at the teeth. I watch her for a few seconds, committing the scene to memory, then go an stand beside her.

—Fuckin *love* dinosaurs, I do, she says. —Even when I was little, like, all thee other girls'd have dolls an toy horses an stuff

70

an I'd have these dinosaurs, these placcy an rubber dinosaurs. I had a triceratops an I painted thee ends of his horns all red to look like blood: I had a tyrannosaurus, he was me fave, an I got bits of lamb from the Sunday roast, small bits of meat, like, an stuck them between his teeth yer know so it'd look like he'd just eaten something?

I smile an nod.

—I left them in there an thee went all rotten an stank me room out. Flies an everything. Me dad went mad.

That's a funny story. That makes me laugh. Imagine her with her toy dinosaurs. Makin them fight each other, makin growly noises in her throat. Her *throat*.

—I was the same, I say. —Used to watch all the films; *Valley of the Gwangi*, remember that one?

—Aw yeh. Brilliant. *20,000 Years BC*.

—Yeh. An I was dead excited when I heard that Steven Spielberg was makin *Jurassic Park*. I was there on openin night, first in the queue at thee Odeon, *dead* friggin excited. Sat on the front row. An when the tyrannosaur came out of the trees . . . fucking *hell*. I was bleedin *terrified*. It was absolutely horrifyin. It was like a childhood obsession come true, like, seein the real dinosaurs. Or ones that *looked* real, at least. I mean, when I was a kid I used to, like, wilfully hallucinate dinosaurs in the school playground, eatin all the teachers an the bullies an stuff an then there thee friggin well were, alive on the screen. Just as mad an terrifyin as I always used to picture them. I sat for most of the film with me hands over me face, hiding like, the little kids in the front row were more interested in *me* than the film. Laughin at me goin: 'Look at that lad.' Thee weren't arsed. Found *me* more entertainin than the bleedin film.

Her turn to laugh. —Little kids, innit. See convincing dinosaurs every day on ther friggin megadrives, don't thee?

—Is right.

We wander round thee exhibits for a while, takin it easy, me waiting for me heart to still which it does temporarily only to shoot up to full speed again when she says somethin strange or amusing or wipes her nose with her sleeve or tucks tresses of hair back behind her ears with her fingertips. Or when she stands

71

before the skeleton of the Irish elk an the huge flat antlers spread out above her like hands offering a blessing. Like hands opening to present her, to drop her to earth as if bestowing a gift.

We follow the circuit back around to the lift.

—Where to now?

—Dunno. The mummies?

She shakes her head. —Been taken into storage or somethin. Ther goin rotten.

—Oh. Aquarium?

Her eyes light up. —*Yes*. That's me faverit *ever* place for coming down.

Is that a general comment or is she actually comin down *now*? Did she do loads of drugs with fuckin what's-his-namey, *Peter*, last night? Am I just someone to pass the time with? Fuck, am I someone to make Peter *jealous* with, in order to win the cunt back or something? Aw fuck, no, not that. That's fuckin, that's *abuse*. That's using people for yer own ends without any fuckin thought at all for ther feelings or self-esteem. Surely to Christ she's not like that. Surely she doesn't have *that* in her. Does she choke Peter as he comes? Does she drag him up into the brightness, the blinding brightness with her hands?

The lift doors clank shut an we descend an she cranes her neck up to kiss me, just once on the lips, more than a peck but not quite a full-blown tonguer. Pressure of her soft lips against me own, how thee yield an spread under mine. And her fingernails on the back of me neck tickling, a stroke an then her palm raspin across me face an her fingers around me throat clutching an then a twitch of pressure an I gasp, all thee air in the lift seems to fill me lungs in half a second an for that time the bulb in the ceiling burns brighter, buzzing, an she's looking at me, not at my eyes but somewhere in the region of my mouth. Christ, her soft fingers encircling me throat. Squeeze me, Kelly, grasp me tighter, make me fucking gag for breath God choke crush hold press *wrench* –

The doors rattle open. I'm following Kelly out of the lift into the green gloom of thee aquarium. It's empty except for a family, a mum an dad an three little kids standin on tiptoe to see into one of the tanks. Ripple of water across floors an ceiling

72

and drifting, darting shadows. No sound except the bubbling of air jets an the chatter of the children.

—Where? I can't see it! I can't see it!

—*There*, look! In the corner!

—That's a *stone*, divvy!

—No it's not, it's a crab! Dad, tell him!

I stand still, stroking me neck gently. My God, just that small pressure from her an what it does to me. Incredible. How can she do it? Like nothing I've ever known before. How the *fuck* does she do it?

Kelly waves me over to one of the tanks.

—Comen see the conger eel in here, Victor. Great big feller. Spends most of his time under that big rock in the middle but sometimes he sticks his head out. Keep lookin.

Staring into the glass, into the water behind the glass. Bubbles rising, weed waving. I like the coolness, the gloom down here but I'm tired of lookin through glass, at lookin at things *behind* glass. It's all fuckin barriers in this bleedin city. It's all screens. All me life I've had to interact with people through barriers: confessional screens, across desks, thick bulletproof perspex in shops an offies an DSS offices. Always somethin between you and other people. Always. An if nothin concrete then there's always somethin else, a class barrier or somethin, some reason for people to look down ther friggin noses at me cos I talk this way or look this way. Small hatches in burger vans or flaps in steel doors in tower blocks or windows reinforced with wire mesh, all these fuckin barriers always there. Yer can never speak to people face-to-face. Yer voice is forever muffled or dampened or distorted, by glass or perspex or iron or mesh. Or even just the barriers of people's own lives, ther loss or craziness, head-voices, the threat an peril thee imagine comin off you in waves. You're forever isolated in the world. You're always fuckin alone. An to make yerself feel a wee bit better you try to communicate with others an they turn away from you an that's worse, it makes you feel worse. Makes yer feel lost. No fuckin wonder that the dark water draws yer. No fuckin surprise in the fact that this city's full of screamers, howlers, people who do nowt but roar.

I want to say all this stuff to Kelly, tell her of all this inside me an I turn to her to do so but then she starts to talk herself; she points to a large, unhappy-lookin fish an says:

—These things don't care that it's a new millennium, do thee? Ther just fish. Thee live in the sea. Ther not bothered by dates. It means fuck all to them, it makes no difference at all. All thee wanner do is eat an swim no matter what day it is. Fuck all to bother them down there, in the water, apart from bigger an tougher fish. An if thee only thing to worry about is stayin alive then . . .

She's quiet for ages. Then she finishes her sentence:

— . . . there's nothin to fuckin worry about, is there?

I'm waitin for more but she doesn't continue, she just closes her eyes slowly an leans to rest her brow on the glass. The big sad fish approaches an nibbles, sucks at her forehead. Her face green in this light. Green an utterly gorgeous. Her lower lip droopin slightly to show a glint of her teeth, light rippling across her skin as if *she's* the one underwater.

I could stay like this for ever. Standin here watching her. The way the pressure of the glass has pushed back the skin of her brow to form small crescent bulges at her temple. Complete peace, complete calm. No worries, nothin. Just her an the green light an the curious fish driftin around her resting head.

—*Right* then.

She pushes herself away from the tank an turns to face me.

—I've got charlie in me pocket an it'll soon be dark. Let's go the pub.

I grin at her. —Is right.

We leave the museum, stand at the top of the stone steps in the drizzle.

She takes my hand an it's like sinkin into softness. Suds or something. A cushion. A *cloud*.

—Where'd yer wanner go?

—Erm . . . I shrug. —Not bothered. Anywhere.

Anywhere with you. Fuckin *anywhere*. I'd walk into Dixie Dean's Bar wearin an Ian Rush shirt with you holdin me hand. I'd wear an Orange sash in the main bar of the Volunteer on 17

March if you were with me. Probly get the cack kicked out of me, but still.

—Where'd *you* fancy?

She wrinkles her nose. —Tell yer what. Let's start off in Matthew Street, the Grapes an Flanagan's an that. Few bevvies an a few toots, set arselves up, cut off somewhere else. Yeh?

—Sounds fuckin ace to me.

—Alright then.

We flip ar hoods up an head out into the rain, up towards the touristy area, Dale Street, Matthew Street. A hive of Yank an Jap tourists an muggers, weaselly scallies in the alleyways waitin to pounce. Like hyenas or somethin, jackals thee are, fuckin bullying thugs like but yer can't help imagining how yer guts would burn when yer walk past Wade Smith's window displayin a £400 shirt an you in yer trackies tucked into yer socks an yer socks in yer £8-a-pair mismatched trainies from Aldi. Can't help wondering how that burning would release its energy. Out of which longing thee acids would gush.

And it feels so fuckin right, this, walkin through the city alongside Kelly. The tip of her nose peeps out from thee edge of her hood, her hand in mine clammy from the rain. So fuckin right that for once I'm not confused as to what I've done, what virtue I possess, to deserve her. She just appeared an I couldn't take me eyes off her an I've only known her for a couple of days an I've never met anyone like her before an I know I never will, in the future when I'm not with her any more, an how will that come about, what will be thee event or fizzle that drives us away from each other? I can't imagine anything along those lines not because it scares me to do so but because I can't see in her anything I might one day grow to dislike, or I can't sense any one thing between us that someday might curdle and rot. She's fuckin wonderful, *I'm* fuckin wonderful when I'm with her, not least because I know what may happen later when I'm coming an she's got her hands around me neck. Squeezing. Starving me brain of oxygen so that the lights flash, the fucking sun bursts. An just for a second everythin is alright, the whole friggin world an all in it could never be improved.

Kelly. Aw fuck aw God here is Kelly, holding me hand. What the fuck did I do, how could I ever have been happy, before I met you?

As we approach the White Star the sky opens an the rain *really* starts to come down, the drizzle's suddenly a downpour, so we duck into the pub. Love that fuckin smell of beer an toasties an fag smoke. The Beatles playin, 'Hey Jude', always the bleedin Beatles in this pub but I suppose thee do it to entice the tourists in after they've visited the Beatles museum further up the road. Get heartily fuckin sick of the Beatles in this area of the city; the Cavern Club, Lennon's Bar. Cheap tacky tat, Fab Four scarves an all that shite.

—Get me a lager, Kelly says. —I'm just off to the bog.

I watch her go. Her arse in the denim skirt. Like I'm wrapped in a bearskin rug.

—Yes, mate?

—Two pints of lager.

I take the drinks over to a table in the corner by the window which is now runnin with the rain, the people passin it outside just blurs, just moving smudges beneath umbrellas an hoods an hats. Safe an warm in here. Safe an warm in here with Kelly. Yellowed pictures on the walls of massive ships, taken when this city was a thriving port. Unloading, loading. Bound for places like Caracas, New York, Sydney, all over the fuckin world. The White Star is, or was, the name of a shippin company or somethin, I think, but it has significance for me now cos it describes what's in me head. Or *will* be in me head, later. A fuckin supernova. A megaton burst. Maybe my skull will crack. Maybe my heart will break.

Kelly returns from the toilet, sniffing and wondrous. She sits down by me an takes a gulp of her pint an swallows an sniffs an sighs an catches me looking at her and her face, her gorgeous fuckin face, explodes in a grin. One of her nostrils is running an red-rimmed an she wipes it with the back of her hand an sniffs again, hard.

—Wharrer you lookin at?

—You.

—Why?

—Cos yer lookin at me.

She pulls the cuffs of her fleece over her hands an wipes her face an digs in her pocket an hands me a wrap under the table.

—Eeyar.

—Ta.

—Charlie cut with bill. It's not bad.

—Who'd yer buy it off?

She goes to say something then seems to change her mind. Her face darkens slightly.

—Just someone Roz knows. It's alright stuff.

—Roz?

—Me mate. With the bleached hair? She was with me in Magnet thee other night.

—Oh yeh.

I go to the toilet an lock meself in a cubicle an tip some of the gear out on to the cistern top, crush the grains an chop them with thee edge of me cash card. If I wasn't with Kelly now I don't think I'd be doin this; I mean, I've been full of drugs for the past month or so since I decided to jack the job in and I'm feelin the need for a bit of a rest, clear me head, like, get rid of the jitters, but Kelly is here an I wanner enjoy every friggin moment with her, enhance every last moment with her as much as I possibly can. She fills me with the desire to push things, to push *myself*, as close to the limit as I ever have; to sharpen the world, make it more dangerous, more threatening, more fuckin exciting. To make all the colours brighter. All the sounds louder. To fuckin *improve* it, I think, that's what's at the centre of all this; Kelly unwittingly forces me to create the kind of world which seems suited to her, to be her natural habitat. One which doesn't seem outshone or feeble when she's placed at the centre of it. A place louder an brighter an stronger an sharper an just fuckin *bursting* with offerings. More intense, more mad, more promising. *Better*.

I divide the powder into two thin lines an snort one for each nostril through a rolled-up tenner. Lean back against the door, swallowing, sniffing, me face numbed an tingling in that unique cocaine way. Me pulse speeds up an me gob dries an me

77

scalp starts prickling. Good gear, friend of Roz. Friend of Roz, yer've made me feel nice. An with me eyes closed I remember in perfect, pore-clear detail how Kelly looked sittin on thee edge of the bath, gleamin wet from the shower an me face between her legs, the smooth downy skin of her inner thighs an the neat triangle of thicker, darker hair beaded with water like dew. Every flap an fold of her fanny, the darker outer lips an the softer pink within, the delicate membrane hood covering her clitoris an her pierced belly button opening an closing like a mouth as her stomach muscles tensed as I licked her, her breasts heaving, thee undersides of them full creamy crescents an her ribcage an her throat all taut cos her head was thrown back. Arched insteps, trembling, her feet resting on the toes. My God. I recall every last fuckin detail of her, how she looked, how she was at that specific moment. The tearing sensation at the back of me throat cos me tongue was reaching, stretching, *yearning* to slurp up more of her. And then how she slid down on to my dick. And how she bit my face an ran her hands up over me body to encircle me neck. And the memory of how the light split an burst is strong enough, complete enough to affect me physically, to make me gasp an buckle at the knees an roar in thee ears, me hands involuntarily begin to scrabble up me pumping chest towards me throat. It's fucking frightening. It fuckin terrifies me, the power of this, what Kelly can do. Jesus Christ, what am I in? What unstoppable fuckin thing am I on?

Kelly. Get back to Kelly.

I rinse me face at the sink an go back out into the bar. Kelly watches me move towards her, her mouth upturned at the corners.

—Alright?

I sniff. —Not bad, yeh. Not bad at all.

She takes the wrap back off me an puts it in her purse.

—Yeh. Some of the best beak I've had in a *long* time.

—Is right.

Chemical burn in the back of me throat an I neck half me pint in one go to get rid of it. I notice that Kelly's glass is empty.

78

—Jesus. Yer drank *that* quick.

—Yeh, I know.

—D'yer want another one?

—Nah. Wanner go, to be honest. It's a bit too friggin . . . *Scousey* in here. Gets on me wick.

—Yeh. I laugh. —I know what yer mean.

—Beatles an that.

—The great port we once were.

—Jerry an the fuckin Pacemakers.

—Stan bastard Boardman.

She laughs at that one an I finish me lager. Stan Boardman, the Harry Lauder of this city. Over the rim of me glass I see a bloke at the bar wearin a baseball cap who can't take his eyes off Kelly, except to throw thee odd puzzled glance at me. He's thinkin: What in the name of *fuck* does a bird like that see in *that* scruffy get? An I'm thinkin: More than yer'll ever know or understand or realise, yer brain-dead bleedin goon. In yer Lever Brothers baseball hat an yer antwacky stonewash jeans.

I put me empty glass down.

—Alright. Where to, then?

—Flanagan's.

—Flanagan's it is.

We get up an go. As we draw level with the baseball-capped no-mark he goes to say somethin to Kelly beginnin with 'Ey, gerl' but she dead-heads him an walks out the door an as I pass him I can't stop meself from smirking. I hate meself for doing it an I feel momentarily like the kind of smug smarmy cunt I usually can't stand but it's done an gone in an instant. Smirk. Look what *I've* got. Walk on. An *you* want it, don't you? Leave the pub.

Tosser, you, Victor. Prick, yer are.

Around the corner to Flanagan's Apple. All dark wood an smoke, filled with people steaming, shelterin from the rain. A group of drunken ahl dears in the corner by the jukey are cacklin an croakin loudly along to 'The Day Delaney's Donkey Won the Half-Mile Race', which is a stupid friggin song. Kelly takes the wrap out of her purse an slips it in me pocket.

—I'll get the bevvies in, you goan av another line. Lager, yeh?

—Yeh.

I go downstairs to the toilet an snort one fat line in the cubicle where I once shagged Michelle during the '94 World Cup after Ireland beat Italy an spring tingling back up the stairs to the main bar. The wifies are now bellowin along to 'Wild Colonial Boy'. I see a flash of white in the gloom, Kelly waving, an go over to her an hand her the wrap an she goes off to the bog. Me legs are twitchin jittery an I don't wanner sit down but I do, takin rapid sips at me lager an drumming on the table top with me fingers. Waitin for Kelly. There's so fuckin much ahead of me. Kelly will come back an we'll drink an snort an talk an laugh an later on tonight I can touch her anywhere, any part of her body, all over, I'll touch an lick every pore, every crease, I'll probe every last follicle. She'll turn me life, she'll turn *me*, into an explosion. A big bright boom. I'll be like the friggin sun in her hands, like an explodin star. Kelly is an angel bringin fire an light. There's a group of four office girls at the table opposite, all of whom are leggy an lippy an sexy an one of them keeps nudging her friend an noddin over to me an ther all attractive, fuckin *rides*, like, but I'd sooner be in bed with Kelly for one single minute than with all of them for an entire day. God, I've had far, far worse than the least attractive of them in the past but now I've had the best an to be perfectly fuckin honest I don't know what the fuck I'm gunner do after this. Everyone will fall short. Every bleedin *thing* will fall short. Kelly is untouchable. Unreachable. Good God, I might as well die. I might as well give up, roll fuckin over an let it happen.

Kelly comes back, walkin across the floor, weavin in an out of the standin drinkers with her hips swaying. Thee office girls are appraising her, lookin her up an down, one of them givin her looks dirty enough to need disinfectin with Dettol. Which should I suppose be flatterin but it really doesn't touch me. I'm just not arsed. Kelly's sittin six inches away from me an that's all, that's it, that's everythin I need or want for ever.

—Alright?

—Sound.

She rummages in her bag for ciggies an puts one in her gob an offers me one an lights us both up. Me whole body's trembling, quiverin with the drugs an her proximity. I can smell her. I can hear her talkin, I can hear meself talking, just meaningless words an sounds an she's laughin. I'm laughin. Sometime later I'm up at the bar buying more drinks, aware of thee office girls or one of them at least watchin me, there's eyes on me, an I hope it's Kelly's gaze I can feel too cos that's all I really need to know through the haze that Kelly is watchin me, fuck all else matters, fuck *all*. It's like I've never been whole until now, like I've never been *me* until now, not properly, not completely, it's like what you hear about twins who don't know that they *are* twins, an that when thee finally discover ther one of a pair that explains to them the unshakeable sense of loss they've always had, the sense of bein somehow incomplete. That's how I feel. That's how it's always been with me an how it isn't any more because there's Kelly sittin over there not ten yards away waitin for me to come back to her with the drinks.

—Yes, love?

—Two pints of lager please.

—What lager?

—Heineken.

And *fuck*, what's fuckin wrong with me? There *must* be something wrong, cos I've only known Kelly for a couple of days, and how the fuck can I feel like this after only knowin her for a day or two? We've had sex twice. We've been out once an this is that single time. It's not healthy, it's not friggin *safe* to feel this way so soon. What's wrong with me? There *must* be somethin wrong.

—Three eighty, love.

But it's like my life would be unsung without her. That's the proper word, that's the *only* word – unsung. Unsung.

I take the pints back over to the table. We drink them an each nip to the toilets for more snorts an drink some more an sometime later night has come down an we're in a taxi drivin down towards the docks through the lit-up city. Me head's whirling an I'm lookin out the window at the people, at the traffic, at all the lights seepin through me eyes an into me spinnin head. Kelly is touchin me. She's got her hand on me thigh. I've got my hand on hers. There's a little Francis Jeffers shirt hangin from the rear-view mirror an Kelly is singin quietly:

—*There's a bluenose over there . . . over there . . .*

An then we're in thee Albert Dock among jazz music an then we're in the Blue Bar, drinkin cold bottles of Beck's at a waterside table. Lights on the water. It's freezin friggin cold. I'm sittin opposite Kelly an holdin both her hands in both mine in my lap an we're both tremblin in the cold night air, the icy cutting wind off the Mersey.

—Fuck me stiff, I'm freezing, I say through chatterin teeth.

—Me too. Wharrer we doin outside?

—Let's go in.

We take ar beers into the bar an find a place to stand, next to Jamie Redknapp an Louise Nurding. Kelly twigs who she's standin next to an I'm half expectin her to say somethin girly an *Cosmo*-ish about how good-lookin he is simply because that's what most girls seem to do but she doesn't. She glances at him an leans close to me an says: —Mind yer don't nudge him with yer elbow. He'll be out for the rest of the season with an injury.

I smile. Drunk an I wanner say somethin to Jamie, some praise or thanks or something, but I don't cos there's nothin more scally than pallying up to a footballer in the Blue Bar or anywhere else for that matter when pissed. And in any case he an his missus move over to a table when a group of suits gets up to leave it. One of them lags behind to shake Jamie's hand an slur somethin in his ear an he just nods and half smiles. The suit leans on the table to burble somethin at Louise an she nods an half smiles as well.

—Must be fuckin terrible, mustn't it, in many ways, Kelly says.

—What?

—Bein famous. Most people seem to assume that thee can just interrupt yer life whenever thee feel like it. Just, yer know, come up to yer in the pub an you've got to be civil to them.

Yeh, but *I'm* famous with *you*, Kelly. Famous in the city or at least it fuckin well *feels* that way. As if everyone knows my face an nudges each other as I pass wonderin who I really am, why I have that aura, that fuckin *glow*. Shining through them all an all the dark brick streets.

—Yeh.

—Come ed. Kelly sucks at the dregs of her bottle. The way her lips bulge around the glass. —Let's move on somewhere else.

—Alright.

Then we're outside in the cold black air again an then we're in a taxi again an we're touchin each other again, groping each other, I've got me arms around Kelly's small waist an I'm squeezin her to me tight an me face is buried in her neck her skin smooth like satin against the tip of me nose an me cheek. Her hands on me back stroking, kneading, she's whisperin things in me ear too low for me to properly discern but the buzz an tickle of her whispering is raisin goosebumps on me arms, making me want to squirm but she's holdin me to her an I can't. I picture the tattoo on her shoulder blade, the big black flower with the thorny stem. I'm humming, I'm crackling with the drugs an the feel of her, the warmth an presence of her, how fucking *here* she is against me an there's a stirring in me jeans. Even with the gear an booze an doin nowt more but hug fully clothed there's a friggin stirring in the crotch of me kex.

—Just here'll do yer, mate, Kelly says an the driver stops an we pay him an get out an we're in Chinatown beneath thee immense elaborate gates. Kelly gazes up at them an mumbles something about Shanghai an then we're in the Nook, snortin more in the cramped toilet, drinkin more. Then we're in the Brewery among a roaring crowd, huddled in the corner beneath the big screen, stink of weed smoke in thee air, drinkin bottles of Newcastle Brown. It's heavin an noisy an we have to shout at each other to make arselves heard an ar shoulders are hunched up to ar ears it's so friggin chocka an I'm gettin jostled incessantly, feel like a bleedin pinball so we go an then we're downstairs in O'Neill's which is a bit of a crap pub but quieter at least an it smells of onion gravy, what thee serve with the colcannon an the soda bread an I'm in the bog snortin another line off the gurgling cistern then I'm sittin with Kelly again talkin about anything, everything, then I'm back in the toilets standin at the urinal with me knob in me hand staring unsteadily down without focus into me own falling murky stream an I'm talkin to meself, I'm sayin something like:

—I'm gunner fuckin tell her . . . I am . . . what's the friggin point in keepin quiet about it, ey . . . Jesus, soon we're gunner be nuddy together so what's the fuckin problem, ey, what's the big fuckin deal . . . just fuckin tell her . . . just go out there an sit down by her an tell her . . . fuck, life's short . . . might as well be . . . yer know . . . got to be fuckin honest with people, like . . .

I shake off an button up an wash me hands thoroughly, horrible thought of sullying Kelly's skin with pissy fingers an go back out into the bar. Kelly's not in the seat. She's done a fuckin runner. I scan frantically around for her an see her up at the bar buyin two more bottles of Brown so relax an retake me seat an she comes back an hands me a bottle an I take a deep gulp at it an the foam fizzes over on to me hand. Me fuckin heart's thumping. I watch Kelly drinking, see her epiglottis bob as she swallows. She puts the bottle down an looks at me an I'm leaning close to her staring into her face, the bridge of her nose, fuck me she's beautiful I would cut me heart out with a Stanley knife an give it to her spurting.

—Kelly.

I'm talking. This is fuckin me fuckin talking.

—Kelly. I'd do fuckin *anything* for you, Kelly. Anyfuckinthing. I've never met anyone like you. Yer fuckin . . . you're amazing to me. I don't know what to do. Yer make me feel like I might explode.

She's listening to me her eyes are twinkling an she's smiling.

—I'd do fuckin *anything* for you, Kelly.

—I *know* yer would, Victor.

—I mean it, fuckin *anything*. Nobody I've ever . . . I've never met anyone like you. All thee others . . . thee mean fuck all to me now. It's *you*, Kelly, it's fuckin you. This is . . . I know I've really only just met yer like an that but I've never felt anything like this before. You're . . . fuck, you're . . . I'd do anythin for you, Kelly, I mean it, fuckin anything.

—I'd *make* you.

—You're . . . fuck, you're . . .

I can't say anything else. Words are cloggin in me throat like gristle in a cheap burger. They've given me a sour, a *wrong* taste in me gob so I drink more beer to swill it away.

What the fuck did she say? '*Make*' me?

She puts her arms around me neck an leans close to look in me face an sing some kind of childlike little song:

—*Victor, Victor, funny name . . . funny name . . . funny name . . .*

Then her lips are at my ear again an she's whispering things, making me burn red-hot:

—I'm gunner make you come so much . . . I'm gunner make you do things you've *never* done before . . . things you've never thought that yer *could* do . . . yer gunner beg me to stop an beg me to carry on at the same time . . . yer gunner fuckin *explode*, man, yer gunner fuckin *burst* . . .

Flash. One blinding bright blue flash half a second long like lightning.

—We're goin back to mine. Come on, you.

An then we're in a taxi again, heading up Hardman Street. Kelly has her hand between me legs an is squeezing my balls so hard it hurts, squeezing them in a kind of 'you're fuckin *mine*' way an I'm sitting here, my lungs in me throat. Breast booming. A wobbling in me knees not due in any way to drink or drugs. At the traffic lights three pissed-up lads stop an one bends to peer into the cab. I hear a kind of drawn-out scream an then Craig shouting:

—It's Vic! It's fuckin Victor with that bird from Magnet! Derm, Quox, comen see this, it's ar fuckin Victor with that judy! Look!

Three faces pressed against the window, makin loud noises. Kelly waggles the fingers of her free hand at them an thee roar an then the lights change an the taxi pulls away.

—They're . . .

—Don't talk, snaps Kelly an squeezes my balls tighter. I gasp. Me hands are flat on the seat at me sides an I'm just lettin her do this, I'm just letting her hold my balls like a vice an tell me what to do. Why? What the fuck's wrong with me? Why aren't I resisting? She's squeezin me bollox so hard that me fuckin *knees* hurt an I'm just sittin here, lettin her do it. In the back of a taxi, heading towards Toxteth. Somethin like fire crawling up me spine. Flame beginnin to approach me head.

We stop outside her house an she lets go of me to take coins out of her purse an it's like I deflate, like some unbearable pressure leaves me an I slump back in the seat breathing again, heavy breathing, my chest heaving in an out. Do I enjoy this, is this a relief? Fuck knows. I want, no, *need*, Kelly's hands back on me again but that's a different matter altogether. All I know at this moment is that without her touching me, *hurting* me even, the night is dark, Toxteth is pitch fuckin black an the street lights cast no yellow.

Inside the house, climbing the stairs to Kelly's flat an it feels like I'm about to collapse. Me leg bones have turned to jelly. Kelly is behind me with a hand flat on me back to, what, support me, steer me, control me, something, an there's a tiny whimpering in me throat an I feel sick with apprehension, fear, longing, an excitement like nothing on earth. Almost like relinquishing all will an terrified, both terrified and ecstatic at what new fuckin freedoms may come. An also horny as fuck cos me knob's like steel in me jeans. Nothing like this before. No previous experience has prepared me in any way for this an I don't know what to do, it's like something else possesses me an directs my actions an thoughts. Like I leave myself, go somewhere else. *Become* someone else. An uncontrollable force inside.

Kelly lets us into the flat an she goes into the kitchen an I go into the bathroom, I don't know why, nothin I want to do in the bathroom, no need to pee or anything but I just don't wanner stand there waitin for Kelly like a fucking idiot. Me fingers stink of ash an spilled beer so I wash them at the sink, noticing on thee edge of the bath (Kelly's arse perched on there, her legs spread, her cunt good Christ her cunt) a small see-through lid of a body-spray bottle (the musk that Kelly smells of) with a small brown smudge trapped inside it. I lean closer an focus an the smudge becomes a spider, a small brown spider trapped inside the lid. Kelly comes into the bathroom.

—Wharrer yis lookin at? Oh shite, the little spider. Is he dead?

She bends an gives the lid a wee flick an the spider moves a leg.

—Ah, he's still alive. I caught him before an must've forgotten to throw him out. He's been stuck under there all day, the poor little get.

She slides the lid to the edge of the bath an holds an open hand under it to catch the spider as he falls. He drops into her palm an unfurls his legs an begins to crawl sluggishly across her hand. She holds him up to her face an watches him for a few seconds then takes him to the window an slides it up an holds her hand out an shakes the spider off into the night.

—Go on. Be free. Goan eat flies.

She closes the window, rubs her hands together an turns to face me.

—Where were we, Victor? Where were we up to?

She's standin in front of me.

—You were . . .

—I was what? Her face is *very* close to mine. She's moving her head, examining me face from different angles. Her hand snaps out an grabs my balls hard an I groan an everything speeds up again. I buckle back against the wall. —Doing this?

—Nnnnn.

—Is *this* what I was doin?

She squeezes harder an my head lolls sideways on to me shoulder. Fire in my guts aw fuck aw God aw never let go.

—You like me doing this?

I can only nod. Skin aflame.

—Tell me what yer think I should do, she's whispering. —Tell me what I should do to you.

Punish, hurt, damage, scare. This arouses me so much not

because *it* is obscene but because *I* am obscene. Terrify. Make me reel under the detonations in me head.

—I want yer to tell me . . . what I should do.

Punish hurt damage scare. Use, abuse. Tear into shreds an trample them under yer feet. Piss on them. I'm useless. Spit on them. Spit on *me*.

—Spit on me.

—*Spit* on you?

—Spit on me. Spit in my face.

Who is this talking? It's not fucking me. It's not me talkin through my mouth, lookin through my eyes. It's not me I am a puppet but fuck how I want it so.

Me eyes are tight closed an I hear Kelly hawk in her throat an then my face is clogged an warm. *Too* clogged. *Too* warm.

—Aw Christ! Not like that! Just spit, not a big friggin greenie!

Me balls are released an I open my eyes an see through sticky strings of mucus Kelly bent over, laughing. I find meself joining in, opening me mouth to laugh an me face covered in her snot. My tongue snakes out to taste, just a wee taster. Nowt but the slightest tang of salt.

—I'm sorry . . . Kelly stands upright smiling, her eyes damp an shiny. —It just, it just came natural. It's just fuckin automatic like to hoik up before I spit.

She wets a flannel in the sink an wipes me face with it. Wipes it once, twice, three times. My ears buzz. Memories of my mother cleanin me face with a spat-on hanky. I dry me face with a towel an when I look up again Kelly's hand is around me neck an pinnin me head back against the bathroom door an it's like I'm bein lifted, like me feet leave the floor, like I've become hot shimmering air rising upwards, hoisted skywards by me gulping neck.

—Is this what yer want? Is *this* it?

I just nod.

—Yeh?

Just nod again. An croak: —Frighten me. Scare me. Make me tremble.

And in a flash she is behind me, one hand holding my hair

an thee other grabbin me belt, I am barged out of the bathroom an down the hallway an into the bedroom thrown an landin face first on the mattress, bouncing once an turnin over to face upwards, me head an face pulsing hot with each tremendous mad beat of my heart. Aw fuck. Aw *fuck*.

Heat. This overridin sensation of an all-devourin heat.

—Take yer clothes off.

Kelly's standin above me, her left side illuminated by the light from the hallway, her right side in darkness. In thee alleyway outside I hear a dog bark four times.

—Take *all* yer fuckin clothes off.

I sit on thee edge of the bed an she watches as I undress. Trainies, socks, fleece, T-shirt, jeans, boxers. Aware of meself all white in the gloom, pale, the swiftness of my breathing. Dread. The biggest fuckin excitement I've ever known, too fuckin much for the world to hold.

—Lie on the bed. On yer back.

Without will or volition I do, I lie back naked on the bed an things move very friggin quickly now; Kelly goes over to a chest of drawers an takes out four scarves or bandannas an ties me hands an feet at wrist an ankle to the bedlegs, me ankles bent awkwardly an painfully down over the bottom edge of the mattress, that position causing me pelvis to thrust upwards. Balls crawling an dick as hard as steel. I'm observing all this, detached like, it's like I'm just watching not actually participating except the burning I feel beginnin to bloom an spread is only too real, so fuckin hot, sharp, razored, napalm burning *too* fuckin real. Unable to move I look up at Kelly, watch her as she strips. How her back curves inwards an her arse sticks out as she pushes herself out of her skirt. The definition in her belly. The hip bones. The ribcage. The wide muscles of her back spreadin like wings as she reaches behind herself an up to unclasp her bra. Thighs moving in the half-light. Her breasts fall an create a cleavage in thee air as she straddles me legs an leans forwards to take my nipples in her fingers an twist, hard an sudden enough to make me yell with the shock an pain an she presses her mouth to mine, powers her tongue into my throat to stifle my noises as she continues to twist hard at me chest an I'm falling through space. Through a blackness with swarmin pinpricks of searin light I'm falling. Her breathing fills the room, presses outwards against the walls, turns them convex. She sits up an releases me an the pain goes an she shuffles further down my legs, away from my face, her arse all warm on me shins an staring into my eyes, her eyes dark, deep-set, she takes my bollox in one hand an fuckin *YANKS*, wrenches, an me knees try to jerk up towards me stomach in protection an pain but bound thee can't an the sudden pain smashes, blunders up scalding through me stomach to scorch my roaring fuckin heart, further upwards to hiss an sizzle in me head like flame. Like light. Terrifying wonderful fire. A light I am in dread of but which I cannot resist bein drawn towards, hot, blinding, this is sex this is dying this is bein fuckin born. This is fuckin everything between each pole. All frenzy on this planet. Ice sheets forming an volcanoes spewing. Red churn of war zones this fucking is. Kelly's fingers are stabbing, probing, delving in me ears, exposed armpits, a whole hand is stretching my mouth knuckles ripping me lips I taste blood, I taste soap. Gagging, gasping, panting as the fingers leave me an reach to flutter over the engorged head of me iron prick an down between me spread legs to stab an viper ther way into my arse, to rend an rip, wrench. To pack me full of flame. I am crying out. Unable to open me eyes until the fingers exit me, withdraw from me an forcibly tear me eyelids open so that I can do nothing but stare into the eyes of Kelly an inch away from mine. An inch. All the blood lacing at her tear ducts. All the cross-hatching of her irises. An the shapes I see in her black an gapin pupils, the light an the shadow, the play an panic of each like things running in terror before a wall of flame, like a forest fire.

She flutters her tongue tip across me open lips. I gulp like a dying fish. She reaches down behind an under her an between us to guide me blood-stuffed knob inside her. Flash of meaningless memories in me brain: me mam handin me a bowl of cornflakes, me sister Jean bulgin pregnant, Quockie juggling a ball with his knees on an empty five-a-side court. Oh the wet warmth I'm sliding into. Meaningless memories flash once and are gone, swamped by the breakin wave of light as Kelly begins to thrust down hard an I cannot move, cannot fuckin protect meself even if I wanted to from her swoopin hands which dive an lock tight around me neck an squeeze, squeeze. Tryin to swallow past that blockage, that constriction an I can't, air is trapped in me throat swelling an me skull roars for oxygen a redness crawls up over me eyes a searing scarlet swallowin me which spreads an intensifies, movin from red through orange to yellow to golden, fuckin golden a blinding golden light too bright to bear I cannot stand it I want to plunge into it gasping, gagging for breath for fuckin *life* I am it's like I'm dying an falling into that bright bright golden sea which appears to spread open as if in something very like welcome. Me back arched, me whole friggin body is craning upwards, skin scraping at wrist and ankle I feel me guts pulsing, me dick spasming like artillery firing shells of what I know must just be spunk but which feel like me innards, me lungs an stomach an heart oh Jesus Christ I'm coming, God I'm fucking coming harder harder than ever before, me heart blasted out an falling in an arc, sinking into that golden cloud a giant white hand slowly opening to catch it. A giant white hand. Like I've been launched over thee edge of the earth an into the light of thee end and an immense white hand is opening to catch me. Somewhere in that scorching brightness which promises thee end of all fear an loss an pain an that's why this is so fuckin terrifying, the removal of all I know an hold to me it scares the fuckin life out of me me eyes are blind I cannot see I wanner come back I wanner come back let go of me Kelly, let me breathe I must fuckin breathe I must fuckin COME BACK.

An I do, gasping and heaving an buckin on the bed, against the binds my body bucking, coughing an spluttering, Kelly biting her bottom lip an pummelling with both fists on me chest as she comes. Calling me names. Air gushin into me body an me whole body friggin snapping an gulping, me skull deflating as that light leaves it an the night slides back in, the night air trapped in the room an the car alarm sounding outside, shrieking. A colossal fuckin sense of loss. Of very fuckin nearly reachin somethin beautiful an then bein snatched away from it again. All loss, bereavement. Deep fuckin stupidity of this body, this fuckin brain. I want to cry. Curl up in the corner an put me head in me hands and cry. Like a fuckin *baby*.

I want to go there again, where I've just been.

I want to go there an stay there.

I want to get a fuckin gun.

I come back to meself fully, feel meself livin in me body again. Feel the pain of bruising in me throat an of scraping, raw flesh bared at ankles an wrists. I open my eyes an all's I can see is the top of Kelly's head as she is lying on me, her face sideways on me chest, hair tangled, matted, sweaty. Waitin for things to return to normal cos I've, we've, fallen very fuckin far, very fuckin deep. Come back from somewhere very far away.

Our breathing, heavy together. Fast an so deep but slowing now, becoming shallower. This fucking sense of loss. What the fuck is it? Why the fuck is it here?

Kelly rolls off me an stands, her torso gleaming with sweat. She unties me, legs first then hands, an I sit up groaning an rubbing at the raw spots, skin chafed red, small spots of dark blood even beading on the surface. I hug me knees to me chest an look up at Kelly. Unable to make out her facial features properly in the half-light, only the twin tunnels of her flared nostrils an the white of one wide eye an the glint of tooth, when she says:

—Turn over. Lie on yer belly.

An I do. Just two small movements: turn an lie. Arms, legs spread. God fuckin help me, this is what I do.

Me face buried in the pillow all I can smell is Kelly's apple shampoo I can see nowt. All there is is darkness. I feel meself tied again, me arms an legs pulled an secured, the scraped skin complaining, re-rubbed. Hear me heart an how it booms. I hear Kelly's bare feet pad out of the room. The car alarm stops screaming. A dog barks again. Loud voices in thee alleyway below. Kelly's bare feet pad back in. Soft slapping of her soles on the bare lino floor, muffled for a beat of three as she walks across the rug. Almost leavin meself again an Christ the excitement of that, the nearly unbearable excitement of that like totally givin up all fuckin responsibility for me life an me mistakes an puttin all I am into someone else's hands. Kelly's hands. Haulin me upwards, towards the fuckin sun. *Into* the fuckin sun. Which I want, *need* her to do again an I gasp in expectation an hope as I feel her restraddle me, the weight of her in the small of me back, her arse shifting as she settles an makes herself comfortable. What's she goin to do? What the *fuck* is she goin to do? Her strong thighs scissoring me waist. What is she goin to do? I can't see a thing. I hear her sigh, a soft an almost plaintive sigh. My heart booming. What is she doing, what is about to oh Jesus fuckin Christ me back is on fuckin fire it's fuckin burning blistering some fuckin blowtorch trained on it or a needle of flame pure screaming an scouring through skin an flesh hot fuckin agony draggin downwards oh Christ she is killing me she is murdering me she is digging through an into my fuckin back to gouge out my heart help me oh fuck Christ help me.

I twist my head. Writhing. There's some pillow in me gob an I scream through it:

—KELLY! PLEASE FUCKIN STOP KELLY! PLEASE STOP KELLY YER FUCKIN *HURTING* ME YER *HURTING* ME! DON'T! FUCKIN DON'T!

I twist me whole body, writhing an wriggling, bucking like a wild horse to try an throw her off but she steadies herself with one hand pressed down on the back of me head drivin me face deeper into the pillow an smotherin my screamed words an the pain goes on, on an on, burning, boring into me, horrible, awful, like fuckin flame being tattooed into me skin. Oh my good fuckin Christ Kelly is a monster she is a killer she is rippin the skin off my back in slabs. Oh fuck she is tryin to flay me alive. She is goin to kill me. She is ripping my entire back open. I feel me belly all hot an wet with the piss I'm voiding me hands an feet swellin with engorged blood as I try to escape, try to drag them out of their bonds. The fucking pain goes on. Please God make this stop. Make this stop oh please oh fuck this is too fuckin much she is goin too far she's mad she's fuckin psychotic please don't let me die this way not this fuckin way tied an helpless skinned an screaming in a pool of me own piss an blood oh fuckin help me make this stop. Like a carcass in a butcher's shop, flayed an raw an bleeding an seeping, whatever the fuck she is doing to me please make it, her, stop.

Please.

My face burrows even deeper into the pillow wet with sweat now, digging an burrowing as if tryin to escape the pain the burning an all the horrible noise. My consciousness becomes vague, seems to not exactly leave me but become somethin else, to change into somethin more accustomed to this red world of terror an pain, growing an fleeing to a height so spinning, so sickeningly elevated never even approached in drugs or in drink as if the horizon thee atmosphere is hurtlin towards me as if my heart has been torn out an exposed on a desert floor under a gloating merciless sky, all heat an parch, a scorchin merciless sun. All is height an speed an bareness. Naked, racked. Soaring upwards an soaring across, no hope of protection or mercy, none. I am crying now. I can feel me chest throb with sobs, taste me salt on me lips, me tongue. Me whole body awash with me own spent fluids. If this isn't dying then what is it? It's wet. It's wet an painful an terrible that's all it fuckin is nothing more, *nothing* fuckin more.

The pain goes on. An some time later I am aware that it has ended. Or, no, it has moved to a different place; *here* it has ended, in me *back* it has ended, but elsewhere it will pulse on an on for fuckin *ever*. Some place will throb an bleed for ever an that will be me, my pain. On an on. Throbbing. Leakin blood. On and on and on.

And now a sudden coolness, a soothing in me back. I hear a moist sound, a soapy sound; Kelly rubbing cream into me back an into whatever fuckin wounds the mad bitch has made. Strokin the pain away with gentle swipes, softly flutterin the pain away. Whispering in me ear: —There . . . ther not too deep . . . it's okay, Victor, it's all okay. Poor Victor . . . *my* Victor . . . don't worry about anything . . .

Numbness of what can only be a tidal wave of adrenalin. Pain now only a flashin red beacon behind me eyes yet a sign, a badge I will wear for fuckin ever. An through that signal I can see her face as I saw it that first time in Magnet, the red/white lights an her lovely face in them, even now her lovely face, her eyelids drooping an her lips all dry an cracked after the millennium celebrations, red an then white, red an then white. The fuckin millennium celebrations; another two thousand years of this, this bondage, this torture, this bleeding, this surrender. How can we live through this? How can I go on?

Slowing of me heart. Slowing of the world. A tingling overtakin the burning an I feel I could lie here for ever but the wetness, the clammy friggin wetness I'm lying in makes me pivot me head over me neck an say:

—Can I go now?

Such a small voice. A small, quiet voice. Pathetic twat, Victor. An Kelly's quiet answer:

—Not yet, Victor, no. There's somethin else I need to do. Won't be long.

I strain me neck to look over me shoulder, see Kelly a shape on me with her arm held in thee air, catchin the moonlight all white an shining as if she's wearing a glove or as if her arm is covered in some kind of cream, some white cream up to thee elbow. A white film on her arm from fingertip to elbow. Then that arm swoops an plunges an I feel meself bein probed, penetrated, then I feel meself bein fuckin split an plundered an there is a fire again inside me a flame so hot so fuckin *hot* a flame not within but without bein forced inside me, fuckin *packed* inside me I feel meself fallin open just collapsin an splitting an it is a terrible pain an it's like I'm bein hoisted, hauled outside of meself, hoverin over the bed an leavin me broken body an witnessin meself spread an pinned below with the girl on top of me beautiful, fuck, still fuckin beautiful no matter what she does the beautiful bare girl on top of me the black flower flexin on her shoulder blade as she buries that arm inside me forcing the flame of the world inside me an my smashed self pushin back against that arm wantin more, God fuckin help me more, more pain, more splitting more fucking *feeling* until I am completely filled so fuckin stuffed that I cannot feel any more, it would be impossible to feel any more altho there is pain much fuckin pain somewhere I can feel flesh ripping an surely that can't be good but beneath that pain I know I am coming once again, good Jesus I am fuckin coming I am coming this pulsing heat between wet belly an drenched mattress oh my God I cannot stop I am fuckin coming once again. Coming. Coming. Shredded an invaded, splitting apart an suffering an coming like a fuckin cannon impossible to stop it. An still fuckin coming when the pain or thee unbearable light inside me makes me croak:

—Stop . . . please stop . . . please let me go, Kelly . . . I can't fuckin stand it any more . . .

And I truly can't. I truly fuckin can't. Can't stand this rocking on thee edge of this abyss. Can't stand this heat, this light. Can't stand this dismantling of myself. This pain. Can't fuckin stand Kelly. Can't fuckin stand Kelly doin this to me, rippin me apart like a lion. I want all this to be over, fuck, I want all this never to have happened. Can't stand the feel of her inside me, stretching me. My God, we must be both clothed in blood.

There's a slurping sound an then it's like I cave in on myself an I suddenly feel so empty, so fuckin *scoured* an hollow, emptier than I've *ever* fuckin felt before. All me essence wrenched out of me it's like I am nowt but a shell, a husk. Just fuckin nothing. This utter feeling of emptiness. Gutted an drained, scraped out. How can I go on living now I am so hollow? In what way can I exist now, bein so full of nothing?

I can smell myself in thee air, in the room. Smell me own insides. Putrid.

Kelly's bare feet leavin the room again. Water runnin somewhere, for quite some time, two minutes perhaps, three. Water runnin somewhere an more wetness on me face. More sobbing. Then the sound of approaching feet again an then me arms an legs are free, *I* am free, I can fuckin move again, I can fold me arms across me chest an hold meself, I can cross me legs tight around my splitting. Conceal me open wounds. I can rub meself, soothe meself, I can protect meself against the scalding in me back an guts, I can fuckin *run* if I want to. I can stand an not meet Kelly's eyes. I can pull me jeans on, step into them an feel thick fluid flop into the crotch of them as I do so. Like hot syrup. Drips of lava.

I cannot meet her eyes. Cannot look up at her. Just get fuckin dressed. Put yer clothes on an fuck off. Get out of here, away from her. She's a fuckin demon. She's insane. What the fuck has she done to me.

I pick me fleece up from the corner by the window an hide meself in it. Exhausted an shredded an spent. I turn to face Kelly but keep me eyes downcast to the region of her knees cos I cannot look at her face. I'm pure fuckin exhausted. She's wearing the same dressing gown she wore on the morning after I first met her, after we first fucked. Before we fucked again. Between stars explodin in me head. Shredded I am. One of her feet is restin on top of thee other. I'm fuckin spent. Dark polish on her toenails, plum or something but black in the street light which leaks into the room. Looks new, that polish. She must've put it on this morning, for me. To look good for me. Except I am not fucking who I was this morning an everything in the world is changed for ever. Never, I will *never* be the fuckin same again. *Nothing* will.

That mad fuckin bitch. Crazy fuckin cunt. Wish I'd never laid eyes on your face.

There's maybe something I should say but I don't know what it is an I glance just once up at her face an that glance is enough to see her shake her head. No expression there that I could recognise. She says something, just one word:

—I.

That's it, just that: 'I'. Only once.

Fuck this. Fuck *her.*

I walk past her, takin pains not to brush against her, and out of her flat. Down the stairs an out of the house an into the dark street. About six in the morning, no sign of any dawn over the terraces or even over either cathedral spire at opposite ends of this long, dead road. There's a stinkin heap of black bin-bags awaiting collection by some railings an I hobble over to them an bend over an spew up into them, spew it all out, all the drugs an drink gone sour an torture an madness of this insane fuckin day. A rat runs an I remember Kelly in Kensington, the shadow of rats on her wall. With her ex-boyfriend, what's-his-fuckin-face. Well, whatever the fuck his name was you can go back to him now, yer mad friggin witch. Go an carve *his* fuckin back open. Goan stick yer arm up *his* arse.

Jesus Christ.

I am friggin shredded. Completely fuckin exhausted. Spent. I'm gunner go home, curl up in bed an sleep an hope I never fuckin wake up. I'm never gunner see Kelly again. Kelly, Jesus Christ. What fuckin brought you to me. Why did I ever have to meet you.

Rattle of a diesel engine an I look up an see a taxi, its roof light on. I flag him down an he stops over the road. Fuckin hurts to walk towards it an I'm aware of meself bandy-legged, steppin painfully, gingerly. Like fuckin acid burning up me arse.

I climb in the cab.

—Bloody hell, lad, what happened to you? Kicked in the pills?

—No.

He's turned in his seat to look at me, waitin for an answer. Slight look of distaste on his face cos he's probly thinkin I'm a rent boy or something an I've turned too many tricks so I give him an excuse, the first one to come into me head:

—Got circumcised yesterday. Still hurts like fuck to walk.

He winces in sympathy an drives off. I tell him to head for Lark Lane an I look back through the rear windscreen up at the front window of Kelly's flat but the light's off an I can discern no shape there. It's in darkness. I stare up at it until the cab turns a corner an I can't see it any more an then I turn to face the front again. See where I'm going, not where I've come from.

Curled up in a tight ball under the duvet, shiverin against the cold an the rain hurling itself against the window an the wind howling. Me back on fire, me arse on fire. Violated is the word. Me head's a spinning confused fucked-up mess but there is *one* thing I know, even if I'm lying here wondering who the fuck I am any more there *is* one thing at least that I'm sure of: I can't see her any more. It went too far, far too fuckin far. Can't assess it, can't analyse it, it's just too fuckin much for me to handle. It went too fuckin far an what's sad is that it could've been something so fuckin special, so fuckin important an unique, so fuckin what I've been searching for all me friggin life . . .

But no. It didn't work out that way. It went wrong somewhere, it turned ugly. I just won't, can't, see her any more.

Fuck the whole thing anyway.

But Jesus Christ, it's cold in here. Cold an dark. Maybe I should cover me nakedness, put some shorts an a T-shirt on or something cos it's as cold as the fuckin grave in here.

Sittin in front of Richard an Judy, eatin breakfast. A big bleedin dose of normality, this is what I need; tea an toast an those two knobheads talkin shite. I'm not really listening to what ther sayin, it's just burble, like, nonsense, but this is the real world, this is day-to-day life in all its stupidity an I need a great big fuckin fix of it right now. Crap toast tho; Dermot with his Happy Shopper margarine.

The phone rings.

Oh fuck Kelly. That might be Kelly. Has she got my number? No, I don't think so. Can't remember givin it to her. Oh God, what if it's Kelly. What the fuck will I do. I hope it's not her.

I pick it up. —Hello?

—Ah, Victor, man, yer in. Been tryin to get hold of yer for ages.

Relief. Is this relief? Is it?

—How are yis, Quockie?

—Sound. Fancy workin off some of yer Chrimbo flab?

—Chrimbo flab? Fuck's sakes, Quockie, I hardly ate a thing over bleedin Christmas. Nor did friggin *you* for that matter.

—Inside yer head I'm talkin about, lar, the flab inside yer fuckin head. Exercise, like. Must be all kinds of shite inside yer head after all that partyin.

He's not wrong there. —What've yer got in mind? Only I'm not fuckin helpin yer build another fuckin New Year's dragon again. Not after last year's balls-up, fuck no.

He laughs, probly rememberin as I am last year's Chinese

99

New Year celebrations, the giant caterpillar/dragon thingio fallin in two on the steps of the Blackie an all the people inside it tumblin over each other, a great big human pile-up. Chaos. An it was ar fault as well, mine an Quockie's; we'd built most of the fuckin thing. Got bollocked by his uncle, Snake Tong Tony; *not* a man you wanner fall foul of.

—Nah. Jimmy Ho's got the job this year.

—Jimmy Ho? Jesus friggin Christ. He'll build it fuckin upside down or something. Inside friggin out.

—Not any more. He's off the bevvy. All dried out. Clean an sober. Pillar of the community ar Jimmy is now, man. Fuckin PR or somethin for the Sino-Scouse Community, as opposed to the hopeless pisshead he was last year.

—Last century.

—Last century, yeh. Anyway, listen, exercise; we're a man short for the five-a-side. Get yer trainies on an I'll pick yis up in about fifteen.

Five-a-side; that sounds just fuckin *perfect*. Just what I need. Football, running, kickin things, aggression, sweat, panting, male company. Sounds like the right fuckin medicine. Exactly what I need right now.

—Alright well. Which court are yis using?

—Greenbank Park.

—Well, don't bother comin to pick me up, I'll meet yis down there. It's not far. Fifteen minutes, yeh?

—Thereabouts. Be quick like cos we wanner start.

—Alright. See yer there.

I hang up an change into sweats an trainies an a hoody. I'll *run* down to Greenbank, get the heart beatin an all the blood flowin. Blow the brain-cobwebs away, not that there's really any of them left after that, that fuckin, that last mad fuckin night with that last mad fuckin bitch. Cleared me right friggin out she did. Scraped it all out with a trowel. Feels like the lining of me fuckin *veins* has been sandblasted away.

I'm runnin as soon as I leave the house, down to thee end of the Lane an over the road into Sefton Park. Five minutes in an already I'm thinkin that this is a mistake; me ankle bones feel like ther crumblin with each footfall, me knees seem to be poppin an me thigh muscles are sayin 'ow' over an over again. Fuckin daft idea this. Spend over three weeks doin nowt but drinkin an druggin an of fuckin *course* yer body's gunner complain if yer start doin fuckin *this* to it. Christ, I can hardly breathe. The sweat an the rough material of me kex an top are beginnin to irritate me wounds, the rips in me skin an sphincter, an to ease it I start to run a bit bandy like Charlie Chaplin or someone which causes much mockin hilarity among the group of ten-year-old scallies bunkin school an fishin with empty crisp bags for sticklebacks in the duckpond.

—Fuckin state of yer!

—Shit yer kex, mister!

—Fuckin Duckboy over there!

Little bastards. I run, or friggin waddle, around the corner away from them an then think fuck it an slow to a walk, an unsteady, wheezin walk. Bleedin knackered I am. Then I think fuck it again an sit-down on a bench to get me breath back cos it's gone somewhere else. Pressure of the hard, cold wood sendin an ache up me arse. The rips up there. Fuckin mad fuckin bitch.

It's *freezin* fuckin cold. Clouds of steam are leavin me gob with unhealthy rapidity. Like a fuckin train or somethin. A steamtrain. The last time I remember me heart beatin this fast was last night when. When Kelly. When I. When me an Kelly did. The sky is a uniform grey, not one single shred of blue, no clouds or anythin just a flat bland breeze-block greyness. It's all dull an miserable. Leafless trees an frosty grass, sound of incessant traffic whinin over the hedge. One dead flower in that hedge, a wrinkled thing black with deadness. A black flower like the one. Like the one tattooed on. That fuckin girl.

Yeh, that insane fuckin girl responsible for the relentless stinging between me legs as I leave the bench an walk, carefully, over to the Greenbank courts. That mad fuckin bint causin me this pain. What the fuck, I mean, did she think I'd fuckin *enjoy* that shit, that fuckin carvin in me back an the fuckin *fist* up me friggin arse? All that fuckin ripping? Fuckin *torture* it was. No lie. You mad fuckin cow, it's *your* fault I can't walk properly. It's *your* fuckin fault I can't sleep on me back. Cracked fuckin woman, I'll never even *think* of you ever again.

Jesus Christ.

Quockie's waitin for me outside the five-a-side courts with three others; two of them I know, a pleasant enough feller called Beans an a surly fat fucker called O'Brien, or Obi for short, Jedi for obscure, an Big Fat Grumpy Cunt for accuracy (my *Star Wars* pun – Obi Wanker Nobi – never caught on). The other lad is another Chinese bloke who Quockie introduces to me as Paul; he gives me a nod, no grin. Not free with the grinnin, these Chinese.

—Yer look shagged out already, Vic, Quockie says. —Ran here, yeh?

—Tried to, mate, yeh. Out of fuckin shape. Had to have a sit-down halfway across Sevvy Park.

O'Brien snorts an I give him a look. Like to see *you* run across Sefton Park yer fat wobblin monstrosity.

—Eeyar, Vic. Put these on.

Quockie hands me a pair of padded gloves.

—Aw no! Not friggin goalie!

—Have to be, Victor. Ar usual's hung-over in bed.

—I'm friggin *whack* in goal, Quox, yer know that. Member the last time I played in goal? Against that Wallasey team? The twelve-niller?

—I do, yeh, but there's no other choice. Has to be keeper. Obi's defence, me an Beansy're midfield, Paul's the lone attacker. That's where we always play. Now stop yer friggin whinging an get between them sticks.

We go into the court where thee other team are warmin up, takin it all a bit too fuckin seriously, leg-stretches, bends, runnin on the spot, all that shite. I raise me eyebrows at Beans an he tells me that ther in a team in Fazakerly an District Youth League, one or two of them bein scouted by big clubs.

—Youth League? How old are thee?

—About friggin seventeen. Just kids really.

—Ah fuck. We'll get shown up here.

—Nah. Don't worry about it, Vic. The little attacker, see him with the bleached crop?

The bleached crop. Like, what's-her-namey, Roz. Friend of that other girl whose name began with a K.

—Yeh.

—Well, he's bein watched by Everton. So now's yer chance to get one over on a future Bluenose bastard, yeh? *Is* right, man.

He slaps me on the back, right on me wounds, me cuts, an I hiss in pain an wince but he doesn't notice cos he's jogged over into the middle of the court. I rub gently at the sore spot an take me place in goal directly behind O'Brien's abomination of an arse. The game kicks off.

We get friggin hammered. The first few minutes go okay, Paul an Quockie both comin close to scoring at thee other end an O'Brien proving almost impassable; in fact, with the lack of activity me body starts to cool down an I'm even beginnin to shiver but then ther little striker nutmegs O'Brien an slams it low in the corner, too fast for me to even fuckin *see* let alone intercept.

—Oh fuckin nice one, keeper, O'Brien says. —Yer are allowed to fuckin *move*, yer know.

—Yeh an you're allowed to fuckin defend, as well. I pick the ball up out of the net. —Not just stand there with yer legs open like a fat Faulkner Street prozzy.

—Fuck off.

—Play fuckin football, O'Brien. Defend. Yer blert.

Which he tries to do but without any speed or skill cos at half-time we're 4–0 down. Useless. Standin on the sidelines smokin an wheezin while thee other little gets suck oranges an do sit-ups.

—Would've been better off with one of me fuckin boots as keeper, O'Brien says. —Would've been as much use as the one we've fuckin got.

I just stare at the cunt an shake me head. It's a kickabout, knobhead, a game of five-a-side. It's not important. It doesn't matter. If yer feel humiliated by bein turned inside out by a seventeen-year-old then you should fuck off an do somethin else. Get some friggin self-respect. In the past few days I've done things you'll never do in yer entire fat life. I've been places you'll never even know exist. I've experienced life at its most extreme, for good or bad I've seen the fuckin light at thee edge of the fuckin world. An all's you can do is whine about losing a fuckin five-a-side game of football. Jesus Christ.

—The fucker yer lookin at? What's wrong with yis?

His big round face in mine. All worked-up an angry. I shake me head at him an Quockie pulls him away.

—Fuck sakes, lar, calm down. It's just a fuckin kickabout. Gerrer friggin grip.

The game restarts. An finishes 7–1, Beansy gettin ours with a flyin header, a rattler into the bottom of the left-hand corner off the top of his ginger nut, scrapin all the skin off his elbows in the process. Best friggin goal of the game. Not that it matters. To anything. I'm fuckin knackered, wheezin like an old man, feelin like I'm gunner be sick. An hour of living has gone. I've distracted meself for an hour or so an that's enough, that's good enough. It's been worthwhile.

O'Brien's all for teachin thee other team a lesson, especially the little bleached attacker but Quockie tells him not to be soft an to knob off which, muttering, he, fatly, does. Beansy an Paul go off as well, for a pint.

—Wharrabout you, Vic? Fancy a bevvy?

I shake me head. —Nah. Want somethin to eat. I'm starvin.

—Come back to mine well. Pick somethin up on the way.

—Could do with a shower as well tho. I ming.

—Get one of them at mine as well. Come ed, I haven't seen yer since we went to Wales. Fuckin ages ago man.

—Two days. But alright.

We go back to Quockie's place off Ullet Road, pickin up some pasties an butties from Sayers on the way. We eat them back at his an drink tea an smoke a mild spliff an talk bollox for a bit an then I take a shower. Deep stingin of the soap on me back an between me legs, I mean real deep stinging, muscle-deep like, so fuckin deep it throbs in me teeth as the soap penetrates the rips an tears. When will these things heal? I'm not meself until I heal. Marked, branded. That mad hag hackin at me. I could've fuckin died.

I dry meself with one of Quockie's mouldy towels an put me dirty sweatpants back on. Have to go home soon for a change of clothes but at least I *feel* better, cleaner, refreshed. I'm at the sink using Quockie's deodorant an I hear the telephone ring an Quockie talking then he's coming in the bathroom.

—That was Craig. Wants to know if we're . . . fuck me, Victor, what's wrong with yer back?

He reaches towards me an I turn away, don't friggin want him to see.

—What is it, man? Have yer had an accident? Looks fuckin bad, that does.

—It's nowt, man. Just some scratches.

—Scratches? From what, a fuckin tiger?

He tries to move around me to see me back but I turn with him, keeping me front to him. Don't want him to see. Don't want *anyone* to see, what she's fuckin done to me, what I've become. What she's fuckin turned me into.

—I'm serious, lar, thee look dead fuckin deep. Yer should see the doc. Might need stitches.

He's lookin over me shoulder at the reflection of me wounded back in the mirror. I go to put me hoody back on so he can't see, put me head through the neck-hole but the sleeves are all tangled up an inside out.

—Oh, I get it, he says. —It's that new girl. That's what it is, innit? The one from Magnet. She did that to yer, didn't she?

I nod. —Yeh. She's got long nails, like. Scratched me when we were on the job.

—Scratched *fuck* out of yer, man. Looks like she's tried to claw yer friggin heart out through yer back. Claw yer fuckin spine out or somethin. Eeyar, let's have a proper look; it looks like *words*.

I manage to untangle the sleeves an work me arms into them an hurriedly pull the top down over me still-wet stingin back.

—Nah, it's just scratches. Her nails are dead long, like. She loses it a bit in bed. Cos I'm such a good shag.

—Yer not friggin kiddin she loses it. Looks like Darren Taylor's been at yer with a Stanley.

—I know, yeh. Fuckin hurts as well. Me back's in bulk.

—Yer wanner sort that out, man. Tell her to get her nails cut or something. Wear fuckin gloves.

—Yeh. Altho I don't think I'll be seein her for much longer, to tell yer the truth. Maybe not even again.

—Oh aye?

I nod.

—But you were fuckin full of her when we went to Wales, like. Wouldn't stop goin on about her if I remember. What's gone wrong?

I shrug. Wrinkle me nose an I'm aware that I'm copyin someone's gestures but I'm not sure whose. —Yer know. Just fuckin . . . there's not much between us, like. One of them things. An she's a bit full-on. Bit of a fuckin nutter, to be honest.

—Ah yeh. Met plenty of them in me time, man, fuckin tellin yer. Bleedin city's full of them. An yer best off rid; Jesus, I'd get fuckin miles away from someone who could do *that* to me back. Throes of friggin passion or no, I'd put at least a fuckin county between her an me. Can't be fuckin sane, that, man. Not fuckin safe.

—Yeh.

I tell Quockie I need to use his bog an he leaves an I lock the door an drop me kex an take a seat. I need to shite but me guts are a bit blocked an it hurts horrible to push; the rips in me sphincter feel like ther openin up again with the straining. My God, what has she done to me. Maybe I'll take some ex-lax until I heal. Until I *heal*, Christ, I shouldn't be sayin that. Shouldn't have to be sayin that. My God, what she has done to me. I stand an look down at the thin tendrils of blood in the water then flush the chain an take me top off again an turn me back to the mirror over the sink, crane me head back over me shoulder to see. I can't make out anythin except rawness, scabbiness. Red lines, some vertical, some horizontal. Like a psychotic kid might make with a key in a table top or something, just scores an scratches an scrapes, patternless an haphazard. I move closer to the mirror an squint. Maybe there *is* somethin there . . . some form, a letter or something . . .

There's a small round shavin mirror on thee edge of the bath (where she sat, edge of the bath, legs open, *all* of her open) so I take that an hold it up in front of me face so that I can see the reflection of me back in the mirror over the sink. My wounded back twice reflected. *Me* removed from meself two times. The wounds are purple an scarlet an angry-lookin an yes, ther seem to be words, letters or parts of letters, squint an hold the mirror steady an I can just about make them out:

Killy? What the fuck's Killy? And underneath that:

A plus sign. And underneath that:

My name. Me own name carved into me flesh, I'm marked with me own name. Like a sum. An the first word's *not* 'Killy' it's *her* name, her fuckin name, like a schoolgirl with a crush carvin the name of her first boyfriend into the desktop, that's what it says on, in, my back, gouged into the fuckin flesh: KELLY + VICTOR. That's what she carved into my back when I was tied screaming to her bed, before she greased her arm with cream an fist-fucked me. KELLY + VICTOR. My God. You insane, twisted, demented fuckin bitch. You really are warped, aren't yer? What kind of fuckin sickness in yer head to do such a thing. What kind of mad fuckin . . .

KELLY + VICTOR. Carved into my fucking back.

I am just meat.

Jesus Christ.

I go into the kitchen an tell Quockie I've got to go home.

—You alright, man? Yer've gone all pale. Look like yer've seen a ghost.

I tell him that I don't feel very well an have to nash.

—I'll drive yis. Yer don't look well at all.

I tell him that I'd sooner walk, get some fresh air, like, an leave. Back through Sefton Park. A couple kissing beneath a leafless tree an a baghead on the nod on a bench. Go home an get changed into clean clothes, smears of blood on the insides of the dirty ones, pick up some money an go round to thee offy; vodka, litre bottle, an a big bottle of Coke to mix. Back home, make a drink, turn on the telly. Oz soaps an *Countdown*, *Ready Steady Cook* an *Pet Rescue*. Didn't he used to play for Chelsea? The drink tastes like polystyrene but I drink it anyway, I mean, it's not the fuckin taste I'm bothered about. Can't believe what she did. Can't fuckin believe that I'm marked this way. Christ alfrigginmighty. How I lay there bound an fuckin pleadin for her to stop an she hacked her fuckin name into me back an rammed her fuckin hand up into me guts. I remember the pain an the terrible feeling of helplessness an then without wantin to I also remember thee explosion of light in me head, golden an fuckin wonderful, me head bursting with all that light an me heart roaring an it was like nothing on fuckin earth, like I'd known nowt of living until that moment an all those years in school an on the dole an mixin cement on sites or lugging boxes twelve hours a day in chugging factories, the boredom, the fuckin *boredom*, were all fuckin worth it because thee all led to that, that fuckin light, that bright an bursting fuckin rapture. An now that's all gone. No more sunbursts, no more fuckin melting in a wave of gold. Her hands around my neck, takin me to that place. How fuckin . . . *important* I felt.

I turn the gas fire on. It's fuckin well *freezing* in here.

Finish the drink, pour another. Force meself to watch *Friends* an think of nothing else. That Jennifer Aniston one looks a bit like. From a certain angle she. In a certain light she. My chest's beginnin to feel all sticky an heavy like it does just before I'm about to break apart an I don't wanner do that because I'm afraid I'd never be able to put meself together again an with perfect fuckin timing the door opens an in stumbles Dermot, half-pissed, eating from an open bag of chips. Good fuckin on yer, Dermot. My good fucking friend.

—Now, Victor.

—Derm.

He flops down heavily into an armchair. Puts a long thin chip between his front teeth an waggles it at me like a worm. Or a long, thin, yellow tongue.

—That's friggin hanging, Dermot. Stop it.

He swallows it down. —Fancy a chip?

—No ta.

—Sausage?

—No ta.

—Yeer sure now? I bought three.

I shake me head. —Fancy a drink? Vodka an Coke?

—Ah, no. I brought me own from the pub.

He takes a can of lager out of the pocket of his overcoat an cracks it open. Good on yer, Dermot. Good to have yis sittin in the room, all the fuckin drunken chippy *there*ness of yer. Me mad fuckin mate Dermot.

—Which pub were yis in?

—That one just around the corner. The Albert.

—On yer own?

He nods.

—Best friggin company, man.

—Ah yeh. Only I got into a wee row with meself an called meself out. Had to fuckin fight meself in the alley. But it was alright tho cos I won.

He bites a sausage in half an chews an swallows, lookin at me.

—What's up with *ye*?

—Nothing.

—Yer arse. Fuckin gob on yeh, Victor. That new mot, is it?

Good radar on Dermot. Might be a pig an all that but there's a sharpness somewhere inside that addled head.

—Suppose so, yeh. Kind of.

—Kind of? What kind of kind of?

It'd be so easy just to tell him. Tell him all of what happened, the light an the binding an the cutting an the fist an the blood an the spurting an the horror an the pain an the fuckin storm in me head. So easy. No, fuck that, it *wouldn't* be fuckin easy; it might make me feel better, temporarily like, shriven or absolved or something, I don't know, but it wouldn't be fuckin *easy* to tell him, not by any means. In fact it'd be impossible. Fuckin impossible. So all's I say is:

—Too much, like. It was just gettin too much.

He stares at me, chewing, his chin all shiny with grease. —Too much?

—Yeh.

—How? How was it too much?

—Yer know. Too, like, intense. Full-on. Yer know. Only known each other for a few days, like, an it was . . . just gettin too much.

I shrug.

—Aye, but in what way too much, tho? What, talkin about fuckin marriage an stuff, was she? I mean, I'm not fully gettin ye here.

—Jesus Christ, Dermot. Fuckin questions on you, man.

—Aye, an what's yer answer? Was she goin on about a weddin an stuff?

—No. Nothin like that.

—Then in what way was it gettin too much? Was she wantin ye to move in with her?

—No.

—Have kids with her?

—*God*, no.

—Fuck all yer mates off?

I shake me head. His eyes widen in horror. —Holy God, she wasn't demandin that ye go on the turn to fuckin Everton, was she?

I laugh. —No.

His eyes open even further. —Not Man U-fuckin-nited? Aw please God, don't tell me that ye poked one of the Scum.

I laugh again. —As if. Djer really think I would? Nah. She's a good Red.

—Well, thank Christ for that. Then what was it that went wrong?

—I don't know. It was just too fuckin much. It was just gettin, like, out of hand. *Well* out of hand.

He eats the rest of the sausage an folds the chips up neatly an sticks the greasy bundle in his pocket. Then he startles me by sayin, with feeling:

—Shite. Utter fuckin shite. Too much me bollix.

I'm shocked. —Why?

—Because what ye mean by 'too much' is that it was gettin too good. Don't ye? Aye, ye do. An it can *never* be too much, man. *Never* be too much. I'll fuckin well *tell* ye what's too much.

He wipes his face with an oily hand an lights a ciggie an jerks his thumb back over his shoulder at the window and the street outside.

—*That's* too fuckin much. All that fuckin arse out there, man. This morning I had to beg for money from a feller called Tyrone with a gold Nike tick in his ear an explain to him why I don't think I'm suited for the New fuckin Deal he offered me, parkin attendant at Safeway's. An then just fuckin sit there while he tells me that if I don't, I won't get any fuckin money. I've got to help an old lady up off the floor after she's been rolled by three fuckin pipeheads for her pension. An not just a bag-snatch, no, this was the real fuckin deal, ye know, blade at the throat, blacked her eye. An I've got to ferry pints out of the pub to a feller born in the same village I was born in cos he's barred from there after fuckin haemorrhaging all over the pool table one fine night when he nearly succeeded in drinkin hisself to death. Barman tells him to find another bar to die in but he's been drinkin in there for over fifty years, his granda took him in there for his first pint, straight off the boat. He's near on seventy years old. An I'm handin him out pints an whiskies an he just sits there on the step in the freezin fuckin cold. Dying. Which is just the way he wants it. This was all today, Victor. All of this happened today. An nothin out of the fuckin ordinary about it either, no.

He shakes his head. —See what I mean? *That's* too much. All of that's too fuckin much, Victor. There's a difference there that ye should understand, between what is too much an what fuckin isn't. Sometimes what ye think is too much turns out not to be, it's just that ye can't fuckin handle it cos it's somethin ye've never known before an so yeer scared of it. Scared of bein fuckin shocked out of what ye know; all the fuckin shite. Ye with me?

I don't know whether I am. He slurps at his can an says:

—Did I ever tell ye me crackwhore story?

—No.

—I never told ye.

—Don't think so, Dermot, no. We've all got one, tho.

—Haven't we just. Anyway, what happened was, when was this now . . . about a year or two ago . . . somethin like that. I was on one *fuck* of a bender, had been for months. Just jacked me job in at the time, like, an was blowin me last wages. The fuckin works, boy; half a bottle of vodders an a few pipes afore I even dragged me arse out of the bed, that kind of thing, ye know?

I nod. I *do* know, yeh. Only too fuckin well.

—So's I find meself in the Dart down Lodge talkin to this woman. Skinny, like, not a friggin pick on her, those crackhead eyes an skin. *You* know what I'm talkin about.

Yeh. The deadening, the darkenin of the pupils; like some bad force, some demon, is tryin to wipe the life out in them. I know that fuckin look. See it everywhere; on thee underground, down Church Street with its claws out, on St Luke's steps. Fuckin *everywhere* in this city. Dermot goes on:

—We ends up back at my place, I was squattin an old shop near Edge Hill at the time. I gave her twenty quid an shagged her, one of those nothing fucks, ye know, the kind where ye just do it cos ye can't be bothered thinkin of anythin else to do. Nothin comes out like, just a wee dribble. Almost fuckin hurts. Anyway, she said that if I gave her another thirty she'd go off an score some stones for us both, but of course I wasn't havin that, no fuckin way, knew I'd never see me money or her again, like, so I told her to leave her handbag with me for the insurance. She did an fucked off.

He drinks deeply at his can.

—So an hour goes by. I'm in the mood for some rock, like, but I knew by this time that she'd fuckin well done one on me so I thought arses to it, screw her bag, see if I can get somethin from it that might salvage the sitch. Maybe somethin in there

112

I could sell or swap or somethin, ye know. Guess what was in the bag.

—Nowt. It was a dummy bag.

—It was a dummy fuckin bag, aye, which I should've fuckin well known. Should've fuckin *known* that she'd be keepin any valuables in her pockets, like, in case she got snatched. It wasn't empty, but. D'ye know what was in it?

I shrug. —Dunno.

—A cake.

—A cake?

—Aye, a wee cake. That's all. A wee sponge thing in a paper wrapper with pink icing on it, what's that ther called now?

—Fairy cakes.

—That's the one. That's all she had in her handbag, a wee fairy cake with pink icing. What the fuck for, don't ask me, but at the time, like, in me fucked head, the state I was in after all the caning, I started to think that maybe it was somethin like, erm, her fuckin *soul* or something, ye know. Like the sweetness inside her that the drugs an the mess of her life was slowly fuckin sucking out of her. Know what I'm sayin? Like that wee cake was her humanity an she was hiding it, like, keepin it for herself. That's what I was thinkin. At the time, like.

—What did yis do with the cake? Did yer eat it?

—*Eat* it? Fuck *no*, man, how the fuck could I have eaten it? I've just said, I thought it was her bleedin soul. Couldn't eat anyone's soul, man, Jesus.

—So what did yer do with it?

—I left it in the bag an went back to the Dart an handed it in behind the bar. I was hopin she'd go back in there, see, an the barman would spot her an give her it back. Whether she ever did or not I don't know cos I went off to Chinatown that night an bought me *own* fuckin rocks. Got caned with Beansy. Craig an all too, I think.

—Did yis ever see her again?

He shakes his head. —No. God only knows what happened to her. He finishes his can an opens another. —Anyway, that's me crackwhore story. We've all got one, haven't we?

—Seems like.

—So what's yours, then?

I fill me glass, neat vodka this time, an tell him; about how fuckin lonely I was; about the girl an me buyin the stones, goin back to her place to smoke them; how she went down on me an had to break off every three minutes to do another pipe, how I told her it didn't really matter an we could just lie there together cos I was enjoyin meself anyway without the sex an I'd pay her for her time regardless; how we started to touch an caress, soft like, dead gentle; how I made her come with me fingers an how I knew that she'd come because of the way she was afterwards, shoutin at me, sayin that I thought she was nothing but a whore an that I'd never see her as anything else, I'd never see her as a friend or a lover just as a crackwhore from Tocky with five kids in care at the age of twenty-four; about how I denied such accusations an let her beat on me cos that's what she seemed to want to do, that's what seemed to make her feel better, layin into me as I curled up against the wall, an about how after she'd finished she fell asleep in me arms like a baby, pure dead to the fuckin world an I had to go but I wanted to leave her a note but couldn't find a pen or paper or anything so I just sneaked off an felt like the biggest wanker on the planet for two days until I went back to her house to see her only to be told by another pro who lived there that she'd gone, she'd fucked off, didn't know where, she'd just disappeared overnight an that her name was Rebecca, the first time I heard her name, Rebecca. And about how I never saw her since an about how I wished to God I had.

Dermot nods. —Yep. I know *that* feelin. Like yeer the biggest arsehole in the history of the world.

—Is right.

—Even bigger than when yeer told that the job most suited to ye on ther fuckin computer is car-park attendant at Safeway.

—Yeh. Or fuckin dogsbody on some site or in some factory somewhere.

—Exactly. Which is what I'm sayin, Victor; it's all too much, that shite, things makin ye feel that way. *That's* what's too fuckin much, an the world is fuckin full of it, boy. An if ye can find one thing that makes ye feel a wee bitty better about it then ye should fuckin well stick with that one thing, even if it's scary or fuckin, ye know, frightens yeh, cos yer only feelin that way about it cos it's new, ye've never experienced its like before. An given time it'll become, it'll turn from bein scary into somethin ye don't know how the *fuck* ye could ever have lived without. So give it time. Or at least stick with it til it stops bein scary an turns into somethin else, and *then* see how ye feel about it. Give it time, likes.

He finishes his can an burps massively. —Ye with me?

Whether I am or not I still don't know, it's somethin I'll have to think about. But I nod anyway.

—Good man. Ye up for later?

—When? Tonight?

—Aye.

—What's happenin tonight?

—Craig's big brother, Eddie. Ye know Eddie?

—Yeh.

—He's just become a dad. Little boy. We're wettin the babby's head. Legs of Man alehouse, nine o'clockish.

—Alright. How's the mam?

—*She's* sound, yeh, but with the babby it was touch-an-go apparently. Born dead, he was.

—What?

—Aye, ye know that cord thing . . . the lifeline, like . . .

—Thee umbilical cord?

—Aye, well, that was all wrapped around his wee neck, chokin him, like. Eddie said that for a few seconds he was actually fuckin dead, heart stopped an everythin. Doctors had to revive him. Mouth-to-mouth on a newborn baby, Jesus. Fine now, tho; little belter, Eddie says.

He stands up. —Anyway. I'd best get back to the pub cos I'll be missin meself. I'll be all lonely. Legs of Man later, yeh?

—Okay.

Dermot leaves an there's just me an the bottle an the telly again. Not that I'm watchin it; I'm thinking of Eddie's baby, comin into the world already dead. Like winnin the race. The cord around his neck, starvin him of oxygen before he's even had the chance to breathe any. This thought sparks something off, some vague memory at the very edge of me recall, some bright blue remembering which flashes blinding once like lightning an then is completely gone.

Eddie's up at the bar, bein held upright by Craig. People are shakin his hand an rufflin his hair an punchin his shoulders an slappin his back an he's rockin from side to side with thee attentions, great big sloppy grin on his face. Craig holds him up with one hand as if presentin him as a trophy or somethin an points right into his face with thee other hand an yells at the smoky ceiling:

—My brother! My fuckin BROTHER!

Cheers an glasses go up. I raise mine as well an neck half of it. Near on very, very wrecked. Almost a full bottle of Prince Caspian an now all these pints an the bugle in the bogs, six or seven lines now, lost count, not far off ten. Very, very wrecked almost. Me sister Elizabeth is up at the bar with Claire, Craig an Eddie's sister. Ther smiling at Eddie as he breaks into some unintelligible, slurred song. Can't tell what it's meant to be; it sounds like nothing on earth.

God, we're fuckin weird. Strange fuckin creatures, us. A few hours into fatherhood, his own insurance against bein temporary, an Eddie's blottin out his new-found happiness with the bevvy. Lots an lots of bevvy. Knockin it back. His missus is still in thee ozzy with the baby, who is lucky to be alive, an Eddie's makin sure that he himself doesn't *feel* alive for some time cos pretty soon, the way he's goin, he'll be friggin comatose. He can hardly stand already. He's well out of it. Laughin an roarin now but in a short while he'll be as sick as a dog an then forgetful of everythin that's happened in the last couple of days. The new life. Thee escape from death. God, how fuckin peculiar we are, us, the way we live ar lives. The sheer fuckin mystery of us. How we plunge arselves into these rapids, these stormy seas, get so irreparably fucked up when all we really ever want is peace.

—How's me best brother? Fuckin out of it by the looks.

I look up an grin at Elizabeth. —Lizzy . . . you look nice.

—Ta.

—Where's Eddie? I can't see Eddie.

—That's cos he's in the bogs bein as sick as a dog. Craig's with him. He's friggin *well* out of it, man.

—Yis havin a drink with me?

She shakes her head. —Can't. Meetin people in Magnet in a few minutes. We're cuttin off now.

—Oh.

Magnet. The red an the white, the red an white lights. Flashing. On an then off. Redflash whiteflash, in her eyes, on her teeth.

—What's wrong? What's the face for?

—Nowt, I say. —Nothin at all, honest. I'm happy as a pig in shite.

My arse hurts. My back hurts.

—Oh. Made up for yeh well. How's things goin with that new girl?

—What new girl?

—Yer know, the one yer told me about on the phone. Just after New Year's. Forgotten her name now. You were goin on an on about how great she is. Made me friggin sick.

I don't say anything.

—Ah, no. Fucked up, is it? Already?

I just shrug. If I try to say anything I might very well fuckin burst out crying. Or, worse, tell Elizabeth the true story. Everything. Fuckin disaster that would be.

—Ah, Vic. Give us a call or somethin in the week, yeh? We'll go out for a bevvy or something.

—Alright.

—Make sure yer do. An phone Mam an Dad.

—Alright.

—I mean it.

—I will.

She stands on tiptoe to kiss me forehead an then leaves the pub with Claire. I watch them go, watch how the bouncers look them up an down then nod firmly at each other over ther heads. I'd give *that* one, that nod says. I'd fuck *that*. Bleedin wankers. She's fifteen fuckin years old. I see Marblearse come into the pub an make a beeline over to the swayin Eddie. Thee unsteady Eddie.

—Edward, my man! Fuckin well done, lar! Made up for yeh! He pumps Eddie's hand vigorously. Eddie just lets it be pumped. —Large Scotch over here, love!

—Cheers, Marbs, Craig says for his brother who doesn't look like he's able to form words. When the Scotch arrives Craig even has to hold it up to Eddie's mouth, like he's feeding an invalid. Marblearse looks on, beaming. —Go on, lar! Gerrit down yer neck!

Marblearse: so-called because when we were at Our Lady's he had to go to hospital to get ollies removed from his bum. Right inside, like, thee were, up in his intestines. *Right* inside. His story was that he was playing with his marbles in the bath an he forgot thee were there an later he ran the bath an got in it an sat on them. How he managed to sit on six at the same time, tho, he neglected to clarify. Bet it was less painful than a whole friggin forearm, a whole fist an wrist. Fuckin mad bastard bitch of a woman. Wearin me like a friggin puppet. Fuckin invadin me like that, fuckin rummaging around in me guts. All of a sudden I feel the need to see Eddie's baby. I need to see all the pink pissed-off newness of him, smell his hot skin, press me cheek to the soles of his feet, put the tip of me nose against the soft spot on his head. I stagger over to Eddie to tell him just that.

—Victor, man! Nicer yer to join us!

Craig throws his arms around me an without support, Eddie starts to topple. Marblearse an the Beans an some man-mountain who I don't know catch him before he hits the floor.

My head is filled with roaring; Craig in one ear, Beansy in thee other, Quockie somewhere in the middle. Ther shoutin somethin about goin on to the Jacaranda an I'm just noddin along. What was I going to say to Eddie? I was gunner tell him somethin but I can't for the fuckin life of me remember what it was. It's gone.

I wonder if that'll ever be me, celebratin the birth of my first child. I hope so. I really fuckin do hope so. I would hate to die without knowin what that's like.

Fuck it. How stupidly, impossibly fuckin strange we are. Me eyelids closing, slidin down, the darkness all descending. Pouring into me bangin skull.

This can't be put off any longer; I've got to go an make a claim for the dole. There's not much money left in me account an I don't feel up to goin back on a site just yet, at least not until me rips close up, like, so signin on it has to be. The housing benefit's good for another couple of months, no problems there, like, except the cheques go straight to Riverside Housing Association an I don't even get to see them, but for daily expenses all's I've got is me rapidly dwindlin current account, so it can't be put off any longer: DSS. With the emphasis on the SS. Back into ther fuckin system. Back into ther ranks. Stupid an dull. This fuckin world.

I catch a bus down Park Road, get off at the Pineapple where I'll go for a scoop or four after I've done what needs to be done. The DSS building behind the row of leafless trees like tall skeletons all blackened with exhaust is all bland an brown an lifeless like those trees an it looks fuckin horrible, fortress-like, an I don't feel up to it just yet so I go into one of the phone boxes by the bus stop. There's somethin else I have to do that can't be postponed any longer either. Money in the slot, dial the number.

—Hello?

—Mam?

—Victor, son, how are yer?

—Sound, Mam, you?

—Alright. Bit flu-ey.

—Yeh, yer sound a bit snotty. Just a cold, tho, yeh?

—Yeh. This bleedin weather. Innit cold?

—It is, Mam, yeh. Yer off on yer hollyers soon tho, aren't yeh?

—Yeh. Can't wait. Frankie's workin twelve-hour days to get us some spends together. All he does is sleep an work but it'll be worth it in the end, won't it?

—God, yeh. Get some bloody sun an rest.

—That's what I need, Vic.

—*And* deserve, Mam.

—Go 'way. Yer big friggin creep.

I laugh. —How's all thee others?

—Alright. Ar Curtis an Stevie are still down south. Jean an Jocky have named the day.

—About time. When is it?

—Can't remember now. Sometime in October, I think. Djer want me to goan check?

—Nah, it's alright. Tell me some other time. I'll be seein yis soon, probly.

—When?

—Couple of weeks or somethin. It's Chinese New Year next week so I've got to help Quockie an his uncle get everythin prepared. So I'm dead busy at the mo.

A fib. I'm not busy at all. In fact I've never been less busy. I'm just ploddin through life without aim, point, or purpose. Bored an listless an without any illumination.

—Make sure that's *all* yer do for that uncle of Quockie's.

—I will, Mam, yeh. Don't worry. I saw ar Lizzie thee other night.

—Yeh, she told me. Said yer had a cob on. Looked fed up.

—Nah, not really. Just a bit pissed, yer know. Just tired, like.

—Yeh sure?

—Yeh. How's ar Kirk?

—Kirk? You'll never guess.

—What?

—He's got a job.

—Kirk? Yer jokin. No way. I don't believe it.

—It's true. In a warehouse somewhere on the Wirral. He's been there a week an he looks like death warmed up, doesn't know what's hit him.

I laugh, imagining Kirk – who smokes more than an eighth a day, has done for years – workin in a warehouse. The word that springs to mind is 'incongruous'.

—Anyway, when're yer coming over? We'd all love to see yer, Vic. I'll make somethin nice.

—Soon, Mam. After Chinese New Year. Say the week after next.

—Bring that new girl, what's her name . . .

—Ah, the money's goin, Mam. I've got to go.

—Kelly, was it? Or Kerry? You still seein her?

—Mum, the pips have gone. I'll see yis in a week or two, yeh?

—Okay, son. Look after yerself.

—An you. Love to everyone.

I hang up quickly an the phone eats me change, 31p. Fuckin BT greedy bastards. I think about givin me dad a call as well but I don't bother; he'll probly be out at work anyway. An besides, he'll also ask me questions about Kelly that I won't be able to answer an unwittingly throw up images an memories that I'll have difficulty in handling, an I'll also have to make arrangements to see him an Christine as well sometime in the future when I can barely envisage thee end of today, this evening, an the whole friggin thing'll be horrible, as will at the moment makin a claim for the dole so I buy a paper an go into the Pineapple. It's 11.15 in the mornin an the bar's full; right next door to the DSS building, this pub does good business. Best speck in the city. I order a pint of Guinness an take it to a corner table, next to an ahl feller intently studying the racin form. I read the sports pages an drink the pint which is so fuckin nice that I immediately buy another. Then another. When I leave the pub it's chocka with the dinner-time trade, all loud an friendly an I wanner stay in there but signin on really can't be put off any longer, I'll be completely friggin brassic soon, so I leave the pub an go to the dole office an join the long queue at the back an wait.

And wait.

And wait for so fuckin long . . . the security guard's tryin to have a banter with us all, keep ar spirits up, like, an avoid trouble but no one's havin any of it; we're all here for one thing only, only one thing, an nothin else counts or matters to us here, in this space. This space of muttering an shuffling an slow, slow hours. Dead time, rotting life here in this dull an lightless brick box. I hate it. I fucking hate it. It's the enemy of everythin I hold dear; no freedom to move here, no fuckin warmth, no explosions of bright light. Or any light at all. You can feel all thee animation inside yer slidin out of yer shoes like cold curry sauce.

What seems like hours pass. The whole world has slowed to a painful, crippled crawl. What small alcohol buzz I had has now become nowt but a fuzziness in me head an a foul an funny taste in the very back of me throat. Jesus sufferin Christ. Sooner fuckin *work* than this. No fuckin lie.

—Who's next please?

Me. At last it's fuckin me. Get this hell over with an get back to the pub.

I take the spare seat at the desk which bears the name 'Tyrone' on it on a Toblerone-shaped piece of plastic. Dermot's Tyrone? Yes; there's the gold Nike tick swingin from his earlobe. Dermot's Tyrone. Whatever makes yer feel valuable.

—I'd like to open a claim, please.

Tyrone sniffs thee air between us an grins.

—Liquid lunch, eh? Bit of a bevvy this mornin?

I say nowt. Just get this fuckin over with. Tyrone takes details; name, age, address. Last job. Reasons for leaving. All that shit. Reasons for leaving.

Sick of the whole fuckin thing. I mean physically sick, in me stomach, dry heaves as if I've eaten somethin bad, decayed. Maggots, writhing. Meat so rank it's green, flyblown. Dogshit. Fresh dogshit the colour of mustard licked up off the pavement.

—Laid off.

—Oh? From Urban Splash?

—Yeh.

—That job's still ongoing, from what I've heard. Behind schedule, like. In fact ther still advertising for workers. An ther layin people off, yer say? Unusual.

I say nothing. Just give me the forms, Tyrone, you gobby fuckin bastard. Just give me the fuckin forms an let me go back to the pub.

He does: Application for income support, unemployment benefit an council tax rebate combined. Housing benefit as well but I don't need that; I told them I was workin part-time, filled in a fuckload of forms an thee continued with the full entitlement. So many fuckin forms. I buy a biro from the newsagent's an go back to the Pineapple an fill the forms in, answerin everythin except me personal details with a lie. No light in these official pages. The white spaces for me answers are the white of meat fat on a butcher's slab. There's nothing here.

When I go back to the dole office to hand the forms in I don't need to exaggerate me stagger. Give Tyrone a full blast of me beery breath.

On the bus home, no, on the bus to a pub nearer me house I can think of nothing but. Nothin except. Just. Only.

That one.

That fuckin Kelly.

What is she doin now, I wonder. What the fuck is she doin now. Nothing, I bet. But who the fuck cares anyway, not fuckin me, no.

I pick the kettle up to test its weight, see if there's enough water in it for a brew. There isn't, so I work the lead out of its attachment, take the kettle over to the sink – which involves, in this tiny kitchen, no movement other than a 180-degree spin – turn the cold tap on, hold the spout under the flow an keep it there for a count of three. Spin back, reattach the lead, flick the two switches; the one on the wall socket an the one on the kettle itself. I bend an put me ear to the kettle to listen for the rumble, I like doin this, I don't know why; the faint, distant hiss becoming a crackle becomin a rumble as thee element an then the water itself heats up. Something about a certain thing happenin, a specific function bein fulfilled. Kettles do nowt, are good for nothing except heatin water for ar drinks; tea, coffee, hot chocolate, Cup-a-Soups. Pot Noodles. Lemsips if yer ill. Hot water for a shave or a wash if there's none in the tank. That's all thee do, nowt else. Ther ar friends, kettles are. I like my kettle. Under a tenner from Argos. I turn back to the sink to take me mug from the drainin board, me favourite mug with the *Jurassic Park* logo on it which me ex, Michelle, bought for me just after the film came out. Michelle with the dead short hair an the face full of metal. It's clean but I rinse it under the cold tap just to make sure, swill away any small spiders or wharrever an hold it in me left hand while with me right I open the fridge an bend to take out the milk, give the carton a slight squeeze to force the spout open at which I put me nose an sniff to test for freshness. It smells okay. I put a splash into the mug, put the carton back in the fridge, close the fridge an turn back to the kettle an place me mug on the worktop alongside the kettle which is now startin to tremble an steam. From the cupboard above I take a single tea bag from thee open box, Safeway's own brand an put it in the mug with the milk. Turn again an take a teaspoon from the drainin board, turn yet again an look down into the mug. A thin tendril of tea, barely noticeable, just the faintest trickle of brown has leaked out into the white milk. I prod the bag with the tip of the spoon an it crumples a bit an the colour of the tendril becomes slightly darker. The perforations in the bag like pores in skin. Seen close up. Focus, an I can see the tiny filaments in the paper, fibres thinner even than the hairlike cracks in the glaze of me mug. The stains of old tannin over those cracks; smears of brown scored through by the edges of stirring spoons to reveal the white of the porcelain beneath. I stand upright again to watch the nice kettle judder as it comes to the boil. Steam huffs out of it. The lid rises slightly on one edge, just a few millimetres or so to create a small crack from which more steam escapes in a slice, a flat blade of vapour cuttin through the looser clouds that billow from the spout. The kettle shudders madly an looks like it's gunner explode or take off; bet it wishes it *could* take off, soar around the room, turn graceful somersaults in thee air above the cooker. Poor kettle, forever doomed to do one thing only, perform one single solitary function. All the faithful kettles everywhere, uncomplainingly doin ther jobs, providin humans with hot drinks until ther elements, ther *hearts*, burst an thee are thrown away or just simply discarded, chucked, for a newer, better model; one with temperature control an a three-litre capacity an a smooth veneer finish. There is a click an the kettle stops its mad shakin an the escapin steam becomes slower, softer, cloudlike an I pick it up by the handle an pour boilin water on to the tea bag in me mug, the milk-sodden tea bag up to a quarter-inch or so beneath the mug's rim. The water makes that sweet rising-scale sound as the cup fills. I put the kettle back down, pick up the spoon an plunge it into the mug an squeeze the tea bag against the side, squeeze an press it, watch the tea escape an spread, the brown takin over the greyish-white, absorbin it, cloudin an flowin through it turnin it all one uniform colour, light brown. Beige. Say the colour of pine, when it's in furniture, I mean, not tree. Say the colour of the paper the off-licences sometimes wrap yer bottles in. The colour of the coats ahl biddies tend to wear. I scoop the wrung bag out, turn an dump it in the bin by the fridge, chuck the spoon clattering into thee empty sink. From the box of chocolate-chip biscuits by the sink I take three in me right hand, turn an take up me mug of tea in me left, leave the kitchen an go into the livin room which is dead quiet except for the faint splutterin of the gas fire which does very little to alleviate the cold an the damp. It's cold in here as well, half four in thee afternoon an it's almost friggin night-time. It's been rainin all day. Cold an dark. Darkness. Coldness. I put the tea down on the coffee table an sit down on the couch. The biscuits have begun to crumble an melt in me hand so I place them on the table as well, by the tea, the three of them on top of each other in a little stack, crumbs dotted around them like orbitin moons or somethin. I open me hand an look at me palm, see the small brown smears where the chocolate chips have begun to melt, an wipe that palm on the leg of me jeans. I pick up the mug of tea, blow on it, sip at it, an put it back down. That indescribable taste of tea. Incomparable. Only similarity is the taste of iron or copper or somethin, which makes it sound unpleasant but it isn't, tea tastes fuckin wonderful. The whole tea experience is one of beauty an pleasure. Tinglin on me tongue, the back of me throat seemin to sigh as the hot drink slides down. All comforting. Between forefinger an ringfinger of me right hand I take up a bicky an drunk it gently in the tea, just the very tip of it, just thee outer rim of its circular shape.

All of this is movement. Motion. All of it must mean

somethin because it is distraction, it stops me from thinkin of other things. Doing other things. All of this must have some meaning to it because it is what we, humans, all of us, all the time, do. An if it is pointless then so are we.

An I'm not. I'm fuckin well *not*.

I hold the biscuit in the tea an lean forward to examine it closely. Its surface is made up of tiny peaks an swirls, ripples like Artex on a ceiling or a beach after a tide. Tiny hills an valleys in regular lines diagonal across its surface. Minute angular boulders of sugar. An the chocolate chips like the humped brown backs of creatures that live *within* the biscuit breakin the surface like whales, smooth an shiny as if wet. I watch the tea gettin sucked up, dark moisture snakin up into the biscuit, makin the chips of chocolate shinier an the surroundin areas darker an duller of colour. I watch a sugar crystal dissolve; its sharp edges blur an soften an bleed, it loses its opacity an becomes totally transparent, it wobbles for a moment like jelly an then its structure suddenly breaks apart an it disappears, either sucked into the biscuit with the slowly climbing tea or run off down into the mug. It goes completely; one second there's sugar, the next there's not. Blink an it's sugarless, or at least that tiny section of the biscuit is. The chocolate bits too are beginnin to leak in the heat, to lose ther shape an thaw; as I watch, one of them collapses into a cluster of tiny brown worms, wrigglin stiffly down towards the hot surface of the tea. Suicidal. Tryin to drown themselves in a lake of fire. Or no, not fire, lava or something, magma; somethin fluid an extremely hot. As I watch, one of the worms does reach the tea an it melts the moment it touches, turns into a small slick of darker brown. A tiny spillage which disperses an finally disintegrates, becomin one with the tea.

Everythin goin, leavin, dissolving. Or is this union? Neither; it's a fuckin biscuit dunked in tea. That's all it is, Victor; a biscuit dunked in tea.

I lift the biscuit out of the tea an raise it towards me gob but the soggy bottom breaks off an drops back into the tea with a small splash.

Fuck it. I *hate* it when that happens.

Surface of the tea now dotted with wet crumbs, driftin an

squelchy, one chocolate chip which sinks like a submarine. The bottom of the mug, when I reach it, will now be an undrinkable claggy mess; a swamp, a fuckin quagmire of soggy biscuit dough an melted chocolate. When I take the last swig of tea that mess will slide down thee inside of the upturned mug an squash against my lips an I might gag. It does make me gip, that, bicky mush at the bottom of teacups. Or that undissolved powdery sludge at the bottom of Cup-a-Soups. Fuckin horrible. But I can't be arsed makin another cup; even tho it would be motion, an therefore meaning, it would render the makin of this first one pointless an unnecessary so the two actions would cancel each other out, thereby resultin in a big fat round zero. An I can't be doin with that. So I dip the intact half of the biscuit, just once an quickly, in the tea an put it in me gob an crush it against the roof of me mouth with me tongue an it squashes an collapses an bursts sweetness, coats the inside of me gob with a sticky sweet film, gets between me teeth an under me tongue an in that hot dark cramped damp place between yer gums an yer cheek. Every wet crevice, every damp pit filled with this sweet mush. I savour it for a mo then swill it away with a gulp of tea, too big a gulp in fact; it scorches me gullet goin down.

Horrible thought; kissin someone whose gob is filled with biscuit mush. Or any type of food for that matter. Workin it out with the tip of yer tongue, all that friggin spitty slimy food goo. Aw Jesus Christ. Funny how we press those hot holes together. Those orifices which eat an suck an spit an stink an spew an scream an drool an decay an produce foul smells, hot rank stench, an we like to lick them an taste them an sniff them. We like to put other parts in them, parts which we piss out of, shit out of. Bleed out of. All ar reeking, steamin vents an how we like to put them together, suck out an swallow each other's garbage. How friggin peculiar that is. And even fuckin stranger, how it can still be somethin like heaven.

I do the same with thee other two biscuits: dunk (quick), crunch an swallow. Dunk an crunch an swallow. Swill me gob out with tea, of which I leave a good inch or so in the bottom of the mug, an inch of clotted claggy mush which looks like quicksand or slurry. Then I turn the telly on, some children's programme, an light a cigarette.

Suckin the smoke out of the tube, through the filter. The faint crackling, the burning. Somethin about the closest we'll ever get to livin in fire, that most dangerous element but the words won't come. They've stopped. And in fact thee stopped, in a way, since I walked out of Kelly's flat bleedin at back an bum. After she'd fuckin shredded me. Like she also chopped up me capacity to fuckin think an vocalise my thoughts because it seems like I thought different when I was with her. I had better words at my disposal, things I'd never thought before. Even more fuckin unfathomable my life was with her an that's a good thing, a *good* thing, it's somethin I'll one day mourn the losing of.

Kelly, yer fuckin *thief*. No, you fuckin . . . how could you have given so much, an taken so much away? An there's another thing; you've made me sound like Michael fuckin Bolton. Or Bryan bastard Adams, some wank power-ballad singer. Which I'll *never* fuckin forgive yer for. Pure fuckin evil that.

Maybe I *will* make another cup of tea. An a couple more bickies. Or no, maybe a bag of crisps this time, the savoury option. Salt an vinegar. Dermot bought a family pack yesterday; two ready salted, two cheese an onion, two salt an vinegar. Think there's only one bag left tho. Hope it's the salt an vinegar.

An a cheese butty to go with em.

Cheese an tomato.

If there's any tomato in the fridge, which there probly friggin isn't.

Maybe just cheese then. An the tea, of course.

My God, I'm bored. So desperately fuckin bored.

—Dermot.

He doesn't look up from his magazine. *Loaded*, I think it is, or some other lad's tit-mag. Cameron Diaz on the cover.

—Ey, Dermot.

Maybe he can't hear me over the telly. I speak louder:

—Dermot, yer deaf get!

He turns a page an sighs. —What now, my brother?

—Djer know what I've never understood? What I've never been able to get me head round?

—No.

—That fuckin *Blankety Blank* chequebook an pen. I mean, is it a real chequebook, with blank cheques in it like that yer can fill in to pay for things, I mean, do thee give yer money, or is it just a covering for yer normal chequebook? Like a pouch or somethin?

This seems important to me. I don't know why, it just does. Evidently not to Dermot tho cos he just shrugs an holds the mag out at arm's length from his face, appraisin the famous woman on it, whoever it is.

—Don't know, Victor. Don't care, either. Turn the fuckin thing over if it's botherin ye that much. Watch somethin else. Can't fuckin stand that Lily Savage one anyway; fuckin sure it was her I poked last month.

Now *that* I can believe; not that Dermot gave Lily Savage one, but that he shagged someone who looks like her. Not too fussy, Dermot, as regards to bed partners, especially when he's had a bevvy. Not like me. Not like me, no, who recently found a pearl, a flower, a fuckin sunbeam in the darkness. Not like me.

Jesus Christ. Listen to yerself, lad; 'pearl'. Fuckin 'sunbeam'. 'Flower'. What's all that shit about? Get a fuckin grip, Victor, yer losing it. Fuckin 'flower' my arse. Catch yerself on, yer knobhead.

I point the remote at the telly. —Whatjer want on then?

—Anything. Try that Channel 5; there's normally a wee bit of porn on there, this time of night.

—Alright.

I flick it over to Channel 5; in between programmes at the moment, there's just the 5 logo in the corner of the screen, but a voice informs us that after the break we'll be taking a peek behind the lace curtains at sex in suburbia. Dermot puts the magazine to one side an begins to lick an glue Rizlas together.

—Fancy a smoke, Vic?

—Okay.

Bored to fuckin death, I am. Quockie's makin preparations for the Chinese New Year parade in a couple of days' time, Craig's with some girl he's been seein off an on for about a year. Haven't been able to get hold of Beansy or anybody else. I even phoned Elizabeth up on her mobile, see if she wanted a bevvy or somethin, but it was switched off. Probly out at a club somewhere, on one. Seems to be incessant with her these days, the E. So it's a night in with the telly an Dermot, who's just being Dermot; piggin out on pizza an chonga, starin vacantly at the TV screen or at pictures in magazines. He seems to enjoy this, doin nowt; he seems to slip right into it very comfortably, very well. Wish *I* fuckin did. Be nice, that, to be able to do fuck all an enjoy it; just see what life brings yis. Not to search or long or feel relentlessly friggin dissatisfied with everythin yer see. As if it's all colourless. Dull an dark an drab.

—Face on ye, Victor, Dermot says, crumblin resin. —What's botherin yeh?

—Nothin. I'm just bored.

—Ah no. Look at yer woman, there.

He nods at the telly an I look up at it; an overweight woman with a muzzy, dressed in skintight leather gear, is showin us through her house. Typical suburban home with aspirations to class, or glamour of some sort; satin bedspread an Klimt reproductions on the livin-room walls. Some chrome stuff in the kitchen. Makes me a bit sad, that, these movements towards individuality resultin in nothin but uniformity. As if all ar efforts to imprint arselves on the world are doomed to failure an will end in exactly that predictability that we long to avoid. As if we're nowhere near strong enough. Except that here, in the bathroom on the telly, is a masked, otherwise naked man on his hands an knees frantically scrubbin the floor tiles. An interesting ornament. The big woman's standin in front of him, hands on her hips, berating him, calling him all the useless bastards under the sun. His whimpering muffled to a squeak behind the leather mask. She moves behind him an plants a powerful fuckin welly right between his legs; he an Dermot an me all three together go: —Oooooff.

130

—Fuck sakes, Dermot says, lightin the spliff. —I don't see any need for that humiliation. Sure, there's enough of it about without ye havin to fuckin *pay* for it as well. The kick up the arse, aye, I can see the attraction in that; but scrubbin the fuckin floor? Sod that, man. That's goin far too fuckin far.

He takes three quick pulls at the spliff an hands it over to me. I lean forward in the chair an reach. Be easier to stand an walk the three steps or so over to Dermot but then he'd see the bulge in me kex cos I've got a hard-on. I can't help it. I'm aroused. That woman imperious, bossy. It's got nothin to do with her looks an everythin with the way she carries herself; so self-assured, so confident, so fuckin cocky. Like Kelly grabbin me balls hard in the back of the taxi. Holdin me at head an belt an marchin me into her bedroom, throwin me on her bed.

Aw Christ. Fuckin *iron* in my jeans.

The woman sits on the toilet seat, her bare painted toes in her chunky high-heeled shoes only an inch or so away from her slave's masked face. She lights up a ciggie an flicks thee ashes on to his bare back, utter contempt in her face. My knob pulses. I think I might come in me kex. But then she begins to hum 'Another Day in Paradise' an me dick instantly deflates, from hard-on to soft-off in two heartbeats. Droop. I could take the name-calling, the arse-kicking, the hot ash, the disdain, I could maybe even take the scrubbing; but someone hummin a Phil Collins tune in me ear? Fuck that. I'm submissive, not fuckin *abject*; I do have *some* self-respect. Jesus Christ.

I hand the spliff back to Dermot.

—Ye meet a lot of women like that, nowadays, he says. —That sexually aggressive, like. Don't know what it is, but in the last few years women have become much more fuckin demandin, much more fuckin confident, like, in what thee want. Used to be they'd just lie there an open ther legs, like, now it's all 'Do me from behind', 'Do that til I tell ye to stop'. Real fuckin predators, like, knowmean? An thee won't let ye come until they've come first; they all make sure thee get at least as much out of it as *ye* do. Don't ye reckon? Have ye found that, Victor?

I just nod. —Yeh. Suppose.

—Like that one, what's her name, friend of that one ye were seeing . . . Victoria, that's it. Close to bein fuckin psycho, her, man, tellin ye.

He shakes his head at the memory. I think he's waitin for me to prompt him, ask him questions, like, find out more, but the subject's uncomfortably close to Kelly so I don't. Dermot talkin about Victoria would make me think of nothin but Kelly; Kelly in Magnet, the red an the white on her face. That first time I saw her between Victoria an that other one, Roz. The way she smiled an laughed. Long strands of hair curlin down on to her cheeks. The gemstone choker. The big tattoo on her shoulder blade.

My God, my belly's burning.

Dermot leaves the room an goes upstairs. The masked man is now talkin into the camera, sayin how he feels free, released from all responsibility, a new an better person when he's nuddy on his knees scrubbin the bathroom floor of a woman who stands above him callin him pathetic, a pathetic, pitiful, useless cunt. He feels, he says, absolved of every bad thing he's ever done. He's got a wife an three children.

I change the channel.

Some cow thing – a wildebeest or a gnu – is bein savaged by lions, one hangin from its neck with its jaws clamped around its windpipe, thee other tearin an rippin chunks out of its flanks. It staggers an reels an bellows an finally collapses in the long grass, one twitchin leg an hoof protrudin over the top of the grass, kickin an shudderin as the big cats tear it apart. What a horrible way to die. Those vast jaws, an you disappearin into them. Claws the size of friggin bananas rippin yer bit by bit out of the world. The terror on me when I was strapped face down to Kelly's bed an she was hackin at me back, rammin her whole fuckin fist inside me an I thought I was gunner split down the fuckin middle, fall in two on her bed in a wave of fluid. Blood an bile. It's not the dying so much as thee actual bein dead, all the things that won't be there any more; that initial chemical buzz at seven o'clock on a Friday evenin, money in yer pocket an the whole friggin weekend ahead. Just that walk, that slow, wide pace yer can comfortably

132

carry off when yer leave a restaurant havin just stuffed yerself full of good food. Sex. Happy dogs waggin ther tails. The smell of another's skin an it so smooth, clear an unblemished. Beatin the Scum again; I would *hate* to die before seein that at least one more time. Hate to die before we're back to beatin the United fuckin filth again. Maybe this season. *Maybe* this season.

An then there's the darkness an dissatisfaction an the dullness, thee everyday fuckin *dull*ness, an will bein dead be any different, any friggin worse? Cold an dark an alone. The coldness an the darkness an just you, only you, no companionship no support just you on yer own howlin for ever in blackness. No fucker to hear. Or care.

But there'll be no lions.

Yeh, an what a fuckin world without them. What a fuckin emptiness, what a great big friggin hollowness without them.

I hear Dermot thumpin about up the stairs. On the telly, a huge snake slides into a burrow an I can hear muffled, frantic, terrified squealing. The snake's thick tail disappears an the squealin gets even more panicked. Then the squealin stops.

God, I've just fuckin *got* to see Kelly again. I've just fuckin well *got* to. It's the least lonely I've ever felt, bein with her. Her inside me, her openin me flesh, me skin. She's seen parts of me that *I* never will. I'll remain more unknown to meself than I will to her. An there's somethin in that, that fallin open . . . like she fell open as well, like she, we, parted like storm clouds or somethin an I saw somethin shine through, some lovely fuckin thing I've been searchin for an never managed to even glimpse. And if I *did* only glimpse it with her, only that an nothing more, then that's still one *fuck* of a lot more than I've ever got out of anythin else. Ever. Except there *was* one time, tho, wasn't there . . . when I was very, very young. It's on thee edge of me memory. The circumstances around it have faded almost completely away, but I *do* remember an explosion of blinding, beautiful light, a quick an sudden glimpse of somethin heartbreakingly lovely that lies somewhere *outside* this life an this world. That same light I saw when I was with Kelly, when I was broken in her hands. What it was then, when I was very young, the first time I saw it, like, I have no fuckin idea. An what it

133

was when I was with Kelly, I have no fuckin idea either. But the two things seem connected. Fuck, yes. Maybe fate is the word. Maybe she was put there, in Magnet, for me to meet cos the thing I experienced as a child (no, earlier; as a *baby*), set a precedent, a pattern for me life to come an I'd go on searchin for it until I found it an some force, some kindness, arranged things so that I would meet Kelly an she would meet me, we'd come together on the planet. Except the result was torture an terror an torn flesh an what the fuck's *that* got to do with any kind of fuckin kindness?

But it *has*. In a way I don't understand an never fuckin will it *has*. I'm sure of it.

Dermot comes back into the room, carryin two video cassettes.

—Here we go, Victor. Yeer entertainment for tonight, the feature pree-sen-tayshun: *Spankin Sisters* or *Lesbian Piss Party*. Got em off Eddie. He's gettin shut of all his porn now that the wee one's here. Got some bleedin crackers an all.

—Dermot.

—What?

—D'yer believe in fate? That things are meant to happen?

He looks somewhat disappointed. What the fuck with? —Ah no, Victor. Not the deep thoughts again. Lay off the weed, my man. The only thing we're fated to do tonight is eat pizza an watch porn. I'm havin a twelve-inch pepperoni. What's yours?

—Seafood.

—Big one?

—Medium.

—Garlic bread?

—Yeh.

—An we'll share a big bottle of Coke.

—Alright well.

He picks up the phone an dials. Local pizza delivery round the corner on Lark Lane.

And it's like . . . I mean, even if I was to die sometime soon, I know that I'd see her again. In a hundred years' time or so I'll be on some fuckin buildin site up a scaffold an she'll walk past, look up at me an stop an recognise something, remember something. Ar eyes'll meet an there'll be a moment of we don't know what, unexplainable, but I *know*, with certainty, that were I to die tonight I'd see her again. Somehow, some way. Everyone's got one, one partner-never-to-be-forgotten, one always-burnin flame. As cheesily sentimental as that sounds I know it's fuckin true. Maybe she's mine.

Maybe I'm hers. What, I wonder, is she doin now. What is she doin with her hands. An her face an her legs an her shoulders. An the bolt through her belly button.

Dermot puts the phone down. —Pizza's on its way. What's it to be first? With the vids, like?

—Not bothered, I say. —Put whatever yer want on.

He does. Women peeing on each other. Wouldn't be so bad if one of them didn't look like Rod Stewart.

I keep findin meself staring into artificial light. I'll go to the fridge to get milk out an I'll be there ages, squattin by thee open door, staring into the light spillin out into thee otherwise pitch-dark kitchen. The manky smell of the dirty fridge in me nostrils an the skin on me face turnin numb in the waves of cold. Me eyes beginnin to sting an water as thee stare unblinking. Or I'll be walkin to the pub or thee off-licence or the chipper after dark an I'll stop an crane me neck, look upwards at the bright street lights, stare into the fallin sodium light until me neck is aching an there are fuzzy black spots floatin through me vision. The neon above thee optics behind the bars in town, or thee optics themselves an the way thee reflect light off ther glass, catch it an throw it back, bounce it back into me eyes. The yellow lights on the rooves of taxis or in the little windows of cigarette machines, the lights in shop windows closed up for the night, left burning to show off the wares, the clothes an electrical appliances an stuff. All the stuff I find meself lookin beyond an through to seek out the source of the light or drop me eyes down to look into the glare of the slanted spotlights on a level with me knees. The bright an sharp lasers shootin from thee old tower restaurant; these yank me eyes up, not to the stars but to the lasers themselves, ther vivid red beams shootin

135

across the black sky. The light needs to be artificial, it seems, sun an moon an stars have no magnetism, I don't know why. Maybe theer not bright enough. Not as bright as the fluorescent tubes on the night buses or thee underground trains or in the tunnels of thee underground itself or the shoppin centres as well, so fuckin garish, so brightly friggin lit, throbbin an hummin an far too fuckin bright, all the man-made illuminants of this city. And yet not one part of it gives anything; I find nothing, *get* nothing, nothing fuckin happens except a pain at the back of me eyeballs an a blurring in me vision, me sight. That's all. Nothin more. Except a persistent headache which thumps in me forehead, sendin black shocks into the bridge of me nose with each dull an heavy beat: thud, thud, thud.

Dermot's not in; he's left a note Blu-tac'd to the telly screen, sayin that he's gone to thee Albert to watch the football. Some international friendly, unimportant, certainly missable. So that gives me a couple of hours at least in the house on me own. Time enough.

Me heart picks up speed. I can *hear* it.

I leg it upstairs to me bedroom. Breathin deeper. Close an lock the door an take all me clothes off, everythin, the coldness in here tryin to register in me brain but I'm fuckin feverish, hot, this *must* be fuckin done. It *must* be fuckin done. I've got to try it, got to try an recapture, there's an emptiness, a terrible fuckin impoverishment an I'll never know if this works or not until I try it an I'd fuckin *hate* that never-knowing. Besides which it's all cold an it's dark an it's dull an there's too much bleedin space in me head.

I thread the belt out of the loops on me jeans. Tremblin fingers. I make a hole with the belt, a noose, an drop it over me head around me neck an feel blood immediately rush into me groin, hot an hectic blood pumped from me thumpin heart. There's a whining in me throat, a kind of grunting whine. A humming in me head. It's almost like. Almost like I remember it. I fall to me knees an tie the loose end of the belt tightly around the leg of the bed. Turn my back to the bed an start to stroke meself, knead meself. Get hard. Panting. Whacking, then I *lean*, I lean forwards until the belt is pulled taut an the noose of leather around me neck begins to tighten, tighten. Rock hard now I start to pump. Pump with me hand, me fist. Lean further forwards an me breathing becomes laboured. The constriction around me neck more severe an me lungs workin hard for air, me whole fuckin breast booming an burning in me guts an balls an me brain pressin against me skull as the lack of oxygen to it makes it expand, makes it search, makes it fuckin thrash for life an fuel pulsing fast in unison with me hand. I can hear nowt but me own wheezing, gasping an gurgling an I lean still more an me vision blooms red, bright fuckin blood red but that's all that redness shot through with black branches like veins, I need more I need more struggling more fighting, gaspin for fuckin breath to remain alive to find again that light ignited by Kelly to detonate again in my screaming head an heart me whole fuckin being that fuckin bright bomb of beauty but it's not here, I can't friggin find it, only this redness an choking each tortured breath a fuckin death rattle. Kelly, think of Kelly; the bolt in her navel an her face in mine an her tongue an her legs spread on thee edge of the bath an the wet warmth inside her an the sinews taut on her inner thighs an on the backs of her knees. Think of her hands, her long slim fingers an now imagine that hand bunched into a fist, imagine that fist fuckin plunging inside, powering inside yer secret places or holdin a knife like a pen to carve her desires into yer skin, an you helpless on the fuckin bed, my bed is moving, it is being dragged across the floor I am pummelling at meself an pulling the bed with me neck I can't breathe my head is about to explode or collapse this cannot fuckin be borne it is too fuckin much an it is not good it is *not* fuckin good an the red haze has parted to let in a trickle of sickly yellow like piss murky with chemicals or illness, a slow sludgy trickle fuck this is not worth it the slate colour of Kelly's eyes an her hands encircling me neck squeezing ever tighter my dick inside her. *Inside* her. Her squeezin the come out of me like toothpaste an all that whiteness, that fuckin pure filling my head where is it where is that fuckin whiteness that brightness, that clean apocalypse in me skull not here, not fuckin here this ooze of clotted custard or pus darkening an fading becoming blacker as if rotting rapidly as me brain begins to shut down this is NOT my belt it is Kelly's fingers an it fuckin hurts me when I come, it stings like I'm draining a wound a spot infected weeping sore, sticky an tepid on me fingers me brain fuckin screaming *screaming* then sighing as I lean back slightly an relieve the pressure, the blackness receding replaced by something that is not light only this fuckin cold dark bedroom inhabited by nothing only the pale an skinny ghosts of myself. Air roars back into me body, gushing an gurglin an I can taste blood, me lungs an head are fuckin shrieking for oxygen, snatchin an gulpin at the world an I fuckin THROW meself forward spent an soft-knobbed an so hideously disappointed I hurl meself forward an the knot snaps an I SLAM into the wall an reel sideways, curlin up tightly around my coughing an spluttering an hacking, gobs of phlegm flying out of me gob, cracklin in me ears as the world torrents back in an me ribs bellowing an each gulp of air scrapes raw an grates down my scoured throat. Curled up, balled me hands clasped between me thighs feelin the clammy leakage from me dick an thee uncontrollable tremblin in me feet an elbows. Shivering, shuddering. Teeth chattering. Snot from me nose an me eyes all hot an stinging, pathetic stringy skinny creature stinking an dripping foetal on the fuckin floor, the belt trailin from me neck like a giant suckin leech an I will know nothing of anything other than this for the rest of my fuckin life, this pure abjectness, this true fuckin awfulness *this*, here, is me, crying an coughing almost fuckin dead I might as well be in the ground because I can feel meself rotting inside, me heart turnin scabby, flakin away, fuck oh God oh Jesus Kelly this is me for ever, me for ever, what the fuck can I do. Everything is shit. What the fuck have I lost.

The postman brings only one letter, a manila envelope addressed to me. It's from the DSS. I open it in the cold kitchen; regret to inform you. Application for unemployment benefit, denied. For income support, denied. Any fuckin benefit, denied. If you would like to appeal against this decision please write to.

Oh you fuckers.

You absolute cunts.

I telephone thee office, ask them why thee've refused me application. Can't tell me over the blower, thee say. Have to call in in person. Which I intend to do this very fuckin morning but in the shower, soapin meself, gettin clean, I start to change me mind because I really won't be able to bear goin to that fuckin place today, standin in the queue for hours, fuck all to do, listenin to thee angered shouting or urgent, quiet desperation of thee other claimants, the telephones ringin an the dry heat in there an the long, slow-moving, shuffling cowed queue. Fuckin nightmare in there it is. Pure friggin hell. I might crack in there today, might just start screamin an smashin things. I feel *very* fuckin close to the edge today, hysteria bubblin in me throat, threatening to boil over. *Very* fuckin close. One little thing, one tiny friggin instance of unwelcomed humiliation or insult might do it, might very well fuckin tip me over. Spend the rest of the day in a cell. Or worse: sectioned. Livin fuckin hell that would be. Quick to section people in this city, the doctors are. No lie. An just the fuckin *journey* to the DSS office itself would be too much to bear an a waste of fuckin time anyway cos I know what thee'll say, I know the reason thee'll give for turnin down me application: that I left me last job voluntarily. So it's six weeks from when I last worked until I can next sign on. And it's been, what, three? Four? Have to wait another two, at the very least. Another fuckin fortnight an I can try again. Cunts.

'Voluntarily'; that's the word they'll use. As if I didn't fuckin *need*, as if it wasn't utterly fuckin *necessary* to have some free time, some friggin space to meself to spend the money I'd worked ten fuckin hours a day every day for months to earn, mixin the cement, carryin the bricks, diggin footings an layin concrete an all the fuckin time breathin in the fumes from thee endless stream of traffic enterin the Mersey tunnel below, hundreds of feet below. Free time isn't a fuckin luxury, it's a fuckin necessity; I'm young still, I wanner enjoy me time on this planet. Don't wanner give all me time an energy over to some cunt else. Come home in darkness stinkin at the foot an armpit, ravenous, knackered, time just for a shower an some food an then crawl groanin into bed an fall instantly asleep until thee alarm screams a few hours later an I'm out into the coldness, puttin on dirty clothes, on the bus an at the site an liftin heavy things before I'm even friggin awake properly, before it's fuckin daylight even. And it was fuckin 'voluntarily' that I walked away from that? That I needed a break from it? I wasn't, like, forced by the desire, the need to live at least for a short time in the way I fuckin *want* to live? To live me life in a way that I don't see every last fuckin hour as a waste? As a moment that I'll scream an plead to have back as I'm dying?

Arseholes. Fucking arseholes. 'Voluntarily' me hole; *nothing's* done fuckin voluntarily. It's all force an compulsion an threat an submission. It's all friggin compromise, all surrender. Fuck all voluntary about anythin. Fuck *youse.*

I hear the doorbell ring downstairs. Turn the shower off an step out steaming. Dermot bellows: —VICTOR! IT'S FOR YOU!

Then another voice, ar Kirk's, shouts: —It's me! Hurry up, Victor lad, cos I'm in a rush!

I dry meself an get dressed an go downstairs. Kirk an Dermot are in the kitchen, Dermot makin tea an wearin only jeans hangin halfway down his milk-white arse. A big green shamrock tattooed under the hairs on his big white belly. Kirk's sittin at the table, smoking, in a nice new O'Neill snowboardin coat, every last inch the scally with cash. Couple of hundred quid's worth on his scrawny back. A job, yer see. That's what fuckin workin does for yer.

—Alright, Kirk.

—Brudder.

—Not workin today?

—Nah. Spewed it for today. Called in a sicky.

—Can't be arsed, yeh?

—That, an also I'm seein this new woman from Halewood. Promised to take her an her kids to Knowsley Safari, like, an today's thee only day she can take off.

Dermot laughs. —Aw good fuck. Sooner look at lions an hippos all the day than lug boxes around a cuntin warehouse. *Too* fuckin right. No competition there, son.

Kirk nods. —Is right.

—If only ye could get paid for doin that, eh? Best job in the world.

—David friggin Attenborough does.

—True.

—And that bearded cunt Bill Oddie.

—Also true aye. Sadly. Very fuckin sadly.

Dermot makes the tea an me an Kirk make small talk about the family, about Jean's coming baby, about ar Lizzie's escalatin drug habit. About ar mother flyin off to Greece in a few days an how excited she is. Then:

—Anyway, Vic, this isn't just a social call.

—Oh aye?

He nods.

—Ah no, Kirk, I've stopped dealin the weed an I'm fuckin skint. Anyway, I thought you had a job now?

—I do, yeh. That's what I'm here about. Djer want one as well?

—What doing?

—In the warehouse, with me. Over in Birkenhead. Some big fuckin loads comin in soon, like, an we're a couple of men short. I told the gaffer that yer'd probly be interested.

I sigh. Something settles inside me, I feel it; not in comfort or relaxation, more in resignation. Defeat, even. Like I'm lyin down an givin up.

—What kind of work is it?

—Just stackin stuff, yer know, general warehouse work, like. Stackin boxes. Can yer drive a forklift?

—Yeh. No licence or anythin, like, but I've had experience.

—That'll do. Yer'll probly be doin half a day on the forklift, thee other half on the floor. Heavy friggin work, like, but some of the lads're okay. I've done a fuck of a lot worse, like. Pay's wank, but yer can make it up in ovies. It's alright. It's work, yer know. Do it for a few weeks, get some money in yer bin, if yer don't like it . . . He shrugs. —Sack it. Easy, lar.

Already me fuckin body feels heavy. Slow with exhaustion anticipated. Prickly with days surrendered, given over to someone else. I say:

—Okay, well. Yeh. When does he want me to start?

—Soon as. Tomorrer?

—Can't tomorrer. Chinese New Year this weekend. *Got* to be around for that, man. Best friggin bender of the year, bar none. Monday, tell him. Start Monday.

—Alright. I'll say yer workin yer notice some place else an can't come in til next week.

—Alright, well.

—I'll give yis a ring over the weekend. I'm pickin a car up on the Saturday so I can come for yis on the Monday. Bright an early. Seven o'clock.

—*Seven* o'fuckin clock? Jesus, Kirk, this isn't like you. Can't fuckin believe this, man, *you* with a job. Seems fuckin unnatural.

Kirk holds his arms wide. —Ey, Victor. I'm wearin expensive gear. I'm off for a day out with me new sniff an I'm pickin a car up at the weekend, only *one* fuckin previous. It's money, lar. Makes a dead nice friggin change, know wharram sayin?

I nod.

—Right, I'm cuttin off. Monday mornin. Make sure yer ready for seven.

—Sound.

Kirk goes. I sit at the table an Dermot hands me a mug of tea.

—Back to work, Vic, ey. Stackin shite in a warehouse. Drivin a fuckin forklift truck. All yer days spent in the one building which isn't yer home. Still, if ye need the money, like . . .

—Which I fuckin *do*, Dermot.

—Understood, yeh. Don't get narky. But I bet ye wish ye'd stuck to the dealin now tho, eh?

—Yeh.

Altho I don't, really; too many bad, sparky people involved in *that* friggin game. Yet there's a sensation in me, unwanted but unshakeable, a small creepin sensation of somethin approachin shame; as if I've somehow offended someone in acceptin Kirk's offer, in settling for that. That someone I deeply respect an admire an maybe even love is disappointed in me because I've settled for that. I didn't try, I didn't fuckin *strive*, I just plumped for the first temporary solution that came along. Settled for thee ordinary. Saw the mediocre an thought: 'Fuck it, that'll do.' Fell without fighting into the cowardly compromise, an someone important somewhere is gritting his teeth at me, shakin his head in disappointment. He expected more from me an I let him down.

I'm useless. I'm really bleedin useless. An no more dole breakfasts, say tara to the lovely dole breakfasts; Happy Shopper bread, Happy Shopper marge, Happy Shopper tea, Happy Shopper milk, a platter full of shite but the *time* yer can spend eatin it . . . just sittin there in the kitchen, radio on, readin every last word in the paper . . . hours goin by . . . more toast, more tea . . . them marathon dole breakfasts. How fuckin lovely. Spend ages over them. All that lovely time to yerself.

No more, no. Never again.

Fuck it.

—Come ed, Victor. It's only fuckin work, man. Don't look so bleedin glum. Sack it off if ye can't hack it.

—Nah, it's not that, I say. —I'm not down. Not havin a lowey. It's just that I'm thinkin, well, it's Chinese New Year startin tomorrer. We could start the hooley today, don't yer think?

Dermot grins. —*Now* yeer friggin talkin. Man after me own fuckin heart, you. I've got a rent cheque to cash, I'll blow half of it on snort. Yeh?

—Sound.

—Just give me half an hour to get meself ready.

He gulps at his tea. An uncontrollable force inside me.

—No, Dermot, you take yer time. Meet me in thee Albert. I'll goan have a pint in there with a paper or somethin an you do yer stuff an meet me in there when yer've made yerself look lovely. About three days' time, yeh?

—Cheeky get. Alright then.

He goes off up the stairs for a shower. I pull on good trainies an fleece an get me stuff together – ciggies, lighter, cash card, all the shite – an leave the house. A dark morning, rainy. A day for drinkin, for sittin in pubs an drinkin, snortin lines off the cistern in the cold, drippin bogs. Dark an dingy protective pubs. I go to the cashpoint, get a balance, then go into the bank an draw out every last penny above the pound needed to keep me account open. Enough for one last bender, one last mad fuckin blow-out binge.

Here I go.

Reeling, rocking. Unsteady on me feet an about to fall. The fireworks burstin in the night sky above, above Chinatown, all the closely packed people lookin up at thee explosions in the night sky, the red an white an green explosions. Fallin stars, planets plummeting. Showers of meteors all different colours. The Chinese flag flyin above the gates, more, smaller stars yellow on the red background above the huge gates on which people are clingin like monkeys, shouting an whistlin an waving banners. The dragon undulates past, bendin an bowin an thrashing its head like a cross between an alligator an a worm. I can see the feet of the people inside it below the hem, shufflin, stamping. Quockie's in there somewhere. I squint an try to recognise him by his feet but I can't. Theer just feet, in shoes; anonymous.

I take a half-bottle of vodka out of me pocket an suck at it. Dermot's not here to share it with, I lost him in a crackhouse somewhere in Toxteth sometime yesterday, out of his brains an droolin over some livin skeleton which I think was female. So I'll just have to neck his share as well.

A hand takes the bottle away from me as I raise it up to me lips. It's Quockie's uncle Tony, the Snake Tong man, wearin a dark suit an a green baseball hat an lookin at me as he takes a swig out of me bottle. I wait for him to finish an then hand it back to me. He hisses through his teeth an wipes his lips with the back of his hand.

—How you, Victah? How you do today?

I just nod, nod an smile. Got to be careful around this man Tony. Triad Tony. Tony Snake Tong. I always feel like an innocent bystander when I'm standin next to him an think of phrases like 'caught in the crossfire' or 'stray bullet' or 'tragic blameless victim of Liverpool's ongoing bloody turf war'. Or even 'missed ther target' or 'assassination gone wrong'.

—Drunk, Victah?

I nod again. He's right; I'm *very* fuckin drunk. Barely-able-to-friggin-stand drunk. But this nodding I'm doin, just this stupid noddin without words, I'm aware of how fuckin rude it might look so I say: —I like the dragon, Tony. Done a great job this year.

He snorts an says somethin but a firework bursts an smothers his words.

—Pardon?

—I say. He leans closer. —I *say*, we got on vair well this year. Not with *your* put-in, hah?

Oh fuck. I stammer an apology, somethin sorrowful-soundin about last year's fiasco but he just grins an pats me on the back.

—Take easy, Vic.

I watch him go. Little feller in suit an baseball cap. A small, extremely stocky Chinaman as wide as he is tall comes out of the crowd to walk alongside him. Looks like Oddjob. He adjusts his stride so that he matches Tony's exactly. Bodyguard or somethin.

Another firework bursts. Fills the sky like a nova, an explodin sun. Red an white stars fall whining to earth. The dragon begins another circuit, drums beatin manically, shoves its demonic leering face into a group of schoolchildren who scatter screaming.

I sway an stumble. Pissed-up fucker, drunken oaf. It's only the ingested rock an charlie keepin me upright so I stagger over to a litter bin, a Chinatown litter bin designed like a pagoda, an lean me arse against the top of it. The spike digs into the crevice of me arse almost into the hole an reminds me of something. What is it it reminds me of. What does this pressure make me almost remember.

I'm giggling. I'm muttering to meself. People are movin away from me an starin at me sideways. Apart from one who is actually coming towards me, actually seekin me out an approaching, now standin at me side.

—Alright, Vic. What's happenin, kidder? What's the Bobby?

—Craig, man. I'm slurring. —The fucker you?

—Not as wellied as *you*, lar. Look like yer about to topple.
I nod. I am.

—Eeyar, tell yer what *you* need. He looks around then takes
me arm. —Eeyar, come with me.

He leads me through the huddled crowd up some steps an
into the doorway of a block of flats. I lean back against cold
bricks. He turns his back to the festivities an takes a wrap out
of his pocket, bunches one fist an tips some small grainy lumps
out into the fleshy hollow between his thumb an forefinger.
He raises that powdered fist up to me face an puts his other
hand on the back of me neck to hold me head steady.

—Go ed. Take a good snort.

I do. Clouds of drunkenness part in me head, things clarify.
The sounds of the crowd an the drums an the bangin of the
fireworks start becomin sharper, louder. The drunkenness leaves
me brains an slides down to me belly an knees, me stomach
sizzling an a jumping in me joints. Fingertips all fiery.

—Feeling better now?

I sniff. —Aw yeh. Fuckin top.

—Boss.

He snorts a couple of bumps himself, his head thrown
back while he sniffs. He makes a noise of pleasure, a kind
of throaty sigh.

—Where's Dermot?

I shrug. —Dunno. Lost him sometime yesterday.

—Been on one, yeh?

—*Fuck*, yeh. *Mad* one.

He surveys the crowd from ar elevated position, hands on
the railings, like the captain of a ship. Lookin over it all. Then
he moves close to me side an points with one arm down at
the gates, the twinkling, crawling Chinatown gates.

—Seen who's over there?

—No. Who?

—Look, there. Under the gates. See where I'm pointin?
Foller me arm.

I do, but can't make out one single specific person in the
crush. I shake me head.

—Look, there. See? Next to the cunt with the sparklers.

146

That sniff you were seein. The one from Magnet. See her? In the long purple coat.

Another big rocket bursts an in that fallin curtain of red an white light I see her. In a second all drunkenness gone an a cold fist clamps my heart an me balls shrink up inside me body. There she is over there in a gltterin cloud of sparks an she's grinning as the dragon bucks past her, every last fuckin thing about her as beautiful as I remember as I could never fuckin forget. Her hands are in the pockets of her long maroon coat an she's wearin the same denim skirt an trainies as she was on that day, *that* fuckin day when she ripped me all to bits. A rocket rises an she watches it rise, her head cranin upwards, sinews on her neck pullin taut like cables and her mouth openin in a smile. She blinks an flinches as the firework bursts an then follows the stars down to the ground, slowly falling, one side of her face red an thee other white, whiteness whiteness once burning in me head an her painting it on to the insides of me eyes.

—Gunner goan have a word with her, Vic? I can tell yis want to, like. Look at yer grid. Can't take yer friggin beams away from her, lar.

He nudges me with his elbow. —Go ed. Goan talk to her.

I can't do anythin but stare. I can't fuckin move. Her friend with the big hair, the prozzy, Victoria, she clocks me staring an nudges Kelly an points over at me an Kelly follows her pointing an sees me an the smile leaves her face. Her eyes on me like swords through me lungs. She nods, just one quick tip backwards of her head an whether that's a beckoning or not I find meself moving, moving towards her, down the steps an through the crowd me eyes locked on her, seein nothin else, just her ahead of me an only her gettin closer, growin bigger. Tunnel vision. Just her lit up an all around her black. An the promise of such a bright burst of dazzling fuckin bright white light at thee end of that dark tunnel.

The words carved into me back, still unhealed, are hurting.

The rips in my arsehole start to sting.

Everything seems to scream an tremble in a curious pale blue haze.

—Hiya, Kelly.

—Hiya, Victor. How are yis?

—Alright. I shift me weight on to me left foot an stumble a little. —Bit wrecked.

—Yer not kiddin. On one, yeh?

I nod. Don't know what to say so I tell her somethin about startin work on Monday an havin one last mad one before I do. I'm findin it difficult to look at her eyes, I can't meet her clear an almost cold eyes an I'm takin in her chin with its shallow cleft an her ears like white whirlpools with the danglin pearls in ther lobes an her eyebrows, her thick dark eyebrows the left one with a thin scar runnin through it on the diagonal an the way her cheeks smooth away from her nose, her nose which descends from her forehead straight down with no bridge to it, it's like a supportive strut for her high brow. She's so fuckin *real*. So fuckin *here* in front of me, better than I remember, more solid, there's so fuckin much to her. She's a lifetime of exploring. Me heart's trippin over itself an me head's spinnin with the drugs an the drink an it's all I can do to stop meself grabbing her, holdin her tightly, fuckin *crushing* her to me an buryin me face in her hair, her neck. Takin her hands an placing them softly around me throat an asking her to squeeze. She makes me want to, I don't fuckin know, run, scream, headbutt brick walls. She turns my blood to boiling milk.

Kelly. Fuck sakes, Kelly, how can I have gone through the past days without you an still be here, walkin around, talking. Living. It just doesn't seem possible. Like I'm still doin things an me heart's been dragged out through me fuckin back.

She stares hard at me face. I look up into her eyes now, see the fallin fires reflected in them, red in one an white in thee other an the big an secret powerful things castin ther shadows behind them. Whatever huge shapes are movin through her mind.

—Could yer go another line?

—Oh yeh, I say. —Can always go another line, like.

—Come on, then. Come ed.

She says tara to Victoria who winks at us both an then she takes me hand, squeezes it hard an leads me out of Chinatown an through the crowds. I see a pair of bizzies eyeing her up.

Without talkin we turn down the next side street an go into Pogue Mahone.

—Vodka an Coke, she says to me an goes off to the bog. I get drinks from the packed, heavin bar. Vodka an Coke for me as well. Two vodkas an Cokes.

Here I am again. Here I fuckin *am* again. The whole bleedin world openin up ahead of me, I'm drunk an drugged an me brain is bleary yet colours are suddenly stronger, sounds louder, everythin much clearer an sharper as if newborn, new-made. It's all so fuckin new an undiscovered an excitin an untamed. Not knowin what Kelly's gunner do to me, an just that wonder itself sums up the wonder about every fuckin thing, all of it, the Chinese New Year an the fireworks an thee Irishmen in this pub in clusters an everything sharper, grander, so much more fuckin valuable than it was yesterday, today, fifteen fuckin minutes ago. How fuckin important all this is. Unique an special an never to be understood even if yer could live for ever.

Fuck. I feel sick.

An Kelly's here again, takin me hand, passin a wrap into it. Without lookin at me she nods an picks up her drink an sips at it. I go off to the toilet, lock meself in a cubicle an do the never-changing drug stuff; chop, snort, sniff, sigh. Feel the chemicals bludgeon my brain, an *what* fuckin chemicals *are* these cos I actually stagger back on me feet under ther impact, me tongue cleaves to the roof of me gob an concrete teeth an skull all heavy an numb an slack. Jesus Christ. What the *frig* have I just snorted. Fuck.

I plonk meself down on the bog seat an wait to get some feeling, some locomotion, back. Fuckin horse tranks or some such shite. Some strong sedative. But that sensation quickly passes an the stimulant it was evidently cut with kicks in, the beak or speed or both, jitterin in me knees an wrists an underneath that this slowness in the blood, this narcotising of the functions. Interestin. An typical of bein with Kelly this mixture, not only in the commingling of effects but just generally in the newness of it, the very fuckin unknownness of it. Never experienced anythin like Kelly ever before. Never friggin will. Part of me wants to leg it back into the bar to be beside her, an part of me wants to sneak out the side door an just fuckin do one. Run away. What do I do? The cutting of me back, the fuckin *invasion* of me. The wrecking of me body. But that beautiful brightness claspin me head, an me friggin coming like a geyser. Those things an which of them do I go for? What do I do? God, Jesus, what do I fuckin do?

I'm askin 'what do I do' over an over again all the way out of the toilet an up the steps an across the bar an through the crowd to stand next to Kelly. WhatdoIdowhatdoIdo. So close I can feel her warmth against my face. I slip the wrap back to her. She finishes her drink an crunches ice an swallows.

—Drink up. We'll goan flag a cab.

—Why? Where're we gunner go?

Sucking an ice cube, she just looks at me. *Into* my face. Her cheeks all drawn in. Jesus Christ, her face. All she says is:

—I've missed you, Victor.

And that's enough. I neck me drink an we leave the pub, left at the top of the road to the bombed an burned ruin of St Luke's Church an the taxi rank there. We get in one an she speaks her address. The cab pulls out into the traffic. Moving slow in the thick traffic an I can't keep my legs from twitching, can't keep me ribcage from booming.

Past the Chinatown gates. The crush of people an the leapin flames. Up on to Duke Street, climbin out of the city an the vast bulk, the man-made mountain of thee Anglican cathedral in its mist of pale blue light. Lookin past Kelly's profile at this colossal form an me vision blurs an for a moment it's like Kelly's head an the cathedral become conjoined, one sprouting from thee other, the two shiftin in an out of each other like in a dream.

Christ my fucking heart.

—Kelly, I whisper an she nods but does not turn her head to look at me. —Please don't cut me again, I say. So fuckin *small* a voice. —Please don't use a knife on me again.

A small shake of her head.

—Don't . . . please don't put your arm inside me. I couldn't fuckin stand that again.

She stares straight ahead, at the back of the taxi driver's head. He's wearing a flat cap. I want her to look at me, I would *love*

for her to fuckin look at me but all she does is say, quietly:
—I won't.

Still drivin past the cathedral. So friggin big it fills the sky. Swallows us up an gulps us down like pills.

Blinded. Me hands and feet tied tight. Spread out an defenceless as if on an altar. Only booming I can hear. And sirens an distant explosions. A hand on me chest, a warm hand, tracing down over me ribs, me skin jumping at that touch an the hand comes to rest on my belly.
—Are yer crying?
—No.
—Are yer crying?
The hand moves down.
—Nnnnnnnn . . . no.
—I'll *make* you cry.
—*Nnnnnnnn.*
The hand has become a claw.
—I want to *see* you cry.
—Nnn . . .
—There. Yer crying *now*, aren't yer?
Claws. Talons.
She can't see my eyes I am blinded I cannot see her.

A rigid finger inside my mouth, rubbing a grainy, sandy substance around an into me gums, between me teeth, under me tongue. That finger stabbing, jabbing, forcing hard grains into every crack and hollow in my mouth.

The finger leaves an I close my gob, run me tongue around me teeth, tasting the grains. Salty an chemical an soapy. Strong.

A hand lifts my head an threads something under it an ties it over my mouth. Blinded an made mute I am. The world too much on my face. I'm convulsing against it, tryin to throw the fucker off.

I hear a snort. Then a door creaking open then that door slammin shut.

The grains dissolve.

151

I am a firework exploding, a blizzard of flame.

Me head is thrashing an me throat is raw I must have been fuckin screaming. No I *am* screaming, screamin shapeless sounds against the gag. Pullin at my binds. Explosions still soundin outside an above me is the clatter of a helicopter. Hearing is all I have left. My last fuckin sense, just one giant ear I am floating in space. And as well this howling on me skin, me bare body ridged with goosebumps an the bareness an thee emptiness of it no hands on it, it *howls* for contact.

What the fuck. Kelly.

Just trapped night air so cold on me crawling skin.

I think I am screaming again.

Points of warmth; both me hands, both me feet, both me thighs. Blood, blood an piss not good no fucking hell. The wet warmth on me thighs trickles down underneath me an turns cold. Me in a swamp of my own making. What the fuck. Floppin like a fish tryin to walk in a pool of my own ooze. Let me fuckin go.

KELLY KELLY FUCK SAKES KELLY COME BACK NOW YOU FUCKING DEMON DEMENTED FUCKING WHORE COME BACK COME BACK AN LET ME FUCKING GO YOU INSANE FUCKING IDIOT LET ME FUCKING GO PLEASE LET ME GO I WILL DIE LIKE THIS I CANNOT DIE LIKE THIS I CANNOT FUCKING MOVE I AM SINKING GOING I AM FUCKING LEAVING HERE DO NOT LET ME DIE LIKE THIS YOU FUCKING CRAZY BITCH YOU WHORE YOU MAD FUCKING DERANGED PSYCHO CUNT WHERE THE FUCK ARE YOU WHERE HAVE YOU GONE YOU FUCKING PSYCHOPATH LEAVING ME HERE LET ME FUCKING GO I WILL FUCKING KILL YOU WHEN I GET OUT OF HERE WHEN YOU LET ME GO I WILL FUCKING KILL YOU I WILL HUNT YOU DOWN AN STICK STEEL IN YOU LET ME FUCKING GO THIS IS TORTURE THIS IS TORTURE TURNING ME INTO MEAT CUTTING GOUGING YOUR NAME IN ME RAMMING YOUR FIST INSIDE ME WEARING ME LIKE SOME FUCKING PUPPET DEMENTED YOU PSYCHO YOU FUCKING WHORE YOU CUNT LET ME GO LET ME GO LET ME MOVE LET ME STAND LYING HERE IN A POOL OF MY OWN PISS ALL COLD AN CLAMMY PATHETIC

AND DISGUSTING I CAN FEEL BLOOD AT MY WRISTS AN ANKLES
YOU MAKE ME BLEED YOU TEAR ME OPEN AN YOU STRAP ME TO
YOUR FUCKING BED I CANNOT MOVE MY MUSCLES SCREAMING
MY THROAT SCREAMING MY HEAD SCREAMING I AM ONE SCREAM
YOU FUCKING WHORE YOU CUNT YOU SLUT YOU CANNOT TREAT
ME THIS FUCKING WAY THERE ARE SO MANY THINGS I WANT TO
DO COME BACK COME BACK AN LET ME GO I WILL TEAR YOUR
FUCKING THROAT OUT WITH MY TEETH HACK YOUR HEAD OFF
AND IMPALE IT ON THE CATHEDRAL SPIRE NO CUNT TREATS
ME LIKE THIS AS IF I AM NOTHING AS IF I AM STUPID AS IF
I AM TO BE USED AND ABUSED YOU WILL PAY FOR THIS YOU
INSANE BITCH I WILL MAKE YOU FUCKING PAY FOR THIS YOU
WILL FUCKING PAY FOR THIS YOU WILL SEE THIS RAGE INSIDE
ME IT WILL COME OUT WITH CLAWS AND VOMIT YOU WILL BE
SORRY YOU WILL BE SORRY I WILL MAKE YOU WISH YOU'D NEVER
SET EYES ON ME THAT TIME IN MAGNET WHEN YOU LOOKED SO
FUCKING LOVELY YES SO COMPLETELY FUCKING BEAUTIFUL AND
HOW YOU LOOKED ABOVE ME TOWERING AND ME SPREAD OUT
BELOW YOU YOU ARE GORGEOUS YOU FUCKING WHORE COME
BACK COME BACK I WILL FREEZE TO DEATH STARVE BE EATEN
BY RATS YOU DEMENTED FUCKING SLAG YOU FUCKING PSYCHO
BITCH YOU FUCKING sick an twisted terror you come back now
an let me ————————— go

please

Is this sleep
    or is this dying
    barkin dogs an a helicopter rattling
    death to the sounds of sirens and singing outside there in
the city
    tied spreadeagled inside these sounds head humming with
drugs with stillness an the rush of me blood an the thud of me
heart like this I never thought too young too young a hard-on
on me an nowhere to put it these sounds pushing outwards at
thee insides of my skull an screaming into my fuckin gag
    taste of soap
    or shampoo

is this dying

too young too young

this darkness this loud darkness LET ME FUCKING GO KELLY YOU
MAD INSANE BITCH WHORE come back an let me go let me live let
me do all the things I've ever wanted to do an never been able to
live by a lake with you you demon let me see my mother again
let me see Jean's baby let me fall over on the grass let me

GO

LET ME FUCKING GO

is this sleeping

is this death

with gravity sucking all me guts down into me back except
for the blood in my hard–on pulsing hot an throbbing pulsatin
like there is too much inside for my one body to hold it will
pop like a balloon it will burst and I will fall so far what is
this rising, this soaring all spinning all whirling the helicopter
returns an circles clattering a car alarm whoops shrieking it is
not rain it is champagne the power is in the blood I can taste
I have bitten me tongue I have broken the skin I am bleeding
I can taste it my own blood I leak too much too much of me
seeps out I can't feel me hands or feet thee have gone numb
or been hacked off they have gone completely away like me
me too am going away I am soaring again will not explode
will not burst will rise will rise too hot to bear cannot survive
this height this soaring the human will dissolve away maybe it
has an this is me my heart my core a whiteness a brightness a
rising brightness a sun a moon everything ever here is me I lift
it I carry it from plankton to me it is all here in this soaring
spinning what is it it is nothingness or

is it the sweet

ness

is it the me

ness

And at the centre of it all this tiny spark. Stripped an tied an
robbed of every last fuckin thing at the core at the heart is this
tiny spark. Birth an death of all, this spark. *Look* at this tiny
spark. Look *into* this tiny fucking spark

what is it is it
me

let me fucking rebuild myself

Presences here in the room. Sensed fuckin presences in this room. Thee can't see me like this naked an helpless the blood an the piss an the drool on me chin hands an feet rubbed raw from my writhing. White an naked I am. Stripped of everything except myself. They must not see me like this but I can hear them an ther whispering, make out ther voices Michelle an Elizabeth and Kirk an mother an father an Dermot an Craig an Quockie sniggering and a priest tutting, a tutting priest, only a priest can tut like that. All these ghosts these people these presences standin then soaring over me like bats an leavin with a WHOOSH

whoooooooooooooooooooooooooooooooooooooooooosh

fuck
FUCK
let me

Am I sleeping?
yeh.
I think I'm sleeping.
still hurts even through the haze. let me fucking go let me fuckin
GO.

I can hear a breath. Is there someone there? Just one breath in the darkness. A breath, a sigh which isn't me. Maybe it's someone. Maybe it *is* me. Nothing in the darkness but this one breath.

Sudden light burning in me eyes even through the blindfold it *burns* my fuckin eyes. Either Kelly come back or an angel. This light is very fuckin real. So real it drives spikes of flame into me head, through me eyes an into me head. I immediately begin to thrash an buck an roar against my gag but a soft hand puts spread pressure on me flopping chest an I hear then a voice:

—Ssshhh . . . lie still, Victor . . .

And I do. Only me chest heaving, me throat gulping. I can feel the wounds on me back reopened, the scabs ripped off. Those words existing again, that legend once more readable. Visible. That voice again, Kelly's voice:

—You'll never leave me again. Will yer?

I shake me head. That's all I can do.

—No, I know yer won't.

The hand leaves me chest. Takes hold of my dick an even now in this stripped state I feel meself expanding. Growing.

—The state you're in, Victor. My poor fuckin boy. Reduced to this . . . ah fuck what have I done . . .

Stroking, pumping. I'm groaning.

—I'm sorry. I'm so fuckin sorry. Let me put yer back together.

The hand leaves an then instantly there is wet warmth. A sucking. Me insides, everything's bunching an bein drawn towards that point of suction. An somewhere a spark beginnin to flicker. Flicker into flame.

The suckin stops an firm legs straddle me, a hand grabs my dick again an guides me inside, oh fuck yes inside Kelly. Every second of me existence fallin away apart from this one, this wet an pumping fuckin wonderful one. If this is all I am then all I am is enough.

Me hips thrustin up to meet the hips thrustin down. From down an from up an meeting in the middle in this amazin fuckin explosion soft an warm an clutching. Yet again me belly burns.

The spark flickers stronger.

Hands. Yes yes hands yes. On my belly then on me heavin chest. Movin up, gentle rasping of skin on skin. Moving up. Me armpits. Me shoulders yes yes higher. On me collarbones.

Around my fucking neck.

No spark now but a flame. A candleflame in darkness. Bigger, brighter. *Burning*. A sun.

The hands begin to tighten. I gulp in air once, twice, then cannot gulp again. Those tightly squeezing hands. A panting in my ear. Hands squeezing. Tighter Kelly fuckin *tighter*, squeeze me fuckin tighter you gorgeous fuckin lovely fuckin as ar thrusts speed up, tightening an closing *crushing* my fuckin neck an me brain now roaring an me lungs now bellowing this pressure pressure stronger stronger everythin now stuffed into my balls about to burst outwards an the flame now a fireball, terrifying, amazing, crackling an blinding an fuck there is a shape in it somehow I remember this, I've seen it before this shape this shape has visited me before I remember it somehow an it is the same so sorrowful, so raging an I am moving towards it so fuckin fast panting for air an the hands ever tighter an me dick swelling all my skin so taut that light is all an that shape in it reachin for me too bright too burning no it's not it's fuckin perfect an the whole world an all in it this bright light burning an me balls burst an in me head I yell an roar

I AM THE LIGHT
red Kelly white Kelly
Kelly coming out of the steam
Kelly under the bones
Kelly inside me
me inside her and her on me give me my sight back let me see your face
to the light, this light
is everything
I am rising
I am rising
out of reach of everything
oh Kelly oh Jesus
I AM THE FUCKING LIGHT
I'm coming I'm coming
I can breathe again
oh Christ oh Kelly
I'm come

KELLY

May those who know me see the marks of biting
And bruises which betray a happy love.
In love I want to weep or see you weeping;
To agonise or hear your agony.

Propertius

THERE'S A BLOKE over there starin at me. He won't, or can't, stop starin at me. At first I wonder if it's because he knows me or something so I take a glance over at him an no, I've never seen him before in me life. The red an the white flashin lights (always fuckin red an white here, in the downstairs bar at Magnet; gets on me friggin wick after a while) blur then illuminate his face, blurred in the red an all lit up in the white. I'm certain I've never seen him before. I'd remember if I had, I'm sure of it cos he's got such a gentle face. Gentle an sort of sad-lookin. Thoughtful an quiet among his loud an sparky mates, gobbin off thee are, showin off, like, thee look like thee've been on one for days like I have an are still up for it but the lad who keeps on lookin over at me seems all spent an lonely, a bit depressed. Such a nice face.

Roz leans over the table a taps me on the shoulder. Shouts over the loud music: —How're yis feelin, Kel?!

—Alright! I shout back. —Bit fucked!

Victoria cackles. —'Fucked'?! Yer don't know the friggin *meanin* of the word, girl! Me, last night, *that* was fucked! Could hardly bleedin *walk*, tellin yer!

I laugh, rememberin the man-mountain bouncer Vicky pulled at Voodoo last night. The fuckin size of him. He took her out to his Shogun in the car park an Vicky came back in the club twenty minutes later, bow-legged, big friggin grin on her kite. Roz asked her: How was he?, an all's Vicky did was hold her hands a foot apart with a kind of pained grin on her face. How she manages to distinguish between all the fellers she's had, I'll never know. She's had hundreds. Thousands. Most of them have paid for the privilege as well; one of the most in-demand prozzies in the city, Vicky is. Upmarket, like; I mean, she's no crackwhore on the corner of Granby Street, she calls at men's houses, like, goes to visit them in ther big posh fuckin houses in Blundellsands or Bebington. She keeps tryin to get me to go with her but as yet I haven't, I mean I'm no fuckin virgin, like, but . . . I dunno, I mean gettin *paid* for it; something inherently sleazy about that. I'd feel like . . . well, a whore. And the punters all fat an sweaty an slobbery an middle-aged pantin on top of me . . .

He's lookin over at me again. I'll give him a smile.

I smile at him, *right* at him. He looks a bit surprised for a moment an then I can't see him any more cos a big feller is standin in front of him an bein hugged an jumped on by his mates. I can hear one of them, I think it's thee Oriental-lookin one, shout a name; sounds like 'Dermot'.

Victoria looks up.

—Did someone just shout 'Dermot'?!

Roz points him out an Vicky squints at him then nods.

—Yep! I *thought* so!

—Yer know him, Vic?!

—Don't *know* him as such, no! But I did him a couple of weeks ago! He paid for the hotel an everything!

Me nose starts to run so I sniff up, hard. Swallow the snot an whatever chemical residue was hangin about up there as well. It's been a hard few days since thee Otterspool party, a hard an long good time; I'm coming into the new millennium feelin fuckin wasted, me face fried with charlie, me head buzzin, me guts all ravaged with the seas of bevvy I've put away. Feel like I could sleep for weeks. Horny as fuck as well, I usually am on a comedown: the urge to feel an grab flesh. Grab a big swollen cock an twist it hard. *Bite* it. Stuff it inside me, feel it stretching me wide.

So fuckin horny on a comedown.

Victoria's tellin us a story:

—He was one of them ones who . . . well, yer can just tell the type, like, yer get to know em after a while! Thee always want *you* on top, like, thee always want *you* to call the shots! An yer know that what thee *really* want is to be tied up an spanked like little friggin schoolboys, I mean really fuckin punished, like! Humiliated!

Vicky's high hairdo is beginnin to wilt. The tins of gel an hairspray she uses to sculpt her hair up like Marge Simpson's have begun to crystallise on her forehead. She still looks fuckin good, tho. An Rosalind next to her with her hair cropped number-one short an bleached white, thee couldn't look more different, shoulder-to-shoulder an me leanin in towards them. How fuckin *ace* we must look, the three of us. Altho how fuckin *wrecked* I feel, like ashes or somethin, something used an exhausted.

He's lookin over at me again. That bloke. Out the corner of me eye I can see him lookin over at me again. I'm smilin at his mate's back, that Dermot feller, because Vicky's tellin us about her session with him an I'm tryin to imagine him tied up bent over the back of a chair with a dildo up his big hairy arse.

—An I was floggin the bastard as well! Vicky's sayin, laughin her head off. —With his own friggin belt, like! An he was goin: ooh *harder*, ye bloody bitch!

She shouts this last in an exaggerated Oirish accent an we all laugh. The four blokes suddenly spin in ther seats to look at us an I see *that* bloke, the one who keeps lookin at me, flap his hands with a shocked expression on his face an his mates as one turn back to him. What's all that about? Why that quick an sudden gawp? Maybe that Dermot one is tellin his mates about Victoria, just as she's tellin me an Roz about him. Funny, that, the two of them sittin not ten yards apart, not sayin a word to each other an yet spillin all private stuff to every fucker else, tellin em all thee did together an yet not communicatin with each other at all. Which is just how we live, I suppose, innit? Huge fuckin barriers between us all the time. We can tell ar secrets to others, but definitely *not* to them who we do secret things with. Bet he leaves out that bit about the dildo up the ring, tho.

—It's mainly the Catholics, I've found, Victoria's sayin. —They're the ones who go in for the punishment beatins, like! Especially the friggin priests! Can't get enough of it! Ther backs an arses all swollen an red an ther fuckin shoutin for more, often not fuckin happy til ther runnin with blood! Honest to God! Thee seem to fuckin *hate* themselves, I'm tellin yer!

Roz yells somethin about original sin an Vicky nods.

—Maybe, yeh! That's what fuckin Coggy schools teach yis,

innit, that yer worthless an useless an stupid! I know for a fact that *mine* fuckin did!

I have to agree.

Vicky leans in closer. —Tell youse what, tho! Sooner have the friggin priests as punters than thee others, like! The Prods! One time I did this fuckin Orange Lodge function, fuckin *knew* I shouldn't, like, but the money was sound an I needed it so . . . thought why the fuck not!

She shrugs.

—Only wanted to fuckin piss on me, didn't thee!

—Go 'way!

—Serious! No lie! Fat sashers got the fuckin plastic sheetin out, wanted me to strip off an lie down on it! Be a fuckin *bog* for them! Cunts!

He's standin up, now, that lad, the one who won't stop starin at me, him with the sad face; he's standin up. As surreptitiously as I can I watch him move across the dance floor, his hips swayin in a kind of wasted an sexy way. There's a certain style to him. A certain class. He's got a way of carryin himself, unless of course he's puttin it all on which would then make for a contrivance which would then make for a pretension which would then make him a knobhead. But no, it seems genuine, cos he stumbles an trips over the single step that leads up into the bogs an I bet he feels embarrassed. Bet his face is burnin hot now cos he's picturing me watchin him, seein him trip. But he even stumbled with a certain kind of stylishness; he held his palms up an away from his sides as if challenging the step or his own misfortune to a barney. It looked good. I like that. I like *him*.

—What did yer do?!

—Told em to fuck *right* off! I know some who are willin to do watersports, like, but not me! An with *those* cunts, the Lodgers, it's not about gettin off or anythin, it's about treatin someone like dirt! Makin them feel like shite!

—Is right!, I shout.

Roz agrees: —Yeh! Probly made sure that thee got a Catholic girl, like! Probly screened yer first, checked that yer had the right credentials! Did thee still pay yis?!

Vicky purses her lips an shakes her head. —*Fucks* did thee! I had to do a fuckin runner anyway! Thee were gettin aggressive, like, just done ther friggin march an all pissed up! Got out of there fast as I fuckin could! Not lettin meself get wee'd on for no cunt! Not unless I *ask* em to, like!

I'm wishin I'd never heard that story. I'm imagining the fear, the squalor . . . all these big angry rat-arsed men wantin to take ther dicks out an slash all over yer. Pure fuckin nightmare.

Wanner go to bed. I'm fucked, I'm knackered. Wanner just curl up an go off to sleep. No, I wanner just curl up an go to sleep with someone else, feel them sleepin by me, ther body all warm an peaceful. Someone not like that twat Peter; someone not like every bleedin bloke I've ever fuckin met. I'm gunner be comin down hard in a bit, parro an depressed an tearful, an that's much fuckin worse if yer on yer own. It's horrible. Desolate. An I've got to fuckin watch meself here cos I know from past painful experience that in this mood, with the comedown in the friggin post, I'll pick up any ahl fucker, take anyone home, any selfish arrogant ignorant smug fuckin arsehole just for the company, like, an it'll be, like always before, a sheer fuckin disaster, it'll turn out far worse than if I had've stayed on me own. Got to watch yerself here, Kelly. Yer in danger. But there's always Roz an Vicky, I suppose; Could all three go back to one of ar flats, carry on drinkin, continue the party. Not Roz's place, tho; she still lives with her mam. But even the company of her mother, the tea an the Jammy Dodgers she still gives us whenever we go round there, would be better than thee alternative; just such a fuckin horror to be alone.

I see that friggin balloon-head Darren Taylor an a few of his divvy mates go into the toilet, swaggerin like dickheads, all of em walkin like that soft get Liam friggin Gallagher. Who the *fuck* do thee think thee are? The bloke who's been lookin at me hasn't come out of the bog yet an I hate the thought of a face as gentle an sweet as his confrontin the scowlin kites of Darren friggin Taylor an his lackies. Maybe I should go an see if he's alright.

I stand up.

—Where yis off, Kel?!

—Need a wee! I shout, an move towards the toilets. Across the dance floor an into the dark corridor where the bogs are. Fuckin Darren Taylor; shits me up, that bastard does. Damaged fuckin goods. Yer look into his eyes an there's fuck all there, there's nowt goin on. Just blankness. A lizard's eyes, that fucker's got. I was in the Grapes last season when he glassed a Blackburn Rovers fan after they'd knocked us out of the FA Cup at Anfield. Didn't actually see it, like, luckily I was down in thee other bar when it happened, but I heard the commotion an the screams an saw all the blood splashed up the fuckin walls. Fuckin psycho. Head-the-ball, that prick. Hope he's not gone in the bogs to sort somethin with the nice-faced feller; pure awful that would be. That sad an gentle face all cut an hangin open. Heartbreaking.

What am I gunner say to that face, anyway? What the fuck am I doing, standin here? Haven't got a scooby what to say. Or do.

Then he's out an walkin past me an I'm tappin him twice on the shoulder. Hard muscle or bone me finger touches. Me heart is beatin a wee bit faster than normal but, God, it's been doin that since the last bleedin century, four friggin days ago. He turns to face me, his eyes big an he's got a face like yis might see in a dream. Like I *have* seen in a dream. I say thee only thing I can think of, have to shout it over the music: —Are yis alright?!

His jaw wobbles as if he's tryin to swallow. His eyes look at my neck.

—Yeh! Why like?!

—Cos I saw yer fall over the step like an I thought that yer might be feelin unwell or somethin! Sick or somethin! So I came over to see if yer needed any help or anything!

He smiles a little bit an mumbles somethin that I don't hear. I lean towards him.

—What?!

—I said, no, thanks! I'm fine! Just dead tired, like!

His breath smells like mine must; chemicals an beer an fag smoke. Not very nice, but I don't mind, not one tiny little bit.

—I'm just the fuckin same! I shout. Tired of yellin but the music's so bleedin loud. —Been a good long party! Gone on for a week! No sleep or food an I'm fuckin knackered!

He nods an shouts somethin which again I don't catch.

—What?!

—I said: You! *Know*! It!

Know what? What the frig's he talkin about? Oh, he's just agreein with me. So I agree with him back: —Yeh!

I lean still closer towards him. Can't help it. It's like I'm being pulled to him by a strong thread. I can't keep me eyes off his face, how boyish it seems, how kind of gently surprised. He's very good-lookin. Not in any conventional sense, no chiselled cheekbones or anythin like that but to me, here, at this moment, he looks very fuckin good. The red an white lights on the right-hand side of his face. He's just staring at me, staring into my face. Without knowin I'm goin to, I ask him if he wants to go upstairs where it's quieter but he doesn't hear me, so I have to repeat myself:

—I said! I put a hand on his shoulder. Feel his skin hot beneath his shirt an the muscle hard beneath that. Grab an squeeze an suck. —I said! Do you want to go upstairs! It's quieter! I'm sick of havin to shout at people!

—Okay! Yeh!

I walk across the dance floor, empty except for a staggerin lad in a Carlsberg shirt reelin all over the place. The bloke with the sweet face follows me an it's like I'm presentin him with me arse an me waist an so what the fuck if I am? I've got a good arse, I've got a good waist. Behind me an he must be able to see the big black flower tattooed on me back, £40 at Birkenhead Pete's two years ago an every man I've ever known finds that a turn-on. But I *am* slightly surprised at meself, tho; surprised a bit at how much I *want* it to turn him on. Want him to find me, *all* of me, a big turn-on. Which if he doesn't now then he soon friggin will.

One of the lads he was with, the Chinese or Japanese one, jumps on him an grabs his head, roaring. I look at his gorgeous face bein squeezed between those two rough hands an just point upwards at thee upstairs bar an he nods an I climb the stairs. I should really say tara to Roz an Victoria but when I look over at them ther talkin to two blokes in suits so I don't bother, I just climb the stairs past a group of silent baghead scallies who follow me with ther eyes an I turn left into the main bar, just as packed an hot as the downstairs one but much, much quieter cos there's no music up here, just voices. Three-deep at the bar tho, but a barmaid I know, a Manc girl called Sadie, smiles an nods at me an I order a bottle of apple Source for meself an what for him? Lager or Guinness, *all* blokes drink lager or Guinness but lager at the tail end of a four-day bender is a bit fuckin rough so I order him a Guinness. Think that's what I saw him drinkin downstairs, anyway.

There's something a bit . . . *different* about this one. We've only exchanged a few sentences, like, but already I can tell. Most blokes, I mean all's I have to do is grunt at them an look at ther faces an thee'd follow me fuckin anywhere; not cos I'm so fuckin gorgeous or anythin like that but because most blokes are such friggin dogs. This one, tho . . . there's something different about him. Not that yer can ever tell for sure, like, but he seems so gentle. Soft, in a *good* way. Nowt hard or horrible in his eyes. I want to fuck thee arse off him.

He's standin by my side. I smile at him an hand him the Guinness. Looks a bit disappointed as he takes it.

—Sorry. I didn't know what you were drinkin, so . . .

—Nah, this is fine.

—Saw yer drinkin Guinness before, see, so I thought: Safest bet.

—Ta.

He sips at it an pulls a bit of a face. He's got full lips an green eyes. Hair kind of straw-coloured an messy, short but messy. Stubble on his face beginnin to grow red at the sides. He's beautiful.

I look around for somewhere to stand cos it's chocka at the bar. See a hole in the crowd by the big windows that face the street.

—Eeyar, there's a space over there.

—Alright.

I move over to the windows, Hardman Street behind them.

It looks mad out there; traffic bumper-to-bumper, big groups of people runnin around wearin party hats an all kinds of mad stuff, jumpin on each other's backs. It's like everything's changed in the past few days; like people have at last started to live in the way ther supposed to. Like they've finally realised why ther alive.

—God, look at it all, I say. —It's like the world'll never be the same again.

Stupid fuckin thing to say. Feel a bit bleedin embarrassed. Daft divvy thing to come out with.

I can feel him lookin at me, studyin me face an I like that so I continue to look over me shoulder out the window, lettin him look. I hope he's appraising. Which I'm sure he is cos the way he's lookin at me it's like he's gulping me, storin me away. Which usually makes me feel robbed, molested somehow, but with him I don't mind. It seems, it *feels*, right. Good. Nothin wrong here.

Except I don't know his name. Nor does he know mine.

A big feller in the street outside pulls a funny face at me through the glass, stickin his tongue out, rolling his eyes back in his head. I smile at him then turn back to this feller I'm with an tell him my name an ask him his. I'm not sure what he says but it sounds like 'Victor'.

—Victor?

—Yeh.

Strange name. —That's not very common. Never meet many people called Victor.

He tells me a funny story about his dad bein a big fan of gladiator films an about naming him after some actor, some macho actor who turned out to be a big weed. It's a funny story an *he's* funny tellin it; his hand gestures, the faces he pulls. I'm startin to like him more an more. He can shag me if he wants. I'll let him fuck me, if he wants to. I like him.

—It's a good name, I say. —Victor. It suits yis. Better than the usual borin fuckin Dave. Or Steve.

—Yeh.

I drink half me Source off in one go. He sips his Guinness. Small talk, but the questions I ask him I do, genuinely, want

171

to know thee answers to; want to know how he spent thee important date. What kind of a feller he is.

—So how was yer millennium? What did yer do?

—Loadser stuff.

Good enough answer.

—Did yis go the docks? The Creamfields, like?

I shake me head. —Nah. Seventy quid? Fuck that. There was a party out in Otterspool, spent New Year's Eve there.

I say somethin about bein able to see the fireworks on the Mersey an how impressive it looked.

—Even better close up, he says. Victor, that's his name. Vick-ter.

—Was it worth the money, then? The Pier Head do, like?

He shrugs an smiles, tells me about his mate having some kind of clout or somethin, some *Mixmag* connections which got them in free. —I mean, we had to go somewhere, didn't we? Town was friggin *dead*.

I have to agree with that. The place was bleedin deserted right enough. —An good on em, the punters, for stayin away, I reckon; the landlords were too bleedin greedy; twenny quid to get in, three or four quid a drink . . . fuckin rip-off. People sacked it all off an made ther own entertainment. An good on em, *I* say.

I'm aware that that sounds a bit fuckin workin-class rebelish, so takin the piss out of meself a bit, I grin at him an say: —Power to the people, eh?

He just smiles back.

Stuck for somethin to say now. Me head's addled, too blitzed to think up conversation. I start to peel the label off the Source bottle with me thumbnail. He's drinkin his pint and, again, lookin at me over the rim of the glass. What's he thinking? It's like he's sizing me up. Or maybe he's havin second thoughts. Maybe, in the brighter light in this upstairs bar, he's beginning to think that I'm not as good-looking to him as I was downstairs an he's workin out how to extricate himself from this situation. But I doubt it because, as I suck at me bottle, he lets out a tiny, barely discernible whimper an his stare, his direct stare at me face, says only three words: fuck an sleep an together. I'm pleased. I turn me head to look directly at him, catch him staring an he gives a wee embarrassed cough an wipes his mouth with the back of his hand. I smile at him to let him know that I don't mind him looking, that he can go on the fuck ahead an look all he wants. I wanner say something to him, something that may make him realise how special an strange he seems, but all's I come out with is:

—You look exhausted.

He agrees an says something in reply but I don't hear it cos I'm thinking: you stupid fuckin cow, Kelly. Is that all yer can come out with? 'You look exhausted'? Jesus Christ. Where's yer friggin brain?

Thee answer to which question is: frazzled into a porridgy mush.

Fuck this. Fannyin around.

I finish the bottle an put it on the narrow window ledge behind me. —Come ed, I say to him. —Come back to mine. Back to me flat.

I turn an walk out an feel him following. This is much fuckin better, Kelly; decisiveness, self-confidence. *Much* better. A prelude to the, the roughness, the friggin violence which I know will always come as soon as I'm in bed with him. I can't help it, it always comes out. I can feel it buildin up inside me *now*, already. Grab an pull an pummel.

Outside is a smack of icy air in the face an thee immediate city noise, cars honkin, fireworks, loud shouting. Cymbals clashin somewhere and I can smell chips and the sea; both of them not too dissimilar. I glance over me shoulder an see Victor behind me, lookin all lost an worried in this new heave so I reach an take his hand an squeeze it tight. He glances down an seems to nod an I lead him through the traffic to thee other side of the road, outside the gates to the Picket out of which people are spilling, singing, staggerin. The world seems fuckin crazy. But I mean crazy like it *should* be; as if life is to be enjoyed, not suffered. Like we've finally fuckin realised that, after all these years of drudgery.

Victor asks me how far it is to my gaff an if we should get a taxi there.

—No, I say. —It's not too far, a cab'd be good, like, but we'd have to walk all the way down to Chinatown to get one an if we do that then we might as well walk. It's about the same distance. Why, like?

He shrugs.

—Yer alright, aren't yeh? Can manage it, like? Ten or fifteen minutes?

He nods an gives me a great big, wrecked smile. I squeeze his hand again. It feels clammy with chemical sweat. He says:

—I'm fine.

—Good.

We go down Hope Street, a cathedral in front an a cathedral behind, both of them so fuckin giant an lit up all misty blue, clouds around ther steeples (not that the Catholic one *has* a steeple as such, like, but . . .). There's rubbish everywhere, party rubbish; streamers an banners an bottles an confetti, popped balloons now just coloured rubber. Groups of people are either ploddin along without words, absolutely cabbaged, or swayin an singin on corners, beneath street lights. It looks fuckin ace. Like the tail end of the best party ever. But, in me comedown, I start to think about how it probly *was* the best party ever an that I'll never see anythin like it again, that, from now on, it's all down-fuckin-hill. This thought isn't perhaps somethin I should share with Victor, me prospective shag (prospective? It's signed, sealed, an delivered, Kel), but there's fuckin *contact* in it, isn't there, there's some form of friggin connection, like, so I start to tell him about when I was little an how the year 2000 seemed like this massive, special time, a magical age:

—When we'd all be drivin around in floatin cars an livin on pills. Havin holidays on Mars an stuff. Everythin was gunner be, like, different, all fuckin science fiction, aliens livin in ar cities an us on ther planets an stuff. But what's changed, tho, really? Nowt. An it *won't*, either. It's all gunner stay the same. Nothing's any different.

—Apart from the livin on pills bit, he says. —*That's* come true.

Which makes me laugh. —Is right. An that fuckin millennium bug; what the fuck was that all about? Nowt went wrong

174

at all. People talkin about catastrophe, war, an look what's happened. Fuck all.

—You *know* it.

This is good, this, this talkin, this bletherin, it's good an it's unusual because it seems like he's actually friggin *listening* to me, he's interested in what I've got to say. Which is a fuckin first. Most blokes, ther obviously just waitin for yer to stop talkin so thee can go on again about themselves. Drives me fuckin mad, that does. Ignorant tossers, self-obsessed. But this one, tho, this Victor, it's like he fuckin *leans* into my words, like ther important to him, like he *really* fuckin *wants* to hear them. There's somethin about him. Despite this rapidly accelerating comedown an despite the fact that I've only known him for about fifteen minutes or something, he's makin me heart soar like nothin else ever has (apart from maybe that bit of rock me an Roz an Vicky smoked on New Year's Day). I turn to him to tell him somethin, I don't know what, somethin that might please him, but he seems all sort of sad; lookin down at the ground with his forehead all in lines. I ask him again if he's alright. He looks at me an nods but doesn't smile.

—Yeh, just really fuckin tired, that's all. Comin down *hard*, like.

He starts strokin the back of me hand with his thumb so I do the same to him. Feels nice. I ask him: —Are yer always this quiet? Or is it just cos yer crashin? He looks a bit worried so I try to reassure him: —No, it's alright, it's not a criticism. It's just that I noticed in Magnet like how yer mates were bein all loud an gobby but you were just sittin there all thoughtful-lookin. Like a, erm . . .

Like a what, Kelly? Burbled yer way into a corner here, haven't yeh?

—Like an, erm, oasis or something. A patch of calm, like.

Daft cow. Stupid. He doesn't seem to mind tho cos he strokes me hand again an says: —Ah. That's nice.

We turn right on to Bedford Street South, my road. A much quieter road, this; lifeless, in fact, apart from a big rat leggin it away from some burst bin-bags.

I point. —A rat, look. Size of him.

We watch it run down an alleyway. It puts me in mind of when I was livin in Kensington with Peter (a horrible life; horrible area, horrible house, horrible fuckin boyfriend), an there was a binmen strike an the rubbish piled up an up an the place was overrun by fuckin rats. I tell Victor about this (leavin out any mention of Peter), aware that I'm beginnin to ramble but I can't help it, I want his interested face, I want his eyes wide and his fascination.

—Yeh, scurryin all over the fuckin walls thee were. An the council was payin people to kill em, like, fifty pence a tail, so yer had all these little scallies with cricket bats an carvin knives wadin through the rubbish. An the *stink*, God. Horrible. Whole flat was full of it. It fuckin reeked. Yer could even *taste* it, in the back of yer throat, like. Made me friggin gip.

—Jesus. Why were yer livin in Kensington? Rough bleedin place, that.

I shrug. —Cheap rents, innit? I was workin in a shop at the time, like, an the wages were shite, so Kenny was all I could afford. Whores below, junkies above. But dead cheap.

He asks me if I'm working now. Oh God, fuckin work; back to that fuckin newsagent's in a couple of days' time, ten hours a friggin day behind the bulletproof perspex. Scratchcards an ciggies, that's all anyone ever buys from there. And porn. Borin fuckin job it is. An the lecherous fuckin boss with his BMW an brown fuckin apron . . . Aw Jesus. Back to work. Back to pure fucking monotony. The year 2000 an nothing's fuckin changed; sooner thee build a robot shopgirl the fuckin better, far as I'm concerned.

—Same shop, I tell Victor. —Newsies off Parliament Street. But not for fuckin long, tho, I'll tell yer that. Not for fuckin long.

Christ no. A couple more weeks, get a wee bit of money together, an I'm sackin it off. Sooner be fuckin skint than put up with that shite. New millennium, new start; an I'll start it fuckin free. Skint, like, but free; tied to *no* fucker.

Shack's song 'Streets of Kenny' starts runnin through my head, I get to the second chorus then we're at my house. I have to let go of Victor's hand while I get me keys out of me pocket an open the door. Inside the hallway an I close the door behind us an me pulse starts to race; I can feel that familiar aching in me hands and throat, thee urge, the fuckin *yearning* to grab an twist an pull an wrench. Always this fuckin roughness in my sex. I can hear Victor's footsteps behind me as I lead him up the stairs to the top floor an I'm imagining where we'll be in a few minutes' time, him beneath me an inside me, me leaning to bite an to grab. Pulling. Punching. Always this fuckin violence in my sex an I don't know where it comes from. Most blokes seem to like it, tho. Most blokes can't seem to get enough. And I, personally, wouldn't want it any other fuckin way.

We reach me door an I begin the slow process of unlockin the five locks. I'm a bit nervous, shakin a bit even, an this makes me drop the keys but only the once, then we're inside an I'm slightly disappointed to notice that thee incense stick I lit yesterday hasn't managed to mask the smell of the fried-onion butty Victoria had for her breakfast. Smells a bit manky. Like a friggin hotdog stand outside Anfield or something. Place is a bit of a tip as well but fuck that. Don't give an arse. It's been one long fuckin party.

I throw me bag on to the couch an Victor sits in the chair by the window. He's lookin around, takin it all in; that interest again. The walls, floor, ceiling, telly, he takes it *all* in. I go through into the kitchen an ask him if he wants a drink.

—Alright.

—What?

—Alright.

—No, I mean what d'yer want?

—What are *you* havin?

Aw God, I *hate* it when people ask that. —Whiskey. Jameson's. I look in the fridge. —Haven't got anythin else anyway. Except some flat cider.

—Whiskey, then. That's good.

—On its own?

—Sound, yeh.

I pour the whiskeys, two big ones. I'm thinking: I'll go back in there an kiss him. Lean over him an smash my gob down on to his. Bite at him, *gnash* at him, snap, snatch, fuckin grab his head in me hands an suck at his face, suck the breath out of his lungs, stretch me tongue down his throat as far as it will go, make him gag an hang his gob open for more. His sweet face an his gawkiness, I really fuckin want him, I'm horny as a bastard but not for just anyone only that Victor with his sad face an green eyes an slender cabled neck. *Bite* that neck, chomp at that fuckin neck. Have him craned below me, exposed, I'll pounce on him like a wolf. Pull his balls. Suck his dick. Bruise him with my grabbing, see his skin flushed red with risen blood. How sweet he seems an gentle an I want him on his back beneath me.

My God. I'm *so* fuckin horny.

I knock back one of the whiskeys an pour meself another. Tastes fuckin awful but once in me guts it glows an smoulders. Go back into the livin room, give a drink to Victor, whose right knee is now jiggling as if he's fuckin terrified. He looks up at me, a taste of what's to come which makes me cunt start to throb then he throws the whiskey down his neck an I can see his throat jump as he gags, a reflex which he tries to hide by falsely coughing. His eyes are all watery.

—Went down the wrong way, Victor, yeh?

—Nah, it's not that, it's just . . .

He trails off an puts the glass down next to me spider plant and, like a child, pulls the cuffs of his fleece down over his fingers an wipes his eyes. Such a sweet movement, a sweet thing to do. I can't make the move now, not right now, not after he's just done that. Can't leap on him after he's just reminded me of a little boy. I sit on thee end of the couch closest to him, on thee edge of the seat so that ar knees touch. He's staring down at his knees, his arms folded an tucked into his belly. I take a sip of the whiskey an put the glass down.

—Sure yer alright? I ask him again.

—Yeh, I . . . He shakes his head. —Just took too big a gulp, yer know. It's been one long bastard party, like . . .

He wipes his eyes with his cuffs again, that same gesture – once is touching, twice is a turn-on. I'm fucking *on* him. Me hand on his nape pullin his face into mine an me tongue in his gob, lickin, slurpin, tryin to pull his friggin teeth out by the roots. Whiskey-taste, tobacco-taste. His lips crumple an give an roll back over his teeth an me heart is surging like some giant wave, he puts his arms around me an I straddle his legs an press me breast to his, rub me fanny up an down his thigh, everythin goes, it all vanishes except this grunting an groanin boy beneath me, I taste his noises an feel him writhe, me hands holdin his face locked to mine I suck him all out an into me. Want to bite an crunch. Feel flesh yield an split, fill me mouth with hot blood. I'm whimpering inside, whimperin under thee intensity of me yearning for him, to have all of him spreadeagled an exposed completely new an undiscovered an pure fuckin helpless. Pillage an rape an penetrate. Fuckin well *shred* him, tear the bastard to bits.

Without releasin me hold on the back of his head I move me mouth down to his ear. Me voice is a quiet roar:

—Aw God . . . I'm gunner fuck you so hard . . . yer gunner love fucking me, you are . . . yer'll never want another woman ever again . . .

Which he won't. I'll make double fuckin sure of that. He's about to experience something which he never would've imagined.

My God, feel my heart.

I push meself off him an we stand up. I nod me head backwards in the direction of the bedroom an walk towards there an he follows me. I'm grindin me teeth. I'm almost fuckin *growling*. A thumping, a thrashin inside me, this aggression always appears an I can't help it it just comes out. This desire to mash an maul an bite. Suck. Tear with me teeth. Rippin at his clothes, draggin his fleece up over his head an he raises his arms to let me do so, I shove him back on the bed an pull his trainies off an his socks an rip open the button fly of his kex. Smells rise, I can smell him, sweaty an unwashed, but I don't care about that, it just makes him more fuckin *real* to me, more complete, more of a well-made an entire thing to dismantle, smash through. Fuckin, fuck yis fuckin *fuck* yis. In one movement I drag his jeans off an throw them over me shoulder, small change scatters an rolls, I'm wrenching at his black boxers clawin at them with me nails an his dick springs free, flat against his belly pointin upwards at his own face already so fuckin hard, so throbbing an vein-laced an thick I punch his legs apart an see his balls wrinkled tight like walnuts, wanner bite, rip them fuckin *off* an I snatch at his dick an yank it down to point at *my* face an pounce on it gob open like a shark must do to prey or a panther. Hard on my tongue. Bulging spongy against the back of me throat. I work the foreskin back with me teeth, not gently, hear him moan an feel the whole friggin mattress contract as he clutches it in his hands. I'm groanin too. Love this. Fucking *love* this, suckin hard, tryin to suck his guts out his heart out through his urethra suckin so fuckin hard me head spins, wantin me teeth to meet through this stuffed flesh an feel the crunch an the split an the salt, the wetness burst inside me mouth all over me teeth, me tongue. Fuckin *love* this. I look up at his face, see his head loll loosely back on his shoulders an his lips hangin open an his eyes gone in folds. Picture of ecstasy. The very image of pure fuckin ecstasy. As if only he an he alone is caught in a bright blindin beam from the sky an he is dyin in a fuckin rapture. Looks like his whole face is about to dissolve. His cock so hard, spasming in me mouth as if he's about to come an I want him inside me burstin like a cannon so I spit him out an stand up an cannot take me gear off fast enough. A band of street light falls across his prone body, diagonal from left hip to right shoulder. I will tear him to pieces with my nails and teeth.

He raises his head up off the bed an croaks words: —Johnnies . . . I've got none . . .

I shake me head. —Fuck that. *I'm* willin to take the risk. I can tell yer clean.

Then, to put his mind at rest, I tell him that I had an AIDS test recently an that it came up negative. —So don't worry. Don't worry.

An then, to put his mind in a turmoil, a pure fuckin frenzy I straddle him an shove his rock-hard cock up inside me as far as it will go, feel it stretchin me an bumpin up against me uterus, *inside* me he's so fuckin far inside me it feels like I might choke. Choke. Chokin me choke *him* . . .

Clean, I called him; clean. And he is. So clean an spotless I will cover him, in blood an come an spit.

Nowt in this room except me an him, just the pulsing of him inside me an his hands grasping my tits, reachin up to grasp my swelling breasts. I want for nothing other than this, I will *never* fuckin want anything other than this. I could fuckin die now with him inside me, him below me all spread out an offered I could give it all up now perfectly fuckin happy. Like this is what I've always wanted, always fuckin needed. Nothing else but me an him.

I grab his shoulders, squeeze, try to punch me fingers through his skin. Rocking back an forth faster an faster. Heat in me ankles. I lean down, me face an inch or so from his, me teeth gritted:

—God, you fuckin . . . you cunt . . . aw fuckin God fuck me you bastard . . . fuck . . . you fuckin cunt . . . *fuck* me . . . *fuck* me . . .

He is *so* fucking hard. Like white-hot steel inside me, scorchin me, scouring me. I am a blur to myself, the whole world of me life up to this point is just one blur an like thee always do my hands scrabble to seek out his neck, spread an encircle an hold. And, then, squeeze. Squeeze really fuckin hard. Then squeeze even harder, feel his frantic swallowin throbbing against me palms, feel his windpipe tryin to open to take in air an hear him panting an gasping an whining I open me eyes a fraction to see thee utter bliss on his face, all his muscles slackened an loose apart from that one inside me which recoils an then fuckin *bursts* open, powerin into me like a missile an squirting fire all the way up into my skull. Thee always come this hard when I'm chokin them, always, like ther transcendin themselves an doin what thee usually cannot do but only Victor I want to do this to, all thee others are forgettable an as nothing compared to him an his bursting, his ecstasy, the bright bright place I've taken him to this lovely clean an dirty fucker squirting, spouting inside me an the heat in me feet explodes an envelops me my entire skin tinglin like one giant itchy scab bein slowly peeled off an I come so hard it feels like me cunt has sucked everything in, Victor the bed the room the city the world. For one instant nothing but me an my pleasure an then for one more instant just me an my pleasure an Victor, him below me wheezing, his breast barrelling as it gulps in thee air I've deprived it of. Fucking . . . fucking *come*, me legs in lava, liquid fire runnin in me veins drippin out of me in a stream of sparks.

I collapse, go weak. Me bones move away from each other an I fall sideways on to the bed, next to Victor. Lyin on me back facing the ceiling. Warm sweat crawlin all over me.

The room stops spinning. Slowly.

—Is that . . .

Very small, his voice is. Sounds sore. Probly is after the friggin choking I've just given him, but I've never seen a face as blissful as his when me hands were around his neck. Never.

—Is that . . . I mean, no protection . . .

—I've *told* yer, I say, harsher than I intended. No need for that harshness, like, but fuck the place I've just been to was pure fuckin beautiful. An now I'm not there any more.

—I'm clean.

—No, I mean . . . babies, like . . .

I shake me head. Quite vigorously. Let me fuckin go back there. —I've just come off the pill. I was in a long relationship. Should still be working.

Too ambiguously phrased, that; I mean, did I mean that the contraceptive pill should still be working, or the relationship? He's probly thinkin the same thing. Maybe I should reassure him. But I can feel exhaustion beginnin to overtake me so when I feel Victor turn his head to face me I stand up an leave the room cos I'm utterly lacking in thee energy to explain meself to him. Altho, to meself, I explain that I was referrin to the pill, *not* the friggin relationship cos *that* never fuckin worked from the kick-off. An nor did fuckin Peter. Altho *one* good thing came out of it, I suppose; the diazzies I was prescribed after we split up an I was fucked up for a bit. The downers which I fetch a few of now from the kitchen. Need for sleep now. Completely friggin wasted. I hear some drippin sounds on the kitchen floor between me legs; I look down an see two little grey pancakes of come on the lino. Victor's come. All the potential wee babbies on the floor, dried to scale in the morning. Tricklin down me inner thighs an turnin cold an clammy. I fill a glass with water.

Pure fucked, I am. In two ways. Probly more than two if I think about it which I refuse to do cos I don't need that low-ey. Just sleep now while I'm happy.

I go back into the bedroom an hold me palm out with some pills in it. Victor looks at them an sits up an shakes his head. That little body.

—*More* E? Fuck *no*.

—Ther just downers. Diazepam. Help yer sleep, like. Want one?

—Alright then.

He takes one an I give him the water to wash it down with, then take the glass back off him an swallow mine. I climb into the bed, the side nearest the wall. All warm under the duvet. The faint aftertaste of the diazepam reminds me of unhappiness so I hold me arms out towards Victor an he moves into them an I wrap them around him. Feel his deep breathing, his slowin heartbeat. Dogs bark outside the window, in thee alleyway below. Distant sirens an fireworks. Copper chopper rattlin overhead. All that stuff outside, all that bleedin madness out there an just me an Victor in here warm an safe in bed. Holdin each other. I wish I had thee energy for another shag cos I'm *well* fuckin up for one despite the tiredness but I'd fall asleep halfway through, I know I would. Sexy, sweet Victor. Lovely fuckin Victor. I'm glad he's here; I imagine him outside in the cold night city surrounded by angry dogs an sirens an helicopters an that thought makes me squeeze him tighter. Victor all alone in the big city. Lovely fuckin Victor, never go, you bastard.

He jerks as if suddenly rememberin something.

—Ey, djer have an alarm? I've got to meet some people tomorrow in thee Everyman.

—What time?

—About two.

—Oh, that's alright. I'll be well up before then.

Which I will be; light sleeper, me. Even tho sometimes I wish I could sleep for years an years I can never usually sleep more than six hours per night. Don't know why, just can't.

—Okay, he says. —We're off to Wales, see, we arranged it ages ago. A wee comedown holiday, like.

—Oh, well, have a good time.

Which I won't have, comin down alone, like. Fuck it. Nowt I haven't endured before. I peck Victor on the lips, his cracked, dry lips, an roll away from him, into the wall. He shuffles up against me, presses himself to me an I feel his hot breath on me back, his too-hot breath as if there's a furnace inside him. Me brain shuts down. Me body, me tinglin body, shuts down. Tight skin, throbbin skull, pleasantly stinging fanny, thee all shut down. Like fallin into foam. All soft an lovely. Like a cloud around me an I dream of bein on a cloud, cross-legged on a cloud, miles high above thee earth altho I can see all the people crawlin across it like ants, busy little things goin about ther business. Scurryin in ther millions. Far below me an my peace, calm here on my cloud in me blueness. Except I'm all alone, entirely alone, an I want the people below me to stop ther frantic scurryin an thee do. Just like that: Stop it I think an thee do. Then I wish them to start again an thee do. Stop again an thee do. Rise towards me an thee do, thee begin to float up towards me, all ther little white upturned faces gettin closer, gettin bigger. An one among them, green eyes an straw-coloured hair an cracked lips, risin faster than all thee others, hurrying towards me, *zoomin* up towards me but he's goin far too fast, much too fuckin fast, the skin on his face beginnin to bubble an blister with his speed, thee air-friction, his eyes are running I mean melting an I'm gesturing for him to stop, screamin at him to stop, willin with all me heart for him to stop but he won't, he continues to rise an accelerate an break apart an I can do nothing but watch him burn, break apart in fiery chunks. Die.

Horrible fuckin dream. Which I'm woken from, thankfully, by a tiny prick of pain on me back, just a tiny twinge, maybe a gnat biting or a flea. I forget where I am for a moment an then the heat of Victor against me back makes me remember an I turn slowly to face him. He's asleep. Breathin deeply. How fuckin lovely he looks like that. I hear the wind howlin against me window, so cold, an I feel that I must touch Victor, must feel the heat in his skin so I do, I take hold of his upper arm an curl me fingers around the bone. Hold on to him so that cold wind cannot carry him off, take him away while we're both asleep. Keep him here. There are things I could do with this Victor. Things I *will* do with him. Things I will do *to* him. To just see the happiness in his face.

Sleep again, deep an sated an unbroken until nothing but the daylight wakes me. I'm on me back, one of Victor's arms flung across me torso, just under me tits. He's quietly snorin, breath whistlin in an out of his nostrils. I lie an stare at the ceiling an work out what I'm feeling an realise that it's an absence, a *nice* an welcome absence; thee absence of that self-loathing an disappointment that I've always invariably felt when I've woken up hung-over next to an unknown bloke. It's always been *Oh fuck, what have I done* an *Oh fuck, what do I do now*. Two horrible questions neither of which I'm thinkin at this moment, the weight of Victor's arm across me. Neither of which are close to me mind. Only a sense of pleasant surprise. Discovery. Some mild shock that it could be this way. That's all.

I gently move Victor's arm away an he grumbles an rolls over. I look at the back of his head, the short hair spiky with sweat an the slope of shoulder that the duvet doesn't cover; the smooth white skin, dotted with four faint fingertip-sized bruises. Marks of my hand clutchin hard. Always that friggin violence, that aggression. Still with me even, cos as I look at those light bruises I feel good, glad, that I've marked him. Like I've branded him or something, marked him as mine. I want to do it more. Wanner bruise him, bite him, fuckin *cut* him . . . Something wrong with me. There's somethin wrong with me. Not fuckin right, this aggression. 'Wanner cut him' . . . Jesus. I'm not right.

I sneak out of the bed quietly, so as not to wake him up. Smell from me armpits, crotch, feet. Cheesy an awful, so I go into the bathroom an turn the shower on an wait for the steam to billow then step under, into, the hot an cleansing rain. Feel the muck slide off me. I scrub meself with lavender soap until me skin hurts, wash me hair twice, twizzle a flannel into a point an work it into me ears, belly button, nostrils. I must be clean, I have to be clean. I *must* be fuckin clean. Feel the sudden need for a dump so I climb out of the bath an have one drippin wet then climb back under the water again an give me arse a good wash. Every crack, every cranny, soaped, scrubbed, scoured. Everywhere that dirt can gather (which is, in this city, *every*-fuckin-where). Flakes of dead skin an twists of hair, exhaust-soot an dried sweat, come-scabs an winnits all down the plug an into the Mersey. I'm clean I'm clean I'm clean.

Out of the shower, dry, brush teeth, deodorant, talc, all that stuff. Nice I'll smell for Victor. Can't wait to fuck him again. Make him lick me, make him work his tongue up into my insides. Feel him swellin inside me, feel him explodin with me hands crushin his neck, the rapture on his face. Men never come harder than when I'm choking them. It's like ther bodies, bein so close to death, are tryin desperately to cause some kind of life. Propagate ther genes before thee die, an cos ther so *close* to dying thee have to do it as quickly an as forcefully as possible while thee still can. Somethin like that. Whatever the fuckin reason is, it feels fuckin . . . *magnificent*, that's the word; mag-nif-i-cent. An the groans thee make an the faces thee pull, almost like ther givin birth, except of course without most of the pain. Ther eyes glazin over an closing. Victor's eyes, Victor's green eyes, glazin over, closing. His green, green eyes.

I go into the front room, take down *The Boatman's Call* an fast-forward it to the last song, 'Green Eyes'. Gorgeous fuckin song. Perhaps corny to play at this moment with Victor in the bed, like, but fuck that, I don't care, it's gettin played. I hum along to it while I make tea. Useless old fucker, this twinkling cunt. Doesn't care if he gets hurt. Which *I* bleedin well do but the point is it's worth it; even if I went back into the bedroom now with the tea an Victor wasn't there an I was never to see him again, the disappointment an upset would be worth it because of last night. Because of the sight of him in his fuckin heaven an the feel of him inside me. If he wants to go, then he can bleedin well go; I'll hate it if he does, like, but for the moment sounds seem louder an sharper, colours are brighter an richer an that's enough, that'll do. It's all fuckin worth it.

The boiler clicks on to heat the water but I don't turn it off. Victor can use the new tank to get a shower, get himself clean. Clean himself up before I fuck him again.

I take a tray of tea things into the bedroom. Victor's on his back with his arms flung out, his eyes open an staring at the ceiling.

—Oh, yer awake, I say. —I was gunner give yer a nudge cos it's gone twelve. I've made some tea.

I put the tray down an sit on thee edge of the bed. Glancing sideways at his face for some clue an all I see is a little unknown smile. 'Green Eyes' finishes an the tape clicks over on to side one. 'Into My Arms'.

—How d'yer have yer tea?

—Just milk.

—Good cos I've run out of sugar anyway.

He sits up an I pour two mugs of tea, give me favourite mug to him, the LIVERPOOL CHAMPIONS OF EUROPE mug that me dad bought me before he died ages ago (ages since we were champions of *anything*, let alone bleedin Europe. But maybe this season; that new French feller seems to be doin something right). He smiles an takes it an blows on it an sips it. He smells rank. His eyes are all blood-shot an crusty an his skin's all pasty, a white scum on his lips. How fuckin gorgeous he looks. Completely friggin shaggable.

—D'yer want anythin to eat?

He shakes his head.

—Good, cos there's nowt in. House's bleedin empty, I haven't been shoppin for ages. It's been one big fuckin hooley. One *fuck* of a party.

I'm just sort of ramblin to meself. Which I can feel meself wantin to do more of so to stop meself I ask Victor some direct questions:

—Did yis sleep alright?

—Yeh.

—D'yer want some more? Another hour or so?

He shakes his head, tells me again about having to meet his mates – Craig an Quockie, ther names are, I think – to go on

187

an arranged comedown trip to Wales. For two days, he says. Two whole fuckin days.

I'll miss him. —Yeh, I remember yer sayin last night.

I fuckin well will miss him. I would love nothin more than to be with nobody but him for the next couple of days. —D'yer not have to go back to work soon?

Shouldn't've mentioned that fuckin word, 'work'. He winces an it's made me feel bad as well, that shop, that barrier, that fucking boss. The real an ugly world intrudin.

—Jacked it in, he says. —I was labourin on that new Urban Splash thing, that warehouse development like down by the Kingsway tunnel.

—Oh yeh?

—Yeh. Signin on as well, like, saved up a bit of cash for this millennium party. Still got some left in the bank. Enough for a few weeks still, I reckon. So fuck work.

—Is right.

I'm findin it hard to imagine him as a labourer. His little body an all those machines around him. All that danger. He's sayin something about the millennium bein a new start or something, a good time to make a change, like, an I'm just noddin along with him, agreein, thinkin of his flesh in me hands an his dick inside me, his blood-filled flesh inside my mouth, between me teeth. Throwing him, plungin me hands inside him. Rummaging around inside his body, squeezing his heart, yankin it out spurting in me hands. All these things an more so I just ask him if he wants some more tea.

—Nah.

I smile. —Is there anything at all that yer *do* want?

Cos *I* want *you* below me, inside me. *I* want *you* bleedin an pantin an coming like a fountain. Yer face meltin like wax.

He says 'nah' again an scratches his head. A smell like rotten catfood wafts out from under his armpit.

—There is, I say. —Or there's something that yer *need*, anyway.

I smile to let him know I'm not offended. An that I'm not gunner fuck him again until he smells better.

—What's that?

—A shower. Yer fuckin ming, lad.

He laughs. —I know I do, I can smell it meself. Not one drop of water has touched me body so far this century. Apart from rain, like.

He pulls the duvet up over his nose an takes a big sniff. —Aw phyew Christ. Tell yer what, tho, I'm not gunner have time to go out to Lark Lane an get a shower an get back in town by two. An besides, Dermot's back so the house'll be a fuckin pigsty. Can I get a shower here?

That's what I meant. What I meant was: Get in the shower, get clean, an I'll fuck yis into heaven. I'll take yer to a wonderful fuckin place.

—Yeh. No problem. I left the boiler on anyway so there'd be some hot water.

—Nice one.

—Just help yerself, like.

—Where is it?

—First on yer right.

—Ta.

I take the tea stuff back into the kitchen, hear Victor pad into the bathroom an close the door behind him. I hope it doesn't whiff in there from me crap before; should've sprayed some air-freshener. I hear the toilet flush, suspiciously soon; he must be havin a dump as well an pullin the flush to drown out the noises, altho it can't mask his deep groan of relief. I smile to meself an rinse the teapot out. A pong drifts down the hallway, strangely smelling just like mine did with all the recent booze an chemicals gone rotten, then I hear a hiss an the whiff is followed by thee air-freshener smell an the toilet is flushed again. His shit stink so soon after knowin him an I'm not bothered. It makes me feel nowt but, what, closer to him somehow. Like I'm already acquainted with what's inside him. All his secret smells.

I hear him sigh again; he must've stepped into the shower. So nice, that, that feeling of hot water on a minty an ravaged body. Like bein reborn or somethin. I go over to the window an look out, see the cathedral turrets over the wet slate rooves. Think I can hear bells ringin from one of them but I'm not sure. Strange city, to have two cathedrals. The two of them so bleedin big an facing each other, as if sizing each other up. Ther like cities in themselves, the size of them; you could spend a lifetime explorin one an never see all of it. So how the fuck were thee ever built?

By using up hundreds of lifetimes, that's how. Thousands of lifetimes in ther construction.

The drizzle on the window, runnin down the glass. I slide the window up on its sash an rest me elbows on the sill, feel the rain light an cool on me face. I can smell the sea. Somewhere down the road dub reggae is thumping; some brave, or crazy, soul refusin to let the party die. An fair fuckin play to em as well. Soon, the parties will just happen at weekends an everything'll be back to normal. Or as normal as it could ever be. Which is to say not very fuckin normal at all. Which is to say, mad an desperate an so very fuckin deeply deeply deeply fucked up.

Victor. Will I still be with Victor this time next year? I'd like to think I would but I've got an idea that I won't be. I mean, there's a little voice inside me, it's pointin out how fuckin fast things've gone already an how if anythin ther gathering momentum, an *nothing* can continue at this pace, this velocity, this fuckin rate of acceleration. It's too fast; it'll break up. Disintegrate. We are not built to withstand these speeds.

So make the fuckin most of it while yer can, then, Kelly. Make the fuckin *most* of it. Get from it everything, friggin *everything* yer can.

Close the window. Cross the room, down the hallway, into the bathroom. Thick fog of steam. Victor's hand is reachin out towards me from the steam. His fingers outspread. His eyes are screwed shut, probly against the soap an the shampoo on his face an his hand is reaching, reaching out. I take it an he instantly yells an snatches it away, immediately holds it protectively around his knob an balls.

—Oh shit! Sorry! I didn't mean to scare yeh!

He opens his eyes, blinking fast. Ther rimmed with red an look sore. He's naked before me, wet an naked, all of him exposed.

—I, erm, I must've forgot to lock the door . . .

I shake me head. —There *is* no lock on the door. But I didn't mean to scare yeh. I thought yer could tell I was here like an you were, like, *reaching* or somethin. I didn't mean to scare yeh.

I can't help but smile. Gettin turned on really fuckin fast. His face seems to relax an kind of soften. Like acceptance or something. His eyes suddenly go darker an his lips fuller. He focuses not quite *on* but sort of *through* my face an his hands fall away to his sides. His knob's already half-hard. Water runnin off thee end of it in a steady stream. My smile gets bigger, an slightly harder at him an his exposure. I'm gunner torment him for a bit.

—An what d'yer want me to do with *that*, then?

He swallows so hard I can hear it even over the shower.

—Ey? What d'yer think I should do with *this* thing?

I flick thee end of his dick, hard, like, an it rises faster an he falls back groaning against the runnin tiles. My God, just that one tiny friggin touch . . . His lower lip droops down an gathers a tiny pool of shower water. Falling backwards he is, only supported by the wall. Soft-boned. All of him wet an on display, his skin clean an gleaming an at the very centre of him this big hard veiny dick, pointing right at me. Singling me out. I want that dick inside me, I want to make it, feel it, *burst*. Want fuckin *all* of him inside me until only his feet are visible. Be able to put me fingers down me throat an tickle thee end of his nose. God yes.

The towellin gown slips off me shoulders an pools at me feet. Victor's eyes run all over me an then settle on the barbell through me navel skin. Another turn-on for men, that piercing; maybe thee see it as an advert or somethin, a declaration of me intentions, a boast that I am willin to be penetrated. I suck me belly in, thrust out me tits. He's gunner be on his knees between mine. He's gunner do whatever the fuck I tell him to do. His arms come up to reach for me an I tell him, no, I fuckin *order* him to put them down an he does an I see his face burn red an there is a humming inside me ears. Me heart beats stronger, louder. A fluttering in me guts as if I've eaten birds.

This makes the world worthwhile. All those days of drudgery an long nights of waiting, they were all fuckin worth it if thee all led to this.

I step into the bath, into the fallin water for the second time this morning an park me arse on thee edge, me back straight to keep me tummy flat an breasts lifted an me legs open, on tiptoe. Displayin meself. Holdin thee entrance to me open for him, showin him thee access. *Look* at me, Victor. *Look* at me. Now fucking *lick* me.

—Lick my cunt, Victor.

A need so fuckin strong. All over my skin. Like a deep, deep itch inside me somewhere this pure fuckin *need* like a healing wound in me womb.

He falls on to his knees. His face is between me legs, I can see the spine-knuckles in his bent back an feel his hot breath on me fanny. What's the bastard doing, he's fuckin conductin an examination or something an I'm here rigid as a friggin steeple so I grab the back of his wet head hard an slam his face into me. The shower drums bass on the muscles of his shoulders.

—*Eat — me — out.*

His arms go around me waist to pull me even closer to him an I feel meself gape open an then that hole is stopped by such a lovely fuckin warm suction, lip to soft lip sliding an nibbling on me clitoris so fiery an in the middle of it all this reachin slurpin muscle, tracing liquid flame all over the walls of me cunt, sparks shootin from every flap an fold. Like all I am inside, all me guts an stuff is bein drawn down to this soft sucking fire an I strain to push it all down into his mouth, to expel everything into him, stuff him full of me lungs an heart, fuckin all of it. There's a catch in me throat which I groan around an it could be the tip of his tongue, lapping, licking. Christ, I can taste him at the back of me tongue. Fuckin wonderful I am scratchin at his back all bent an wet an trying to crush his skull in me thighs.

Close to coming but I need to be filled with more than his tongue so I grab his face an lift, draw the fucker up on his knees an hold his face in front of mine, his lips an chin wet not with water. A red haze creepin into me field of vision an always this aggresion:

—Oh yer fuckin bastard, you pure *cunt* . . . you little fucker, you fuckin *cunt* . . .

I slide down thee edge of the bath, reach under me arse to grab his engorged dick. Guide it up into me an I yawn down there to engulf him, swallow him, he's inside me so big, so hot. Fucking on *fire* I am. Biting his shoulder, mewling in me throat like a cat, his hips jerk as he tries to get deeper inside me an I want to sink me teeth into his flesh, feel his skin split, his blood burst. Fuckin rend an wrench an rip. Peel his skin away, bare his beatin muscle. Me hands are hackin at his back grabbin fistfuls of skin an yanking an I'm wantin to put them around his neck an strangle the fuckin life out of him, see his face in rapture an feel him coming like thunder inside me but he himself takes hold of my hands an places them at his collarbones, around his neck. He *wants* me to do it, the mad bastard, he really fuckin *wants* me to do it . . . Squeeze as *hard* as I fuckin can. Want his face to turn blue, see his tongue loll out all black an swollen, his eyes spun back to white. I'm squeezing an his dick's swelling even further, I can feel it stretchin me inside. His whole body is shivering an tremblin uncontrollably as if he's freezing or terrified an he's gaspin an gulpin for air like a fish, his neck has become hard in me hands. I've compressed it to fuckin iron, I can hear him wheezing an whimpering, feel his chest expandin against mine as he tries in vain to suck in air, an I push me elbows into his chest to make it even more difficult for him, to make it even more fuckin ecstatic for him an he's like somethin alive inside me, kickin like a baby filled with frantic life I am heat spreadin from me toes to absorb me whole body, scalp prickling, an I'm shouting as I come, come around him, melt into syrup an flow around him an over him an down his pulsing cock an into him. All muscles gone me hands leave his neck an flop limply in thee inch or so of water in the bottom of the bath. Dimly through the haze I feel him coming inside me, spasming an bucking, sense his whole body go rigid an hear his frantic panting. The whooshin gulps as he snatches at air. His hips leaping, his shoulders shudderin. His spunk shootin up into me an poolin blue. An then the rapid thaw; him collapsing, shrinkin, his spent dick contracting, only his chest left tensed to draw thee oxygen in.

Sudden awareness of cold. The shower's runnin cold. I reach over an turn the taps off. Only ar double breathing to be heard now, my head on his shoulder an his on mine, me strokin the back of his head. His hair all damp an tangled as if in reflection of the confusion beneath it, inside that skullbone.

Me skin crawls into goose pimples. His does too; I can feel it creepin against mine. This is good fuckin sex. This is *great* fuckin sex. The best sex ever. We seem to fit like jigsaw pieces.

He murmurs me name but I can't answer. He says it again, in a question:

—Kelly?

I just make a noise.

—Kelly. This is erm . . . this is . . .

I don't want him to say anything; I mean, the sex speaks for itself, there's no need for words. Theer inadequate an useless compared to what we've just done. There's no point to them as there's no friggin way thee could describe what we've just done, thee'd only subtract somethin from it so to prevent Victor from talking I kiss him on the lips an climb out of the bath an put me gown on.

Feel peculiar, standin here, gowned an Victor naked an shiverin an dripping below me. Feel like, I dunno . . . a fuckin violator or something . . .

—You'd better go, I say. —It's not far off two.

His face lookin up at me. Damp strands of hair in his eyes an those eyes too big. He nods an inhales deeply then abruptly doubles over in a coughing fit, his bruised throat inflamed by the steamin air. He's folded sideways into the bath in an inch of cold water, thin an naked an tremblin an coughing his guts up, his face turnin purple. He looks pathetic an I suddenly feel like shite, watchin him; I mean, look what the fuck I've done to him. Look what I've turned him into.

I leave the bathroom an him still spluttering, hacking, his head held in his hands. In the bedroom I change into a baggy jumper an some faded old black jeans, but the rough denim

194

irritates me sore fanny so I take them off an put on a pair of shorts an then pull the jeans back on again, over the shorts. Go into the front room, past the bathroom where I can hear Victor brushing his teeth, write me phone number on a piece of paper an stand with me back to the window, waiting.

Knowin so much about someone so soon. So fuckin much of them bared. How far yer can take them. How far they can take *you*. Like I've just discovered somewhere new an lovely an plundered it already an now I'm gunner plunder it some more. Victor so new an so known.

He comes into the front room. Dressed, his hair all spiky with wet. A wee bit embarrassed he looks, sheepish, like. I can smell him an he smells nice an I give him the piece of paper.

—Eeyar. That's me number. Ring me when yer get back from Wales.

—Okay, yeh. I'll only be a couple of days.

—Whenever yer get back.

He pulls a face, a quite sad face. —Don't really wanner go any more, to be honest with yis. But it was all arranged ages ago so I suppose I've got to, really. Can't let people down, can I?

I look at the clock. —Yer'd better leg it. It's nearly quarter to.

—Ah, they'll be late anyway. Thee always fuckin are.

He folds the paper up into a square an puts it in his pocket. I kiss him quick on the cheek an put me hand on his shoulder an at that touch he catches his breath an his pupils instantly expand an I can feel the blood under his skin begin to speed up. This makes me feel horny as well an I wanner jump on him again, strip an bite an suck an clutch, so I take me hand off him an shoo him to the door.

—Go on, then. Gerrout. Yer gunner be late. Have a great time an give me a ring when yer get back.

I open the door an he goes out on to the landing. He smiles at me, that lovely face, an we say tara an he waves over his shoulder as he goes down the stairs. Want to run after him. Wanner call him back. But I close the door an go straight to the window, the pane still runnin with rain. This silence in here. Thee empty day ahead. I press me face to the glass an watch Victor far below me move off towards the RC cathedral, his hands in his pockets an his hood up over his head. I watch him until he turns the corner an I can't see him any more.

I make more tea. Sit on the couch an roll meself a spliff. Turn the telly on: weather forecast; rain. Oh yer don't fuckin say, mister. I smoke the spliff an drink the tea an then pour more tea an drink that with a bowl of Rice Krispies. Just starin blankly at the babblin telly. Funny; Rice Krispies have never tasted this good. Just the sweet crisped rice an the cold milk which even though it's on the turn, still tastes spec-fuckin-tacular. An it's not due to the chonga cos it's never enhanced simple food *this* much an it was a weak spliff anyway. It's fuckin lovely. An the people on the telly, I'm not really listenin to ther words but just the *sounds* of ther voices, Australian accents I think thee are, it's like pure fuckin music. Wonderful to listen to. An all these colours around me . . . a sensory friggin riot here, I'm tellin yer. I've never seen the world like this before. Just this room, this one small room seems to me a palace.

I take the dirty dishes into the small kitchen an wash them up in the sink. There's a stingin in me fanny when I move, when I walk, but all that does is make me feel randy again. I'm for some reason very aware of me tits pushin out at me jumper, very aware of me own bare feet. Never been turned on by me own bare feet before. Just to feel meself move I go into the bathroom an stand starin down into the bath. A few pubes are curled around the plughole, whether mine or Victor's I don't know, an I swill them away with water. The wet impression of a foot on the bathmat. Towel draped over the door, tie-dyed with dampness. I take it an hang it up in thee airing cupboard an hang another dry one in the bathroom, over the radiator. Go into the bedroom an look down at the rumpled bed.

Best fuckin sex.

Best sex ever.

I straighten the sheet an punch the pillows. Wee spot of dried come on the sheet like fish scale, like hardened glue. I pick at it with a nail an it comes off whole, restin on the tip of me finger like a cloudy contact lens. I blow at it an it drifts away, seesawing like a feather. Throw the duvet over the bed then pull the duvet straight with thee edge of the mattress. Go to stand at the window, look down into the back alley.

Best bloke.

Best fuckin feller ever.

Like sometimes some things just fall an click together. Yer didn't know it, yer had no idea but it happens an you think to yerself: Jesus, this is what I've been lookin for. This is what I've been searchin for all me fuckin life an I didn't have the faintest friggin clue an now here it is an I must be fuckin blessed. I will want for nothing ever again.

Possible problems, tho: 1) pregnancy. Nah; haven't long come off the pill, I should still be safe. Infertile. Me hormonal balance is probly still overloaded an I'm still infertile. If not then I'll worry about it when I know for sure. Cross that bridge should I come to it. An 2) the virus. Again, nah; Jesus, if I haven't got it yet after some of the dogs *I've* friggin slept with then I'm sure I won't be gettin it off Victor. I can't imagine *any* poison of any sort in him. He's purity. An if I'm wrong then, again, I'll worry about it when I know for sure. But I really don't think I'm wrong.

So; no problems. Nowt wrong. There's fuck all to be worried about.

I put some shoes on an a woolly hat an go down to the corner shop for some ciggies an some dinner. Thee Arabic feller behind the counter is all smiles:

—And a Happy New Year to you, my friend.

—An you, mate.

—You have good time?

I give him a big smile. —The *best*.

He smiles back. —I am very, very glad to hear it. And glad to see that the millennium bug did not eat you.

I laugh. —Yeh.

The prayer mat hangin up over the clock (nearly three; see Victor among mountains) is a design of incredible intricacy, like a spider's web or something. All the swirls an loops. It looks fuckin beautiful. I decide to eat out instead so I just buy the ciggies an a paper an go to the caffy around the corner, buy a mug of coffee an some orange juice an thee Arabic breakfast: falafels an fried eggs an feta cheese an olives an coriander an pitta bread. Me belly, unused to food, protests at first but then opens to welcome it an I wolf it down an then order a fried-mushroom butty an eat that as well. The paper's chocka with reports of the millennium celebrations around the globe; nothin kicked off, no explosions or disasters or anythin, just one great big bleedin hooley. Just as it fuckin should be. I think of gettin drunk again but dismiss the thought almost instantly; got to come down sometime, haven't I? Or at least wait until tonight, anyway.

I go outside an phone me mother.

—Mam? It's me.

—Ah, love. Happy New Year.

—An to you, Mam. Did yer enjoy yerself?

—Certainly did, love, yeh. Dean took me to a do over on the Wirral, on some farm or something. Big firework show an free food an stuff. It was really good. How about you?

—Yeh, had a good time. Just friends an that, yer know. How's Dean?

—Alright to be goin on with. Poor replacement for yer dad, like, but . . . who isn't? No, I shouldn't say that; he's a good man, Dean. Wharrabout you? Have yer seen Peter recently?

—No, Mam, I haven't an I'm glad. I've met someone else.

—Oh aye?

—Yeh.

—What's he like?

What *is* he like? Like no one I've ever met before. Like something I never would've believed existed until I saw it for meself. He's so fuckin unique to me, so fuckin peculiar that I want to rip him open with me bare hands to see what makes him work. Ah yeh, an he's the *best* fuck I've ever had in me life. Bar fuckin *none*.

—He's nice, Mam. Really nice. His name's Victor.

—Victor?

—Yeh.

—Funny name.

—Innit, yeh. His dad named him after some actor in an old gladiator film or somethin.

—What does he do?

—Who, his dad?

—No, divvy. The boy. This Victor one.

Fuckin *hate* that question. What the fuck does it matter what he does for money? On the bins or on the board, it all comes down to the same bleedin thing.

—Dunno, Mam. Didn't ask him.

—Yer didn't ask him? So yer could be gettin involved with a gangster or a drug dealer or anythin?

—Christ, Mam, no. He's not like that.

—How d'yer know?

—I can tell. He's dead kind an gentle an stuff. An anyway, Peter was no angel an yer liked *him*, didn't yer?

—Aye but he had prospects, Peter did. He was goin places. Ambition, like.

—He was a wanker, Mam.

—Yer shouldn't say that. He was in bits when you left him, Kelly, bits. Came round here in tears, he did. Hell of a state.

Good. I'm glad. Peter cares about nowt but himself. He would sell scourin powder to little scallies an tell them it was coke, laugh when he heard that thee were in hospital, ther sinuses burnt away. Justify himself by pretendin that he was teachin them a lesson, warnin them off hard drugs. He would anally rape me with an Impulse canister when we were drunk an I refused to put up with the shite that he was full of. He was a control freak, a tyrant. A complete arsehole. With that smarmy charm that mothers always fall for, buyin her chocolates on her birthday, sendin her flowers. 'Bits', she says? Christ, I wish I *had* left him in bits, I mean literally, the kind yer make with an axe.

—Anyway, that's all over. He's gone now, Mam, an I'm a lot happier.

—That's the main thing.

—It is, yeh.

—So are we gunner meet this new one, then? This Vincent one?

—Victor. An I dunno; maybe. Dunno when, tho. Couple of weeks.

—Yeh. Bring him over.

—Alright. Is ar Adam there?

—No, love, he's with his girlfriend. A new one. Phone tomorrow an yer might catch him in.

—How is he?

—Fine. Doin well at school.

—Makes a change.

—From *you* it does, aye. Little bleedin horror you were. Lost count of the times I was called up to that school.

I laugh, but it's false cos I still remember school; hated every last fuckin thing about it. Tried to burn it down, once, me an Roz. Weren't grabbed for it either an it caused thousands of pounds worth of damage. It was in thee *Echo* an everythin.

—Anyway, Mam, got to go. Stuff to do.

—Like what?

—Just stuff, yer know. Clean me flat an things.

She sighs. —Okay then, love. Comen see us soon, will yer?

—Yeh, Mam, will do. Love to Dean. An Adam when yer see him.

—Okay.

—Take care of yerself.

I hang up, relieved. Always a strain talkin to me mother. She's interfering; she always has been, like, it's in her nature, but she's become a wee bit worse since me dad died. Which is only to be expected, I suppose, but I can't help it if it gets on me wick. Still love the friggin bones of her, tho.

I go into the video shop, next door but one to the caff. Racks an racks of shite. I get out *Human Traffic* cos it's funny an I like the music an I'm thinkin that maybe, hopefully, John Simms will remind me of Victor. Somethin similar about the nose. Maybe in the smile. Or maybe the frown. On the way out a familiar tall overcoated figure comes through the door; the remembered snotty headback strut, lookin down his sharp nose at the world so everyone can see his bogeys. He stands in front of me an flings his arms wide.

—Kelly! Is it, my God, yeh, it is! It *is* you! Thought yer'd left the city. Long-time-no-hear-from, eh?

—Hiya, Peter.

—Is that it? Just a fuckin 'hiya'?

I just nod. He's gettin fuck all from me. I do not step into his open arms an he drops them back to his sides, buries them in his pockets.

—Didn't spot yer at Creamfields thee other night. What did yer do with the ticket I gave yis?

—Used it for roach material.

A dark cloud passes over his face; where it once would've stayed there, gettin darker, now it just blows over for a few seconds an is gone. He forces himself to smile again, shakin his head.

—Yer haven't changed, have yer? Cut yer nose off to spite yer face, you would. No lie. Your loss, tho, yer missed a superb fuckin night. Best gig *I've* ever been to, anyway. What've yer got there?

I tilt the video box so he can see the cover. He pulls a face. How *I'd* love to pull his face. With a pair of pliers.

—Immature. Thee attempts at magic realism fall flat an are pure fuckin embarrassing, to be honest. It's supposed to be a *drugs* film, for fuck's sakes. Like the Howard Marks bit, tho. Eeyar, here's somethin to make it a bit more watchable. Or bearable, at least.

He looks around, delves in his pocket an transfers a small wrap into me hand. Don't like the feel of his skin against mine. Slimy, sends a shudder down me spine. His fingers linger on the back of me wrist an I pull me hand away.

—Just a toot or two of beak. I've got plenty more, like, maybe we could, yer know . . . watch that film together or something . . .

I shake me head. *Fuck* no. —Nah. Don't think so.

—Why not?

I just shrug.

—Oh, I gerrit, he smirks. —Yer friends. Ther comin round. Never really *did* like me, did thee? I was always a wee bit too

201

much for them, I suppose. Couldn't quite handle me, could thee? Could never quite work me out.

Oh, thee worked yer out alright. Worked out that yer a total fuckin loser snidey gobshite fuckin toerag an Jesus Christ that smirk on yer fuckin face. I see that smirk in my nightmares. That smirk above me in the darkness an me tied immobile to the bed. That smirk never leavin, not even when I cried an told him to stop. Fuckin wanker.

He's shiftin from foot to foot. Seems nervous about somethin. I think he *is* nervous. I feel *meself* startin to smirk. Peter ill at ease in front of me is a totally new experience an I like it. He can't take his eyes off me face, he's got his hands back in his pockets an is now lookin worried an I can feel something goin out from me, emanating from me to swamp him. Drown the cunt. For the first time ever I'm seein him uncomfortable, threatened even, an like everybody else does he looks twitchy an dead small an pathetic.

—Are yer seein anyone at all now, Kelly?

—Yeh.

—Who?

This is fucking great. This is fucking top. —Yer wouldn't know him, I say. —He's lovely. He's perfect.

A glow here in me chest. I can take this even further, an I do:

—He's the best lad I've ever met. He's absolutely fuckin brilliant.

Peter nods, tryin to look firm an unruffled but yer can see all his composure leggin it out the shop. This is fuckin ace. —Oh. An he's who yer watchin the film with today, is he?

—Maybe.

—Oh. Well. He sniffs an squares his shoulders. —Enjoy yerselves, won't yer. Enjoy the fuckin film. Enjoy *my* bleedin cocaine.

He flounces off down the shop an I have to stop meself from burstin out laughin. Where did *this* come from, this new strength in me? Completely unflustered in there I was. Fuckin cool *as*. Totally calm an in control. Peter was the one all worried an ruffled. *He's* the one who'll feel bad all afternoon, hating himself, hating the weakness he exposed in himself, the lack of self-confidence, the chink in his armour. Jesus, why the *fuck* do we obey laws, other people? Why don't we crave, with all ar hearts, freedom from another's will an whim? Maybe cos without it, we're chaos; us, the ones with bugger all, the ones with nowt but a great big fuckin yearning, maybe we need the demands of others to stop us coming apart. But I can't think of anythin more ugly an destructive to yerself than surrenderin yerself against yer will, against all yer own instincts. Pure fuckin hideous that is. Black, disgusting, a stain on thee earth.

Fuckin Peter. You twat.

I'm chucklin to meself all the way home. Home, where I chop up an snort deeply a thin line of Peter's beak, enjoyin it all the more cos it came from him free whereas up until recently it would've come with an obligation, an 'expression of gratitude' as he used to put it which would usually involve pain and/or humiliation. I wash it down with a shot of watered whiskey. Flop back in thee armchair feelin fuckin great an put the film on an John Simms does *not* remind me of Victor, not one tiny friggin bit. Can't imagine why I thought he would've, really. I mean, no one could remind me of him. That uniqueness. Completely fuckin unfamiliar. Think of him tiny among mountains. Think of his eyes rolling back in his head as yer take him to the point of ecstasy. The way he is, so completely himself an at the same time so, like, vulnerable; all small an at risk in the world. With the best fuckin smile I have *ever* seen. An I mean fuckin *ever*.

Can't fuckin wait to touch him again. Press him hard to me, grab an clutch an stroke. Twist an pummel, oh fuck yes, see the bruises bloom. Know that it's me an only me who's marked him, marked him for ever.

Feelin friggin horny now. Hot inside me belly, between me legs. I move me hand down there to stroke but at that moment the doorbell rings, makin me jump. Maybe it's Victor. Maybe the Wales trip fell through or something an he's come back to see me. Fuckin *hope* so. I spring to the window an slide it up, lean out to see who it is, me heart thumping fast but then it rapidly slows cos it's certainly *not* Victor, not unless he's suddenly taken to dressin up in a fake fur coat an fake leopard-skin platform thigh-boots. Only one person I know dresses like that.

—Victoria!

She looks up. Her face caked in slap. —Hiya! Come down an let me in quick!

—I'll throw yer the keys! Hang on!

I chuck the keys down to her an she catches them an lets herself in. I can hear her footsteps echoin through the house in the big boots, booming louder, gettin nearer. This must be what her tricks, her subs, hear as she approaches them. Christ, how ther pulses must start to race an ther throats to dry. An, yeh, ther dicks to harden like steel.

The door creaks open an she comes in. Fuckin *all* of her.

—On yer own, Kel?

—Yeh.

—Thought yer might still be with that lad. The one yer picked up in Magnet last night. Yer dirty whoo-er.

I laugh. —*Me* a dirty whoo-er? Yer cheeky cow. An I suppose yer off to visit yer ahl granny in *that* fuckin get-up, are yeh?

She unbuttons the coat, swings it aside to reveal a shiny PVC catsuit with a heart-shaped hole over her tits that shows her cleavage.

—Yer look like someone out of a porno.

—Sometimes I friggin well think I am. She sits down on the couch. —So where is he, then?

—Who?

—This new feller.

—He's gone off to Wales for a day or two with his mates. Chill out in the mountains, like, by the sea.

She nods. Christ, her make-up is *so* thick. She looks like a fantasy, a dream made real. Not one of mine, tho.

—One of his mates tried to tap up Roz last night. After you'd left, like.

—Which one? The Chinese one?

—No, thee other one. Think his name's Greg or somethin. Roz was havin none of it, man. Didn't wanner friggin know.

—Why?

—Dunno, really. Yer know Roz; fussy cow. That's why she's never got a feller. *I* would've given him one, personally like, but . . . that's just me. She rubs her hands together. —So come ed, then, tell all. What was he like? This new bloke?

—Nice. Lovely, in fact.

—Yis gunner see each other again?

—Hope so. Think so. Yeh.

—Better than that fuckin Peter, anyway.

—Oh God, yeh. Be hard pressed to find anyone any worse, tho, wouldn't I?

—You know it.

She starts to ask me things about the size of Victor's knob an stuff but I tell her to sod off an she presses so I tell her about meetin Peter earlier on an about how brilliant it was to see the cunt squirm an to feel that I was on top, in control. She listens an lights two ciggies an hands one to me.

—An yer liked that feelin, did yer? That bein in control, like?

—Yeh. Specially over *that* knobhead. Yer should've seen him, Vix; he didn't know *what* the fuck to do.

—An d'yer wanner feel it again?

She's gettin at something here. She's buildin up to something, I can tell. This isn't purely a social call. —What d'yer mean?

—What d'yer mean, what do I mean? I was just askin if yer wanted to feel it again, that's all. Christ. Why so suspicious all of a friggin sudden?

—Bollocks, Victoria. Yer buildin up to somethin, don't try an deny it. I *know* you, there's somethin yer gunner ask me, isn't there? Just fuckin out with it an stop fannyin around.

—Erm, well . . .

She tells me that one of her clients has requested a session with two women, Vicky an someone else. He's a sub who likes to be tied up, whipped, abused, spat on. The usual stuff, nothin *too* extreme or distasteful, she says, just the general bog-standard punishment scenario. Hundred quid for a half-hour's work. Each. She tells me that he's a businessman who's had a particularly successful week so he's feelin the need to be particularly successfully punished, treated like shite for a while, a bit more than his usual session, like, so hence the request for two women, not one. Easy money, Vicky says, a piece of piss.

I shake me head. —*I* can't do that, Vicky. Yer *know* I can't. Ask someone else. Ask Roz.

—Roz isn't in. An anyway, *you're* more suited to doin this than *she* is.

—Oh aye? I am, am I?

—Yeh.

—An why the fuck's that, like?

—It's not an insult, Kels. Don't get a cob on. What I mean is that you're more up for experiencing new things, y'know, seekin out new experiences, like. I mean –

—Yeh, but I don't like the thought of bein a prozzy. I ain't bein no whore for fuckin no one, Vicky. No offence, like, but I don't want some fat ahl businessman fuckin thinkin he can buy me. That he can have me just cos he's got the fuckin money, like.

—But that's the thing, see, he won't even *touch* yeh. Won't lay one fuckin finger on yis. Be hard pressed to bleedin do so seein as how I've left the daft twat in the stocks.

—What? The *stocks*? Honest?

She grins. —Honest to God. Straight up. He's got a set of stocks in his basement an he's in them now. I was round there before, like, thrashin fuck out of his lard arse, an that was when he asked me to go an get someone else. A partner, like. Double the punishment. Honest to God, Kelly, he won't touch yer once. Yer won't even have to see his face, he's in a mask. All yer've got to do is hit him with a cane an call him a few names, that's it. It's dead easy fuckin money. Hundred sheets for the half-hour, smackin fuck out of some rich bastard. What could be easier? It'll be a laugh.

—A *laugh*?

She nods. —Yeh. No lie, it's dead funny. Makes yer feel like a headmistress or something, it's friggin bizarre. An here's this rich bastard with more money than yer'll ever see in yer life beggin yer to cane his arse. Tears runnin down his face an

206

everythin an he's askin yer for more. Think of every fuckin boss yer've ever had, every bastard bizzy yer've ever had hassle off, every control–freak cunt that's ever made yer life a misery. It's yer chance for revenge. One of those fuckers is *giving* yer money instead of takin it away from yis, an all's yer've got to do is smack fuck out of his arse an call him a dickless cunt a few times. Tellin yer, it's *dead* easy.

I'm beginnin to be tempted, I must admit. Very much tempted, in fact. It was that notion of revenge that got me goin, as well as, of course, thee amount of money on offer; I mean, I'd have to work three days, three long days in that God–awful shop to earn a hundred quid, with that twat of a boss breathin down me neck, an here I've got the chance to earn it in thirty minutes. An the novelty aspect of the whole thing can't be dismissed, either, it'll be . . . unusual, to say the least. An face it, Kelly, yer sexuality is an aggressive one; just ask friggin Victor. Ask his bruised throat. So yer might as well get paid for it, mightn't yer? It could be a chance to release all yer frustrations, take it all out on someone, a sort of compensation for every time yer've been used, abused, hurt an humiliated by some cunt with more power an money than you. An there've been fuckin *hundreds* of them. Plus, it'll be somethin to fill the time, all thee empty hours ahead, before Victor comes back. Somethin to relieve this terrible fuckin boredom.

Victor, tho. What about Victor.

—Yis up for it, Kelly? Yer'll do it? Yer thinkin about it, aren't yeh?

—Erm . . .

—What's up? What's the matter?

—It's just this new feller, like. The one I met last night.

—Wharrabout him?

—Well, he's dead nice. I like him loads.

—Yeh, and?

—Well, it's like . . . like fuckin cheatin on him or somethin. An I've only just *met* him.

She snorts. —Is it *fuck* like cheatin on him. Cheatin on him would be if yer went out tonight an got canned an fucked some scally who yer'd probly never see again. *That* would be cheatin on him. *This*, tho, this is earnin good, easy money. An not even bein touched. If it makes yer feel any better then think of it as, I dunno, a friggin burglary or somethin. Cos in many ways that's what it is. Or, or like gettin into a brawl an winning, for once. Yeh, a battle with some gobbo boss over not enough pay or something an him giving in.

I nod.

—An anyways, what's all this fuss about fuckin cheating? Not somethin that's ever bothered yis before.

—I know, it's just ... I shrug. —This new one. I like him loads.

—Well, that's nice. An he never needs to find out, if that makes yer feel any better. No one else has to know apart from me an you.

—Alright.

—An yer never know ... it might turn him on. If he *was* to find out, like.

I smile. He doesn't need any more assistance in *that* department.

—So yer'll do it then?

—Alright. I nod. —Yeh.

—Aw fuckin nice one, Kels. It'll be a friggin laugh, don't you fuckin worry about it. It's hilarious, honest. After *my* first session I pissed meself laughin for days after.

I can't deny I'm excited. New things, thee unknown, thee unfamiliar, a place where I've never been, thee all make me feel like this; all hot an fast inside. And, also, like me days are bein lifted up; which probly means fuck all but seems to express how I feel.

—What about clothes, tho? What should I wear?

Vicky looks me up an down, takes in the faded kex an the holey old jumper. —Well, he likes trainies, this one, he gets turned on by girls in trainies. Trainies an nice dresses. I think it adds to it for him, yer know, the feelin of bein treated like shite by what he sees as a social inferior. But fuck him, tho, wear whatever yer feel comfortable in. Anythin.

—Trainies, yeh? Well, how come yer wearin *them*, then? I gesture at her mad boots.

—Well, that's what I've just said. Wear what yer feel comfortable in. An I feel fuckin *ace* in these. Have men crawlin on the deck to kiss them, these do.

She raises one leg an flexes her foot. PVC creaks an groans.

I go into the bedroom, get changed into a tight knee-length backless black dress that I wear for weddings an christenings an stuff (too sexy to wear for funerals) an a pair of Adidas Gazelles. Never havin worn these two things together before, this dress an these trainies, I stand an look at meself in the dresser mirror, the way the dress clings to me body, the springy feel of me bare legs in the trainers. I feel fuckin gorgeous an I look just the same. I feel sort of strong, powerful; I feel like I could rip everythin apart with me bare hands. I tie me hair up into bunches, one on each side of me head. Put some slap on. I feel every muscle move, tight an toned under me skin. I feel fuckin amazing. Like I amaze everything. I wish Victor was here now, to see me like this. I wish he was on me bed spreadeagled, his whole body bared an laid out like a sacrifice for me teeth an nails. Wish I could feel him comin like a fuckin thunderstorm inside me. *Bursting* apart inside me. There's a noise an I suddenly realise it's me, *I'm* makin it, growling in the back of me throat so I cough an swallow an stop it. Smooth the dress down again over me body an go back into the front room, stand with me arms out in front of Victoria.

—Whatjer reckon?

—Oh yes. Gorgeous. Could fancy yer meself. Yer feel alright, yeh?

—Yeh. I shrug. —Suppose.

—Yer sure yer wanner do this?

—Hundred per cent.

—Positive, now?

—Can't be any more positive than a hundred per cent, can I?

—Not unless yer a football manager.

—Yeh.

—Right then, let's get a move on. Poor bastard's probly fuckin frozen to death by now. Or starved.

—Where've yer left him? Where's his house?

She grins. —Lower Heswall.

—Yer kiddin.

—Nope.

—All that bleedin way?

—Yeh. He's been in them stocks for about three hours. Don't worry about it. He fuckin loves it. Left him in them all night once; I sat in his livin room drinkin his brandy an smokin his cigars while he shouted an pissed hisself in the cellar.

I laugh, an there's an edge to me laughter, a sharp an cruel edge. It makes me feel like a conqeuror, a victor. I move like a big cat, puttin me coat on, collectin me stuff up, ciggies, keys, cash card. All me muscles movin. I could lay the whole fuckin city to waste like this, in this mood.

We leave the house an get into Victoria's car. She takes a half-bottle of vodka from the back seat an passes it to me an I swig at it as she pulls away an into the city, the lights beginnin to go on, still big groups of people driftin in an out of the pubs, ther denial of parties' end evident in ther wasted staggers, ther hooded eyes. We drive down towards the Kingsway tunnel; I look out an up at thee Urban Splash development as we pass, imagine Victor up there, on the high scaffold, in a hard hat. His little thin body. Covered in brick-dust, his mucky clothes flappin in the wind. An then him tied naked to me bed panting with his dick like stone lying flat against his belly. His balls all exposed, unprotected. Me hands curl around the vodka bottle an grip it hard, so hard that I'm scared it might shatter but I fuckin love that feelin, of somethin hard an unyielding against the palm of me hand, pressin in, diggin in, almost puncturing the flesh. I cross me legs an love the muscled silky feel of me bare calf brushin against me bare knee. I am *so* sexy. *So* fuckin strong. I could do fuckin *anything*.

We enter the tunnel. I look sideways at Vicky, see the yellow tunnel light glitterin like diamonds in the gel in her hair. She nods at the tape player.

—Put some sounds on if yer like.

—What kind?

—Ah just press play. Me tape's already in, me goin-on-a-job tape. Songs to get me in the mood, like.

I press play: Cypress Hill, 'Highlife'. Fuckin brilliant, pure brilliant. Me head is buzzing. I'm *so* friggin excited.

—What's it like, Vic?

—What's *what* like, Kel?

—Bein a prozzy.

—I wouldn't know. Never been one.

I laugh. —Yer arse. Yer've been one for ages.

She shakes her head, her expression all serious. —No, I haven't.

—*Yes* yer bleedin have.

—*No* I bleedin haven't. I've been a prefessional dominatrix, a mistress, *never* a bleedin prostitute. There's a difference, a big fuckin difference.

—Oh aye? An what's that?

—That me body remains me own. No one ever has me body, no, I've never in me *life* been paid for lettin someone screw me. No fucker even *touches* my body, unless I want them to, unless I say thee can. An that'll be through personal choice, not cos some bastard is payin me to let them do it. *They're* the ones who offer ther bodies to *me*, it's *not* thee other way round. Never has been. They can't have me. They can't buy me. I've had some of the sad bastards grovellin on the floor, beggin me to let them have one touch, just one tiny touch.

—An what d'yer do then?

—I give them another ten. She smirks. —With the cane, like. *Really* fuckin lay into them. That's what me job's all about, yer see; about bein, like, untouchable. That's essential to the whole thing, the whole fuckin slave scenario. If I let them touch me, I mean even if I wanted to, like, then that would destroy the whole fantasy. It'd all fall apart an it wouldn't work.

—Haven't yer ever wanted to, tho?

—What?

—Let one of them touch yeh. I mean, hasn't there ever been one that yer've fancied?

She shakes her head. —Nah. Not really. It doesn't work like

that. Ther just money. Thee give me money. It's like . . . I dunno, it's like, to fancy one of them would be a breach of professional ethics. Know what I mean?

I nod, but I don't, really.

—Besides which it's never really a sexual thing for me. Never really turned me on, like, altho I *do* enjoy it in other ways. But, I mean, it'd be like a breach of contract or something. Can't really explain it. I mean, thee pay me to remain distant from them, untouchable. The whole thing is based on me bein better than them, that I think ther pathetic an useless. With tiny dicks an all that stuff, nowt that I find attractive about them whatsoever. That's what thee get off on, bein made to feel like utter shite. I tell them ther as thick as my shit an I've seen bigger dicks on a mouse. An if I let them touch me, or if I touch *them*, in a tender or sexual way, like, skin-to-skin, then the whole thing would be undermined. It's finely balanced, really. Well, kind of. All yer've got to think about is that, in the normal way of things, *these* bastards wouldn't think twice about causin a fuckin catastrophe in yer life. Thee don't give two fucks if ther actions in business or politics or court or wherever make yer homeless, or take away whatever yer've got an worked hard for an leave yer with absolutely fuck all. Thee don't care, like. Just keep that foremost in yer mind; that this cunt's yer boss. Usually, day-to-day like, he thinks yer lower than him, he's convinced that yer fuckin inferior to him. He thinks yer scum. An now here he is trapped, his fat fuckin arse in thee air. An *you're* the one with the big fuckin stick in yer hand.

I reach down an scratch me ankle; me skin so smooth, so clear. Delicate bones beneath it. The way me calf bulges, pressed against me knee, the tunnel lights gleamin off it, an me thighs outlined in the tight black dress all clingin to the big long muscles. I am fuckin gorgeous.

We leave the tunnel into Birkenhead. The sun is setting through the cranes that line the waterfront like giant skeletons.

—Got any change, Kel?

I dig coins out of me purse an give her a pound coin an a ten-pence piece. She throws it in the chute at the toll gate an the barrier lifts an we drive under it an through Birkenhead, past Prenton Park, towards lower Heswall.

—Wharrer yer thinkin, Kelly? Yer excited?

I shrug. —Kind of, I suppose, yeh. No, I am, defo. *Dead* fuckin excited, to tell yer the truth.

—Well, what's the face for then?

—What face?

—*Your* face. Gob on yer like a wet weekend.

—Nowt. It's just that I'm thinkin, like, well, it's not *really* you in control, is it? Not *really*. I mean, what it all boils down to is that you're still doin what *they* want yer to do because they can afford to pay yis to do it. I mean, physically yer in control, like, yeh, but that's all. You're still ther fuckin employee, aren't yeh?

—Maybe so, yeh. But think of any job yer've ever had, every fuckin jumped-up twat of a boss yer've ever had; if yer had the choice of bein paid to do *that* job, whatever it was, an workin for *that* boss, or kickin seven kinds of shite out of yer boss, an bein paid miles better for doin it, then which would yer have chosen?

I smile. —I see yer point.

—Too friggin right yer do.

She checks in the rear-view mirror for police cars then takes the vodka out of me lap, gulps at it an returns it, licks her lips. Her thick plum lipstick goes all shiny. I lick mine as well. Vicky goes on: —But I see yours as well.

—My what?

—Your point. I mean, there *is* an element of truth in that, like, of yer know, them still bein in control, as yer said. It's like thee drag yer into ther obsessions, ther twisted fantasies, like, because thee can afford to. *They're* rich an *you're* skint. They've got the money, an know that you need it, so . . . She shrugs. —But yer learn, like. Yer learn what to avoid, what yer limits are. I mean, when I was first startin out there was this headmaster from Chester an his thing was, what he liked to do, like, was put on a pair of schoolgirl knickers – white, like, thee *had* to be white – an a little pleated school uniform skirt an then . . . well, guess what?

—I dunno, what?

—Shit hisself.

—Shit hisself?

—Yeh, he'd shit hisself. Put the school uniform on then shit hisself into it. An, worse, he'd pay women to kneel down behind him an peel his shitty knickers off while thee called him all the useless dirty cunts under the sun. That was how he'd get off, like. That was his thing.

—Jesus Christ.

The images in me head. The smears an the stench.

—Is right. But I knew some women, one or two, like, who didn't mind doin stuff like that cos *they* weren't bein touched or slobbered on or fucked or mauled or anything. So thee didn't really mind. Said yer get used to it, an the money was good. Weren't particularly *keen* on it, I mean thee didn't friggin *like* it or anything, but . . . easy money, for some of them. Not somethin *I* could've done, tho. Ew God no. Bein *that* close to someone else's shite? Aw Jesus.

We crest a hill an I see the Dee estuary in front of me, the mountains of Wales in the mist beyond it, huge an awesome. That's where Victor is now, over there, somewhere in those massive mountains; small-bodied in those immense rocks. Without a fuckin clue as to what I'm doin at this very moment. Or to what I'm gunner do. If he's thinkin about me at all, which of course he mightn't be.

How my heart is beating.

Vicky goes on: —I mean, stuff like that is vile. Blokes with those kinds of fantasies, thee should fuckin sort themselves out instead of draggin other people into ther dirty fuckin obsessions. They'll kid themselves that ther not harmin the women any, but of course thee fuckin are; theer offerin *poor* people money to acquaint themselves with ther shite. That's friggin disgusting. But the stuff *I* do, tho, the stocks an the bondage an the whippin an stuff, I've got to say that it's a fuck of a lot better than any other job I've ever had. Partly cos it's so well paid an partly cos it's, well, if yer feelin pissed off, if the job's gettin yer down for whatever reason, then yer can take yer anger out on yer boss, if yer wanner see the sad bastard in that way. The cunt who pays yer for doin what he wants yer to do, in *this* line of work, yer can beat him til he bleeds. An begs yer to stop.

We turn down on to a long coastal road, a few big houses built on the banks of the Dee. Nice houses, overlookin thee estuary; me an Victor could live in one of them, just us two with cats an dogs. Nowt to do all day but walk an swim an drink an shag. Just us two. Take a big jug of vodka an orange on to the shore, watch the sun go down, listen to the seabirds calling. Victor all mine, *just* fucking mine. How fuckin happy I would be.

—An it's like Natasha keeps saying, Vicky says.

—Natasha? Who's that?

—I've never introduced yer to Natasha? Yer've never met her? Friend of Elaine's, from down South somewhere, lectures at the university?

I have a vague memory of a horsy-faced woman wearin beads an laughin like a drain at some party somewhere sometime in the past but I shake my head. —No.

—Well, anyway, *she* says that *all* forms of deviance, includin sexual ones, like, are in some ways a valid protest against the, what did she call it, yeh, the normalising absolutes of mainstream society. *Her* words, like.

—An she's a lecturer?

—Yeh.

—From down South?

—Yeh.

—Then what the *fuck* would she know, then?

Vicky thinks for a minute an then nods. —Yeh, yer right. I agree with her, like, in a way, but I think you're right. What the fuck *would* she know.

That's friggin wick'd me off, that has. Fuckin lecturers. Get on me bleedin nerves. She might have the words to sum it up, like, but what the fuck does she *really* know about it? Vicky's the one in men's houses. Vicky's the one doin it, livin it; Natasha does nowt but talk about it, that's *all* she fuckin does. Fuck *her*.

We turn, crunching down a gravel driveway to a huge

house, all granite stone an chimneys an arched windows. For some reason, an image of Victor with no clothes on flashes up in me mind. The perfect dimensions of his dick. The perfect way he is in sex. I'm missing the bastard so much it hurts. I hope he's not with another woman right now, over there in those mountains across the waves. I'll fuckin lay those mountains low if he is. With him, and her, fuckin buried under them. Only just friggin met you, Victor, please be what I hope with all me heart you are. Please be what I pray for you to be, what I hope I've finally found.

—This is it.

I look out the windows at the house as Vicky drives around it to a little car park at the top of a huge lawn that slopes down to the water. —Bleedin size of it.

—I know. Friggin yowge, innit.

—It's a fuckin mansion.

—Not far off half a million quid's worth.

She parks the car an we get out. Strong sea smell; I love that smell. The ground crunches under me feet. Me throat is dry, spitless, an there is prickly heat behind me eyeballs, in me skull.

—Yer alright, Kel?

—Sound.

—Sure?

—Yeh.

Like acids bubblin in me stomach. Big birds flappin about in there. Nerves an aggression both mixed up an I want to lick the skin I've scratched an torn.

—It'll be alright, don't worry. Just enjoy yerself. Honest, it'll be a laugh. An think what yer can do with a hundred quid.

She opens the back door an we go into the kitchen an she closes the door quietly behind us.

—He likes to leave the door unlocked, Vicky explains. —It's part of the thrill for him, the possibility of bein discovered. Turns him on, the little turd. Next time I'm gunner go to Garlands an get a bunch of butch queens an drive them over here an let them fuck him stupid. He'd probly friggin love it. Pay me extra.

The kitchen is all chrome an stripped pine, spotless, gleamin. Shiny surfaces an cleanliness. A fridge-freezer that hits the ceiling. Bowls of fruit. Crockery displayed an everythin a kitchen could suggest, every appliance from juicer to dual microwave. I shouldn't fuckin be here. This isn't my place, an the glee an mischief I feel cos I'm in it is fuckin ace. Fuckin give me a bat an I'll turn it to dust.

—Is he married, this feller?

Vicky shrugs. —Not sure. I *think* so, cos there's women's stuff in the bathroom. Never once mentioned his missis, tho. Not that I've ever really heard the fucker speak, come to think of it. He's nearly always gagged. Only ever heard him beg an groan, really. An scream.

I follow her out of the kitchen an into a room with a huge bay window that overlooks the estuary. It's fuckin amazing. A great big couch along one wall, a giant telly with DVD an video as well an a hi-fi system in the corner, speakers as tall as me. There's nothin in this room but enjoyment; you would never do anythin yer didn't want to in this room. Yer could die happy here, lookin out over the sea. If I lived here with Victor. Just me an him. Both of us on that couch drinkin cold gin an lookin out at the water, some good music on, some great film on that vast TV. Only me an Victor, only me an Victor. Just us two in here. God, I would fuckin kill for that. It's worth fuckin killin for. The fuckwit who owns it probably has.

Thousands of CDs on floor-to-ceiling shelves across the far wall. I move over there, me leg muscles rippling, an scan the titles.

—Nowt of any interest there, Vicky says.

—Yer not fuckin kiddin. Look at it: Phil Collins. Chris de bastard Burgh. Whitney Houston. Ah Jesus: Celine fuckin Dion.

—I know, yeh. Vicky shakes her head sadly. —Tasteless tosser in a place like this, eh. Pure friggin waste. Not fuckin fair.

—Is right.

—An comen look at this. Yer think this is bad, this is even fuckin worse.

She leads me out of the room into the hall. Between the

front door an the foot of the stairs is a glass frame hangin on the wall. Inside that frame is a Man U shirt, neatly folded, a few seasons old.

—Aw for fuck's sake.

Vicky points, her fingernail long an red like a claw. —Look closer.

I do. The fuckin thing's signed by Eric Cantona.

—Right, that's fuckin *it*, I say, with real anger, real disgust. —Where is the little prick? I'll take the fuckin skin off him.

Vicky grins. —Yer ready then, yeh?

—Yeh, I say, an I am. Me hands have curled into claws at me sides. Adrenalin has turned me skin to sparks. Rip an rend an crush an tear.

Bloodspurtbloodspurt.

—Yer positive, now?

—Fuck, *yes*. Let me at him. That cunt's gunner regret askin you to get a partner.

—Yeh. If at any time yer've had enough, for any friggin reason whatsoever, like, just tell me an you can go an I'll finish the job meself.

—Don't worry about me, Vicky. Only thing yer've got to worry about is whether I murder the little get.

She grins. —Nice one.

She spins an thumps on her chunky soles to a door set in the wood-panelled wall under the staircase. She yanks that door open an I stand at her shoulder, lookin down a set of stairs which descend into a cellar. Faint blue light spills upwards. My heart booms an rumbles like distant thunder. Me gob an throat are completely dry, totally without spit. I feel fuckin . . . what? More than human.

—YER READY NOW, YER LITTLE PIECE OF FUCKING SHIT?! Vicky yells. —YER READY FOR SOME MORE?! I'M BAAAAACCK!

I can hear a muffled whining risin from the cellar.

—YEH, AN THERE'S TWO OF US NOW, YER USELESS FUCKIN PRICK! TWO OF US! ARE YER READY FOR THIS?!

We go down the stairs, Vicky in front, ar feet very loud on the wooden steps, especially hers, thudding, clattering. The whining gets louder. More urgent. The cellar is a warm stone room with a slate floor, all the walls lined with wine bottles, ther glass bottoms catchin the light like a thousand eyes. An in the centre of the floor, directly beneath the hangin bare bulb that glows blue, is the man, naked white an flabby, his masked head an hands trapped in a set of stocks, authentic-lookin stocks, grey splintery wood an heavy rusty hinges. His leather mask swings towards us as we stand there. The whining accelerates, becomes almost hysterical.

Vicky totters over on her heels. Circles the trapped man, so tall she is in her boots.

—Little fuckin wanker . . . look at the fuckin state of yer . . . call yerself a man . . . yer make me friggin *sick*!

On the last word she plants a boot in thee upturned an defenceless arse. The mask squeals. The knees knock.

Vicky beckons to me. —Come over here. Comen see this little shit. See how fuckin useless he is, how fuckin *pathetic* . . . nothin but a fuckin wanker . . . little fuckin turd . . .

Observing myself. As if above all this part of me is lookin down on the scene – the struttin, spitting Victoria, the bound an quiverin naked man, me steppin over towards him. The powerful movements of me thighs in the tight black dress, me back muscles ripplin under the light as I move. The man's tremblin intensifies as I stand in front of him; the flab wobbles at his sides. I bend with me hands on me knees an peer into his face, his masked face. Holes for his eyes an his nostrils, a zip for his mouth. Bulging eyes an the nostrils like tunnels gaping, flared, snorting. Thee expression in those wide eyes should be impossible; such need mixed with such terror. The two things should not be able to coexist in one person but thee do, here, in this trapped man's eyes.

I have no pity. I am fuckin merciless.

—Oh yeh, I say, me face about three inches from his. —My friend's right. I've never seen such a pathetic little prick as you. Useless little piece of shit yer are. Stuck here with yer fat arse in thee air . . . insignificant little wanker, you . . . I bet you *are* a wanker, as well, aren't yer . . . what, ten times a fuckin day? Worn yer little dick down to a stump? Thinkin of women like me?

I look up at Vicky. She smiles an nods. I'm doin alright. Me heart seems to have grown to the size of a boulder, hammerin away inside me, powerin thick boilin blood to me legs an arms. Power which I feel in me face. For some reason I'm exaggeratin me accent, I have no idea why, but fuck how it adds to this strength.

I look back down, into the bulging eyes.

—Yeh . . . this is the closest yer'll ever come, innit, the closest yer'll ever be to women like us . . . we'd never waste ar time with a useless prick like you unless yer were payin us . . . think we *like* bein close to a dirty little cunt like you? Sexy fuckin women like us? Think we *wanner* fuckin be here?

The head's noddin frantically. I'm gettin into this.

—Think we'd *ever* fuckin let you touch us, ey? Ever think of yer as anythin other than completely fuckin laughable?

Vicky's givin me a sign, an O made with her finger an thumb. I am racing, speedin inside. All me senses alert, finely tuned, colours an sounds so bright an sharp, the blueness of the light cracklin above an sparkin off the wine bottles on the walls an thee anguished fevered whining behind the mask, desperate, pleading.

—What's that yer triner say? Triner tell me somethin? Are yer, yeh? Well, let's fuckin hear it, then, eh?

I undo the zip an instantly a bad-smellin storm hits me in the face:

—PLEASEPLEASEPLEASEPLEASEPLEASEPLEASEPLEASEPLEASE-PLEASE

I zip it shut again. The leather swells with air, with his desperation. Swells an bulges. I can do anything. The world all under me.

—Here, K. Catch.

Vicky tosses me a thin whippy cane an I catch it one-handed an stand before the man strokin it, caressin it, sneerin into his eyes. It's like I've done this a thousand times before; I know exactly what to do. I know how to cause thee effects. It's simple. It's natural. The fucker's head is noddin madly.

—Want this, do yer?

Madly nodding thee eyes so wide.

—Yeh, I thought as much. Pathetic little twat.

I move around to the back of him. Vicky's there with another cane, swishin it, whippin it through thee air to make quick whooshy sounds. His arse is wobblin. White, hairy, huge. The fat white arse of all oppression it is, saggy an sat on, a smug, self-satisfied arse, used to shittin out expensive food all over the heads of those who never had a fuckin chance, of those who missed out on the luck, born in the wrong place at the wrong time with fuck all. God, if this cane was a *sword* I'd fuckin use it. If it was a chainsaw, if it was a gun.

—Don't hold back, K, Vicky says. —Give it all yer've friggin got, girl. Fill yer fuckin boots. Now's yer chance. Watch me.

She takes her coat off an drops it on the floor an nudges me to one side with her hip an raises the cane up over her shoulder an brings it down so incredibly fuckin hard on thee exposed arse. Crack like a gunshot an the mask howls an the whole big body trembles an a red weal rises instantly. She does it again. An again. All the red slashes rising. An then she goes on doin it, raisin the cane an bringin it down, a series of unremittin CRACKS red stripes criss-crossing, a roaring in me ears, the big body shudderin an strainin at the wood of the stocks an a howlin voice behind the mask the words all muffled but the same three shouted over an over soundin like NAKED SCREAMING FREEDOM over an over repeatedly, screeched with every vicious crack of the cane. All me skin is burning, me throat is dry an there is pooled heat at me groin an then *I'm* the one using the cane, the weapon, hoistin it high an swoopin it down as hard as I possibly can all the muscles of me shoulder an back behind each swing each impact tingling in me jawbone an in the bundle of nerves behind me ears, the blood I see risin an the skin on him in places beginnin to split an the red to run an fuck I am frenzied, a fuckin tornado, every moronic moment of my life from the day I was born paid for by this thrashing every last hour of enforced boredom an frustration now compensated for in this battering I inflict. Sensation overwhelming, pure sensation overfuckinpowering, I stop for a moment panting an sweaty an expect to see Victor in me swimmin vision an when I don't, only that juddering flayed arse I lift the cane the weapon again an it rises an falls, rises an falls over an over. Lost to meself I love myself I fuckin burst with what I can do. Meaningful life, some purpose here layin the body beneath me to waste. Fat fucker, cunt you rich greedy cunt your skin will come off in strips you'll regret your life you'll hate what yer've done greedy fuckin twat pay for it pay for it you evil get pay for it all, this is what I am *for*.

Me hand is grabbed in mid-air, prevented from striking again. Victoria's face, flushed, there's a smile on it but a worry, a shocked concern behind that smile.

—I think that's enough, Kel, she whispers. She moves my arm gently back down to me side, prises the cane from me grip an removes it an throws it clatterin into a corner. —I think he's had enough. Look, yer've made him piss hisself.

The roarin leaves me ears an I hear a spatterin sound. The man's feet are in a pool, a yellow pool on the flagstone floor. Rivulets down his left leg, his bent back racked with sobs. My God, his arse is fuckin massacred. Like red ink scribbles on white paper. Some of them runnin freely. He's bleeding. I've made the fat get bleed. His whole body seems to be drooping floorwards, kept upright only by the stocks. He's shredded, fucked. He looks completely beaten. Broken. I mean as in defeated.

—You alright?

She's peerin in me face, Vicky is. I'm panting, sweat runnin down me body. I manage to nod.

—How d'yer feel?

—Sound. I nod again, take a deep breath. —Fuckin top.

Which couldn't be any truer. 'Top' is fuckin *right*; on top of everythin, the world, me life. For once it seems like nothin is runnin out of me control, I can reel it all in, sort through it, keep what I want an sack what I don't. I feel like I can do anything, absolutely anything. Like things will not be taken from me.

—Sure?

—Yeh, God, yeh. Stop worryin. I'm fine.

I smile at Vicky an she smiles back, a smile of relief, it seems.

Her cheeks are flushed pink under the make-up an her mascara has run slightly an strands of gelled hair have broken free to hang in blonde corkscrews around her face. She looks fuckin great. A warrior or somethin.

—What happens now, then?

She nods at the wreck of a man. He's still sobbing. His arse looks like it needs hospital attention, stitches or somethin. *My* destruction, *my* work. *My* fuckin achievement. —We release dickhead here, she says. —He wanks off in front of me, tho *you* don't have to watch that, if yer don't want to.

I shake me head.

—He gives us a shitload of money an we frig off. An that's it; job done. We goan get somethin to eat while he bandages his arse up the best he can an sits, no, *stands* wonderin why he's such a fuck-up.

—Sounds good to me.

—You can wait in the car if yer like.

—Alright.

—Say tara to *that*, first, tho.

Me legs are surprisingly steady as I move to the front of the man again. Bend down again to stare into his face. His eyes in ther holes are sunk in tears, snot has dribbled from his nose an slug-trailed down the leather of his mask an behind the zip he is still whining, I can still hear him whinin. I grin into his masked face. Pure pleasure, pure fuckin strength in this grin.

Know that there are people like me, you fucker. Next time yer swannin round in yer great big fuckin car or treatin people like the shite on yer shoe, *know* that people like me exist. When yer've healed up enough to be able to sit again behind yer big fuckin desk or in yer fuckin executive box at Old bastard Trafford, *know* that I'm in the world alive an that I hate you. With all thee organs in my beautiful body I hate you. Fuckin *know* it, man.

—See this? I stand up straight an run me hands over me body, smoothin me dress down tight to me skin, me flat belly, me strong thighs. Victoria's grinnin at me. —See these? I cup me tits up towards me chin, stroke me fanny. Bend again to

223

stare into those wide an swimmin, red-rimmed eyes. —Yer'll never . . . *ever* . . . have any of it. Yer'll never touch one part of me in yer entire miserable life, cos all yer are is one fat rich cunt in the stocks. With an arse like half a pound of cheap mince.

Vicky snorts with laughter an I purse me lips an blow him a slow kiss. He starts to whimper again.

—See yis in the car, Vix.

—Alright.

I leave her unlockin the stocks an go back out of the cellar an through that clean an gleamin kitchen. The temptation is there to skank somethin but I don't bother cos there's no need; just thee act of stridin through that antiseptic room in me tight dress an skin, after doin what I've just done, seems like some kind of theft in itself. Or if not that then repayment or somethin, reparations. The gypsies on me dad's side used to say that in ther language the words for stealing translated as something like 'taking light', an that's what it feels like now, takin light into meself, absorbin it, storin it away. Takin it from one who has too much an wants still more. I'm glowin, I am. So fuckin bright an powerful.

In Vicky's car I take a deep gulp at the vodka bottle an light up a ciggie. Me hands are shakin as the hurricane of adrenalin starts to leave me. Me pulse slows back down to normal, moisture comes back into me mouth. I can feel meself a bit wet between the legs, just a wee bit; some sex would be good now. Sex with Victor. Hard an rough an dirty. God, if he was here now I'd fuck his bleedin brains out, fuck him dead. Only with him the world explodes. I feel like I can do anything. I want to fuckin roar. Burn this great big posh friggin house down an stand among the cinders roarin an beatin me chest, me gorgeous chest, like a gorilla. Never been this strong in me life. Never before felt like I could possess this power . . . I am an avenging angel. Trailin fire. Everything in my hands.

I'm laughing. I'm *really* fuckin laughin. Me shoulders are shudderin, there's a chuckling in me chest. That fat man in the stocks, his knees knockin, pissin hisself in terror. An his arse like a butcher's slab. *I* did that, didn't I? Yeh, I fuckin did. An he's gunner *pay* me for doin it. God, that is funny. That is so fuckin funny.

Vicky gets in the car. —What's the matter with you? she asks, lookin closely at me face.

—I can't help it, I say. —That whole thing . . . so friggin funny, man . . .

She grins. She hands me a roll of money. Not a big roll but a roll nonetheless.

—There's a hundred an twenny quid there, she says. —Sad twat gave us extra.

Me laughter picks up. This is not far off a week's wages. For half an hour's arse-whipping. This is completely ridiculous.

—What's so funny?

I shake me head. —Nowt, really . . . just the whole fuckin thing . . . all this bleedin money just for whackin fuck out of a fat feller's bum.

Vicky starts to snigger as well, infected by my laughter, hunched forwards in her seat with her hands on the steerin wheel.

—Did yer see him wet himself?

—Oh God, yeh.

—I thought you were gunner bleedin kill him.

—So did fuckin I.

We're both laughin openly now, freely. Laughter from right deep down in ar bellies, ar beautiful, flat, pierced bellies.

—He won't be able to sit down for a week.

—He'll have to use one of them cushions. Them special ones like giant doughnuts for people with piles.

—Oh God, yeh. Me nan had one.

We're roaring.

—What's he gunner tell his missis?

—Oh my good friggin God.

—He slipped over on some barbed wire.

—He got attacked . . . by a wild animal . . .

We're *roaring*.

—An arse-eating fox.

—A bum-burrower. Some kind of evil rabbit.

225

We're in friggin *fits*. Victoria's bangin her forehead on the steerin wheel, I'm clutchin me belly an stampin me feet. I'm gunner wee me knickers. I'm laughin so much that there's no sound, just me gob hangin open an me eyes closed an me whole body shudderin. How fuckin odd it all is. Strange an daft an absurd.

—He wants yer back, I hear Vicky say. —He wants yer to cane him again.

—Don't . . . aw don't, Vicky, don't . . . I'm gunner fuckin *die* here I am . . .

—He says . . . he told me that . . . he said you're . . .

I can't talk, I'm flappin me hand at Vicky for her to stop. I can't bleedin stand it.

—He said you're . . . told me to tell yer that you're . . . his . . . his QUEEN!

That's it. I've never laughed so much in me life. Didn't think it was friggin *possible* to laugh so much an not die. I can't bloody breathe. Me skull is splitting, me chest is gunner burst. All me abdominal muscles cramped up an knotted. Yer whip a stranger's arse to shreds, call him all the useless cunts under the sun, make him pee hisself with fear an he pays yer a hundred an twenty quid an calls you his queen. Wants yer to do it again. That is *so* funny. That is *soooooo* fuckin funny. I've never heard anything so stupid in all me born days. People are truly insane.

Me laughter starts to die away when Victor's face rises up completely unbidden in me mind, his sweet, gentle face. His eyes rolled back to white as he comes, as I *make* him come with me hands around his throat an his knob explodin inside me. The whole world bursting, as it only ever has done with him, the two times we've shagged (two?). I'm pretty sure about that; we've only fucked the twice, like, but I know it wouldn't happen that way with anyone else. He's like a, what, he's like a fuckin sun. So much sensation with him. All me skin sparking. He's over thee estuary somewhere in Wales an I miss him so much I'm incomplete an I can't wait to see the daft bastard again. Can't wait for that fuckin feelin again, me skin all on fire, me whole life worthwhile. God, when he comes back

I'm gunner fuck him so hard. *So* fuckin hard. He's mine he's mine he's *mine*.

I'm wipin me eyes, smearin mascara everywhere. Me face aches from all the laughin. Fuckin mad.

—Have yer finished? Vicky asks, still grinning.

I nod. —Yeh. Jesus . . .

—Told yer it's funny, didn't I?

—Yer did, aye. Wasn't friggin expectin *that*, tho. Thought I was gunner cark it with laughin so much.

—Yeh, so did I, the first time, like. Wears off after a while, tho.

She pats me shoulder an starts the car an we drive off away from the house. Up through Heswall, on to the main road, towards the Mersey.

—Yis hungry?

I realise suddenly that I am; I'm friggin ravenous. —God, yeh. Starvin. Could eat a scabby head.

—We'll stop at that Afro-Caribbean place in Tocky, pig out. Alright?

—Sound.

—Rice an beans an stuff, carbohydrates, that's what yer need. Replace thee energy, like.

—Alright.

We're quiet for a minute or two, just drivin like, then Victoria says:

—So would yer?

—Would I what?

—Do it again, like.

—What, with the cane an stuff?

—Yeh.

I think about it for a bit. The cash feels fuckin great in the pocket of me jacket, an the laughin felt friggin wonderful, an for a brief moment there it felt like I could do anything. But it's too soon to say whether or not I'd repeat thee experience. It's too soon to know what I feel about it all, really.

—I don't know, I say. —Ask me again in week or two. Give me time to, like, think about it, yer know.

She nods. —Assimilate it.

—Yeh. Work it all out, like.

—Fair enough. Tell yer what, tho, Kels; yer really fuckin went for it, didn't yer? Really friggin gave it some, like. I was gettin worried for a bit, I thought you were gunner bleedin kill him. Either that or oust me from me position as the most in-demand dom in the north-west.

—No chance of *that*, Vicky. In yer friggin element in there, you were. Fitted the part perfectly. An there's no friggin *way* I could do it for a livin, like.

—Why not? It's easy fuckin money, innit? An *lots* of easy money as well.

—Yeh, but, it's just . . . I shrug. Findin it difficult to explain.

—It's no different from *all* work, really, is it? In some ways it's just like every other job I've ever had. Yer need money so yer go somewhere yer don't wanner go, do somethin yer don't really wanner do with people yer don't really wanner be with. Not meanin you, like, I'm talkin about the, yer know, customers, clients, punters, whatever the fuck yer call them. An why? Cos yer need money to live, that's all. There's no difference, basically, when yer think about it.

—Yeh, but the pay's much better. Yer need to work half as hard doin this as yer do at anythin else, an for *twice* the friggin money, usually. An there's other perks as well.

—Such as?

She glances at me, a small, wry smile on her face. —I saw the look in yer eyes down in that cellar, woman. Don't tell me that there wasn't a part of yer enjoyin it.

That surge of power. That wave of strength in me. In *being* me. —No, that's true but . . .

—But what?

—Well, that's not all there is to it, is there? It can't all be as easy as that, surely. Bloke in the stocks an all yer've got to do is cane him on thee arse. Some of them must want *other* things. Things yer not *really* completely comfortable with doin.

—Like what?

—Well, *I* don't know, do I? You're the professional. *You* tell *me*.

She doesn't answer. Just stares straight ahead through the windscreen.

—I'm right, aren't I? Victoria?

—What?

—I said I'm right, aren't I?

She purses her lips. —Suppose so, yeh. To an extent. But *I* can handle it. Maybe *you* wouldn't be able to like but *I* fuckin can.

—Yeh, an that's fair enough. Don't get narky. I'm not friggin gettin at yer or anythin, I'm just sayin. You asked me why I couldn't do the job full-time an I'm tellin yer, that's all. Because I don't think I could handle it. There's me answer. There's yer reason.

We drive into the gloom of the Queensway tunnel. Car headlights play across the curved yellow walls an look like reflections ripplin on water which is exactly what I thought thee were when I was a kid. I thought that yer could see the water of the Mersey through the walls.

I'm gettin images. Me mind's bogglin.

—I've *got* to ask, Vicky.

—Ask what? She looks at me then smiles. —Oh, I know. Yer wanner know what other things the punters want, don't yer? What vile an horrible things thee ask me to do. Yer just eaten up with curiosity, aren't yis?

—Wouldn't go *that* far, like, but . . . well, I'm interested. Yeh.

She shrugs one shoulder. —Well, most of them want the same thing; bit of abuse, bit of CP, like. Yer know.

—CP?

—Corporal punishment. Canes an stuff. Sometimes whips. Probly got the taste for it in school. Bit of bondage maybe, set of stocks, like yer saw. It's mainly the power thing, yer know; thee wanner feel powerless, like, helpless. Thee wanner be told what to do, bossed around an humiliated by a woman ther sexually attracted to an know thee can never have. Especially if thee see that woman as ther social inferior. It's all about humiliation; the pain's just a part of it. Don't ask me why. It's a puzzler. I have one or two theories, like, but I can't

229

be arsed goin into them now. Probly a loader shite anyway. Light us up a ciggie.

I do, an hand it to her. She sucks at it an blows smoke at the glass in front of her. Goes on: —An anyway, there are some things I'd *never* do, no matter how good the money was. Never in a million years. Yer've got to have boundaries, like, got to draw the line somewhere, haven't yer? Like that dirty get I told yer about before, the fuckin sleazoid, remember him with the shite an the schoolgirl panties?

—Wish I fuckin didn't.

—Would friggin *never* do somethin like that, man. Fuck no. I'd be friggin sick. But there are worse things, tho, I've gorrer say. I've been asked to do worse things.

She sucks so hard at the cigarette that her cheeks collapse. It burns down to half its length an she exhales very little smoke. She asks me somethin which I don't quite catch.

—What?

—Ever heard of 'crush' videos?

—'Crush'?

—Yeh.

I shake me head. —What're they?

—I'll tell yeh.

She finishes off the fag in one drag an then stubs it out in thee ashtray. Never known anyone to smoke like Victoria does. She attacks them, devours them.

—I had a client once out in Formby. About two years ago this was. Into the same sort of stuff that most of them are, like yer one we've just visited; abuse, bit of whippin, yer know. Bog-standard sort of stuff, like. This one day, tho, I goes out there, an he's got all these boxes in his cellar. Shoeboxes, like, ther lids held on tight with laccy bands. An inside each one was a little animal; mice, hamsters, gerbils. A rat or two. Even a squirrel.

—Ah no. He didn't want yer to . . . ?

—What, do a Richard Gere on him? Nah, that wasn't his thing. Think that's an urban myth to be honest with yer. Never come across it in real life, ever. No, what this twat was after was much, much worse; he wanted to make a crush video. He'd bought me some new shoes, these nice sexy platform-soled sandals, like, an he wanted me to do me feet up, polish an toerings an all that stuff, put these new shoes on an stamp on all these little animals. While he filmed me doing it. Wanted me to crush all these diddy cute fluffy things an film me feet in close-up, doin it.

Jesus Christ. Me heart seems to sink in me chest. —That is friggin *sick*.

—You *know* it. Big market for that type of film, apparently.

—That's fuckin disgusting.

—Innit, yeh. Somethin fuckin wrong, there, am tellin yis. Not fuckin right that shit.

But all too friggin common. The world's full of sadistic wankers. Wantin to see defenceless little animals bein crushed an all that fuckin matters to them is the fulfilment of ther sexual obsession, whatever the fuck it is. Ther personal fuckin frenzy. Like that cunt I work for, him who owns the shop; if he catches a mouse or a rat in his stockroom he takes it out the back an cuts it up with a Stanley knife while it's still alive. I put my fingers in me ears so I can't hear the squeals. I asked him once why he doesn't kill them quickly, so thee don't feel any pain, like, an he said that thee need to be taught a lesson. Glassy-eyed fuckin grin on his face. One sadistic twat, that. Back to work for that fuckwit in a couple of days, I am. Shite. Too many like him in this friggin world.

—What did yer do? Yer didn't *do* it, did yer?

—Fuck *no*. D'yer really think I'd be able to do a thing like that?

I shake me head. —Just checkin.

—Nah, what I did was, I told him that I'd do it but he'd have to know what it felt like first, that I'd have to tie him down an walk over him in these new sexy shoes. Little prick got all excited at that, like, so I tied him up dead fuckin tight, gagged the cunt as well, then took all the boxes out into his garden an let the little animals go. Fucked off an left him there all tied up, unable to move or shout or anythin. Probly still fuckin there for all I know. Starved to death, like.

—All he fuckin deserves.

—Is right. Sick bastard. Hope his friggin missis caught him like that, tied up in the nud. Would've friggin loved to've heard thee explanation.

—Should've stamped on the fucker's balls. Crushed *them* instead of the animals.

—Nah. Twisted cunt would've fuckin *loved* that.

We exit the tunnel an drive across the city, along the dock road to avoid the traffic an up through Chinatown. The new gates loom up over us an all the buildings around them, huge an amazing. Yer look at them an yer think 'Wow', then yer look behind yer an see thee Anglican cathedral all lit up in the night sky an yer think 'Oh my good fuckin God'. An then yer think about how fuckin impossible we are; how we can build the gates an the cathedrals an also conceive of things like crush videos, even fuckin get off on such things. We can generate the *need* for crush videos an also the *need* for the gates an the cathedrals. How the *fuck* can we do that? What's goin on here? How can the two things coexist? What, what, *what* the almighty *fuck* is fuckin wrong with us?

We drive up Upper Parliament Street an park up at the kerb outside a row of shops. Me belly rumbles.

—Jesus. Was that you?

I nod. —I'm starvin.

—Sounds it. Come ed, let's goan stuff ar faces.

There's a group of young black guys millin around outside the takeaway. A couple of Rastas, a couple of Yardie types. Thee nudge each other an nod over at us as we get out of the car in the clothes we're wearin, me in me tight black dress, Victoria's leopard-skin an PVC. We strut past them, Vicky flickin her fingers at them an shoutin in patois, just messin around:

—Mmmmmm*ash* it up, bumba claat! You all dat? Me gwaan get dat curry goat, seen?

Thee look at her bemused, answer her in pure Tocky Scouse:

—Yerwha?

—The fucker *youse* goin on about?

We laugh an go into the takeaway. Order up a fuckload of food: rice an peas, saltfish patties, jerk chicken an ackee, mackerel callaloo; fried yams, fried plantains. I'm fuckin starvin. Ravenous. A bottle of lemo to go with it. While we're waiting, one of the fellers from outside in ridiculously baggy kecks an his hair done up in cornrows comes in to stand beside Victoria an just stare at her face. Ther noses about three inches apart. Vicky just stares at him back an says: —Iya.

He doesn't answer. She says it again: —Iya, you.

—I know you, doan I.

Vicky shakes her head. —I don't think so, mate. No.

—Yeh, I do. I met yer once in the Jac. Yer know my mate Adam.

—Adam?

—Adam Sinclair. Sinky.

She nods in recognition. —Oh aye, yeh. I remember now. Sinky, haven't seen him for a while. How is he?

The black guy shrugs. Says nowt for a few seconds then goes: —He *likes* you. He *really* fuckin likes *you*, Sinky does.

—I know he does. He's a nice lad. Next time yer see him, tell him I was askin after him, yeh?

The bloke nods an then leaves, just like that, no tara or anythin. He just nods an turns his back an walks out. He says somethin to his mates then thee all head off up the road, into Toxteth proper.

—Jesus. What the fuck wa *that* all about, Vic?

She shakes her head. —Tell yer in a minute. Take the scran back to your gaff, yeh?

—Sound.

We collect the steaming placcy bags an foil trays an drive up the road to me flat. Vicky's car fills with lovely smells an I'm so fuckin hungry that I'm almost drooling. Must take a lot out of yer, takin a cane to someone's arse. Must burn up a lot of energy smackin frig out of someone's bum with a cane cos I'm absolutely bleedin famished.

We park up outside the Deutsche Kirke an go into my house, climb the stairs to me flat. Behind some of the doors, the flat doors, like, the party is *still* goin on; sounds of music an people shoutin in slurred voices. This will continue for another couple of days until thee intervals between the parties get longer until eventually thee begin only on Thursday nights an stop on Sundays. Which is the way it's always been. Then Chinese New Year will come along an the madness'll begin all over again.

Inside me flat an I think I can smell Victor. A faint lingerin whiff of him, his natural body scent. I ignore it an turn the telly on, fetch forks an glasses from the kitchen while Vicky opens the food. The smell is just amazing. Amazing. In three seconds I've filled a plate and am crammin it in me gob.

—That guy back there, Vicky says, —in the takeaway. He's a mate of a client of mine. Or an ex-client, I should say. I had to stop seein him cos he was gettin obsessed.

—With you?

—More with what we used to *do*, I think. He *thought* that he was obsessed, in love, like, with *me*, but *I* reckon that it was just with what we used to do. It was startin to get hold of him, like. Takin over his life.

I eat half a patty in one bite. —An what was it?

—What?

—That yer used to do with him. That he was gettin obsessed with.

She forks rice an peas into her callaloo an mixes it all up. —He's a nice lad. Young, like, couple of years younger than me. Born an brought up in the Banff, yer know them flats? That big Coggy community?

—I know it, yeh. And?

—And what?

—Aw Jesus, Vic. What was it yer used to do to him? That he became so obsessed with? I'm dead interested here.

She forks food into her mouth with her left hand an holds up her right in a fist. I'm puzzled.

—What, yer used to *punch* him?

—God, no. Altho some of them *do* like that. No, Adam was . . . he had this thing about bein penetrated.

It hits me then. —Oh Christ. An yer used to *fist* him?

She nods, chewin. —Yeh.

—Yer whole friggin arm?

—Until he told me to stop, aye. Which'd normally be about . . . She places her left index finger on a point halfway up her right forearm. —Here.

—Jesus Christ.

I try to imagine what that'd feel like, to be filled so much. To burstin point, like. It makes me feel heavy inside, like I need to go the toilet. Peter used to do things to my bum, more often than not against me will, like, but that was body-spray canisters an cucumbers an stuff, not a complete fuckin arm. Surely there'd be, like, splitting. Surely something would rupture.

—I thought yer said yer didn't touch any of them?

—There are exceptions. Very fuckin few. But he was one.

—What was it like?

An *arm*. Jesus.

—For me or for him?

—Both.

—Well, I think for him it was like being . . . it sounds daft, but he had some kind of crucifixion fixation. I think for him it had something to do with that. To be, like, speared or somethin. She shakes her head. —I dunno, it's not somethin I spend a great deal of time thinkin about to be honest with yis. I just do what they pay me to do, within me own boundaries, of course. But the things he'd say an stuff, this Adam one . . . it was all built around sacrifice, with him. *I* reckon. Funny lad, really.

I nod. Somehow, I understand what she's talkin about. Somewhere inside me what she's sayin is makin some kind of sense. I can't explain it or even describe it in any way other than to say it just clicks into place somewhere deep down inside me.

I take a big swig of the lemonade. Jerk chicken's like eatin fuckin lava. Nice, tho.

—An wharrabout yerself? I ask.

—Well, for me, it was like . . .

—Smelly, I bet.

She laughs. —There was a bit of that, yeh. Not as much as yer'd think, tho. He'd give hisself an enema beforehand, like, so it wasn't too bad in thee 'ick' department.

—What did it feel like?

235

—Hot. Dead, dead hot. Squishy.

—Ew, God.

—And, to be honest, quite fuckin amazing. Honest. I mean, to be so fuckin far inside someone else's body . . . it felt like I was doin the impossible, yer know, somethin that shouldn't be allowed, that I shouldn't be capable of doing. Imagine it; yer whole hand inside someone else. The feel of ther insides, like, against yer skin. The parts of someone that only the fuckin mortician'll ever see. Feels amazingly soft. Almost like friggin silk or something.

She thinks for a minute, chewing. She takes a bone out of her mouth an puts it on the side of her plate. Then she says:

—But d'yer know what I'd really like to do? I'd like to do it to someone that I really, really care about. To get that close? *Inside* them, like? Fuckin incredible that would be I reckon. I mean, yer not far off touchin ther actual fuckin *heart*, are yer? Yer part of them, *inside* them, like. Couldn't get any closer, physically, I mean. She takes a big swig of the lemonade out of the bottle an burps. —Funny fuckin state of affairs, innit? I mean, here's me thinkin that it's been a long friggin time since I've liked anyone enough to want to put me entire arm up ther ring. Jesus.

We both laugh at that. A telephone starts to ring an me heart instantly lurches, thinkin that it might be Victor but then the ringin changes to the tune of 'Hit Me Baby One More Time' an Victoria takes her mobile out of her coat pocket an answers it.

—Hello? . . . oh hiya.

She says 'okay' a few times then puts the phone back in her pocket.

—I've got to go, Kels.

—Who was that?

—Natasha. Neurotic cow's havin another crisis again an wants me to goan help her sort it out. She's half-pissed in the Philarmonic pub.

—Fuckin middle-class lecturer's problems, I say, with real disdain. *Justified* fuckin disdain an all. —Probly findin it difficult to pay the fuel bill on her friggin Aga or somethin.

—Is right, yeh. Still, tho, I'd better go. Don't wanner read about her in thee *Echo* obits tomorrow, do we? She's tried it before, like. Toppin herself. Paracetamols.

She shovels down a few more forkfuls of food then stands to go. —Thanks for yer help today, Kelly.

—Alright.

—Nah, I mean it. You were a big help. An yer feel okay about it, yeh?

I shrug. —Sound, yeh. Think so, anyway. Certainly don't feel *bad* or anythin.

—Good. I'll give yis a ring soon an we can have a good natter about it, yeh?

—Yeh.

—Nice one. When's that new feller of yours comin back? Tomorrow?

—Tomorrow, yeh.

She smiles. —So next time I see yer yer'll be walkin bandy-legged.

I laugh. —Hope so, yeh.

—A real man, eh. Yer lucky bitch. There's not many of them around.

She goes an I finish the rest of the food, just automatically forkin it in, watchin some game-show crap on the telly. The flat, empty now except for me, just me, starts to press in against me head an the night sky outside the window looks like a black blanket, starless. I draw the curtains. Take the food cartons into the kitchen, crumple them up an put them in the bin. Wash the forks an glasses an plates. That warm cellar. That naked man. Smoke a cigarette, think about buildin a spliff, decide against it. His head an hands in the stocks an that bulgin leather mask an that big white arse raised up. Build the spliff after all an smoke it. That cane, thee impact of each stroke in me shoulder. So hard, hittin him so hard. The noise it made. The noise *he* made, behind his mask, squealin like a rabbit in a trap. Go into the bathroom an have a dump. The friggin *state* of his arse. So red. An his piddle dribblin down his legs an the money he gave me an I don't know what the fuck his face looks like but the daft twat thinks I am his queen.

My God. The things I've heard today. Knicker shite an crush videos an fistin, sacrificial. The things I've fuckin *done* today.

Christ, I'm knackered.

I wipe an pull the chain. I'm gettin the giggles again. Laughin to meself. The total fuckin madness of it all. The stupidity, thee absurdity. The things I heard today, the things I *did*. Fuckin mental. An, it must be said, a bit depressin as well; I mean, what the fuck *is* it with men? Why are so many of them so, what, so fuckin warped an twisted in ther sexuality? Wantin to be caned, mercilessly; to shit themselves wearin schoolgirl knickers; wantin to be friggin fisted; fuckin crush videos for Christ's sake. Crush videos; one of the sickest things I've ever heard. Have men always been like this or is it just now? An if it *is* just now, then why? Why so feverish an sick in ther desires?

All a bit of a downer, really, this whole fuckin day, if truth be told. All of it an insight into the darkness of men. Put me on a bit of a lowey. And as I'm washin me hands at the sink an starin into the fallin water there's suddenly a picture in me head, a clear an sharp picture of the sea, a dark sea, a sea at night-time, the moonlight on the waves an the waves softly crashin on to a pebble beach an the pull of it all, the draw, the dark permanence of it an the strange desire to be a part of that, vast an black an for ever. Where did this come from? What the fuck's all this about?

The phone rings.

I'm on it in two leaps.

—Hello?

—Kelly?

His voice oh thank you fuckin thank you, thank you God for makin him phone. Thank you Victor it's you thank God thank fuck it's you.

—Victor?

—How are yer?

—Where *are* you?

—I'm in Wales. In the middle of Wales, like. A place called Aberystwyth. Lively enough little town, like. Just bought some chonga an Craig an Quockie have bagged off, it looks like.

Only Craig an Quockie? Well, what the frig are *you* gunner do then, on yer own?

—I'm gunner have a walk on the beach an a smoke. How are yer?

Bastard can read me mind. —Alright.

All blokes together, gettin wrecked together, thee'll all fuckin pick up women together, nothin surer. Ther all the bleedin same. Probly some slag waitin outside the phone box right now, as he talks to me.

—What have yer done today?

I almost burst out laughin. Christ, if only he knew. How would he react? With shock? Amusement? Arousal? Best just keep it neutral.

—Not a lot, like. Went out with Victoria.

—Who's that?

—Victoria? One of the girls I was with in Magnet thee other night. With all the piled-up hair?

—Oh aye, yeh. I remember.

Yeh, I went to see one of her clients. A fat, Scum-supportin businessman. Took the friggin skin off his arse with a cane. An found out about crush videos an men who like to take a dump in schoolgirl knickers an the world is not the same, it is less an you sound so very fuckin far away. He asks me if I had a good time an the laughter nearly pounces up out of me. I smack it back down with a cough.

—Alright, yeh.

—Where'd youse go?

—Just for a drive an stuff, yer know. Over to the Wirral. I could see Wales. Where *you* are, like.

An wanted to be over there with you holdin yer fuckin face so tight in me hands that I could feel the bones shift under me palms. An they can all fuck off; Peter, Man-in-the-stocks, Crush-video-cunt an Shitty Knickers, Adam Sinclair with a hole like the Mersey tunnel. Only *you* matter, Victor. Only *you* count. Your voice is so fuckin clear an miles, miles away.

—Kelly, I . . .

I wait for him to say somethin else but he doesn't. He just breathes.

—What's up?

—Nowt. Just a bit tired, that's all, he says. But there's somethin else he wants to say. That he's not going to say.

—At a bit of a loose end, really, he goes on. —I'm on me own.

Maybe he's tellin the truth. Maybe he really hasn't picked anyone up. I want to ask him outright, like, but God, I've only known him for a couple of days an if he's anythin like every other bloke then the very asking of that question will give him licence to go an do precisely that. An anyway, how the fuck would he feel about what *I* did today? How would he react to knowin about my day as a dom? Yer've all got fuckin secrets, Kelly. If Victor's got one, yer'll find out about it. Eventually.

—Suppose I'll just have a walk on the beach an get wrecked, he says in a small, sad voice. —Kip in the van, like. It's nice here, the beach. Stones an shingle. With a great big hill all lit up at one end of it.

Little Victor on that beach, beneath that big hill. Little Victor. Come back to me an let me rip chunks off you with me teeth.

—Kelly?

—Yeh?

—What's up? Are yis alright?

I shake me head in an attempt to clear an still it, calm it, stop it friggin bouncing around everywhere, all these fuckin pictures rushin in in a torrent; Victoria an leopard-skin an big houses an split flesh an runnin shit an dead animals, ther guts trailin from ther mouths an balls of flame an streams of fluid, blood an piss, dark waters an the strength to bend iron an Peter, that cunt Peter, how I went out with him for a matter of years an in all that time felt for him not one tiny thing not one fuckin shred of what I already feel for you, Victor, sweet-faced skinny Victor, broken beneath me gasping ecstatic an me biting at you. Peter in the shop, feelin a fool, lookin a fuckin fool. Foolish fuckin Peter. Knobhead Peter, creepy Peter, bastard bastard bastard.

—Kelly?

—Ah, just something that happened today. Give him thee

edited version, Kel. Edit it heavily. —I saw Peter. Remember thee ex-boyfriend I told yer about?

—No.

So much worry in that one word. —Well, he's a knobend anyway. An arsehole. But just seein him like, yer know, it was weird.

Change the subject now. —When are yer comin back?

After a pause he says: —Tomorrow.

—What time?

Too eager.

—Dunno. Depends on Quockie, I suppose, cos he's drivin.

Aw *fuck* too eager. —Early or late?

—Haven't gorrer clue. Probly early cos Quockie's got to get back to arrange somethin for Chinese New Year or something. Don't know quite what, like.

Sound eager. Fuckin *be* eager. Tell him, Kelly, just friggin tell him. —Okay, well. Meet me somewhere.

—Yeh. Where?

Fish. Weapons. Bones. Somethin somewhere that was before me, before Victor, before me and Victor. Livin things, dead things. Flesh an machines. Old bones. God, me fuckin head is all over the place. —Natural History Museum.

—Sound. What time?

—Two o'clockish?

—Alright.

A little jump now in his one word. —If yer can't make it then give me a ring, I say. —Otherwise I'll just see yer there.

—Okay. I . . .

My God, his voice, his voice it makes me ache. Before I can stop meself I say: —Hurry back. Take care, an hang up. The telephone just squats there like a shell.

I'm all over the place. I'm in the kitchen, the bathroom. I'm in the bedroom, straightening an already straight sheet. I'm rollin another spliff, I'm smokin another spliff, I'm watchin shite on telly. I'm readin a paper two weeks old, last century's news. I'm lookin at the clothes hangin up in me wardrobe. I'm gazin out the window. I'm watchin some scallies in the street below breakin into a car. I'm back in the bathroom again, pullin matted hairs out of the plughole. Changin the towels. Pickin at the peelin varnish on me toenails an wonderin whether I should paint them again. Then paintin them again. Lookin at meself in the dresser mirror, then changin out of me nice black dress now crumpled an sweaty into trackie bottoms an a jumper. Watchin the clock. Brushin me teeth. Thinkin of dead animals. Pools of shit with faceless men writhin in them. I'm havin a wee. Emptyin ashtrays. Rubbin the shoulder of me right arm, me cane-swingin arm. Swallowin a diazepam. Sittin on the couch wonderin who the fuck I really am. What I might become. Noddin off on the couch not givin a toss. Standin, swayin, staggerin into bed. Fallin asleep.

Waking up.

I have a cup of tea an two slices of toast an jam while the bath's running. Watch a bit of Richard an Judy. Put the dishes in the sink then take me gown off an get into the bath, the hot suds all tight on me skin, lovely, like heaven. Fuckin love havin a bath, I do. Love that feelin of bein clean. I wash everywhere, inside an out, a real good scrub. Want to be washed all over. Want to smell nice all over. Scour everythin away for Victor, rinse it all down the plughole, Peter an the man in the stocks an the cane an the crush films an the shitty knickers an that lad whose name I've forgotten that Victoria used to fist, everythin not me all scrubbed off me an swilled away down the pipes an under the city an out into the Mersey an I climb out of the bath just me, pure me, nowt on me except me skin an hair an thee ink of me tattoo. Oh yeh, an the metal through me skin an this massive fuckin ache. All over me this fuckin ache.

Don't worry, Kelly. Be patient. He'll be here soon. Less than two hours.

I put lily-of-the-valley talc on me feet an bum an fanny. Deodorant on me pits, perfume, just a dab, on me neck an wrists an behind me ears. Spray meself with Boots musk body spray. Notice a little fat brown spider on the side of the bath so trap him under the transparent lid of the body-spray canister; I'll throw him out the window later. Pluck me eyebrows. Worm a cotton bud into each ear. Small zit on me jaw, I scratch the head off it then rub raw soap into it. Dab some witch hazel on it an on the bolt through me navel, it's been feelin a bit itchy recently. Hope it's not gettin infected. Put a wee bit of slap on, just around thee eyes, like, then go into the bedroom an get dressed; trainies, long denim skirt, tight cropped T-shirt an then a fleece over that cos it'll be bleedin freezin outside. Look at meself in the dresser mirror. Alright. I look alright.

The money I earned yeaterday is lyin in a loose fan on the dresser. All those queens' heads. A lot of fuckin money. I put half of it in me purse then put thee other half in as well. Bulging purse feels like a concealed weapon on my hip, a gun. It feels good. It feels fuckin *great*.

I fetch the wrap of coke that Peter gave me yesterday, go into the livin room an chop up a line on the coffee table an snort it. It's good, clean coke; instant facial numbness, sudden rush. Turn the telly off an click the radio on, tune it to Crash FM, some DJ babble an then Boss Hog, 'Itchy an Scratchy'. Superb. I read recently that ther gunner use this song for the next Levi's advert, which wouldn't fuckin surprise me; I mean, everythin becomes a brand, sooner or later. Or if not *becomes* a brand then gets used by one, absorbed by one, which is more or less the same friggin thing. Look what happened to the Clash. Everything, sooner or later, is robbed of its individuality. All sensation, *true* sensation, like, bleached out of it. No fuckin lie.

Except this bleedin cocaine. This is top. I have a little dance around the room, not too energetic like cos I don't wanner work up a sweat. Clean an coked I am, off to meet a lovely man. I'm happy. I am, I'm fuckin happy. The song finishes an some God-awful boy-band cover toss comes on so I turn the radio off, brush me teeth again, pick up me keys, leave the flat an then the house.

Rain. Well, drizzle. Bugger. Dirty city drizzle. I pull me hood up an set off, down Faulkner Street an down Hardman Street (prophetic, I hope) an on to Bold Street, into the city proper, which is friggin chocka cos of the January sales. It's heaving. Shoulder-to-shoulder on the pavements an no one seems to be enjoyin themselves; ther scowlin, hurryin,

243

scurryin, weighed down by cumbersome packages an armfuls of carriers. Ther tuttin an snarlin an dartin into shops, jumpin queues, elbowin each other out of the way. It's manic an oppressive. Everything's for sale; the Gap, Ikea, River Island, Body Shop, Schuh; everythin can be bought. Billboards an posters advertising not things, not products, but a sense of community, belonging, self-respect, which is a fuckin laugh considerin the desperate fevered mass tramplin over each other to purchase such things. It's one great big fuckin mess. New fuckin millennium an sod all's changed. In fact, in some ways it's got worse; the millennium itself is now bein used as an advertisin technique, employed as a gimmick to sell everythin from toasters to cars. It's a fuckin joke. I've always hated it, this high-street brand-name bollocks; always hated that fuckin Nike tick, that fuckin tick everywhere, gigantic on billboards above buildings or barricadin thee end of a road. Fuckin tattooed into people's skin even. Daft fuckin images that people worship. Skinny women in expensive clothes on posters in shop windows an the whole thing's so fuckin cold an empty. It gives yer nowt but a feelin of inadequacy; yer feel friggin useless cos yer don't look like that an could never afford to look like that, so yer told more an more that yer pathetic an thee only way to improve yerself is to wear these clothes, smell of this perfume, drink in this fuckin coffee shop, until yer don't know what yer really, truly want any more, or even who the fuck yer are. Yer *told* what yer want, yer *told* what yer are or what to be. What yer should *want* to be. Yer taken out of yer life an put into another one, one that's got fuck all to do with you an yer private, personal needs, an most people are so fuckin miserable that ther happy to accept this, perfectly happy to become part of the faceless fuckwit mass. Yer nowt if yer don't consume.

Not me, tho. Oh no, not me; I'm coked an clean an off to meet Victor.

God, that cocaine's good. I'll say one thing for Peter, an one thing only: he deals the best friggin beak in the city. Bar none. That's thee *only* good thing I can say about that twat.

I cross the road on to Church Street, walk under the huge

steel Christmas tree that Norway presents to the city every year (somethin to do with the Second World War, I think). The steel struts all gleamin with rain. Next door to Schuh is a clothes shop an in the window is one of the best long coats I've ever seen; about knee-length, made out of some sort of coarse canvassy material. I'd look dead friggin cool in it, I would. It's of a deep maroon colour that'd go ace with me hair an skin tone. I'd look sexy as fuck in that, oh yes. Cool an sexy for Victor. I go into the shop an approach one of thee assistants who's hangin bra-an-knicker sets on a rack. Me mind tries to picture a pair of those knickers clingin to a big fat hairy male arse but I don't let it.

—That long maroon coat in the window, I say. —How much is it?

She fingertips her hair back over her ears. Her cheeks are all pink an she looks flustered.

—It's on sale price at the mo. A third off. Ninety-nine ninety-nine.

—That's with the third off?

—Yeh. It's nice, innit?

—It is, yeh. How long's the sale on for?

—Til thee end of the week.

A hundred an twenny in me purse, I'm thinking. That'd only leave thirty quid. Don't get paid until thee end of next week. Bit in the bank, like, but not enough on me right now. Could always go out an cane another fat cunt's arse.

—Can't yer afford it, no?

I look at the girl, but she's not bein snotty, she's not havin a dig. She's only about sixteen or somethin an she's got kind brown eyes.

—No, I say. —Well, I *can*, like, but . . . I'd leave meself skint. What if I pay half now an thee other half at thee end of next week an yer keep it for us until then? Can yer do that?

—Erm . . . not really, no. Sale stops on Saturday, see, an then everythin goes back up to full price. Tell yer what I *can* do, tho. She looks around then back at me. —Give us half now an I'll put it by for yis, put a note on it sayin that yer owe fifty. If the boss asks I'll tell her yer paid full whack.

—Brilliant.

I give her fifty quid an me name an address.

—It'll be here for yer next week.

—Nice one. Thanks very much.

—Yer alright.

Sound girl. I leave the shop, back into the crush of people. Lookin at meself in the shop windows an imagining how I'll look in that ace coat. Then I realise how ace I look now, the denim skirt all tight to me legs, an I notice blokes lookin me up an down, ther eyes as always goin to me chest first then when thee realise that me baggy fleece doesn't reveal anything thee look at me legs an then a quick offhand glance at me face an then ther heads turn to follow me arse as I walk past them. That's ther order of priority: tits legs face arse. An it'd probably be arse before face if it wasn't on the back of me body. If only thee knew, if only thee could know what I am. What I did yesterday. What I'll do tonight. I wonder if it'd turn them on . . . wonder if they, too, like to be beaten, abused, humiliated. Like to shit themselves in front of scolding women. Like to watch women stampin on small animals. Or if thee'd like to be fisted, fuckin impaled on some woman's arm. There's a million different kinds of sexuality an some of them are the darkest fuckin things on the planet. Countless secrets. Infinite ways in which people want more, some of them sick an dirty an all-consuming. Ways in which thee wanner friggin *be* more.

Me skin starts to tingle. Me heart starts to thump.

I turn up towards Lime Street. The clock on the Royal Court tells me I'm early so I nip into the Penny Farthing for a quick drink, just a neat double vodka knocked back, kickstart the coke again. Then another one mixed with orange an sipped with a ciggie to stop the slight tremblin in me hands. It works an I leave the pub, wait for a gap in the busy traffic then cross the road into St George's Gardens, across which I can see thee entrance to the Natural History Museum, the wide stone steps an the grand columns like somethin yer'd expect to see in Greece or somewhere, thee ancient ruins, like. Leanin against one of them is a slight figure. Hands in his pockets, hunched into himself. I think it's him. I can't make out any details at this distance but I can't really remember the details of Victor anyway really, just his messy hair an green eyes an smile, but I'm pretty sure it's him. I move closer an hide meself behind the war memorial an watch him. A scally girl picks her way up the steps towards him an thee both exchange a few words an he digs in his pocket an gives her something, probly money. Thee talk some more an then a group of business types, all gelled hair an suits, climbs the steps an the scally girl is quickly among them, hand out. The Victor figure watches her then leans back against a column. I squint at his face. It fuckin is. It's Victor. Seems lost in thought, like a reverie. Wonder what he's thinkin about? The scally girl puts me in mind of a crackwhore I know named Becky, but then I suppose any skeletal girl in a grimy tracksuit would an there is an overwhelmin urge in me now to get up close to Victor's face, take in his features, smell him, touch him, feel the heat of him close an the throb in his skin an I can feel me face split in a grin as I walk towards him waving, he looks up an sees me then stands up straight an smiles an watches me as I cross the road. I take me hood down so that he can see me face. So that I can see his. I climb the steps towards him. I stand right in front of him an smile into his face.

—Iya.

—Iya, you.

Here he fuckin is. Here's his face, so close to mine. His hair all spiked with the drizzle an his eyes, green, the long lashes flickerin as he blinks. All I wanner do is laugh.

—How're you?

—Good, he says. —Ace, now.

I can feel me smile widening. Wanner crush him to me chest but I don't know whether to do that or not, whether it might be sort of clingy, too friggin desperate even, an he evidently feels the same way cos his arms sort of jerk upwards in front of his body as if involuntarily an it looks daft an a bit biffy an he seems a wee bit embarrassed so I just squeeze his arm an kiss his cheek, his aftershave like lemons, an ask him again how he is. I don't know whether he answers me or not cos all I can hear is me own voice tellin me how fuckin wonderful this is, how fuckin wonderful *he* is, how fuckin missed an how gorgeous an even now, already, within me rises the kind of aggression thingio that always comes sooner or later in sex an here it fuckin is already the teeth-grindin desire to punish, *hurt* . . . put him in the fuckin stocks. Whip his back an arse til blood comes. Lovely Victor gorgeous Victor. Presence so strong it's like an assault, so whole against me I wanner tear it to bits in me hands.

Smile at him. Out of the corner of me eye I notice the scally beggar girl watchin us intently, her expression dark. Victor gives her a little smile, a kind little smile, an me an him go into the museum together.

What do I say now? What do I do? Small talk, yeh. Just talk small.

—How was Wales, then?

—Good, he says. —Green an sheepy.

I still *really* wanner know whether he spent last night on his own, to be honest. Whether, like his mates, he picked up some slag. —Did yer have a good time?

He shrugs. —Suppose so. Yeh. Got wrecked. Stoned, drunk. That's about it, really.

He looks so crestfallen that I have to laugh. —Yer could've done that *here*, man.

—I know, yeh, but this was by the sea an the mountains. Made a nice change, like.

—So did it work, then?

—What?

—The trip. To Wales. The recovery trip. Have yer recovered?

He smiles an nods. —Oh yeh.

—That's good.

—What did *you* do last night?

The directness of that question startles me a bit, considerin what I *did* do yesterday. The power in me arm an the marks I made. If I ever *do* tell Victor about it then it won't be now, here in this museum with him again. Wrong time, wrong place. Altho it'll probly always remain a secret, known only to me an Victoria. An of course that twat with the shredded arse. Can't see *him* tellin anyone.

Victor's lookin at me, waitin for a reply. I just say: —What?

—You, he says. —Last night. What did yis do?

—Oh. I put me hands deep in me pockets. Tell him that I just went out with Victoria.

—Where to?

Jesus Christ, all these friggin questions. I give a big, exaggerated shrug. —Just pubs an that, yer know. Nowhere special, the Jac, Magnet. Usual places.

I shrug again, lettin him know that that's all I'm gunner tell him an that I don't much care for this friggin interrogation. An that there's nowt else *to* tell him. That nothin happened, I just went out to a couple of pubs with Vicky an had a few bevvies an that's all there is to it. Certainly didn't go with Vicky over to the Wirral an get paid over a hundred quid for caning fuck out of some sexual slave's arse, God, no. He doesn't ask anything else.

We show ar passes at the front desk an go into the lift. I'm thinking about teeth an claws an ancient history. Giant beasts that once lived here now just bones. I press a button.

—What floor? he asks.

—Three.

I watch him thinking. His eyes light up an he says in an excited voice: —Dinosaurs?

I smile. —Dinosaurs, yeh. Yer won't be scared, now, will yeh? Yer won't run away?

He laughs. —I might do. Might shite me kex in terror.

The lift jerks an we're lifted up into the building. Victor's joke reminds me of that dirty get Vicky told me about, him in the schoolgirl's uniform. The distance between that vile obsession an Victor's daft little joke makes me feel a bit sad. I want to hug him now. Press his face into me shoulder an smell his hair.

He's different. He *is* different. He's not like other men, because most of them – nearly all – don't love anything, not even themselves, apart from ther own fixations. That's all thee hold dear, ther obsessions, no matter how destructive or deadly to others thee might be. Ther utterly unable to love anything other than ther own dark an desperate desires. Why is this?

Why should this be? I don't know. Somethin to do with identity, maybe, or power. Fuck knows. They don't even know themselves.

Victor, *my* Victor, excited about dinosaurs. An coming like a cannon when I strangle him.

But that's me, as well, isn't it? Yeh. That's fuckin *me*.

The lift doors rattle open. Victor gestures at me to leave first so I do, knowin that he's lookin at me, appraising me, like, from behind. I take small steps so me hips sway an me skirt pulls tight to me thighs an I make me way over to the allosaurus skeleton. Its gob open in mid-roar, all of its ferocious teeth. Imagine it with flesh on it, scale an muscle. Imagine its mad voice. What would its *eyes* have looked like.

Victor comes to stand beside me. I look an smile at him then tell him that I've always loved dinosaurs:

—Even when I was little, like, all thee other girls'd have dolls an toy horses an stuff an I'd have a set of placcy dinosaurs. I had a triceratops an I painted thee ends of its horns all red to look like blood. I had a tyrannosaur as well an I got bits of lamb from the Sunday roast, small shreds of meat, like, an stuck them between his teeth, yer know, so it'd look like he'd just eaten something?

He smiles an nods.

—An I left them in there an the meat went all rotten an stank me room out. Flies an everythin. Me dad went mad.

He laughs an I think of me dad, shoutin at me about the flies an the niff then doublin over in a coughin fit, a real hacker. Such fits became more n more frequent from then on, until of course he couldn't cough, or shout, or even friggin breathe, any more. I still remember his face, tho, his face when fightin for breath; the colours it would go, from white to red to purple. Terrifyin to see.

—I was the same, Victor says. —Just the friggin same. Used to watch all the films; *Valley of the Gwangi*, remember that one?

I do, because of the tiny horse in it. —Aw yeh. Brilliant. *20,000 Years BC.*

—Yeh.

He tells me a story about goin to see *Jurassic Park* when it first came out, about how excited he was an scared of the dinosaurs on the screen. All the little kids in the row in front of him turnin round to point an laugh at him. It's a sweet, funny story an it makes me laugh. And wanner fuck his brains out as well, to be brutally honest.

—Thee found *me* more entertainin than the bleedin film.

—Little kids, innit, I say. —See convincing dinosaurs every day on ther friggin megadrives, don't thee?

—Is right.

I imagine him in the cinema, his hands over his face, peepin out from between his fingers. Then I imagine him as a little kid, all curled up in bed, dreamin about dinosaurs. But thee image is a wee bit disturbing cos I picture him with a small child's body but the head is the same as it is now, an adult's. Not a comfortable picture. I shake me head to get rid of it.

We wander round thee exhibits. Victor won't take his eyes off me; he's watchin me every move, listenin intently to everythin I say, seemingly fascinated by everythin I do. Thee attention is pure brilliant; it makes me feel beautiful. I don't feel self-conscious at all, it's like I can be completely meself, I don't have to act out any role or anythin because the person watchin me only wants to see *me*, just me, what I am. No pretence, no falseness, just me as I am. It's fuckin lovely. When we get to the skeleton of thee Irish elk Victor doesn't say a word, he just stands there watchin me staring up at the bones, the huge antlers. Just appraising an admiring he is, we both are. Me the elk an him me. He's standin behind me an I can't see his eyes but I know, completely, how intent thee'll be, all deep green an focused. Shapes movin through them.

Just wait til I get you in my flat, Victor. In my bedroom. Just you fuckin wait.

Like my blood is rubbing against itself.

We go back to the lift.

—Where to now, then?

He shrugs. —Dunno. The mummies?

Don't like the mummies. All that dry an rotten flesh. The grinnin skully teeth an the horribly elongated toes an fingers. I shake me head an tell him some story about how they've been taken into storage cos ther startin to decay or somethin an need to be treated. He suggests thee aquarium an just at the sound of that word I start to feel peaceful an calm. Cocooned in soft green light.

—*Yes*, I agree. —Me favourite place *ever* for comin down.

Which I mean in general terms; I'm not comin down *now*, like, I mean that line of beak has well worn off but I slept well last night an nearly all of the last few days' bingeing has left me now. I don't feel bad at all. Certainly not bodily; in fact I feel quite healthy, healthy an strong, especially with Victor here by me but he seems a bit distant an worried about something so in the lift as it sucks us down to the basement I kiss him once on the lips, just a quick peck, like, his full an soft lips an reach up to stroke the back of his neck with me fingernails an then drag me palm across his face an unable to stop meself I clutch his neck, squeeze slightly, feel his pulse bump against me palm an his muscles tense, I'm starin at his mouth I wanner see it fall open in helpless ecstasy how I wanner squeeze, crush, pulp choke pummel *squeeze* –

The doors slide open an I let go of him an leave the lift. Got a bit fuckin carried away, there, Kel. Me heart is thuddin but it slows as I step into the cool green gloom of thee aquarium, the driftin shapes an shadows, the delicate tinklin sounds of drippin an bubbling water. Like stepping under the sea an bein able still to breathe. Like a dream down here it is. I love it. So many times I've spent hours down here on me own, just staring.

There's three little kids standin on tiptoe to peer into a tank. One of them's shoutin that he can see a crab but another one's tellin him that it's just a stone. Thee make me feel good, ther excitement, ther enthusiasm. I think of the feel of Victor's neck, strong an muscled, an go over to the conger eel tank. Victor's standin behind me, rubbin his neck. I wave him over.

—Comen see the conger eel. Big feller. Spends most of his time under that big rock in the middle but sometimes he sticks his head out. Keep lookin.

No show. Just the rocks an pebbles an wavin weed. A couple of prawny things pickin across the floor, such fragile tiny claws. I glance sideways at Victor an thee expression of sadness on his face is so strong it almost rocks me back on me heels. He doesn't notice anything, he's evidently lookin down deep into himself, his face twitchin as if he's thinkin of somethin that actually physically upsets or stings him, so to distract him from whatever it is he's thinkin of I tell him somethin that I personally find deeply comfortin an peaceful, hopin that he will too, that these fish an prawns an things don't care about the date, they've got no conception of it, all thee wanner do is eat an swim no matter what time it is. That the most important thing to them is stayin alive, an if that's *all* there is to worry about then . . . Ar lives would be truly fuckin blessed, I want to say. I wanner say how awful it is to yearn to shed yer fuckin skin; to feel the fuckin canyons openin in yer heart an all yer've ever hoped for gushin into them, runnin away from yis. These thoughts suddenly make thee inside of me head feel all hot, an everythin that's happened in the past few days begins to glow red burning hot in me skull as does the closeness of Victor, the memory of his face changin colour an his eyes rollin back in his head an my head so fuckin hot, so sizzling, so to cool it I lean me forehead against the cold glass of the tank, feel the water behind it trickle soothingly in through glass an skin an bone an brain . . .

I could stay like this for ever. So calm, so quiet. Everythin fallin away from me then I start to feel empty, hollow inside, like, aching, yearning an Victor's here, his whole body to explore an I want suddenly, *need* suddenly to cram meself full of him an all the fuckin madness of this city an this world. Noise an movement an drugs an drink an faces an voices an flesh, bloody flesh comin apart in me hands. Music, *loud* fuckin music an the taste of blood on the back of me tongue.

—*Right* then. I push meself away from the glass, stand upright an spin to face Victor. His face. God, his fuckin *face*. —Charlie's in me pocket an it'll soon be night-time. Let's go the pub.

He grins. —Is right.

—Right.

I wanner get hammered, hammered off me face an do to Victor things I've never done before. Want to fuckin burst. Wanner see his face as he comes an use that image to scorch everythin else out of me brain. His spunk scalding me insides. His hot an frantic flesh yieldin to me fingers.

We're outside the museum, standin in the rain. I take his hand.

—Where'd yer wanner go?

—Not bothered, really. Anywhere. Where'd *you* fancy?

The way he's lookin at me. The friggin *need* in his face.

—Tell yer what, I say. —Let's start off in Matthew Street, yeh? Few bevvies, few toots, cut off somewhere else. Yeh?

I'm tryin to infect him with me enthusiasm. Which I think I have because he smiles wide an goes: —Sounds fuckin *ace* to me.

—Alright.

We flip ar hoods up over ar heads an head off, through St George's Gardens, towards tourist an thus mugger central. A bus drives past us, painted to look like a giant Cadbury's Double Decker bar, the faces behind the steamy windows lookin vaguely embarrassed. Travellin in a giant chocolate bar. How bleedin ridiculous. I take Victor's hand again, feel in it the need, thee ache. It fuckin scares me. It scares me thinkin how far I might go with him. The things I wanner do with him I don't really know about cos if I let them take shape they might fuckin terrify me. Make me want to run away, from him, from myself, from the two of us together an what we might be. What I might turn him into an turn meself into in the process. I'm fuckin scared. Worried. And as excited as I've ever been in me entire friggin life; the man trapped naked in the stocks an me above him holdin a cane, *fuck* that, it's got fuckin nothing on this. Me heart is cannoning blood through me face.

Outside the White Star an the rain *really* starts to come down so we dart into that pub. 'Hey Jude' playing. No fuckin surprises *there*, then. I need a toot.

—Get me a lager, I tell Victor. —I'm just off the bog.

—Okay.

Inside the toilet, me hands are tremblin as I chop up a line on the cistern. With this worry. This concern. This odd mixture; it's so fuckin ace an so fuckin frightenin at the same time,

Victor out there waitin for me, how he'll be waitin for me later tied to me friggin bed an me swoopin above him like an eagle. Picture me hands around his throat. Picture me hands carryin something, what, some stick, a club, a fuckin whip, my hand bunched into a fist an then that fuckin fist inside him squeezing his huge heart like a sponge. Feel like I'm exploding. Me hand wrapped tight around his dick his neck his balls, a hammer a truncheon a *knife* –

Calm the fuck down, Kelly. Yer fuckin losing it. It's too friggin much, yer goin fuckin crazy.

I chop out a line, roll a tenner into a tube, snort the beak. Feel better instantly; the bouncing of me brain starts to slow down or if not that then focus itself on one thing, one thing only which is me movements as I rewrap the cocaine an put it in me pocket. Me movements as I unroll the tenner an put it back in me purse. Just me as I sniffle an rinse me kite at the sink an look at meself in the mirror, the brightness of me eyes, how nice me hair looks in wet ringlets framin me face, me numb face. Me legs as I walk. The sway of me hips. Me back straight an me head up an me arsecheeks so tight.

That's better. That's *much* fuckin better.

There's Victor, over there, in the corner. How his face lights up when he sees me returning.

I sit down by him an take a big gulp of me pint, washin the coke residue down me throat. I sniff an wipe me nose an grin at Victor cos he's gawpin at me.

—What're yer lookin at?

—You.

—Why?

—Cos yer lookin at me.

I wipe me face with the sleeves of me fleece. Pass the wrap of nose to Victor under the table.

—Eeyar.

—Thanks.

—Charlie. Cut with a wee bit of whizz, I think. It's not bad.

He asks me who I bought it off. Can't tell him the truth, like; can't say that Peter gave it me cos I don't wanner do or say anything that might make him worry, not one tiny little bit. I want everythin to be perfect. A laugh, a good time, a totally worry-free day. Precious fuckin few of *them*.

—Just someone Roz knows, I say. —It's good stuff.

—Roz?

—Me mate. With the bleached hair? She was with me an Victoria in Magnet thee other night.

—Oh yeh.

He goes off to the lav. I watch his small arse move until I can't see it any more. His small, tight wee arse punchin against itself. I sip at the lager an sit back in the seat, me head humming, me face numb, warm expansion in me chest. Wanner close me eyes an smile. Wanner purr like a cat.

—Buy yis a drink, love?

I open me eyes. Tall skinny bloke standin over me. Lever Bros baseball hat, oil-stained, minty stonewashed jeans too tight. Minty bumfluff muzzy.

—No ta. I'm grand.

—Are yer?

—Yes I am as a matter of fact. I'm with someone.

—Who?

Jesus Christ. —He's just gone the bog.

He points back over his shoulder with his thumb. —*That* feller? I *know* him, I do. He's a druggy. Yer don't wanner click with *him*, love.

For fuck's sakes. —Yeh I do. Already friggin have. He's the best bloke I've ever met. An what friggin business is it of yours, then, ey? Never met yer before in me life.

He stands upright, weedy chest out, all aggrieved. —Just lookin out for yer, that's all. Jesus. Excuse *me* for havin a fuckin conscience, like.

—Yeh, well, don't bother. There's no need. I'm perfectly fuckin happy with who I'm with, thanks very friggin much.

I wave him away an he tuts an goes grumblin back to his stool at the bar. Knobhead. Typical of blokes, that, the way thee just assume that thee know what's good for yer, the way thee genuinely seem to believe that only *they* know what yer really want. Which is never, in reality, fuckin *them*. Got to feel sorry for them, really; it's only a lack of self-worth that makes them act that way. Thee know that ther useless an expendable so thee seek to endow themselves with a sense of importance in any way thee can. Still, tho, if someone acts like a friggin divvy, yer treat them like a friggin divvy, don't yer? Regardless of ther motives, like. His fuckin attitude of assumption, it's only a short step from there to shitty knickers, or fuckin crush videos. Yer can only react to people according to how thee act with you. An what the *fuck* would that feller know of me an Victor? Of me on thee edge of the bath with me legs open an Victor's face between them, what the *fuck* would he know? The swirl of hair on the crown of Victor's head. The knobbles of his bent spine. An his tongue snakin up inside me, partin me, muscling its way inside to lap at me uterus, up further into me womb. Feel horny as fuck just thinkin about it. Gettin wet an short of breath just rememberin it. I drain me glass.

God, Victor.

Here he comes. I watch him come.

—Alright?

He sniffs. —Not bad, yeh. Not bad at all.

I take the wrap back off him an stash it back in me purse.

—Some of the best bugle I've had in a *long* time.

—*Is* right.

He necks half of his drink in one go then nods at me empty glass.

—Jesus. Yer drank *that* quick.

—Yeh.

—Djer want another?

I shake me head. Bloke at the bar's staring hard, the piped Beatles are gettin on me nerves. All the pictures of dockyards on the walls, of ships on the Mersey. When this city finally becomes just one giant theme park, this pub'll be the one marketed as offerin thee 'Authentic Liverpool Experience'. Complete with resident gobshite at the bar. Sometimes feel like a friggin cartoon in pubs like this.

—Nah, I say. —I wanner get out of here, to be honest. It's a bit too fuckin . . . *Scousey* in here. Gets on me friggin wick sometimes.

257

He laughs. —Yeh, I know what yer mean.

—The Beatles an that.

He nods, agreein. —The great port we once were.

—Jerry an the fuckin Pacemakers.

—Stan bastard Boardman.

That one makes me laugh. Stan fuckin Boardman; what the fuck would he have done for a career if the German bombers had've missed his chippy?

Baseball hat at the bar is staring over, no, *glaring* over, unashamedly borin his eyes into me. Every now an again he steals a glance at Victor an yer can see it in his eyes, the puzzle, the bafflement; what the fuck, he's thinking, does a girl like that see in the scruffy no-mark next to her? Why the fuck is she with *him*? Why *him*? And, more to the point, why not fuckin *me*? An I'm thinkin, in return: yer'll never fuckin know, lad. None of youse'll ever fuckin know.

Victor drains his glass. —Alright. Where to, then?

—Flanagan's.

—Flanagan's it is.

We get up an go. Passin the bar an the bloke in the baseball hat says: —Ey, girl.

I just walk past, ignorin the dickhead. Go out the door, into the still-falling rain. Feelin a bit shitty; I mean, he was a prick, that bloke in there, but he's obviously a lonely prick an I shouldn't've really turned me back on him like that. Bit fuckin rude; bit fuckin superior. I hope Victor didn't smirk at him, in that 'I've-got-what-*you*-want' way; I would friggin *hate* that, I would. Can't stand people who smirk.

Victor comes out an we leg it around the corner into Flanagan's Apple. It's heavin in here, people shelterin from the rain, steam an smoke an the smell of wet clothes. Fuckin ace; exactly how a pub *should* be. A gang of pissed-up ahl dears in the corner are bellowin along to 'The Day Delaney's Donkey Won the Half-Mile Race'. Theer havin a friggin great time.

I take me purse out, take the droogs out an slip them into the kangaroo pocket of Victor's fleece.

—I'll get the bevvies in, you goan have another line. Lager, yeh?

—Yeh.

He scoots downstairs an I shoulder me way to the bar. One of thee advantages of bein youngish an fairly pretty is that blokes at bars part for yer like the Red Sea for Moses. Or most of them do, at least; there's often thee odd dirty fucker who'll try an rub against yis, or the probly-impotent power-trippin get who likes to see yer struggle. But most of them are sound.

—Eeyar, let the girl through. One massive feller in a Celtic shirt sweeps his mates aside with a tree-trunk arm. —There yer go, love . . . PADDY! He roars at one of the barmen an points at the top of me head with a finger like a banana when Paddy looks up, over the crush of heads at the bar. Paddy nods an looks at me, eyebrows raised.

—Two pints of lager.

—Export?

—Yeh.

—Now.

He pours the drinks, hands them over to me, takes the money. The ahl dears are now singin 'Wild Colonial Boy', which is better, altho rat-arsed as thee are they've slowed it down far too much an are singin 'da dee' an 'da dum' instead of most of the proper words. I see Victor through the crowd lookin around for me, lookin so friggin lost an innocent; I wave to him an he smiles relieved an makes his way over to me, wormin his way through the close-packed people. He returns the wrap to me an I give the drinks to him an go off to the bog. Lock meself in a cubicle, Christ, how many fuckin times have I done this, how many times have I shut meself in pub toilets, breathin in disinfectant an other people's molecules of shit an piss an chopped up expensive powders on the cold porcelain of the cistern? Or rubbed those powders on me gums, or wrapped them up in a Rizla an swallowed them? Or hunched over to be sick? So many times. Too many times.

Chop out an snort two lines. I remember, suddenly, years ago in this very fuckin cubicle, I think it was, bein shagged by a bloke called Stuart. Years ago this was, durin some big football tournament, USA '94 or Euro '96, one of them. A blurry drunken knee-trembler in this very bog. Stuart holdin me legs up around his waist an pantin, whimperin, almost bleedin *crying* into me neck as he came. Not a bad shag, as I remember, affectionate, like, not that I particularly *do* remember it in any great detail; all those years ago an I was wrecked at the time anyway. But one thing I remember, or rather *know*, perfectly clearly, is how inferior to Victor Stuart was, how inferior they've *all* been; how thee all lack Victor's presence, the way he displaces air as he moves, his slim hips, his smile. The bare fuckin *need* in him an the wholeness surroundin him as he comes, his neck gulpin for air under me thumbs. How he looks so fuckin lost out in the world, lost an empty, an how full an found he seems when he's in me an I'm on him an he's coming. There's nobody like him. He's unique. He takes everything in. No man has ever been like him an I'm gunner fuckin keep him, hold him, mark the bastard as mine. I found him an he's mine.

I go back up the stairs, into the main bar. See Victor at a table on his own an make me way over towards him. I feel eyes on me an notice a group of office girls at a table against the wall givin me dirty looks, lookin me up an down. One of them's sneerin, the snotty cow. I stick me tits out an exaggerate the sway of me hips. Give the bitches somethin to sneer about. I sit down next to Victor.

—Alright?

—Sound.

Delve in me bag for cigarettes, give one to Victor, light us both up. Love the way smokin feels when I'm charlie'd, me lungs openin wide, chest swellin. Me knees are jitterin an me fingers are tremblin an I feel absolutely fuckin top. Victor's right by me, smellin of lemons, I watch his hands gesturin as he talks, hear him laughin, hear *myself* laughin. Everythin movin quickly now. Smoke in twin streams from Victor's nostrils. The pupils of his eyes so big, black holes to suck the city in, to suck *me* in. An sometime later he's up at the bar, leanin against it buyin drinks, I'm lookin at his legs an bum an the slopes of his back an watchin thee office girls watch him too, ther all drinkin different-flavoured Hooches an nudgin each other an appraising Victor up at the bar, sizing him up, an I feel a power surge inside me belly, how ace an cool Victor looks how lean an confident up there at the bar an the women liking him, admiring him, an the fuckin things I've done to him the things I'm *going* to do to him, none of those women will ever friggin know. They like him, yeh, thee see something in him that thee evidently like an thee'll never see him beneath them, his face dissolvin in ecstasy. Thee'll never feel him breakin apart in ther hands, an why, cos the fucker's *mine*. He's marked as mine an mine only.

My ache for him starts to throb in me skull. Like a fire in me nape, where spine meets skull. An intense heat. It's a kind of completeness, definitely, but inside that is a weakness an it's thee ache I have for him. The pain I have to feel him burstin inside me is like a weakness in me howlin in me chest an even tho I know I'll feel him later on, his flesh in me hands an his flesh inside me the fuckin rapture on him, it still means that I'm sittin here now not entirely up to strength, some defences down, like, an all I've built for meself, around an within meself has this hole at the centre of it so it could all come fallin down an I don't fuckin like that. I don't, no. It's fuckin dangerous. Not fuckin safe to be out in the city full of drink an drugs when there's an absence inside yis. It's a weakness, there's a fault in there. I'll be stronger. I'll have to build up strength. I'll be as strong as a friggin ox tonight when Victor's all open below me. Too right I fuckin will.

He comes back with the drinks. Drink an more drugs in the toilets, each of us in turn, more drink an spinnin an sounds, no past no future only this lovely moment an sometime later we're in a taxi an it's night-time an the city is all lit up an we're movin through it. Bright clusters of lights an the vast slices of pink then blue as the laser beams an spotlights cut over the city. Victor's hand is on me leg an mine too is on his. His muscle hard on me palm. I notice a wee Francis Jeffers shirt hangin from the rear-view mirror of the cab an I start to quietly sing:

—*There's a bluenose over there . . . over there . . .*

Victor holds his hand up over his face. He's laughin. An then we're in thee Albert Dock somewhere, some jazz saxophone an lights on dark lappin water. It's the Blue Bar we're in, drinkin bottles of Beck's at a dockside table. Victor's face is half in shadow an he's holdin me hands on the steel table top which is freezin fuckin cold. His teeth are chattering. He's lovely. *I'm* lovely. Everythin is friggin great.

—Fuck me stiff. I'm freezing.

—Me too, I say. Then: —What the *fuck* are we doin, sittin outside?

—Yeh. Let's go in.

We do. Find a space at the bar. There are two faces by mine, two faces which I've seen many times flat an shiny on a page or too colouful on a telly screen, lookin too kind of big, too friggin dimensional now, in the flesh. It's Louise Nurding an Jamie Redknapp. I half expect Victor to say somethin bloke-ish an *Loaded*-y about Louise but he doesn't, he just glances at her then looks at me. I lean close to him an whisper:

—Mind yer don't nudge him with yer elbow. He'll be out injured for the rest of the season.

He laughs. A group of suits vacate a table an Jamie an Louise go over an sit down at it. I watch one of the suits return to lean on the table grinnin sloppily an say something to them. Can't hear what he's sayin but it looks drunkenly earnest an a bit friggin embarrassing. He's really fuckin leanin into ther space, like, his flushed face right in thers. Ther just bein polite, like, half-smilin, half-noddin as he slurs. I'm thinkin how terrible it must be, to be famous an all them people presuming that yer wanner talk to them, presuming that yer won't be pissed off when thee interrupt yer evenin out. To be everyone's fuckin property like that. An maybe I say this thought aloud cos Victor's lookin at me, a whole fuckin story in his face, but all he says is: —Yeh.

I finish me bottle. Wanner move, walk, travel. Be somewhere different. Flit around the city like a starling. —Come ed. Let's move on somewhere else, eh?

—Alright well.

Then we're in a taxi again an it's impossible not to touch him, me arms are around him an his face is in me neck the tip of his nose cold against me skin he's holdin me tight, squeezin me to him an I'm strokin his back, kneadin the prominent muscles at his shoulders an I can smell his hair an feel his heat, feel the thump of his heart an I'm tellin him these things, whisperin them close to his ear how lovely he feels against me an how he smells good enough to wrench open with me teeth an feel him trickle all hot down me gullet an how I'd like to fuck him right here in the back of the cab, just rip his fuckin clothes off an throw him to the floor an pounce on him. I can feel him growing, gettin hard against me hip. So fuckin horny I am. But the city is all spread out so big an bright around me an I want the linked shadows of me an Victor to fall across it, drift through it, wreck it, absorb it all.

I see the yowge Chinatown gates through the window. I tell the driver to let us out here an he does an then we're out in the cold air again, the gates towerin over us.

—Shanghai, I'm murmurin to meself. —Shipped all the way from fuckin Shanghai . . . so fuckin far away . . .

Then we're in the Nook, I'm in the tiny toilet tooting more, then we're in the Brewery drinkin bottles of Newky Brown beneath the big screen, shoutin at each other to be heard because it's friggin packed an I can smell weed burnin an we're both bein bounced around by the pissed an swayin crush of people an it's annoyin, a pain, we can't hear or often even see each other. So then we're downstairs in O'Neill's an I'm in the toilets snortin again then I'm drinkin an waitin for Victor to come back from the bogs where he's gone not to snort but pee.

Fuck. The speed of things now.

I'm thinkin that, when he comes back, I'm gunner tell him. No point keepin quiet. Some secrets should be kept but this shouldn't even *be* a secret an if it's not then it should be shared. No room for embarrassment or doubt in a situation like this, yer should be utterly fuckin open an upfront an hide nothin cos if yer do that's what will in thee end drive a wedge between yis. Got to be open, an honest. Honest, yeh that's the word; got to be totally fuckin honest. Just tell him. When he comes back from the bog just look at him an say:

—Yes, love?

I look up, see a barman lookin at me. I'm at the bar. Fuck,

I thought I was still sittin down. Might as well get more ales in while I'm here.

—Two bottles of brown please.

—Newcastle or Mann's?

—Newcastle.

I take the bottles, see Victor sittin back in his seat. I go over to him an give him a bottle an he gulps at it an the foam fizzes over on to his hand. I take a swig, put the bottle down, me heart goin like a fuckin machine-gun then Victor's face is at my ear I can feel his breath all warm on me cheek an he's sayin something, what's he saying, he's sayin that he'd do anythin for me, *anything*, he's never met anyone like me an I amaze him an he'd do absolutely fuckin anything for me. I know he would.

—I *know* yer would, Victor.

—Fucking *anything*. Nobody I've ever . . .

This stuff he's saying. These words. Humming in me head like heat, almost like pain.

—I'd do anything for you, Kelly. Fucking anything.

And it rises inside me. Redness at me tear ducts, I can see the redness pulse in the corners of me eyes, pulsin fast in rhythm with me heartbeat. Feel a growling begin in me throat.

—I'd *make* you.

—You're . . . fuck, you're . . .

His face crumples an he makes a few noises, not real words, just sounds. To stop them he takes a swallow of beer an frowns an he looks so fuckin childlike. So like a little boy. I hang me arms around his neck an sing a daft little song about his name, an he smiles an stops lookin innocent an sweet an starts to look dirty, so fuckin sexy, his full lips parted showin his teeth an the lights in his green eyes all fuckin gorgeous sexy as fuck me mouth is at his ear, the clean bleached shell of his ear an me voice is thick I'm saying:

—I'm gunner make you come so much . . . I'm gunner make you do things yer've *never* fuckin done before . . . things yer've never thought that yer *could* do . . . yer gunner beg me to stop an beg me to carry on at the same time . . . yer gunner fuckin *explode*, man, yer gunner fuckin *burst* . . .

He blinks. And in that blink I see a promise of his face fallin apart, losing itself, all his ego meltin away around him an just him an the moment an his bliss an my insides shattered with his coming, with *my* friggin coming. Clasp an groan an pant an squirm an writhe an roar an bleed, bleed like a body hacked open an the fuckin heart swiped out on a slab. On an altar.

—We're goin back to mine. C'mon, you.

Another taxi an Christ the fuckin *speed* of things now. Goin up Hardman Street, very fuckin apt cos me hand is on Victor's balls an I can feel him hardening an I'm squeezing his balls through his jeans, feelin them against my skin an the fibrous strings that attach them to his body. He's whimperin an his knees are wobblin uncontrollably. His bollox bulge. I squeeze them hard an wanner feel them give, split, crumple. Me heart like a gnashin mouth in me chest. Taste in me throat like copper, like blood. At the traffic lights there's a face peerin in the window on Victor's side, a shouting face.

—It's Vic! It's Victor with that bird from Magnet! Come quick, comen see this it's ar fuckin Victor with that bird! Look!

Three faces against the window now, all of them whoopin an roaring. With me free hand I waggle me fingers at them an the taxi pulls away. Victor goes to say something but I tell him not to talk an squeeze his balls even tighter an his whole fuckin body not just his dick stiffens as if I've just pumped him full of air. This power within me like cracklin neon in me head. A power like nothing, of a completely different kind to that I felt when shredding the stocked man's arse. Different, better, *cleaner* – it's somehow sharper, wider, I can feel it in the soles of me feet, in the secret places inside me, all the wet caves. Not like the power I felt when wielding the cane, fuck no, this is like fuckin *being* the cane, bein somethin utterly itself. Thee air whippin around me an me slicing through it.

I have to let go of Victor when we stop outside me house so's I can get coins from me purse to pay the cabbie. Victor kind of slumps in his seat when me hand leaves him. I pay an we get out an I let us into the house an I'm fuckin shoving him up the stairs, me hand on his back, I don't wanner let go of him, I'm guiding him up, up to the place where *what* will happen? Blood an bursting. Groans. Limbs shakin without control. I let us into the flat an Victor goes off to the bathroom an I go into the kitchen, not for any reason that I know of, I'm just in the kitchen as if I've been led here or something has possessed me, I'm not myself. I don't know who this person is, walkin around inside my body. This person makin me do things, I've never met them before.

The kitchen. A place where things are sliced an burned. Knives an fire in here.

I go into the bathroom. Me hands curled into claws at me sides. Teeth grinding in me ears. Victor is bendin over to look closely at something on thee edge of the bath.

—What're yer lookin at?

I see it; the lid of me musk body spray. Then I remember.

—Oh shit, the spider. He's not dead, is he?

I give the lid a little flick. The wee spider moves one of his legs.

—Good. He's still alive. I caught him before an must've forgotten to throw him out. He's been stuck under there all day, poor little sod.

I slide him off the edge of the bath an into me cupped palm, take him to the window an shake him off outside. —Go on. Be free. Goan eat flies.

Turn back to Victor, that fuckin Victor. He's standin there, watchin me. The fear an need in his eyes. Punish him, fuckin *hurt* him. See the light when he squirms an gasps. I'm gunner go so fuckin far with him. I'm gunner break the boundaries, I'm gunner be fuckin obscene. Just the thought of that obscenity arouses me. I must be fuckin obscene myself, an that thought too turns me on even further. I am obscene, I am *obsceeeeeeene*. Turns me on all to fuck.

—Where were we, Victor? Where were we up to?

I move over to him.

—You were . . .

—I was what? I put my face in his, studyin his physiognomy, the shape of his jaw, his small ears, the tiny wrinkles at the sides of his eyes an mouth. Me hand leaps like a snake an fastens round his balls an he buckles back against the wall, kept upright only by my clutchin hand. —Doin this?

—Nnnnnnn.

—Is *this* what I was doin? Yeh?

Feel my fuckin arm like oak. Squeeze harder, grind, grind his balls against each other. Pain. Cause pain.

—Yer like me doin this?

He nods, just one floppy movement of his head. All his limbs loose, dangling, his gob slack an his eyelids drooping. As if with me hand I'm pullin all the resilience out of his bones an flesh.

I whisper in his ear. —Tell me what yer think I should do. Tell me . . . what I should do to you.

Love this fuckin *love* this. Never so much promise in anythin else ever.

—I want yer to tell me . . . Squeeze. —. . . what I should do.

He groans an his head rocks. He murmurs something which sounds like 'spit on me'.

—*Spit* on you?

—Spit in my face.

Yeh. Use, abuse. Debase, deface. Trample all over this fucker while the world spins around youse.

I hawk up in me throat; it's just natural, automatic, like, to hawk up a big catarrhal snotter. An then blast it out between me lips into his face. Big oyster on his face, green, slimy.

He yells: —Aw Christ! Not like that! Just spit, not a big fuckin greenie!

Streamers of me snot like icicles from his eyebrows an thee end of his nose. I can't help but laugh. I let go of his balls an bend over clutchin me stomach, really fuckin laughin. 'Spit in me face': hawk, ptoo. Snotter. That's friggin hilarious.

Victor joins in. Both of us in fits an his face all gooey with snot.

I tell him, through me laughter, I'm sorry. —It just came natural, yer see. Just fuckin automatic like to hoik up before I spit.

I wash his face with a wet flannel. He turns to dry himself

with the towel hangin on the door an I watch him do that an all laughter leaves me an it's like the demon is in me again tellin me to hurt him, mark irreparably his soft unblemished skin. Make it fuckin mine. He turns an instantly I grab his neck, slam him back against the door. I can feel an hear him gulpin, gurglin.

—Is *this* what yer want? Is *this* it?

He nods.

—Yeh.

Nods again. Says in a strangled voice: —Frighten me, Kelly . . . scare me. Make me tremble.

An then I'm behind him, holdin him firm by hair an belt an shovin him out of the bathroom an down into the bedroom, throwin him on the bed me arms like fuckin pistons powering an he lands an bounces an turns over an there the fucker is below me, all spread, the street lights outside illuminating half of him, the left half. Half light, half dark he is. I will tear him limb from limb.

I order him to take his clothes off. Standin over him like a predator I am. Outside, a dog barks four times. —Take *all* yer fuckin clothes off.

He sits up on thee edge of the bed an I watch him undress. His movements fluid an easy, no awkwardness or hesitation as if he's puttin clothes *on* instead of takin them off. There's his feet. Surprisingly small toes. There's his arms, rising like swans' necks to pull the T-shirt over his head an there's his torso, shadows slashed across his ribcage, flat boards of his pectorals an the scribble of hair around his deep belly button. His legs with ther prominent knees an his thighs swelling. His dick erupting from the top join of those thighs. His balls clustered, I can almost see them moving, crawlin around inside the bag.

Utterly fuckin naked. Exposed entirely an without defence. I feel a trembling in me joints, *all* of me joints.

—Lie on the bed now. On yer back.

He does. I take four scarves from me chest of drawers an tie the bastard up, each limb to a corner of the bed, his feet bent down at ankle over thee end of the mattress an attached to the bed legs so that his pelvis thrusts up, his hard dick an balls raised ceilingwards, offered. Thee accentuation of ther bulging, the demon in me affronted almost at ther proud occupation of space. Crush. Slice. Bruise. Unable to move or protect himself he is all opened out below me an me head reels with the things I wanner do, *will* do, to him. It's like I have all this strange fuckin beauty before me an I can wreck it an it will spring back pristine again like in a cartoon. Mash an grope an twist. The pain that I will see become ecstasy on his face, such precious unknown sensation. Thee only way I can get to know him, to see him like this so open, so friggin exposed, naked an offered, laid out like a sacrifice. Inside him I want to be, *right* fuckin inside him; me fingers, me hand inside him like I remember at Sunday school the fingers of Doubting Thomas inside Christ's wounds, that picture in the bible we had, all garish-coloured an the probing fingers delving, pokin inside the gapin slashes red-lipped an moist like cunts. I wanner know fuckin *all* of him, all about him, what he thinks about when he wakes up of a morning, what his dreams are, what memories possess him an what he was like as a little boy or a baby. What makes him laugh or cry or wanner throw up or yearn for more, for more, for more. Wanner know every last inch of this fucking body tied spread beneath me, every last fuckin inch of it; every pore, every hair on his head an body, dimples pimples, the way the skin pulls in his armpits when he lifts up his arms or the shining pinkness inside his mouth an the stains an chips in his teeth. All the different greens of his eyes. Every last vein on his dick, every goosebump on his balls, his puckered pink arsehole I imagine like a little clenched fist. The sinews taut on the backs of his legs as thee strain now against the bonds, all of this, all of it, all of this an more, there's always more to fuckin know an it's only here that I'll find it, here now in this rented bedroom like this, everythin in the fuckin world that matters compressed to fit now inside these four walls.

Things start to move faster now.

I take me kit off an straddle him. Pull at his nipples hard to make him yelp, crush me mouth to his, suckin at his breath still twistin at his nipples feel his blasts of pain an shock against the back of me throat. I shuffle backwards to sit on his legs an grab his balls an *pull*, hard, feel his legs jerk an thrash in outraged surprise, pull an twist an wrench, wantin to drag them away from his body, wantin to hold them severed an ragged an spurtin in me hand. I'm delving, stabbin me fingers into his gateways, his ears, mouth, navel, armpits, tryin to stuff me whole hand into his gob an then tickling his rock-hard knob an jammin me fingers down between his legs an up rigid into his arse, the clingin heat, muscle resistance blundered through. He is yellin, cryin out. His eyes tightly closed an I put me hands on his face an force his eyelids apart, stare closely into his eyes at the fear an thee ache there, almost like lookin into deep space through a telescope, the vast blacknesses criss-crossed with comets' glowin tails.

I caress his lips. Feel ther full softness against me fingertips as thee flicker at my touch. I'm hangin open, yawning I am, I can feel meself so painfully fuckin empty down there so I reach down under my arse to grab his dick, his iron dick an place the tip of it against my cunt an slide meself backwards on to it, get filled, stretched, plugged. Aw God the fuckin *relief*. Thrustin back on to his hardness I feel him inside me, pushin up into me, feel the walls of me fanny spasming an clutchin an the tight fire in me clitoris as it grinds against his pubic bone, his hips are jerkin spasmodically up against me I see the rapid rise an fall of his chest I place me hands around his gulpin neck an squeeze so tight, feel the contraction in me wrists an the muscle effort straining in me shoulders, *that's* how tight I'm squeezing an instantly his cock swells still further, his balls bulge more an butt up against me slamming arse. The features of his face seem to slide down into the mattress. I'm lifted up as he arches his back up off the bed an I can hear a whining in his heavin chest as he struggles for air, I squeeze tighter fuckin *tighter* me fingers almost meeting at his nape an his eyes roll back to show just white an his lips hang open his breath leaving in one warm wave the bliss in him, the bliss in him he bucks an thrashes the spectrum in his face from white to pink to red the purple veins bulging at his temples such colour he thrashes an explodes inside me, one lightning blast the hot jet of his come imagine it like tracer bullets rocketing through my wet, dark places, feel his dick buck an pulse an then I'm gone as well, dragged into me orgasm, fuckin *yanked* up into it hammerin with me fists on his chest in an attempt to smash me way through his ribcage to his thudding heart an grab that heart squirting an crush it in me hands. I've fuckin melted, all of me, melted an imploded an poured steaming out of me own cunt. I'm shoutin things, callin Victor names. Biting me lip, tastin blood. Hearin him below me coughin an splutterin, whooping as he takes air into starved lungs, knowin that he's been somewhere rapturous an I wanner reach inside him an drag something of that out, see what it looks like in thee air. What shape it is, what colour it is. Stuff it up into meself. Make it fuckin mine.

His face: purple red pink an back to white. Gleaming with thick sweat. I'm bent forwards on his chest, me head resting there. His heartbeat loud an fast but slowing in me ear, his lungs snatchin at air, gulpin in great whoops of it which sound to me like the distant roaring rumble of an avalanche, a landslide beginnin to shift. His slippery chest against me cheek, pressed. Waitin for everythin to slow down.

An everything slows down. His dick, soft now, spent, slurps out of me an I feel a glut of goo follow it.

I'm empty again. So fucking empty.

I push meself off him an stand, lookin down on him. The way he's all spread, the fucked-ness of him . . . I'm fuckin unsatisfied. I want more. Me head is bombarded with images, thoughts, a bright burning light an blood drippin across it, bones snapping, lungs an mouth roaring. There's more I want. I'm knockin against meself inside.

Untie him. He groans an sits up on the bed, rubbin at his wrists an ankles. In this half-light I see skin rubbed raw, dark-coloured. Bracelets of beaded blood. Huggin his knees to his chest an the shape of him, the huddle of him, his eyes so big an wide an the sweat gleamin on his pale skin I want the fucker tied down again, strapped down for me. There's fuckin nothing I won't do. I'm growlin in me chest.

—Turn over, I tell him. —Lie on yer belly.

So fuckin compliant he is. Useless tosser. So fuckin bendable, malleable. A willin sacrifice. My God the shapes I'll put you in. The twisted fuckin shapes.

Retie him. Shove his fuckin face in the pillow. The tensed muscles in his back like stretched canvas an his arse like some fruit, some splittable, suckable, pulpable fruit. Unmarked page of his skin. I become aware of a car alarm shrieking outside which, as soon as I become aware of it, stops. My God all that unmarked skin.

I leave the room. Go into the kitchen. All me blood like molten lead, hot an howling at me pulse points all I can think about is that virgin skin an how I must fuckin mark it, make it mine, the huge fuckin need in me to know as he walks through the world that there is something on him that singles him out as mine, my work, something that declares what we've done, ar connection. Something on *him* that isn't on anybody else an could never be.

I'm like a puppet. This isn't me, this is someone else; here in this kitchen is not me, it's someone else lookin in the fuckin cutlery drawer.

Trance.

And a quick memory, sudden, clear; one of me teenage boy-friends, an uncontrollable nutter called Colm, Colm Downey. How I used to write KELLY + COLM everywhere. On bus stops, on bus seats, or carve it into park benches or the bark of trees or freshly laid concrete. KELLY + COLM all over the city. How I wanted everyone to see it. The pride I had in advertising it, ar togetherness. It wasn't a particularly innocent relationship, like, despite ar youth, not with all the drugs an the fighting an the madness but the pure excitement in it I would love to feel again, the pure excitement of it which is now impossible to recapture so there's nothin to do but trap it, forcibly, twist it, fuckin warp it. Free the purity inside it. That beats inside the memory of what once was.

Trance. My hand reachin out for the knife. Colm Downey long gone, fuck knows where, an Victor strapped to the bed. The knife in me hand. Small vegetable knife. Sharp, serrated. This knife in my hand.

I'm back in the bedroom. Trance. I'm straddlin Victor again, me weight settling in the small of his back. Steel catches the street light an gleams. Trap him in my thighs. As immobile as possible render him. Pool of wet heat between my legs, where my cunt clasps his skin, all that pure skin under me I can't help but sigh at its untouched clean sheen. The bulge of it over the shoulder blade. The blade. So smooth. Blank canvas, flat page. Raise the knife.

Carve.

One vertical stroke bloodless at first then rapid flush black an trickle, spread, Victor immediately bucking an thrashing an howling beneath me tryin to throw me off like an unbroken horse I force his head down into the pillow with me left hand. The knife is digging an cutting the skin parts with the soft sound of torn tissue an the blood black in the sodium light runs an rivulets. Back muscles shift startled an ripple as if attempting to flee the blade, rodeo-me on Victor as he pitches an bucks. The words takin shape, my own brand takin shape, obscured by the freed blood which I smear away with the side of me hand. Screams from him, from his twisted head, from his mouth stuffed with pillow:

—KELLY! PLEASE STOP KELLY! PLEASE STOP KELLY YER FUCKIN *HURTING* ME, YER *HURTING* ME! DON'T! PLEASE DON'T!

Shove his face still deeper into that mufflin pillow. No words from him now just baffled screams. The knife strokes an slashes, a legend takin shape, spreadin dark slick on that white skin an I feel hot dampness on my inner thighs, either *I've* pissed meself or *he* has. *He* has; I can feel it squirting up from beneath him. Me hand moves, the blade carves on. He goes loose beneath me, his resistance gone, flaccid with acceptance. He's crying, I think. I can hear him sobbing in the pillow. God, I could dig right fuckin through him. Take his bleedin heart out through his ribcage. I'm not lookin through my eyes but the booming inside me is *my* heart only, just mine, *my* heart an *my* power an the fuckin mad world I'm standin on.

The last letter, an R. Cut in. The fucker's marked. He's *mine*. Force you to walk topless the streets of this city, displayin your brandin to thee eyes. Human fuckin park bench you, thick-barked tree, a record of baby relationships or wants. I get off him an go over to the dresser in the corner, put the knife on there an take a jar of cold cream back over to the bed an the trussed-up carved-up fucked-up Victor. Most of the bleeding stopped now, the cuts not too deep at all. Should heal fairly quickly, them words in his skin. I scoop some cream out on to his back an start to smooth it in, gentle swipes, like, a soft stroking. His sobs subside, his muscles relax an slacken. Cease ther bunching an straining.

—There . . . it's alright . . . ther not too deep. It's okay, Victor. It's all okay.

Jesus Christ the things I could do. Delve, plummet. Plunge in. Violate.

—Poor Victor . . . *my* Victor. Don't worry about a thing.

Just me an you an your wounds, my marks. Nothing of the world inside here, nothin of it between us, the new millennium world with its noise an intrusion an billion pointless images. Price tags an brands. A bondage dead different to the one here in this room, thick chains an padlocks wrapped around that place in yis in which yer still fuckin sleep against yer mother. Where yer all still new an whole. Hidden places inside yis, all those secrets never to be known. *Inside* yer, deep fuckin inside yer. Deep breathin here an wounded peace an nothin of ther shite, fuckin stupid useless time-wastin jobs an life runnin out an obsessions in yer face forced down yer fuckin throat naked screaming freedom you fuckers you cunts at last for one moment I am left alone. *Inside* you.

Victor turns his head. A movement which sets off a muscle reaction down his shoulders an ripped back an into the muscles of his arse, those big round muscle-sheets at the sides. That doorway into him, into his heart, the boilin brewery of him containin all that he physically is. Such places inside him. Such secret fuckin places. His pure an beatin heart.

—Can I go now?

Such a small voice. I tell him: —Not yet, Victor, no. There's something else I need to do. Won't be long now.

Trance. I cover my right forearm in cold cream, from fingertips to elbow. Pull it on like a glove. To feel his life held in me palm, heavy an hot, throb an pulse, thee ultimate power of him decided in a simple twitch of me fuckin fingers. Thee ultimate closeness. Such sensation on my skin, all over me fuckin skin.

I pull at him an spread him an see a small howling mouth. Or a third eye hidden that sees, sees what? God knows. *I'll* find out.

An uncontrollable force inside.

Me fingers pinched together into a point an then that point inside him. Twist an push, fuckin *shove* against the muscle resistance, *shove* from thee elbow from the shoulder until that resistance gives, snaps simultaneous with Victor crying out one sudden high bark of shock an the startling sudden cling of him on me, so hot an clutching on me disappearing arm I'm wearin him like a puppet an me fuckin head roars. Inside him I am, fuckin *inside* him, me fingers flexing among the vital parts of him an ther heat, ther fiery heat. My wrist is gone. I can't see me wrist. Only a blood-streaked collar of cold cream at the point where I enter him about halfway up me forearm where me an him are joined, his hips are bucking an he is both sobbin an screamin an suckin air in over his teeth as he comes, he's coming again, me arm is *right* fuckin inside him I'm squeezin something that feels like a tennis ball made of wet sand an he's spurting again, dribblin again into thee already saturated mattress. The cling of him, like silk like muscle like tidal mud. Like the time when I was small an I plunged me arm into a wobblin mass of frogspawn in a rain bucket. His heartbeat on me bunched knuckles so fuckin close, I push me arm in still further an feel me fist bump up against something hard like bone. I feel somethin tear, give against me fingers an see two twin trickles of blood run down to me elbow.

He's talking. Sayin something:

—Stop . . . please stop . . . please let me go, Kelly . . . I really can't fuckin stand any more . . .

Pulse racing in me throat, such an intense heat behind me eyes. I withdraw me arm, pull it slurpin an suckin towards me an suddenly it is cold, released, chased by a clot of dark stuff from the pinioned drainpipe arsehole an a thick, soily stink. Dark streaks on me hand, up me arm. The smell. The smell of his inner self where he grows things an nurtures them like compost an muck an a garden after rain.

I go into the bathroom. Don't turn on the light cos I don't wanner see too clearly an wash me hands at the sink, wash them thoroughly, an leave the tap runnin while I sit on thee edge of the bath an frig meself off, a couple of fingertip rubs an I come, unpleasant really, like a necessary purge. Burstin a boil or something. Turn the tap off, put a dressin gown on to cover meself up an go back into the bedroom. See him there tied face down an what the fuck have I done to him. The words hacked into his back. The clouds of blood on his upper thighs an arsecheeks. Oh Christ. Oh fuck. Just look what I've fuckin done.

Coming back into meself now. Runnin back into meself. Taste of iron on the tongue an salt sting in each eye.

I untie him. Wrists an ankles chafed raw, the skin abraded away. I feel sick. I cannot look at him as he gets painfully up off the bed an puts his clothes back on. Turn my face away, catch an accidental glimpse of him in the dresser mirror, his leg bent at the knee as he steps into his jeans, an hear his little moan of pain. I am so fuckin sorry. Jesus Christ, what have I done. Victor, you bastard, what the *fuck* did yer make me do to you with yer innocence an yer fuckin difference. Your fuckin, your rareness. Fillin me with such urges. Such an uncontrollable force. Ah Christ, you fucker, I'll never be the same again.

Fully clothed now he glances at me an I shake me head, unable to meet his eyes. What would I see in them? I say, without really intendin to, one word:

—I.

That's it; just 'I'. Can't say anythin more.

He's shaking. His hands are shaking. He walks past me on delicate, painful steps. I wanner reach out for him an pull him to me but I'm rooted to the spot, listenin to him leave, doors closin, footsteps descendin, more doors closing. Leavin just a smell and an action painting on me sheets.

Jesus Christ, Kelly, what the *fuck* have you done.

What the fuck. Have you done.

Everythin's changed. Changed fuckin everything now.

I run to the window in the front room an look down into the street below, see Victor limping towards a taxi. Victor so bleedin small from this height. He gets in the cab an I watch it pull away, squintin for a glimpse of him through the rear window but all's I can see is the yellow glare of reflected street lights on the glass. I watch it turn a corner, go out of sight.

Wanderin whimperin through thee empty flat. Mad couple of days, *mad* couple of days. Neck two, no fuck it *three* diazepam, knock meself out. Oblivion, not caring that I use the stuff of him his blood an spunk an tears an piss an shit as a bed. It's comfortable enough, if a bit cold. Soft enough to sleep on.

Mad fuckin couple of days. *Insane* fuckin couple of days, take them away take them away, far far afuckinway.

Stiflin an cramped in here, in the laundrette. Behind the little porthole of the machine me sheets tumble soapy, all of his fluids an stuff bein rinsed away, through the plumbin system under the city an out into the river. All of his leaked liquids. Cleanin him away I am. Me black dress is in there as well, the dress I wore to go on the job with Victoria; I must've sweated friggin buckets into it. I sniffed at it this morning an was surprised at how much it ponged. Stale BO an that.

Rain chucks itself against the window. I turn me head to look at it; the city, the world itself, looks like it's bein washed as well as me clothes. Rinsed down, like. All the blood an spunk an piss, all of it swilled away. I watch it for a minute or two then turn me head away cos I don't wanner see it goin through the spin cycle. That would be scary, that.

Mad fuckin spinnin in me head here, tho. Mad fast whirlin around. Rememberin his flesh partin, red words takin shape on his back. The feel of his guts clingin hot to me arm. So much of me so fuckin far inside him. Felt like I was storming somethin, batterin down the gates. Breakin into somewhere bright an intense an fuckin wonderful. Like a palace, no, fuckin paradise or something. Green fields an sunbeams.

Wouldn't've done it if he hadna been so fuckin compliant. Wouldn't've fuckin done it at all if I had've suspected for one moment that he didn't want me to; if he had've given me one sign . . . just one fuckin sign that he wanted me to stop . . .

Not his fuckin fault, Kelly. He screamed an begged, what more of a friggin sign do yer need? A written fuckin affidavit from his lawyer to cease an desist? He screamed, an he begged, an he pleaded with yer to stop. That should've been enough for yis. Cracked, crazy, *twisted* fuckin cow.

Yeh but the way he is. Was. All that odd fuckin beauty of him. The thought of him all alone an vulnerable in this big rough city with all them fuckin nasty forces pullin at him, yankin bits of him off. Dead-eyed fuckers wanting, demandin that he obey them, crawl to them. Among all this he's now marked by me an I could maybe think of that as a charm, like, a badge or somethin, some safeguard against harm.

Except it fuckin isn't, tho, is it? All it is is you an yer insane fuckin lust. Yer not right, Kelly. Yer need fuckin help.

The clothes stop spinning, the machine stops vibrating, an the red light clicks off. I open the door an bundle the wet gear into the basket. A pair of knickers – me sexy black lacy ones – miss an splat on the floor an I'm glad I'm thee only person in this laundrette cos a bloke, any fuckin bloke, in here might've taken that as a cause to leer which I would've taken in turn as cause to chuck a beaker of fuckin Daz into his friggin eyes. Fuckin blokes, ther all the same. Shitty knickers an crush videos, oh whip me you bitch whip me, I've been a bad boy. All the fuckin same. Even thee imaginary ones.

I put the wet things into the dryer. Feed it five 20p coins. Should be enough. All his smells an traces washed away, he's gone, gone, yer won't smell nor see him any more. No more. It, fuckin *you*, everythin went too far yesterday, last night, far too fuckin far. I don't like what he brings out in me, what he makes me wanner do to him. Can't fuckin help meself when he's around. I burn inside. Too much to fuckin handle. I'll leave it. Sack it all off. Plenty more fuckin blokes in this city; plenty more panting dogs. Snotty superior shitheads like Peter or cringing abject loathers of everything like that twat in the stocks. Among them all there must be at least *one* decent one, mustn't there? Must be fuckin *one*, somewhere, unusual an unique. Different to all thee others, surely to Christ.

Pure fuckin *must* be, man.

Close the door. Machinery whirrs an the clothes start to tumble. For an instant me black dress is thrown up against the glass as if it's trying to escape or screamin for help then it's rolled away by the sheets. Get dry. Clean an dry. Smell of nowt but Daz.

Pepperoni pizza for tea. Eat it in front of the news, the heatin turned right up an all the lights on cos it's so friggin cold tonight, the night pressin against the windows, so cold an so dark. An all's I can see on this pizza are the red rings of sausage, red an black-speckled, thee remind me of something but I don't know what. Round an red. A deep red colour. Dark-ringed as if with blood.

The phone rings.

—Hello?

—Iya, Kel, yer ahl friggin slapper.

Relief. Or is it? It's something, anyway.

—Vicky, you whoo-er. What's happenin?

—Nowt, really. What yis up to?

—Same. Eatin pizza. Watchin telly.

—No plans, well?

—None.

—Not seein that feller tonight then?

—What feller?

—Yer know. Him. That friggin what's-his-namey. Him who went to Wales.

Little jump in me chest. —Oh no . . . Saw him last night, like. He's erm, he's off doin somethin with his mates tonight. Dunno what, like.

Maybe I should just tell her, tell her everythin that happened. Might make me feel . . . what? What, exactly? Unburdened, something like that. Kind of fuckin free. But not now, tho, no. Not on the friggin phone.

—Why? D'yis wanner come round?

—Can't, she says. —Got a job to do. Same knobhead, like, yer know the one over in Heswall? Your mate?

279

—*Him* again? Fuckin hell, Vic. Would've thought he'd still be friggin healin up. The skin we took off his arse.

She laughs. —I know, yeh. He can't get enough. Poor twat's obsessed. He wants *you* again, as well. He's asked for yer, like, specifically.

Distant roaring in me head. Grinding me friggin teeth almost. Picture that man immobilised before me an Christ I would do some fuckin damage.

—Ah no, Vix. I couldn't, honest. I just fuckin couldn't.

—Yeh, but he's asked for yer, tho. He friggin *begged*. Yer could name yer price.

—Aw behave, Victoria, will yer.

—Tellin yer; it's true. Yer could earn a friggin fortune here.

—Honest, Vicky, I wouldn't be able to trust meself, like. I'd friggin kill the sad bastard if I went round there, I'm tellin yer. I would, I'd fuckin kill him. I'd get lifed up for murder.

She laughs again. —*I'd* be there, tho, Kel. I'd keep a restrainin arm around yis.

—No, Vicky. Honest. I really don't want to. I'm sick to friggin death of blokes an ther stupid little fuckin perversions. I don't want any part of it. Get someone else.

Vicky goes on tryin to persuade me for a few minutes an I eventually convince her that I'm serious, I'm really not up for it. There's a gnashin gob inside me full of teeth an all I know is that it must not be fuckin fed. It's a great big friggin hunger that is best left unsatiated cos it'll just grow bigger an want more an more an more an where the fuck will that end? With knives an blood an skin splitting open around me muscles. Leave it. Blank it.

—Well, then. If yer completely sure, like . . .

—I am, Vix, completely. Anyway, if he's really a masochist then he'll get off on me refusal, won't he? Me totally ignoring the tosser should be a big, big thrill for the sad ahl get.

We arrange to meet up somewhere next week for a bevvy an she hangs up. I turn back to me pizza, cold an claggy now, the cheese like fuckin leather or something. Them rings of pepperoni. That fat cunt in the stocks. God, I would've taken a sword to that bastard tonight. I would've fuckin killed him, no messin. Chopped the twat up into little bits. Him with all his fuckin money an his great big friggin mansion an his Eric fuckin Cantona signed strip. Useless little prick. An he can pay people like me an Victoria to do whatever the fuck he wants. Drag us into his fuckin obsessions. Twisted, forcin his demented fuckin fixations on the world. God, I would've friggin murdered the bastard an he probly would've enjoyed it as well, sobbing an wanking while I hacked his legs off at the knee. I'll give yer naked screamin freedom, yer fuckin fat blert. Never go within ten friggin miles of yis again, yer insignificant dickhead.

Fuckin men. Some fuckin men. *Most* fuckin men, what bizarre an fucked-up things youse are.

I raise a slice of pizza to me gob. An then I get it, the circle of red sausage; it's Victor's arsehole, raw, bloodied, gaping an bruised when I withdrew me arm. That doorway to him, stormed an battered.

Aw God. Aw Jesus Christ.

I chuck the pizza back in the box an pick up the phone, the receiver slippery in me greasy hands. Dial a number.

—Hello?

—Roz, it's me, Kelly. I'm climbin the friggin walls here.

—Kelly! How the fuck are you?

—Climbin the bleedin walls, girl. Need to be out.

—I was just about to ring yis. See if yer fancied a bevvy. I'm meetin Elaine in Magnet, will I call up for yis on the way?

—How long?

—Ten minutes?

—Alright well. I'll be ready.

—Sound.

I'm in the shower. Thinkin nowt. Soapin, rinsing. Gettin clean. Thinkin: drink. Thinkin: drugs. Thinkin: anythin, absolutely *anythin*, but fuckin *this*. Puttin smellies on; talcum powder, deodorant, white-musk body spray. Tyin me hair up. Puttin on music – Primal Scream – as I put on clean undies, trainies, baggy combats, a black ribbed top. Thinkin nothin in words, just shouts, just bellows. Like a torrent in me ears. Grey fleece over the top of everythin. Buy that maroon coat soon. Jack in the job. Can't fuckin face *that*. Tomorrow, tomorrow. But now pick up keys an money an fags an the remains of Peter's beak an leave the flat as the doorbell rings an go downstairs through the dark an chilly house an open the front door an see Roz.

—There yer are, Kelly.

I give her a big hug. Feel her ribs against me palms beneath her leather jacket. Just good to hold someone, anyone, even another woman like Roz who smells of cheap shampoo an expensive scent an doesn't feel against me completely alien to how Victor felt. *Different*, yeh, but not *completely*; not, like, unrecognisably so or anythin. Same prominent ribcage, same protuberant shoulder blades. Only the bulge of her breasts against mine where his were flat an hard.

—How are yis, Roz? How's the new century treatin yeh?

We head off down the road as Roz goes off on one about her mother again. Always havin a friggin whinge about her ma, Roz is.

—I mean, she's just fuckin on me case twenny-four seven. Won't fuckin leave it alone, Kel, I'm tellin yeh. Get a job, go on a course, do some friggin voluntary work, go shoppin, tidy me fuckin room. Help out around the house, that's her favourite thing, as if I don't lift a friggin finger, like. Honest to God, it's like I'm friggin sixteen still.

I've heard all this before, many times. —Only one solution, then, isn't there?

—Yeh, yeh, I know, move out. Get a place of me own. But how the fuck can I do that with no bleedin money? Need a deposit an a month's rent in advance, yer lookin at four hundred quid, easy. No fuckin *way* can I get that kind of money up. I've told her all this but she just won't friggin listen. Says it wasn't like that in *her* day. Of *course* it fuckin wasn't; she had cheap jobs an cheaper rents, at *my* age. Ain't fuckin like that any more, tho, is it?

—What about the DSS? Have yer tried them? To find yer a place, like?

—Oh aye, yeh, she scoffs. —Fuckin bomb site off Edge Hill or a crackhouse on Princes Road. Fuckin lovely. Went out with them a couple of weeks ago to see a flat out in Allerton. Wasn't *too* bad, like, only one wall pissin with the damp. Liveable if it wasn't for the fuckin non-stop screamin from the flat below.

—Screaming?

She nods. —Yeh. Only a bleedin knockin shop, wasn't it. Fuckin brothel, like. Only a queue of sleazoids to thee end of the friggin road waitin to have ther arses whipped.

I laugh. —Try Riverside, well. The housin association, like.

—Been on ther books for fourteen fuckin months, woman. Low-priority case, yer see; I'm not homeless. Soon fuckin will be tho if me ma doesn't shut the fuck up. Jesus, I'd become a friggin prozzy meself if it meant a roof over me head away from that naggin ahl bag.

—Speakin of which . . .

—What? Naggin ahl bags?

—No; becomin a prozzy . . .

—Oh aye?

—Guess what yours fuckin truly did thee other day . . .

An I tell her. About Victoria an Heswall an the fat fool in the stocks. An the size of his house an the size of his arse an the fuckin frenzy in me as I tore it apart. Thee ache in me shoulder an thee almost beautiful sense of losin all control. An how truly, genuinely, hugely fuckin funny it was. How I near pissed meself with laughter in the car.

—An that's what *he* did, as well, the punter, like; peed hisself with fright. Honest, when I was thrashin fuck out of his arse; all over his friggin floor, pssssshhhhh.

Roz is lookin at me all wide-eyed. Shocked smile. —Straight up, all this?

—Yeh, I nod. —No mess. Not a word of a lie. An a hundred an twenty nicker for a half-hour's work. Can yer believe that? That some sad fuckin musher would pay yis that much money to have ther arse caned?

—Jesus, she says, all awed. —That's how much Victoria charges?

—Nah, I think she normally charges a wee bit less, but this soft get was so impressed that he paid us extra. Knobhead, eh?

283

Vicky's gone back over to see him tonight. Tan his fat arse again, like. Asked me to go along with her but I said no. Once was more than enough.

—Aw Christ, *I* would've fuckin done it! Things I could do with a hundred an twenty sheets, Jesus!

—Give her a ring then on yer moby. Might not be too late.

—Can't, can I? Ran out of credit. Fuckin can't talk much on a pay-as-yer-talk scheme, can yer? If yer friggin skint, like.

—Is right.

—But I'll ask Victoria, tho, next time I see her. Tell her I've got a good strong arm.

She whips an invisible cane an makes a 'swooshing' sound. I picture her, little Roz with the blonde crop, slight-bodied Roz standin over a bound an gagged man, a cane in her hands, a ferocious expression on her face. Then I picture her with money, boundin into Modo or the Jazz Bar, or into Cream wearin nice new clothes. She suits each scenario equally. But nothin in either of bliss, of rapture, of a closeness so fuckin deep that you're joined; nowt in either of yer head burstin, yer heart burstin, fulfilment if only for a moment and a person inside you an you inside them an a fuckin furnace in yer belly. Yer knees tremblin an yer can't control it. Want an need an a longing so fuckin intense . . . nothing of that anywhere, tho, is there? Nowhere on earth except one place, one fuckin person.

Fuck it. It's over.

We go into Magnet. Fairly empty cos it's fairly early.

—Get the drinks in well. Seein as yer loaded, like.

—Alright, I say. —What yer havin?

—Double vodka an Smirnoff Ice.

I order two of them an we take them over to the table at thee end by the fountain where Elaine is sitting, wavin at us. She's all dolled up, Elaine is, blonde hair almost white down to the beltloops of her leather kex an a tight 'D&G Is Love' T-shirt. Heavy make-up.

—Bit togged up, aren't yis, Elaine? What's all this in aid of? Who's the lucky feller?

She gets all on the defensive. —Allowed to make a friggin effort, aren't I? Don't need a bleedin reason, Christ.

Roz shows her palms. —Don't bite me fuckin head off, I was only askin. Just makin a fuckin observation, like, that's all. Fuck's sake.

Tetchy friggin cow, that Elaine. Dead snappy always, like, always on the defensive. Too much charlie makin her paranoid. A labels woman, as well; everythin on her has to be Gap or Nike or Hilfiger or, as her T-shirt says, fuckin 'D&G Is Love'. Which it isn't; it's fuckin claustrophobia.

Never really liked Elaine much, if truth be told. Judgemental streak to her. Like now; Roz is goin on, again, boringly, about her problems with her mother an Elaine's just sittin there, arms folded, smirking, shakin her head. She gegs in:

—Don't see what yer problem is, Rosalind, to be honest. What's the big friggin deal? What's such a big fuckin pain about livin with yer ahl queen? Food cooked for yis, clothes washed an ironed, no bills, no bleedin responsibilities. It's sound. Can't see anythin wrong with thee arrangement, meself, like. Can you, Kelly?

Thee both look at me an I just shrug, take a swig of me drink. Ther both waitin for an answer, like, so I just say: —I wouldn't know. Left home about ten years ago, like, so I wouldn't know anythin about it.

Which is a wee bit snotty, like, but so fuckin what. Elaine stiffens, all affronted.

—An what the fuck's *that* meant to mean?

—Nowt, I say. —I'm just sayin.

—Yeh, an sayin what, like?

—That I left home years ago. That's all. No fuckin dig or anythin, just a simple friggin statement of fact. Fuck's sakes, Elaine, yer asked me so I told yer. Get a fuckin grip.

Daft friggin bint. To get away from her an her parro whingin I go to the toilet, thee upstairs one. Because it's nearest. An because downstairs will remind me, bring it all back to me, the red an the white lights an his face in them an the way he walked an talked an tripped over the step an the way he couldn't stop gawpin at me an Darren psycho Taylor followed him into the bogs an I was worried an so I waited for him to come out an tapped him on the shoulder when he did. An his face. His face in the lights, turnin to face me. Face *me*.

The back of his head an the hair flat an matted with sweat when he walked out of me flat bandy-legged an in pain. His blood. The stuff of him comin out.

I wash me face at the sink. Look into the mirror. From the scar in me eyebrow when I fell off the Sefton Park seesaw as a little girl down to the rest of me face, the signs of recent ravage. It's a rest you need, Kelly. It's been a friggin insane last couple of weeks an it's beginnin to show on yis, yer lips all cracked, yer eyes bloodshot, burst blood vessels on yer cheeks an nose an eyelids givin them a maroon tinge. Doesn't look good. Everythin seems dry; cracked an split hair, skin like sandpaper. Dry an cold an dark. Lifeless. The music piped in here, some Detroit housey thing, sounds harsh an grating. The lights are murky an foggy, like bein under the surface of a polluted pond. It's all drab an flat an uncomfortable.

And back at fuckin work tomorrow, to top it all off, to put the shit icing on the spew cake. The crust on the cack pie is that fuckin shop waitin for me. That wanker of a boss. Life behind perspex. Bollox to it all.

I go into the cubicle, have a pee, tip the last of the cocaine out on to the cistern. Just a few dry granules which I can't even be bothered to chop up an snort so I brush them off into me cupped palm, lick a finger an dab at them like sherbet an rub them into a paste on me gums. Foul fuckin taste, numb tongue. Stupid stupid stupid, more booze, more drugs, more creepin fuckin boredom. All the bastard brightness going. Just feel drained an tired an wanner do nothing but sleep.

No yer don't, Kelly. Sleep's not what yer *really* want, is it?

No. Is it fuck.

Wash me hands again an go back out into the bar. Elaine's not there, there's only Roz at the table an she's lookin at me all concerned.

—Gob on yer, Roz. What's the matter? Where's Elaine?

—She's up at the bar. She's here to meet someone, Kel. I think he's just arrived.

I squint at the bar but thee only detail I can make out among the crowd of people is Elaine's bright hair. An beyond that I can see the big window that faces the street where I stood with Victor. Before we'd done anything. When I'd only just met him. Seems like fuckin years ago.

—It's that fuckin Peter, Kel, Roz says. —That fuckwit yer used to go out with. She's here to meet him. I think ther seein each other.

—Oh, I say. —That doesn't bother me, Roz. Not one tiny friggin bit, honest. Ther fuckin welcome to each other. Thee fuckin deserve each other.

Which isn't a nice thing to say. I don't like Elaine very much, it's true, she's a silly cow if the truth be told, but no one deserves that Peter. That cruel cunt Peter. Sadistic wanker Peter. Winnie Mandela maybe, or Margaret fuckin Thatcher or Ann fuckin Widdecombe, any one of those three would deserve Peter in ther lives. All devils together, like. But not Elaine, really, wicky an selfish as she is; not her. When it comes down to it, all she is, really, is a confused young woman riddled with doubt, an she's done nothin to deserve Peter in her life. That cunt settin up residence in her heart an her head, Jesus; I pity her.

Roz says: —I know, Kelly, I know that. It's just that she might bring him over here like . . . yer know what she's like. Fuckin smug bitch sometimes, isn't she? Takes pleasure in windin yer up, like.

I shake me head. —I won't *be* wound up, Roz. I'm not bothered. Honest to God.

Compare Peter to Victor. Then throw yer head back an laugh.

—Good, well.

Here he comes. Smirky Elaine leadin him an him with *his* fuckin smirk behind hers, the smirky twins, like, and his leather overcoat an his glass of red wine held by the stem. All these fuckin items, put them together an thee spell dee eye sea kay aitch ee ay dee.

—Roz. Kelly.

—Hiya.

—Alright, Peter.

—Oh yeh, youse all know each other, don't yer, Elaine says, her face all mock-innocent. Peter sits down opposite her, by me on the right, an swirls the middle finger of his right hand in a circular motion a few inches above the table.

—Everybody okay for drinks, yeh?

—I am, I say, but Roz holds up her nearly empty glass. She's skint.

—I could do with one.

Peter hands her a tenner. —Whatever yer want. Might as well get Kelly another one while yer up there, yeh?

—Yer alright, Peter.

He looks at Roz. —No, go on. Whatever she wants.

—Same again, Kel?

I just nod at Roz an she winks at me. There'll be friggin quadruples in ar glasses this time, I'll bet.

Roz goes off to the bar. Elaine sips at her drink, simperin at Peter over the rim of the glass. His presence by me, his body in my space. Where once the very fact of him would have made me cringe an cower, obey, it now fills me with an urge to push, shove, banish his big body from my proximity. There's nothing in him any more which is threatening or overpowerin; he's just an irritation. An uninvited obstacle I wanner boot to one side, so it's not in me way. Not even the memory of him buggerin me with an aerosol canister, holdin me face down to the floor can undermine this feelin within me, this feelin of bein above him. Better than him, fuckin *more* than him. He's just a piece of furniture in my path. He's nowt.

—Sorry I'm a wee bit late, he says to Elaine. —Went into the Legs of Man to see a mate. Got caught up in some party there, some private do. Some idiot just become a dad or somethin. Altho why anyone should see that as a cause for celebration is well friggin beyond me, like.

Elaine laughs, too much, too loud. Wasn't even fuckin funny.

—Unless of course he was drowning his sorrows. *Wet* the baby's head? Fuckin *immerse* it, more like. Get rid of it like an unwanted kitten. Nowt more stifling to a young life than the nappies under the sink, ey, Kel?

Elaine laughs again. I just deadhead him an take a drink.

A baby. A child. Maybe *that's* what I need. Maybe *that's* what'd calm me down, like, the responsibility of a kid, somethin to chill this fuckin fire inside me, douse it, cool it into milk. A baby. Life from me.

—I've booked a table in Jalon's, Elaine says, reachin across the table to take Peter's hand. —Nine o'clock? That alright?

He nods an takes his hand away from Elaine's to light a ciga-rette. —Sound, yeh. Classy margarita in Jalon's, innit, Kel?

Why the fuck he's askin me I haven't got the first friggin clue cos I've never been to Jalon's in me life. He's lookin at me face an I meet his eyes an his pupils the size of saucers are swirling, spinnin. He's beaked out of his brains.

—I said, isn't it, Kelly?

—If yer say so Peter, yeh.

—Fuckin *do* say so. Come along with us if yer like an see for yerself.

Elaine gasps. —Table for two, tho . . . for two just, Peter . . . already booked an everythin . . .

Staring at me the twat is. I shake me head.

—No thanks. Already made plans.

—Change them, well.

Fuck all this shite. I stand up.

—Where yer goin?

—Roz needs a hand with the bevvies.

—Sit down. She'll be alright, she can manage.

Elaine looks like she's about to cry. Her big eyes are drillin into Peter's face an her lower lip is hangin on her chin. Get used to it, girl. Arsehole's like this all the fuckin time.

Peter's hand reaches up towards me waist so I move away from there quick, before I have to slap his hand away or knee him in the balls or glass his stupid fuckin grid. Wanker never grows up. On this incessant puerile power trip. It's all friggin mind games with that bastard, it's all to do with control an coercion an I'm dead glad I'm out of it an he can fuck right off. Biggest mistake of me life

so far, that, gettin involved with him. Elaine'll learn. She'll
fuckin learn.

I find Roz at the bar.

—What's up?

I jerk me head back to indicate Peter. —Just had to get
away from knobhead there. He's actin the cunt again.

—Oh is he? What's he up to this time?

—Ah yer know. Just the way he is. Stupid fuckin mind
games, like.

She nods an gives her order to Sadie, the nice Manc girl.
Her boyfriend, Jay, is leanin on thee end of the bar an he
smiles at me an I smile back then me eye is caught by a young
girl standin not far from him to his left, a pretty young teenage
girl an her mates; she draws me eyes cos there's somethin about
her, the shape of her forehead, the way she smiles, the colour
of her eyes, somethin in all these which calls Victor up, shoves
him into me mind, that night I first met him here, downstairs.
It's like he's echoed in her face, his face can be seen under
hers. Like *her* flesh has been put on *his* bones. It's strange. It
sets a squirming up in me stomach. An then a big friggin *kick*
in me stomach as I hear her mention the name 'Victor'. I strain
to listen an she says it again: 'Victor'. Deffo. *That* was the name
she said.

I move around Roz so's I can hear better what the young
girl's sayin. Roz asks me if I'm alright an I just nod. Listen:

—. . . nearly died, yeh. Eddie an Evelyn were friggin gutted,
man. That's why Eddie's so hammered now, like, cos his baby
nearly died.

Names, events that Victor never mentioned, so maybe it's a
different Victor. Coincidental, tho. An not that he mentioned
much at all, come to think of it; my tongue in his gob. A gag.
A pillow. Or too friggin busy groaning. Or pleading.

—Same thing happened to me brother, the girl goes on.
—Ar Victor.

Boot in the belly again, hearing like a razor.

—Same thing, like, that cord thing, what d'yer call it,
Claire?

—Umbilical cord.

—That's it, yeh. Wrapped around his neck it was when he was bein born. Choked him, like. Apparently he was actually dead, clinically dead, like, for a while. He doesn't know, he's never been told cos me mam thinks it might upset him. Doesn't want him to know that he was born dead.

Her friend shakes her head slowly, all shocked. —Bloody hell, Lizzie. An he doesn't know?

—Nup.

—Yer haven't told him?

—Why should I? What would be the point? Might really fuck him up an there's no need, is there?

—Suppose not, no.

—I mean, he's happy, or most of the time he is. Why take the risk of makin him upset?

—Yeh. Yer right.

—Come ed, well. Let's go downstairs.

Roz hands me a drink. A huge vodka an a bottle of lemon Hooch.

—Let's take these downstairs, Roz. Get away from *that* gobshite.

—Alright, yeh. I'll see yer down there, I'll just goan give him his change.

I go downstairs, lookin for the young girls. Ther on the dance floor, givin it large. Just young teenage girls enjoyin themselves. Becomin somethin ther startin to like. Fair play to them as well. The red an white lights flashin across them an ther movements in those lights, ther assertive, confident an sexy movements. Fair do's. I remember when I was ther age, not that long ago really, when everythin was spread out before me all so full of promise an I felt I could do fuckin anything, that anything might happen to me, any bright an lovely thing. Which of course it still friggin can. Not fuckin old yet, Kelly, not by any fuckin means. So many years ahead of yeh. An things do happen that *are* fuckin wonderful, don't thee, Victor up at the bar in Flanagan's an me watchin him or him naked in me bath, even if such things *do* turn sour after a while. An bein a teenager was no golden age, fuck no; all those problems, the zits, the confidence at times slidin off yer like sweat or something. But I remember things as bein somehow much easier then. Less pressures, for one, or if not exactly *less* then different, of a milder type. Altho thee probly weren't, really. Just hindsight, nostalgia colourin things rose. That's all it fuckin is.

Life is easy. It's *easy*.

The pretty girl nudges her mate an nods over to me an thee both look an I realise then that I'm gawping. Standin here gawpin at them like a sad an lonely lezza. So I give them both a big smile, a big toothy grin, like, an a thumbs-up an thee give half-smiles back an I turn an go into the basement bar an meet Roz comin down the stairs. She blows air out through pursed lips an shakes her head.

—What's up?

—That fuckin Peter. What a knobend.

—What's he done now?

—Stormed off somewhere. Don't know why, like, just swept all the bottles off the table with his arm an stormed out in a huff. She taps her temple with her index finger. —He's in here. He's got fuckin problems, man.

—Don't I fuckin know it. What's Elaine doin?

—She's gone out after him. Fuckin crawlin after the prick like a good little girlie. Hangin on to his coat-tails, like.

I sniff. —Typical. But she'll learn.

—I friggin doubt it, Kel. Fuckin proper wee wifie, she is, that's her through an through. That's how it'll be with her for the rest of her life. Bet yer.

I don't say anything. She's probly right, Roz, but I have faith in thee idea that it's never too late to change. That things *will* come along an happen to yer that shock yer out of yer nurtured, preconceived sets of mind an it's never, ever, too late to change. In a hospital bed, breathin yer last, yer might find all of a sudden that yer actually prefer lime juice to orange juice, an that yer've kidded yerself during every bleedin breakfast or vodka-with-mixer night yer've ever had. God. What a friggin shock that would be.

Roz grins. —One thing, tho; cock-jockey forgot to ask for his change before he stamped off. So I can get the next round in.

—Nice one.

—But let's go on somewhere else, yeh? Head into town or something.

Which we do. Don't know where, like, cos the next thing I know I'm staggerin into me bedroom, bouncin me shoulder painfully off the door jamb. Be a bruise there tomorrer. Pissed enough to almost forget that I'm back at fuckin work in a few hours. An not pissed enough to forget to set thee alarm, but pissed enough, pissed enough to sleep.

Such a long queue at the bus stop. Glum white faces lookin beaten an desperately fuckin unhappy. I'm early an it's rainin so I duck into a nearby phone box, lookin out at the bleak faces. Jesus, I'd almost forgotten how truly fuckin miserable a workin day really is. Look at all the people; so fed up thee look, so friggin angry, almost fuckin enraged at the unfairness of bein alive. Might as well give me ma a bell while I'm here.

—Hello?

—Hiya, Mam.

—Kelly, love. How are yer?

—Alright.

—Yer don't sound too good.

—No, I'm fine. Just a bit hung-over, that's all.

—Hung-over? Well, yer up early if you were out on thee ale last night.

—Wouldn't be if I had the bleedin choice. Back at work today.

—In that shop?

—Yeh. Unfortunately.

She makes a sighing sound, theatrical, overdone. This wicks me right off.

—Mam, however much yer hate me workin there, just remember that I hate it ten times more. I can't stand it. An it's no good tellin me to get somethin else cos there's nothin else to get. There's nowt else around.

—Have yer tried?

—Mam, this is Liverpool, in case yer haven't bleedin noticed. Good jobs're a bit thin on the ground here.

—Alright, alright, don't bite me bloody head off. I didn't say a word.

—Yes yer did. An anyway yer didn't bloody have to; I could tell what's turnin round in yer head.

—I know work's scarce, love, but there are other things. Courses an stuff. The dole have this scheme now where thee –

—Mam, don't start. Please. It's half eight in the morning an I'm hung-over an on me way to a job that I hate. Don't nip me head. How's Dean?

—Changin the subject.

—Yeh, cos it's half past eight in the bleedin mornin! I feel like shite!

People at the bus stop are lookin my way. One ahl feller bites into an egg roll wrapped in tissue paper an yolk squirts out on to the pavement like pus.

—Don't shout, Kelly. No need.

I've had enough of this. Stupid fuckin idea, phonin me mother on the way to fuckin work. As *if* she's gunner cheer me up at all. As *if* she's gunner make me feel better.

—Mam, I've got to dash, the bus is here. I'll comen see yer soon, alright?

—Make sure yer do. It's been ages. An yer only a bus ride away, yer know.

—I know, Mam, yeh. I'll see yis soon, I promise.

I hang up an leave the phone box an join the queue. I'm leanin against a wall an me head's fuckin bangin. Then I'm on the bus, crushed between people, all on ther way to a place thee hate. Then I'm off the bus. Then I'm in the shop where I work, my particular fuckin prison, my particular necessary hell. Fat Macca, the boss, is behind the perspex sheeting wearin his usual shit-brown smock an eatin a bacon butty an drinkin a cup of tea, readin the *Star*. Globules of red sauce are caught in his muzzy as if he's been eatin raw flesh, or is bleedin profusely from the gums. Wish he fuckin was.

—Late, he says.

No 'Happy New Year', no fuckin 'How was yer millennium'.

Just that; 'Late'. I glance up at the clock; just gone nine. About a minute past.

—By less than two minutes, yeh.

—Doesn't matter. Still late.

He unlocks the flap an lifts it up an I crawl under it. Behind the counter now I am, behind the perspex walls. An here I'll be until half past fuckin five when I can go home an eat an shower an sleep until eight o'clock tomorrow when I'll get up to come back to this exact same fuckin spot, imprisoned by bulletproof perspex, an the whole shitty cycle will go on an on an on until what? Til I die. Or somethin better comes along, which it never fuckin will unless I bastard well *make* it.

Hate this fuckin hate this. Wanky friggin job. Lifeless, dull an stupid.

—All the shelves need a fillin, Fat Macca says, not lookin up from his paper. —All the sweets, everything. An be sure to fill them up full, like, cos your on yer own today.

—On me own?

—On yer own.

—But it's Wednesday. It's lottery day. Place's gunner be chocka this afternoon.

—Can't help that, can I? I've got a bit of business to take care of in Runcorn.

I'm fuckin pissed off here. —What sort of business?

He looks up at me. —The none-of-your sort. He presses thee end of his red nose with a yellow fingertip. —Keep *that* out an do yer job. What *I* pay yer to do.

Oh for fuck's sake. First day back in this stupid fuckin place an it's gunner be worse than I ever imagined. All bleedin day it'll be a steady stream of shufflin people an thee only ever buy a few things, but hundreds of each; lottery tickets, ciggies, alcohol, chocolate, soft porn. All short cuts to some poor an narrow paradise. Shallow an short-lived. I can't stand it. I can't stand it.

I fuckin well *won't* stand it.

I go into the back room an put on the brown apron that Macca insists I wear an take boxes out into the shop an begin fillin the shelves. Mavericks, Fuses, Twirls, Twixes, Mars,

Bounties, KitKats, Yorkies. So much fuckin chocolate. Do we really need so many different types of chocolate bar? I can feel gaffer-twat's eyes on me as I work. An me head is throbbin sore.

—Thought I told yer to wear a skirt?

Oh here we fuckin go. Don't answer the letchy cunt. Snickers, Crunchie, Toffee fuckin Crisp.

—Oi. I'm talkin to you.

—What?

—I said I thought I told yer to wear a skirt.

Milky Way. I just shrug.

—Well, *do*, from now on. Looks nicer for the customers.

An *you*, yer fuckin perv. Funny how whenever I wear a skirt an awful lot of work needs to be done on the top shelves, isn't it? An funnier still how it's always fuckin me who has to go up the ladder. Scared of heights me hole.

Maltesers. Turkish Delight. Mints, Murray Polo Trebor. All this fuckin condensed sugar. Tons of it. Slidin an gooey, sticky like an immense web.

Too fuckin old for this, Kelly. No schoolgirl any more. The things yer've done, the things yer've seen an here yer are stackin Skittles on a shelf for money. Demeaning, that's what it is, fuckin pure demeaning. Sack it off. Get rid of it.

The fridges are empty, both soft drink an alcohol, so I go into the back room to get the supplies. An here, crouched between Pepsi an Lilt, I decide what to do. No fuss, no buts, I know completely what I'm gunner do an when I'm gunner do it. It's perfectly fuckin simple. So clear, so pure, so easy. I can feel me face split in a smile.

—What's so funny?

—Nowt.

—What's the big grin for then?

—Just somethin that happened thee other day, that's all. Somethin that made me laugh.

He shakes his head. —If yer findin the job amusing then yer not workin hard enough. Don't pay yer to stand around gigglin to yerself.

The door tings open an Macca is up an at the hatch in the perspex wall.

—Morning.

—Twenny Regal an a *Mirror*.

The man is served an he frigs off. Watch him; that's how easy it is, to frig off, just walk out of the shop an close the door behind yeh. Dead fuckin simple.

Macca takes his dishes into the storeroom an dumps them in the small sink there. Taps do not open, water does not run. He takes his overall off an hangs it over the door.

—I've got to be in Runcorn before ten so that's me. Usual thing; lock up when yer leave an post the keys through the letter box. Cash in the safe. Thirty quid float in the till.

—I know, yeh. Done it before.

—Yeh, well.

He takes a tenner from the till an leaves. I watch him go.

Silence apart from me slowly beatin heart. The calmness of decision. This will be so easy, so good.

I wait five minutes or so until I'm sure that he'll be well away then I take off me smock an hang it up, take the money from the till – just over thirty quid or so – an put it in me bag along with a handful of chocolate bars an a few hundred ciggies. So easy. Christ, this is so fuckin easy. How could I have ever thought it would be anything but easy? Leave the shop, lock the door, post the keys back through the letter box. An that's it. I am fuckin free.

—Scuse me, love. Are yer closin up?

An ahl dear in a bobble hat.

—Yeh. Illness, like. Be open again tomorrow morning.

—Ah. I just need some ciggies an the garage is closed n all. Have to walk down to the Londis now.

—What's yer brand?

—Benny Hedges.

—Yer in luck.

I take sixty Bensons out of me bag an give them to her.

—Eeyar. A prezzie.

Her face lights up. The grin on her. —Honest? I don't owe yer anything?

297

—Nup. Ther yours. Go on.

She looks down at the golden packets as she might at a winning lottery ticket or somethin. A disbelieving joy. That's saved her over a tenner.

—Yer sure now?

—Yeh yeh, no problem at all. Ther yours.

—Ah God bless yer, love. God love yeh.

—I think he already does.

An that's it, I'm away. All free. Pure fuckin free. It's like a horrible friggin burden has gone off me shoulders an I'm almost bleedin *skippin* down Parliament Street. So easy, so fuckin simple. Now me whole life stretches ahead of me, all glitterin an new. There's fuckin nothin I can't do. I am reborn. I will go now into a caff an I will eat a great big fried brekkie with loads of tea. Then I will go home an sleep for friggin ages, sleep me hangover away an when I wake up I will have a bath, get all clean an then what? Anything. Everything. There's fuckin nothin I can't do. I am pure fuckin free an there's fuckin *nothing* I can't do.

The Moorfield DSS office is heavin and, despite the signs, choked with fag smoke. It's like a fog, a thick grey fog with shapes moving, driftin through it. And an acrid smell in thee air of burnin carpet where people have ground ther fags out cos there's no ashtrays. An thee atmosphere, God, so tight an uncomfortable, as if physical violence is only one wrong look or word, a simple mistake or refusal, away.

I take a ticket from the machine an find a corner to stand in. Me ticket says '112', the display on the wall says '97'. Be here for fuckin ages, I will. Glad I bought a paper on the way, somethin to pass the time with. The humiliation begins. I unfold the paper an start to read. Read every single friggin word in it, even the horoscopes, even thee adverts.

An I'm so much fuckin older when me number is finally called. So much fuckin closer to death. There's a slice of me life, a big fuckin slice, like, in which I did nowt but lean against a wall in a cramped too-hot room an read a newspaper three times an breathe in other people's smoke an breath. That's all

I did. Wasted that big section of me life, did fuck all in it but kill time, wish it away. It's worse than work, almost. Fuck, it friggin well *is* work. Should get bleedin paid for it. I am older, now. I am more dead than before.

I leave the paper on the floor, go an take the spare seat at the perspex wall. Or the reinforced-glass wall, whatever it is, just another friggin barrier, another bulletproof sheet. Public commerce in this city is always carried out through some kind of barrier, yer can never speak to people face-to-face, never get to feel the breeze of someone else's breathing on yer skin. Which is maybe no bad thing, considerin the halitotic hell some public functionaries put yis through. Priests, teachers, bizzies; breath like thee've been eatin turds.

The woman behind the desk, through the perspex, is bottle-blonde, growin out. A tan that looks bottled as well. Her name tag says 'Kelly', like me; that's nice.

—What can I do for you?

—I'd like to open a claim, please.

She gives me all the forms; income support, housing benefit an council tax combined. I take them over the road to the Coffee Union an drink a couple of double espressos as I fill them in; so many fibs on them when I've finished ther like a work of friggin fiction. Take them back over the road, wait fuckin ages in the fuckin queue again, shrinkin, recoiling, being reduced an diluted an weakened until me number is called. A different woman this time; an African lady called 'Sumea'. I slide the forms through the gap under the glass an she flicks through them.

—Oh . . . your address is Bedford Street South. Liverpool Seven.

—Yeh?

—Well, yer in the wrong office, love. The Park Road branch deals with applications from that area.

—But this one's closer.

—I know, yeh, but it's just the way it works. The city's separated up into zones, y'see, an your zone comes under the Park Road area. Just take these forms over there an hand them in.

Aw no. Park Road. Fuckin miles away. Another friggin queue.

Fuck it.

I take the forms back, fold them up into me bag an leave the building, out into the city. Park Road's fuckin miles away, an a bus ride would be just another boring, cramped, uncomfortable activity, just another fuckin dull an meaningless chore, so fuckin empty it would be unendurable, like everythin else yer don't want to do but are fuckin *forced* to by the general fuckin requirements of existence. I mean, exhaust; concrete an glass; bland, blank faces. I wouldn't be able to handle that today, I'd go fuckin mad. Put it off til tomorrow, well. Sooner be back in me flat at the moment, on me tod, doin . . . what? What the *fuck* is there to do?

Find a cash machine, get a bank balance. Still a couple of ton left in there, surprisingly, a small wad in me purse from the job with Victoria, an the rent's paid a fortnight in advance so there's no real rush yet. No real urgency. Be on the bones of me arse soon, like, but I'm not yet so don't fuckin worry about it, Kelly, don't you fuckin fret. There's bugger all to worry about just yet.

I cross over the road on to Dale Street, headin down into the city centre. I feel okay; the freedom from work is such a fuckin relief. Yesterday, there must've been millions of jobs jacked in all over the country, first day back at work for millions of people after the millennium celebrations, like, an so many million minds thinkin: 'Aw fuck this. There's more to life than this mind-numbin, soul-crushin shite, there's more to life, I've seen the proof.' All them millions of notices handed in. All the millions of bosses told to stick ther poxy jobs up ther rings. All the fuckin dole offices inundated with new claims, tidal waves of forms filled in with fibs. Reason for leavin last employment? Involuntary redundancy, illness, bereavement, some kind of incompatibility. Never the real reason, that for a night an a day the world fuckin exploded into brightness an promise an showed everyone how thee could possibly live, how it is underneath it all possible to live how we're meant to, with arms around each other an heads spinnin an hearts beatin, singin ar fuckin lungs out. An that the way we friggin *do* live is an insult to the notion of how we maybe *should* an that we're wastin ar fuckin lives livin them the way we do. *That's* the real reason why I left me shitty little job. An I would've written it on the form an all except the box provided for me answer was only big enough for me to write the words 'contract ended'.

Turn left on to Church Street, into the shop next door to Schuh. I look for the young girl with the nice green eyes who served me last time but I can't see her. A different assistant comes up to me, black bobbed hair, dead tall.

—Can I help yis?

—Yeh. There's a coat put by for me. I've come in to pick it up.

She takes me name an goes into the back room, reappears holdin the ace, long, maroon coat. *My* coat. —Fifty owin on it, yeh?

—Yeh.

I pay her an she folds it up an puts it gently into a placcy bag. *My* friggin coat now. It'll hang ace on me an I'll look dead cool in it, cool an sexy. The man in the stocks would cream his kex to see me in it. Victor would push his face into me neck if he saw me wearing it. Push his face into me neck an breathe deeply an I'd hold him an slide me hands up his back to encircle his throat an he'd tremble, tremble an whimper. Such a hardness in his jeans, pressin against me hip.

Outside in the street again, the busy street, an I find meself scannin all the passin faces, tryin to glance at every one, lookin for green eyes an a wide grin an mousy, spiky hair. An should I just bump into Victor, like, just accidentally meet him in the street, what the fuck would I do? What would I say? How would I stand, I mean, in what position, would I touch him, would I lean in towards him or away from him? An would he even want to talk to me, after what I did to him, all his leaking, or would he just glance at me once an once only an then look away an walk on? What would he do? What would *I* do?

I really don't friggin know. I haven't got the first fuckin clue. All I know is that just the thought of meeting him, seeing him, like, sets me fuckin pulse racing. Me mouth dries up an other parts of me moisten. Just the very thought. Just the fuckin *thought*.

On the way home I stop off at a newsagent's/stationers an buy a few big sheets of plain white paper, some glue an several papers/magazines: two tabloids, an *Echo*, a *Cosmopolitan*, a *Mixmag* an a *Loaded* with Cameron Diaz on the cover. Lots of bright pictures. Colourful, high-resolution focus. Then I head home, nippin into the Greek deli on the way for a cheese an spinach roll an some black olives an once inside me flat I dump all the stuff on the floor an have a shower an put on me new coat, nowt else, just me coat, an look at meself in the mirror. Admire meself. I look fuckin great. Then I lie back on the bed an wank, rub me clitoris with a flat palm until I come an then I roll a strong spliff an go into the front room wearin nothin but me ace new coat an I turn the telly on an eat some food an smoke the chonga an then, when I'm fairly stoned, I start doin what I used to *love* doin as a kid whenever I was ill or alone or just simply bored (which, if memory serves, I almost always fuckin was as a child): I start to make the monsters. Used to spend friggin hours doin this as a little girl, I did. Get pictures of famous people, cut them up an put them back together again all wrong on a piece of paper – makin monsters. That's what I used to call it. Used to cover me bedroom walls with these grotesque images, probly worried the fuck out of me mam an dad, especially when I decided that I wanted to be called 'Satin' instead of 'Kelly' cos I thought it sounded nicer but thought it was spelled with an 'a' instead of an 'i' so glued a big sign up on the door of me room that said 'SATAN LIVES HERE'. And beyond that sign would be all these images of famous people rearranged as if by an insane trainee vivisectionist or somethin, all nightmarish disproportions an freaky hybrids. Probly disturbed everyone who saw it for life, altho it used to keep *me* entertained; spend hours doin it, I would. I'd kind of go into a trance, snippin an gluing an gigglin away.

Like now; I can't stop laughin quietly to meself. Tony Blair's head on Cameron Diaz's body on Michael Owen's legs. Then two legs, clad in fishnet tights an high heels with the big an bloated tattooed body of some footy hooligan caught in mid-arrest with the head of Angela Lansbury. The head of a horse on the body of a swimmer, then the swimmer's head goggled an capped on the body of the horse. It's dead funny. These mad creations of mine, so fuckin funny an I'm stoned an I'm laughin, laughin, so absorbed in what I'm doin that I don't answer the phone when it rings; 1471 tells me that Victoria was tryin to get in touch. Probly wanted me to go out with her again on a job, cane some sad fucker's arse. Well, not tonight, Vicky. I have everythin I could ever need right here.

Almost.

Sami Hyypia's hair an forehead. Keanu Reeves's eyes. The nose of some young local councillor accompanyin an article about Railtrack or somethin. Brad Pitt's jaw, perhaps a wee bit *too* square but it'll do. That almost looks like him.

Almost.

Sittin, starin down at it, this fucked-up face I've made. Then not really bein able to see it any more cos me vision has gone all blurred.

I rip it up an stuff it in the fuckin bin. If I had a real fire I'd friggin burn it, feed it to the flames an appreciate the suitable drama of that, thee approximation of his face crinkling, turnin black, becomin soot, but I don't so I just jam it into the bin beneath the crusts an wrappers an tea bags an roach ends an ash. Jam it down until it's buried beneath the shit. Torn up an buried. Then I go to the phone an dial Victoria's mobile.

The blood comin out of him. Him strugglin, screamin, unable to get away. Me, elbow-deep in the burning of him an his face fallin when he came. Me hands around his neck, the fuckin *look* on his face. *Of* his face.

—Hello? Who's this?

Vicky's voice barely audible over the background noise. A babble of voices an music.

—It's Kelly.

—Who?

—Kelly!

—*Who?*

—KELLY! IT'S KELLY!

She makes a loud sound of cheering. Evidently already pissed, or thereabouts.

—I'm in the Brewery, Kel! Upstairs, like! There's a party on!

—Whose?

—What?!

—I said: WHOSE?

—I don't know! Just flashed me baps at the bouncers, like, an thee let me in! It's bangin, get yerself down!

Thinkin about it. What I *really* need is a night in, food an sleep an stuff, recharge the wasted batteries, like. Get rested an all that. But it's cold in here, cold an dull an dark an the telly babbles shite an I really don't know what the fuck to do. Except *think*; I mean, that's what I *don't* want to do. Retreat inside me own head an stay there. Soon be bangin me friggin fists on the wall, on thee inside of me skull, *fuck* that.

—Kelly!

—What?!

—Are yis comin down? Free booze an everythin! It's sound!

—Alright then, yeh. I'll be there in twenty.

She shouts somethin about Chinese New Year, how soon it is an how we should start the celebrations now or something like that an I say 'Okay' an hang up. Get dressed an nice-smellin, put the ahl slap on, all that shite, an leave the house. First night out in me new maroon coat, which is somethin to smile about, I suppose. If I didn't have an ace new coat to show off I'd stay in; go to bed early, get some sleep. That's what I'd do, were it not for this ace new coat.

We put the steamin foil cartons on the floor an pile food on to ar plates; lemon chicken, egg fried rice, stir-fried mushrooms an prawn crackers. I'm fuckin starvin. We're *all* starvin; me an Roz shovellin the food into ar gobs with spoons, Vicky delicately pickin up whole dumplings with chopsticks an then swallowin them in one go. Feels good to have food, hot proper food, like, goin inside me; a warm glow down there for a moment, temporarily dispelling this biting fuckin winter cold that seems to have gone bone-deep. This must be the coldest bleedin winter on record; fuckin sure of it, I am. I'm *freezin*. Global warming, me hole; I feel like a bleedin Eskimo.

—Bit fuckin warm in here, Kel, Victoria says. —Can yer not turn the heatin down a bit?

—Yer jokin, aren't yer? I'm bleedin freezing. Teeth are chatterin an everythin.

Roz nods. —Nah, Vicky's right. It's like me nan's house or somethin. Stiflin. I'm bakin in here.

—Yeh, turn the fire down or somethin, Kel. I can hardly friggin breathe.

I turn the gas fire down a wee bit, fetch a cardy an put that on. Never been so cold in me life. No lie; icy I am, right down deep inside, like.

Roz asks if we're gunner put the film on. Something she chose, some sci–fi giant-insect horror thingio.

—Bit early yet, Vicky says. —There's ages yet. See what's on telly first, yeh? Try Five; normally some weird friggin porn thing on there about this time of night.

I do; an there's a feller with nowt on bar a leather ski mask, on his hands an knees vigorously scrubbing the tiles of a bathroom floor. An overweight woman in a tight leather catsuit comes in an starts callin him a wanker, a useless excuse for a man an I can hear him whimperin an then the woman hoofs him up thee arse an he goes 'oooooff'.

—Told youse, didn't I, Vicky says. —Always somethin like this on Five, this time of night. Series of documentaries on prozzies an stuff. No, not prozzies; Sexual Tension Release Specialists, that's what we are. Oldest profession in the world.

—Could make yer friggin *own* series, you, Roz says through a gobful of rice. —Kelly told me all about that feller over in Heswall, the one yer left in the stocks. Didn't yer, Kel?

—Did, Roz, yeh.

—Aw, he's fuckin infatuated with *you*, Kelly. Vicky tongs a king prawn in her chopsticks an holds it in front of her face. It looks like a penis, cut off an fried. —Tosser won't stop goin on about yer. Says he'll pay anything. Fallen for yer big time, he has, tellin yer. Started callin yer his 'angel'.

—So I've gone from 'queen' to 'angel', have I?

—Yeh.

—An why? Cos I caned the sad twat's arse til it bled an he pissed hisself in terror?

—Seems so, yeh, Vicky nods. —Daft as it sounds, that's the reason. *You* work it out. Cos I can't, but it pays me fuckin rent.

An nor can I work it out, not in another fuckin millennium. I mean, look now: the woman on the telly is now smokin a cigarette an flickin thee ashes on to the crawlin, scrubbin man's bare back. Now what the fuck's that all about? Anyone were to use *me* as an ashtray an I'd fuckin leather them one in the fuckin jaw. But this bloke, here, this bloke on the telly on his hands an knees *pays* people to do it. What's that all about? What the fuckin hell's goin on there? The woman's sittin on the toilet seat, sneerin down at the man with utter disdain. She begins to hum a song.

—Aw fuckin hell, Vicky says. —Even *I'm* not that cruel. Singin a Phil Collins song in the poor cunt's ear.

Roz laughs. —That's pure torture. Should get Amnesty International on the case.

—Is right.

—I feel sorry for him, now. Poor bastard. Roz chews thoughtfully for a minute then gulps her food an says: —What's all this about, Vix? Why do so many fellers wanner be treated like shite nowadays? An why are there so many women willin to treat them that way?

Victoria starts sayin stuff about money an power games, all the stuff we talked about in her car on the way to Heswall that time. I can't deny that there's something of Victoria, something of the big woman on the telly too, inside me; I mean, just watchin this programme an rememberin bein in that cellar with the bloke unable to escape, an I can feel meself stirrin below, gettin warmer, wetter, wider. But for me, tho, it's not really about prostitution, not really about the money. Nor is it really about power; I mean, yeh, I *did* make money from it, money that I'm still spending, but that was a one-off an I'll never do it again. It's like, with her clients, Vicky's the dominant one supposedly but the fact of the matter is that it's *her* without the power, it's *her* who gets dragged into other people's desires, fixations. It's *her* who's the one ends up bein used. Bein forced to do things she doesn't really wanner do for money, while those with the money get exactly what thee want. The sick capitalist dynamics remain unchanged, in fact there thee are in ther purest, blackest form. With me, tho, it's different. With me it's just . . . one person. One person only I want, *need* to do everything to. One person only I want to rip apart an put back together again, rebuild. I ripped apart Peter, accordin to me mother, an that twat can stay that way, in bits, like. But *Victor*, now, Victor I want to . . . to mend. Fix. Glue him back together again.

Humpty fuckin Dumpty.

Except maybe it was me who smashed him into pieces in the first fuckin place; maybe it was me that was his great fall. But all I know is that with him there was heat an light an the closest I've ever come to fuckin ecstasy; without him it's just a Chinese takeaway an a crap, titillatin documentary, dark an cold an dull. An I really fuckin miss it, I do, with all me fuckin heart. I miss *him*. Not even sackin off me crappy job has given me one tiny fraction of the freedom I felt when I was with him. His skin parting at me touch and his blood. My hand powerin up inside him to take hold of his thuddin heart.

—Y'alright, Kelly?

I look up. —Yeh, why?

—Just looked a bit pissed off, there, that's all.

—No, I'm fine.

—Is *this* makin yer feel down? This programme? Vicky points the chopsticks at the telly.

—No, I'm alright, honest. Just a bit knackered, I suppose.

—Oh, I know what it is, Roz says. —It's that new feller, innit. That one from Magnet. She looks at Vicky, nods sideways at me. —She's missin him.

—Yeh. Haven't seen him for a few days, have yer?

I shrug.

—Aw no. Youse haven't split up already.

—No, no, I shrug again. —It's just, yer know . . . not that

heavy, like. Not that serious. He's doin his own thing, I'm doin mine. He's busy helpin out with the Chinese New Year party. His mate's uncle or something builds the dragon so he helps out each year.

—Which mate? Vicky asks. —Thee Irish feller?

—Thee *Irish* feller? I think it's more likely to be the *Chinese* feller, Vic, don't you?

She smiles. —Oh aye, yeh. Anyway, the Chinese New Year; we gunner go on one, yeh?

—Deffo.

—Oh fuck yeh. Remember last year's?

—Not at all, Roz, no, I say. —*That's* how bleedin good it was.

She laughs. —Is right.

—Yeh, so we'll repeat it *this* year, Vicky says. —Same as last year, yeh? Meet up in the Dingle, work ar way into town?

—Yeh.

—Follow the trail of bars an beak.

—An boak.

—You know it, Roz.

—Alright then. Vicky puts her empty plate on the floor, the chopsticks on it in a crucifix. —Two days from now, the Pineapple, two o'clock. Sound good?

—Sound to me.

—Me n all, I say. —Can't wait.

An I can't. Already lookin forwards to it *big* time. Get some good rest tonight an tomorrow, eat well, go on a mad one. Excited at just the thought of it, I am. An Chinatown with all the people an the flames an the fireworks an the big snaky dragon thing an what else might I see there? What other delights might I meet in Chinatown, two days' time?

—So it's a date, then? Vicky asks.

—Oh yeh.

—Too right.

—Youse both sure? I mean I don't wanner be in the Dingle on me own, like.

—Positive, Vicky.

So sure that I can take me cardigan off. So sure that I change

308

channels on the telly; some David Attenborough stuff. From a suburban dominatrix to lions eating a gazelle. Not that much different, really.

—Put the film on, Kel, Roz says. —Let's watch great big insects eat people.

—Alright.

We do.

Me wrists are sore. Why the fuck are me wrists so sore? In fact, both me entire arms are painful, from wrists to shoulders, like, as if I've recently swum a long way or played a game of shinty or something. Some muscle fatigue from somewhere. An then, in the shower, I find out why cos as I pick up the shower gel the bottle just bursts in me hands, the top of it just shoots off an all the gel splurges out, a gooey pool of apple-an-rosemary-scented green gunge around me feet. I look at me hands, the crumpled placcy bottle between them, both of them curled around it into tightly clenched fists an I remember yesterday holdin a banana an just about to peel it when it burst too, the skin suddenly splitting an all the fruit squirtin out like thick yellow toothpaste and, yeh, now I come to think of it I remember last night the toothpaste tube also bucklin in me hand an spurtin white spearmint paste all over the mirror above the sink. It's me hands, me fuckin hands; thee want to grip things too tightly. Thee feel kind of empty yet peculiarly strong, thee wanner grab things in the world an feel pressure, me palms closin around things an holdin them, squeezin them. Fuckin *crushing* them. It's like I wanner throttle the world an everything in it, like I wanner clasp the whole fuckin planet in me palms an squeeze until it bursts an all resilience collapses an crumples an gives an I'm left holding nothin but mush. Like I need to push against things, or no, snatch an clutch all fuckin solidity an squeeze it, *squeeeeeeeeeeeeeze* it until it either breaks an surrenders or me arms give in cos thee can't take any more. Which is why both me arms are all sore, like, cos I've been doin that squeezing for days, everythin I touched, grabbed an clasped an fuckin *squeeeeeeezed*. Crushed all to fuck.

Too tense, Kelly. Relax. Just take it friggin easy.

I scoop some of the spilt soap up in me hands an rub it all over me body, rinse it off an then sit on thee edge of the bath while I push the rest of the green slime down the plughole with me foot. The feelin of the bath edge diggin into me arse, FLASH on to Victor bent down on his knees between me spread legs, the shower water fallin, drummin on his back, his head buried between me thighs an the ridges of his backbone bent as he ducked his head an the strong muscle of his tongue strainin up inside me, inside my cunt, slurpin wet an warm across me burning clit an flickin on it, *flicking* on it makin it fuckin spark an all the warmth inside me flowin an drippin an lickin my clit he was where me fingers are now, just there, rubbing, so fuckin sensitive an the light pressure on it fiery an insistent an then his whole tongue up inside my fanny slurpin an slobberin God I felt his tongue right up in my fuckin womb how *open* I was, how yearning yawnin so fuckin wide then I slid down to sit on his hard dick an it forced me even further open an pushed up inside so hard an bulging like oak like fuckin iron him panting an his chest heavin my fingers inside me now this feels wrong somehow like an invasion, a fuckin plundering, like my own cunt doesn't want to accept me own fingers. What's goin on then FLASH to the face of Victor in mine bent back at the neck which buckled in my hands squeezing, crushing so tight so relentless an his eyes rolled back to show the whites an his mouth fell slack an the noises from him one long drawn-out groan quiet an thee ecstasy on his face, the sheer fuckin rapture an the mad bursts of his cock inside me as he came like a cannon booming white hot pulses of bright burnin light an I came then as I am comin now but not like it no cos this is painful, searing, it's like a fuckin drained wound or something an abscess suckin out of me all fuckin energy an vitality it feels just fuckin awful an I slide down the side of the bath an slump under the shower, the water drummin on me skull an I feel fuckin *awful*, I feel fuckin guilty an shameful an sordid an stupid an lost. Lost, last, completely fuckin horrible. A stain on thee earth. Shredded an empty an drained of all good.

Turn the taps off. Feel the steel of them in yer palms, fuckin *feel* it, the four blunt points driving into yer flesh. So fuckin tight that yer fuckin *back* aches. All the muscles in yer body powered into yer grip, clutch so fuckin tight you could shatter granite. Fuckin *feel* it, Kelly. FEEL IT.

Something is about to tear in me wrists so I let go, flex me fingers a few times to restore the circulation an step out of the bath. Dryin meself an I must inhale a fibre from the towel or a hair or something cos suddenly I'm bent double coughin, hackin an splutterin phlegm splatterin on the floor, I feel like I'm choking, gaggin an gulpin for air or to eject wire wool from me lungs, it's fuckin horrible. It's a real hackin fit, I can feel me face turnin bright red an hot, I'm coughin so hard I think me teeth are gunner fuckin fly out, me eyes shoot from ther sockets. Coughs from right down deep in me guts. It's fuckin vile. It lasts for ages an when it finally passes I'm hit with a wave of sadness so deep an intense that I remain hunched over, naked, clutchin me stomach, futility an loss an pain washin over me like a wave of mercury so fuckin dense an heavy I am fuckin crippled under it, me knees are knockin I am dizzy an reelin like all suffering ever is within my skin an me scalp crawls with the horror of it, the colossal fuckin *pain* of it an I manage to push meself backwards on to the toilet an I sit there weeping, scaldin salt water on me face an sobs so hard thee might break my bones I am naked I am weeping me heart is broken there is fuck all to live for ever I am grippin each knee in each hand so hard me knuckles white with the pressure an straining me fuckin kneecaps groaning, threatening to shatter hurting but fuck it feel it Kelly *FEEL* it.

I'll see him again, I think. Can't imagine the rest of me life stretchin ahead without seein him again, at least once. All those days an months an years empty of him, devoid of him, without that strange attractive person an I hate that fuckin thought, I hate it, can't bear to live with that fuckin thought. Me on me own yearning for him or with other men an comparin them to him an them always without exception fallin short an I'll pretend to like them, pretend to enjoy bein with them an I'll let them shag me an I'll pretend to enjoy it an thee'll puff ther chests out thinkin how ace an manly thee are an all's *I'll* be thinkin is: You're fuckin *nowt*. Yer nothing, not compared to a certain one. An I know that feelin will never pass, never fuckin leave me an that's a thought impossible to live with so I'll either implode, wither an die or see him again, see him again just the once, hold his pulse an beat in me hands just once more cos if I don't I know I will I'll fuckin crumple, dissolve an vanish an surely that can't happen so I'll see him again, I'll see him again. Somewhere, some way I'll see the bastard again. This howlin hole inside me. Yawnin so wide I'll fall in fuckin two.

Rain on me new coat, on me new maroon coat an ruinin me hair, all that time I spent over it primpin it in the bathroom mirror, all friggin wasted. An colouring darker me tight, long denim skirt an splashin shite up on to me trainies but fuck it, it's just water, it's only rain; try an avoid it an yer'll end up both wet *and* frustrated, so yer might as well just be wet. Let the fucker fall.

The way it colours everythin the same. It makes the world all just one.

I get off the bus at the DSS office down Park Road. Can't be friggin arsed waitin in the queue so I just go over to one of the desks, a feller behind it with a gold Nike swoosh in his ear sad branded bastard is talking to a client, a customer, a claimant or whatever the fuck we're called now (chubby feller in shellsuit an perm, typical Dingle scally). I ask him if he minds an he says:
—Norrat all, love. You go ed.

I give the envelope to Nike man.
—What's this?
—Claim forms.
—Well, can yer join the queue cos we have to go through these together, like, to see if yer've missed anythin out. It's in yer best interests.
—Can't, I say. —Late for an appointment. Me number's in there, just phone me if there's anythin yer need to discuss.
—Yeh, well, can yer just wait a moment please. I'm busy.

I just walk out. Leave that bastard office. Knowin the grief ahead of me that waits in there, thee endless questions an judging, the fuckin New Deal forced into me fuckin life. Heart sinkin whenever there's a windowed manila envelope in me letter box of a mornin. All those meetings, the Jobsearch an progress reports an havin to remember all the lies I've told.

Fuck it all.

I head down Park Road, towards the Pineapple. Still rainin. Fine, sooty, greasy rain, more a mist than a rain really, holdin in suspension all the smog sucked up from the city an turned to a hissin, driftin mist. Streaks of muck on everyone's face. The rings of dark scum there'll be tonight in every fuckin bathtub throughout Merseyside. This floatin dirt that we walk through.

Nice smell of bakin bread reminds me that I'm hungry. There's a sign in the window of the bakery: HELP WANTED, FULL-TIME. Somethin draws me in there, not just the good smell.

—Yes, love?

—It's about the job.

—Oh aye. REENIE!

I jump. A right friggin screech, that. Sounded like a bleedin pterodactyl or somethin. A woman with curly red hair comes out of the back room, her eyebrows raised at me. This is Reenie, I suppose. The other woman, the screecher, nods at me.

—Girl here's askin about the job.

Reenie looks me up an down. —Done shopwork before, yeh?

—Loads.

—Come with me then.

I follow her into the back room, into the lovely smell an the dry heat of thee ovens an she asks me a few questions an I answer them, most of them truthfully an when I leave there about twenty minutes later I've got the job. Start on Tuesday, workin behind the counter in a pinny an a hat sellin cakes an bread an other baked stuff. How I feel about it I don't really know. I mean, there'll be no continuous hassle off the dole wankers an I won't be stuck in that fuckin shop all day, just me an Fat Macca behind the bulletproof perspex, an I'll have more money than if I was to sign on, but, well, it *is* back behind a fuckin counter again; without a cage an a twat of a boss, true, but a friggin counter nonetheless. But there it is again, the public, dealin with the friggin public, them givin me money for things an me givin them those things. Those transactions, like. I'll be makin nothing, *creating* nowt, fuck all to be proud of, fuck all to look forward to when I wake up in the mornings. No time to meself. This will grind on an on until unhappiness takes over an settles down inside me an I drift aimlessly around in a state of perpetual tiredness. Perepetual *miserable* tiredness.

Feel like I've failed, somehow. Like I've compromised too fuckin much. Worse; like I've fuckin *betrayed* someone. Someone who had great faith in me to *do* something, achieve something that I've always wanted to achieve, is now lookin at me an tutting an shakin ther head. Disappointed an let down. Feel like I've fucked up again.

Nah, Kelly, it'll be nice, workin in a bakery; givin cakes an bread to people, seein them all pleased. Little ahl ladies with ther iced buns an Eccles cakes, ahl fellers on the piss in the Pineapple an the Volunteer comin in for ham rolls an scouse pies to line ther belies. It'll be a *nice* job. Yer'll make people smile. An Reenie seemed sound as well; a bit odd, like, but in a *good* way. An at least it'll be *warm* in there, from thee ovens, like; a cold winter's morning, goin to work in there with the cosy heat an the lovely smells, it'll be sound. It'll be alright. *You'll* be alright. You can't foresee the future or heal the crippled, so do what yer can. Sell people cakes. An bread. An pies.

I go into the Pineapple an there thee all are, at the far end of the bar by the jukebox, a bright an loud collection; Victoria with her hair skyscraper high an Roz an a lovely Jamaican girl I went to school with called Michele. She's the first to spot me an she waves an gives a great big grin. Thee others all look up an cheer. I go over to them. Shop-girl Kelly, baker Kelly movin slinky in her ace new coat.

—Yer late, Kelly. Catchin up to do.

—Just got a job, I tell them. —In a bakery down the road. Start Tuesday.

—A job?

—Thought yer already *had* one, in that newsies, like.

—Sacked it a few days ago, didn't I?

—Ah well then, Michele says. —Let's have a little drinky to yer success.

—Yeh, Vicky says. —A nice little drinkipoos. Forty-eight-fuckin-*hour* drinkipoos.

I tell them I need some money then go back out of the pub an go down Park Road til I find a bank. Go in it, draw out every last penny above the solitary quid needed to keep me account open. Then go back to the pub with me pocket bulging.

One last party. One last mad bastard spree.

Haven't got the first friggin clue where I am. Bright lights an loud music. Somewhere down by the docks, I think, cos it seems I can smell the sea.

I'm leanin against the bar an the bar's wobbling. There's a drink in front of me, something with Coke, a wiltin lemon slice stuck to the side of the glass, an it's probly *my* drink because I'm now drinkin it. Seems like I've been drinkin it for fuckin ever but not really; all it is is another drink in a long, long line of the same. I'm drunk an gettin drunker.

A hand squeezes me elbow. I turn an look an see Peter's ugly fuckin face far too fuckin close to mine. Stubble on his cheeks an chin an black-ringed eyes that look afraid an his breath stinks like somethin rotten.

—How are yer, Kelly?

—Sound, sound. Havin a *great* time.

Without *you*, yer prick.

—Not really, no.

—I wasn't friggin askin *you*. I was tellin yer about *me*.

Cheeky cunt. Thinks the whole fuckin world revolves around him. His hand's still clutchin me elbow, the fingers really diggin in an I jerk me arm free an his hand goes to his pocket. He's strong, Peter is, he's big an has always been physically strong, but it's not a good strength; it begs.

—Who're yis with?

—Victoria an Rosalind. Michele was with us an all but I don't know where she's gone. You with Elaine, yeh?

He just winces an shakes his head an changes the subject. —Is there anythin yer needin? Anythin I can help youse with?

Roz appears at me shoulder an asks me if I'm alright. I tell her I am an ask her if we need any more drugs. She says no, she doesn't think so, but it's not like we need any *less*, is it, so I turn back to Peter.

—Alright. Wharrav yer got? Straight beak, yeh?

He shakes his head. —Christ, Kelly, no. Uncut coke's like fuckin gold dust in the town at the mo. Haven't yer heard?

—About what?

—About the coca tax?

I shake me head an sip me drink.

—Oh yeh, he goes on. As he so fuckin *loves* to do. Demeanour of a world-weary, cynical, seen–it–all reporter. —Coca tax in Columbia. FARC an the ELN have set up a new tax, see. Charlie's gone up to five thousand dollars at source from two thousand at souce in about two months. Oh aye, it might be just a good night out to you an yer mates like but to them it's necessary fundin for ther autonomous Marxist state. Have to support the fuckin revolution somehow, don't thee? An if that means that Westerners have to pay a little bit more for ther nights out, then so be it.

Tosser. Thinks he's a fuckin hero of the people cos he once gave a flim to Shelter. Knobhead. —So what is it then?

—What's what?

—What yer carryin. If it's not cocaine, like.

—Well, it's got a coke *base*. Wee bit of billy thrown in, wee bit of smack. Plus me own secret ingredient.

—Which is?

—Not tellin yer. It's a secret. *And* a prezzie.

As I lift me glass he slips a wrap into me pocket. Then slides his hand down to rest on me hip bone which is stickin out cos I'm leanin me weight on me other leg in an attempt to stay stable. Not so pissed tho that I can't feel the slimy heat of his hand even through me clothes.

—This a new coat? It suits you. Yer look good.

316

—Gerroff me, Peter.

He doesn't.

—Peter, don't fuckin touch me, will yer.

He does, so I turn away from him, but his hand on me shoulder spins me back around to face him again an I pull me drink back to chuck in his stupid fuckin face an he says:

—Kelly, don't leave me. Please come back to me.

His hand still on me shoulder, now creepin up to stroke me neck. I shrug it off an he looks like he's about to cry.

—I really fuckin miss you, Kelly. I haven't been happy since yer left.

I can see Roz an Vicky behind him, lookin at me all concerned. I smile an nod at them to show them I'm sound. Peter's pathetic in front of me, lookin so fuckin useless, his arms hangin limply at his sides an the ravage in his face pitiful. The nice, dreamy side of me wants to feel sorry for him but the cynical side, the harder side, the fuckin *real* side is just enjoyin watchin him fumble an flounder. The shite he did to me, fuckin inflicted on me an now here the twat is, fallin apart in front of me eyes. It's fuckin ace.

—I do, Kelly, honest to God; I'm not messin, I really fuckin miss you. Why did yer ever go?

—*Right.*

I finish me bevvy an put it down hard on the bar. Peter's eyes are followin me every movement, his mouth downturned at the corners.

—D'yer really wanner know? He doesn't say anythin but I carry on anyway. —Remember that time when yer slapped me face so fuckin hard that yer loosened three teeth? Remember that? An I had to go the dentist to get them cemented back in an *you* wouldn't even fuckin pay for it? Even tho yer were fuckin loaded, like. An remember, soon as I got home with me fuckin gob all swollen, sore, full of fuckin blood yer made me give yis a blow job? Remember that time?

He gulps. I actually see his Adam's apple bounce up an down. Never noticed before how big his Adam's apple is. How big an hairy an ugly. Like he's swallowin a friggin bin lid or somethin.

317

—Yeh, but you . . .

—Or the time yer fuckin raped me –

—Raped you!

—*Raped* me with the body-spray canister? Held me face down on the floor, sat on me back so I couldn't move an fuckin rammed it up me arse? Remember that one? Yeh, yer really fuckin *forced* it up there, didn't yer? Really fuckin *jammed* it in, like. I bled for a whole week afterwards, yer know. It was like menstruation from me arse.

He winces. I just shake me head. There's many other things I could tell him but it'd be pointless cos cunts like him never learn, ther obsessed with makin others feel as bad about themselves as *they* do an besides which I'm with me mates an it's Chinese New Year an we're all on a bender an I wanner be with them an not him, I just want him to go away. A good time is what I want an I could never imagine one with him in it.

—Oh, just fuck off, will yer, Peter. I don't give a fuck whether I never ever see yis again as long as I live. Gerraway from me. Gerrout of me life. Just fuckin do one, will yer.

An then I walk away, back to me friends. Don't even look back at the twat once an then we're out again in the city, I can see fireworks burstin around the spire of thee Anglican cathedral in the distance an coldness clasps me face an I can feel an anger inside me, a violence and urge to hurt but the strange thing is it's not Peter that I'm directin these urges towards. Him, I don't give two fucks about. It's that friggin *Victor* who I wanner hurt. Rippin his arms an legs off in me mind. Now why the almighty fuck is that?

Because he's unique. Because he's alone on thee earth. Because I've never met anyone like him ever an he's not in me life any more. I haven't seen him for so long.

Because yer not quite right in the head, Kelly. Because yer need fuckin help. Because sometimes yer not even certain that yer awake; sometimes yer think yer dreaming.

That bastard. That *fucker*.

—Where to now? Roz says, shiverin, her arms wrapped around herself. —Head on up to Concert Square, yeh?

—Fuck that, Roz, no. Vicky's hair sways as she shakes her head. —Be fuller friggin students tonight. Some kind of cheap promotion in Arena or something.

—We'll go Modo, then.

—Cunts'll be in there as well. Get fuckin everywhere, thee do. Should be confined to ther unions an friggin . . . She burps, staggers. —Friggin *shot* if ther seen out in the city.

Three lads walk past wearin Harry Enfield Scouser perm wigs an fake muzzies, lookin like Terry McDermott, circa the seventies. Ther grinnin an shoutin loud in fake Scouse accents.

—Yer see! Vicky points at them. —Yer fuckin *see* what I mean! WANKERS! Hope youse get the shite kicked out of yis tonight! Fuckin student WANKERS!

Thee whirl around to face her, see her there nearly friggin seven feet tall with her high hair an platform boots. She stands above them an fuckin swoops down at them, her clawed hands grabbin for them, gnashing an screechin. Thee run away. I laugh. Victoria shouts some more:

—ARSEHOLES! FUCKIN GOBSHITES!

But it *is* thee Arena bar I find meself in, standin swayin at one of the windows overlookin Concert Square which is a heavin mass of people. Fireworks are burstin over the city, short-lived giant flowers of flame in the night sky. I'm drinkin a bottle of vodka Source but I can't tell what flavour it's supposed to be. Apple, maybe. An here he comes, striding grinnin cheesily over to me, fuckin smug-cunt fat-lipped student in a hooped rugby shirt an what's his chat-up line? What's the first thing he says to me?

—Hi. I'm Dave.

Just that; 'I'm Dave'. Idyit.

—That's a borin name, I say. —Suits yis.

He gets a bit of a beamer an goes back to his mates who point an jeer at him. He sits down with them an I can see him mouth the words 'slag' an 'slut', lookin sideways at me. Knobhead. One of his mates, a taller bloke in a Puma hat an baggy cargo kex, sidles over smirking.

—I, erm, I have to say that I really admire the way you blew out the Dog.

That accent. That fuckin BBC featureless accent. Why do students all sound the same now? An where the fuck does that accent originate?

—The Dog? He said his name was Dave.

—It is, yeh, but the Dog's his drinkin name.

Drinking name? Is this cunt serious?

—He can sniff a woman out at a hundred yards, y'see.

—Oh fuck off.

—No, it's true. He's like a bloodhound. We've all got drinking names. Mine's the Snake.

—Oh fuck off.

—No, it is, seriously. Want to know why?

I go the bog. Chop some of Peter's whatever-the-fuck-it-is out on the window ledge, two lines, an snort.

Fuck me *stiff* this is strong. Me tongue goes instantly numb, me face throbs an me back teeth start to tingle an I swallow chemical goo an me heart's racing. Me right knee is jerkin in time to the music I can hear muffled an there's a deep buzzing in me ears an I can feel the surge of blood in me scalp, a hot rush all over me centred in me face me twitchin face an I rasp the tips of me fingers over me cheeks an forehead an it feels lovely, *I* feel lovely an I press thee end of me nose against the cold wall tiles an murmur.

I hear a door opening, someone comin in.

—Kelly? Is that you?

Roz's voice.

—In here.

—Yis alright?

—Sound, yeh. Flyin.

—On what?

I let her into the cubicle an chop her out a line an she snorts it an then I chop out another an snort that meself an then we're out in the city again an then in another pub an then another an then the cathedral so massive is blockin out the stars an I'm off me face in Chinatown, standin beneath them yowge gates thee built in Shanghai an shipped all the way from there to here an all the people around me are crushed together an swayin an the lights flash an there are explosions an the long dragon snakes past me, buckin an bowin an whippin around on itself an it looks friggin incredible, dreamlike, fantastic an wondrous, its snarling ferocious face all lit up. It circles the cramped crowd, the feet underneath it stamping an shuffling, like a giant millipede from some country visited only in sleep. Fuckin amazing it is, here, now, in the real, mad world.

Stabilised by the drug, kind of. It's taken some of the drunkenness away an I'm firm on me feet now, just a mad whirling in me head. Soaring I am an I feel absolutely fuckin ace. Wonderful. Like an essential part of it all.

I put me hands deep in the pockets of me new coat to disguise the frantic twitching of me fingers. I see a rocket rise up into the sky an I watch it rise, climbin upwards, tilt me head back to watch it climb til it suddenly bursts in a shower of red an white sparks which fall slowly back down to earth again an I watch them fall, fallin gently like snow, all of them dyin before thee hit the ground. Gorgeous. Fuckin gorgeous. I could watch that all night, I could, the climbin flame an the burst an then the fallin stars. So sharp an twinkling in me eyes. I can feel meself smiling.

I feel a nudge, a gentle nudge in the ribs. It's Vicky, lookin moody, annoyed. She tells me that she's just run into one of the Sashers who wanted to piss on her some months ago, after thee'd hired her to strip for them on the evening of ther march.

—What, an the cunt gave yer grief, did he?

—No, he didn't, I don't think he even saw me, it was just, yer know . . . brought back memories. An not very fuckin nice ones either.

I'm a bit shocked to see how shaken up Vicky looks. She looks genuinely upset. She seems to take it all in her stride usually but she's human, it *must* affect her badly sometimes, this wide sickness dragging her in; stocks an caning, shitty knickers, gangs of men wanting to piss on yer, lads with crucifixion fixations wantin yer to ram yer fist up ther arse, friggin *payin* yer to do it. Fuckin crush videos for Christ's sake. It must get to yer after a while, all that obsession, all that illness, no matter how well adjusted an strong of spirit yer are. There are times when it *must* undermine yis; get close enough to make *you* feel ill, as well.

Naked screamin freedom. Skin opening under the mighty power in me arm, terror an obsession so strong it loosens bladders, sphincters. A queen, I am. Some voice called me a fuckin *angel*.

—Kels. Vicky nudges me again.

—What?

—How many Prods does it take to change a light bulb?

—Dunno, how many?

—None.

—Why?

—Cos thee all live in eternal darkness. Seen who's over there? She points into the crowd further down the road, in front of the flats next door to the Blackie. —Staring at yer? Can yer see him?

I follow her finger.

—No, who . . .

—*There*, look. He's fuckin *gawpin* at yer, girl.

Oh my good fuckin God it's him. It's Victor. His face in the crowd in the falling light, red an white falling. He's staring at me, his friend at his shoulder pointin me out to him, an I'm staring at him back an me brain is registering his stare with a fire in me guts an I nod once, that's all I do, the world melts away except for his face in the falling light an I nod only the once an that simple movement that short backwards jerk of the head is enough, enough to pull him towards me. He's coming towards me an I watch him come. Show me your scars, Victor. Show me my name.

Here's Victor, swayin towards me. Standin before me now here he is.

—Iya, Kelly.

He's slurring. He's off his face. His lovely, odd, fuckin infuriating face.

—Hiya, Victor. How are you?

—Okay. He stumbles then straightens himself. —Bit wrecked.

—Yer not kiddin. On one, yeh?

He nods, his head all floppy on his neck. He starts to ramble, somethin about Monday an a new job, disconnected words an nonsense an he can't look at me eyes, he's focusing on me chin an me ears an then the bridge of me nose, unable to meet me eyes an I'm lookin at his thick eyebrows an the way thee rise pointed in the middle an the little cluster of downy hairs that join them an the shallow wrinkles at ther edges an the way his tear ducts gleam an his pupils, his big black pupils reflectin the sky an the bangin, burstin fireworks an all the fallin stars red an then white cascadin slowly across his drifting eyes. I'm not as nervous as I thought I would be, there's no thunderin heart or dryness of gob, in fact it feels so perfectly an completely correct as if all this is meant to be, me an him facing each other off in this big reeling crowd an the dragon plunging over his shoulder an all the coloured stars falling out of the sky. Feels just so fuckin *right*. As if everythin that's ever happened in the world ever from old trade agreements with China to the circumstances of my birth has been geared towards allowing nothing but this, this meeting, me an Victor here, tonight. Just fuckin this an this is fuckin everything.

Thee urge to grab him. Pounce an clutch, snatch, grab, yank him off his feet an squeeze him til his ribs crack. Til his eyes pop. It's all I can do to stop meself.

He's stopped talkin now an he's just standin there, slightly smiling, his eyes kind of unfocused, glazed. His hands loose at his sides. Feel like I've found somethin precious that I lost ages ago; me granny's weddin ring or somethin, me grandad's war medals, some gift from me dead dad. Somethin which I'll never lose again cos it left me fuckin bereft an *this* time I'll never let it out of me sight, I'll wear it on a choker around me neck, pierce it through me ear, stitch it to me skin.

Tie it to me bed.

Sloppy-smiling Victor. I ask him if he could go another toot an he nods an agrees enthusiastically so I tell him to come with me an I say tara to Victoria an take his cold, fragile hand (a labourer's hand, this? Fuck *no*, the softness) in mine an lead him up through the crowds out of Chinatown. Two bizzies eye us up, tryin no doubt to work out why we're staggerin, booze or somethin else, but thee leave us alone an without sayin one single word I lead Victor stumblin down a side street an into Pogue Mahone. Packed fuckin Pogue Mahone, boilin hot an sweaty. I tell Victor to get me a vodka an Coke an I go off to the bog.

An here I fuckin well *am* again. Here I go again. I'm off again, among cold tiles an tinklin water, all sounds an colours sharpened, heightened, cuttin up drugs on cracked white porcelain. Anythin is now possible, it seems. There's nowt I can't do. All the world an all the history of it is compressed into this one city on this one evening, the mad celebration of everythin that ever was even before I was born into this strangest of all possible worlds an everythin fuckin in it is for *me*. Me an Victor, Victor waitin for me up at the bar with booze an drugs again in me face, buzzin in me face like it seems thee always have, the first breath I took was some kind of hit. I raise me hands to cup me breasts, feel them quake with each boom of me heart. Wild an wondrous an terrible.

I feel ace. I feel awful. I don't know how the fuck I feel.

Scared.

On automatic pilot I'm back in the bar, takin Victor's hand an passin him the wrap. I start drinking an he goes off to the toilet, an I'm on me own here now among all these men, any one of which might want me to cane ther arse, carve me name into ther back, force me fist up ther hole. Break them apart an then rebuild. All of them have secrets, wants an needs so strong thee become cravings, obsessions, real deep needs over an above those things ther *told* that thee need, new cars or whatever, tellies, sound systems, yer nowt without a fuckin DVD, these things ther told ther lives would be hollow without an right down deep in the black unexplored chambers of ther thumping hearts ther *real* needs, ther genuine, unadulterated, authentic cravings thee might have been born with begin to curdle an sour an grow twisted, deformed, more n more an worse n worse until they too are locked in stocks while strange girls physically mutilate them, beggin for mercy an beggin for more at the same fuckin time, desperate an frantic an sweaty, all part of the larger fever. This insane fuckin frenzy an at the centre of it all is just one spark, one wee flickerin spark, bright an sputtering an inextinguishable. Only we've been conditioned into wantin everythin so fuckin colossal an deafenin that we can't any longer see such a tiny thing or hear its faint snapping. It might as well not exist.

Aw fuck's sakes. Come back now, Victor. What do we do, what the fuck do we do. What do *I* do. What do *I* fuckin do now that you're fuckin here again, with me. Jesus fuckin Christ.

He's standin by me an I can feel his warmth comin off him in waves. He slips the wrap back into me hand an I pocket it then neck me drink.

—Drink up, then. We'll go an flag a taxi.

—Where're we goin?

I'm suckin an ice cube, tryin in vain to calm the white-hot fire in me face. Look into my gob like a dentist would an you'd be able to see the flames leapin at the back of me throat. I look at Victor's eyes an now he meets mine.

—I've missed you, Victor.

That's all I can say. Through it all I've missed him; through birth an childhood an puberty I've fuckin well missed him. There's nothin else to be said.

He knocks back his bevvy an we leave the pub. Up to the taxi rank beneath the tall charred skeleton of St Luke's, bombed an burned by the Nazis half a century ago, during the last millennium. I remember me granny talkin about it, how it burned like a sun. How people screamed an ran an how the sky rumbled an spat flames. The church burning, a planet of flame, lightin up the whole city. We get into a cab an I give the driver me address an he pulls out into the busy traffic, crawlin along in the tight line of cars all slowin down as thee pass Chinatown to gawp at the gates an the dragon an the people an the fireworks. Victor's leg is jumpin, jittery. I turn away from him to look out the window at thee Anglican cathedral as we pass it, the fuckin sheer *size* of it somethin I can never get used to an the way it swells unstoppable from the ground towards the sky so bleedin immense. Why is it there? Why in the name of fuck is it there? From its top, you'd see the planet's curve; from the top of it, you'd see the ball we're living on.

Growling in me throat. Grindin me teeth together. I hear Victor whisper my name an I can't look at him cos if I did I'd tear his fuckin face away with me teeth so I just nod. Just stare straight ahead at the back of the cabbie's shaven head an nod.

—Please don't cut me again, a small voice says. —Please don't use a knife on me again.

I shake me head.

—Don't . . . please don't put yer arm inside me. I wouldn't be able to stand that again.

I can't look at him. Little Victor, the presence I can feel like an electric fire all down my left side. Grab an clasp an gnash an gnaw.

—I won't, is all I can say.

As he takes his top off I catch a glimpse of the words. Dark in the moonlight but still my cunt burns at the way thee look; raised, the flesh proud, scabbed an raw an full of pus.

I did that. That's *my* mark.

Put the scarf around his face. Tie it tight, *blind* him.

The whiteness of his chest. Risin an fallin like a sea about to storm. An jumping as I touch it, lay me hand flat on it an smooth the skin down over the flat belly, the flat belly supine under me, spread out, laid out, I can do fuckin anything.

Sounds comin out from beneath the tied scarf, the blindfold. Whimpering. Whining.

—Are yer crying?

Thee answer sounds like 'no'. I ask again:

—Are yis crying?

Me hand moves down. Folds itself around some bulging blood-stuffed thing an begins to squeeze.

—*Nnnnnnnn* . . . no.

The voice breaking. Me fingers becomin iron.

—I'll *make* yer cry.

—*Nnnnnnnn* . . .

Fuckin *iron*.

—I want to *see* you cry.

326

Iron sharpened into points.

—*NNNN* . . .

The voice breaks. Shatters like glass.

—There. Yer cryin *now*, aren't yer?

Scarf around his face I cannot see his eyes. Sirens outside, some distant explosions. Victor's body goes rigid an then suddenly deflates, relaxes an will not flinch or twitch no matter now much me clawed fingers pull an punch an stab cos the fucker's passed out. He's left here. Me on me own.

I stand an look down at him, blinded an bound spreadeagled to me bed. How pale an delicate, despite the corded muscles cabled just underneath his skin. His nipples hard an erect in the cold, so pinchable, so fuckin twistable, so attackable with teeth. An his dick an balls the same, the dick softenin now, retreatin back into the small pubic thicket. The things I could do now. All the things I could do to feel the soaring in me head an the bursting in me heart. Things that would change me whole life from now on, things I'd never forget.

Just tighten the knots. Make sure he can't move, can't get away unless I let him. Keep him here for ever, until I'm old an grey an about to die.

I leave him, go into the front room an stand by the window, look out at the partyin city. People in the street below, determined to be happy. There is a shiftin, kaleidoscopic thing inside me now black now white now flat now with depth an what the fuck is it? Why is it inside me an where did it come from? Why do I *like* Victor tied to me bed an the power thrummin all over me skin? All the muscles coiled like cobras. Why this roaring in me ears?

Questions. Worthless fuckin questions, stupid an futile in thee asking because thee answers are not here an if thee were then there'd be no need for the questions because without bein aware of it I'd know. They'd be *in* me. They'd be the colour of me eyes.

A helicopter clatters over an I watch it pass, just two red lights an a noise in the night sky. A searchlight clicks on, sweeps the streets below for a few seconds an then snaps off. A firework bursts, a vast splash of lime green sparks an the chopper appears to fly through it. Fuckin view that would be. What an experience that would be.

Everything in the city. All the lights an sounds an movement.

I go back into the bedroom, sit on thee edge of the bed an take the drugs out of me pocket. Open the wrap, lick me finger an dab it into the powder, then force that finger into the mouth of the tied figure on me bed, the white flat figure that jerks awake as soon as me finger parts the lips, jerks an flexes, tenses. A large amount of the powerful drug on me fingertip an I force it into that mouth, rub it over the gums, under the flappin tongue, coat all the smooth shiny slimy surfaces with this granular powder. In every wet crevice. Withdraw me finger an the mouth starts to gasp an gurgle so I take a bandanna off the floor, lift the head gently an thread the scarf under then tie it tight across the mouth which can gasp an gurgle no more. The whole white body begins to thrash. Buck an twist an writhe against the bonds, convulse like a landed fish an as it does I tip some of the powder out on to the back of me hand an snort it then leave that thrashin figure, out of the room I go, out of the flat an slam the door, down the dark stairwell an out into the street.

Drained, almost. Feel nothin but a need to walk. Skin so tight it threatens to split. An I must be saturated, unable to physically absorb any more cos thee only discernible effect of that last bugle is a small added resilience in me legs, a wee rechargin of the motor. All's I really wanner do is sleep, curl up next to captive Victor an suck his warmth into me an sleep for fuckin ages but me legs, like pistons, fuelled an strong, take me down on to Hardman Street, into the crush. Brightly coloured Ben Sherman shirts an bare, blotchy legs all goosebumped with the cold. No one looks at me as I walk through them, no one acknowledges me preoccupied as thee are with shouting or scrappin or neckin or bein sick or pissin in doorways. It's a heave, a mass, a giant squash of people, all the way down to St Luke's where the steps are stuffed with people in tiers as if at an auditorium or something an beyond them, at thee end of the road, the Chinatown celebrations still goin strong an over it all, over everythin the immense fuckin spire of the cathedral, so fuckin huge that it makes me realise how unimaginably immense thee entire fuckin planet is; like, it's so massive that that colossal red edifice is less than a pinprick on its surface. It makes me, too, feel huge. Giant an booming, stridin through these people like a member of some bigger an better race, one capable of buildin these cathedrals like humans would play with Lego. Just one block on top of thee other. Build it up like that.

My God. My fuckin … how much fuckin longing can we hold? How much more can we *stand*, without fuckin exploding into little bits? Look around an it seems that we must surely burst. Stuffed so fuckin full we'll shatter, any day now, skywards.

Victor on me bed. Unable to move, tied to me bed. A groan escapes me lips an some pissed-up scally stares, stands swaying an starin at me but I deadhead him an keep on walkin down Bold Street.

More drunken crush. Boomin kickdrums from the clubs. A bouncer like a fridge-freezer in a black suit holds some kickin figure by the scruff off the floor, his Vans kickin an pedallin a good foot or so above the cobbles. People walkin on cars, open-topped cars cruisin slowly, blastin out drum n bass an all this stuff goin on around me an I see none of it, me eyes locked straight ahead, just walkin through the city down towards the sea an it's probly not safe, a woman on her own walkin through the city at this time of night but there's a power in me legs an a man tied to me bed unable to move or anythin an I am fuckin invincible. *Nothing* can touch me, no one. Each fall of me feet resonates through the planet, knocks cups off shelves in Australia.

I pass the shop where I bought me new coat, this ace new coat I'm wearin now. A bakery a few doors down from it, the smell of bread in thee air, a smell I'll friggin live among soon. Workin behind a counter, workin in a shop, work's the fuckin same the whole world over an for what? So we can stand in front of these brightly lit window displays an know ther within ar reach. So we can waste ar lives for money to waste in turn on all this fuckin stuff, all these lights an all these clothes, labels, gadgets, all these fuckin things, everythin here orbiting money, all about tryin to make pretty thee ugliness of ar lives an the lengths we'll go to to make arselves feel just a tiny bit better about arselves, we humiliate arselves in order to feel less fuckin humiliated an in doin so we push everythin of meaning to one side. We wanner stumble blindly an unthinkinly through ar days, strip them of authenticity an light an any real joy an it makes no fuckin sense, no fuckin sense. So fuckin terrified are we of death that we make arselves so ignoble an base an petty an vile an meaningless an shallow that when death finally comes for us, there's precious fuckin little for it to take. An in that way we think we've beaten it. But we haven't, an we don't; because we do nothing of worth, live in no fuckin glories whatsoever an when we're gone it's like we were never bleedin here. We've made no mark in the concrete to prove that we passed this way, that we existed. So we don't defeat death, an we never could; we defeat life. Turn it all colourless an tasteless, bland an insipid an bled dry. We settle for mediocrity an we're perfectly fuckin happy to do so, we can't even imagine anythin else, anythin more. Actions without consequence. Let others tell us what to do, do away with the enormity of thinkin for arselves. Offer ar lives gladly to faceless fuckin shadows an let them do with them whatever the fuck thee want to. Forced to conform, to give in. Follow ar own destinies, do what we really fuckin feel the need to do an we'll live moneyless an in misery. We're rewarded if we buckle. Told we're good if we give in.

Can smell the sea now, the river. Salt in me nostrils.

Why the fuck aren't we screaming? Standin with ar arms outstretched on the rooves of tall buildings, explosives strapped to ar chests? Tryin to do somethin, *anything*, to arrest the withering of ar hearts? The bleaching. The shrivellin. Dulled an stupefied by what's around us because we can't see anything of menace; I mean, just fuckin look at it – everythin's lit up, an everythin's for sale. It's all so very fuckin welcoming.

Victor's body, all laid out an exposed. The things I will do to it when I get back home. Sunlight on me skin.

The Pier Head ahead of me. Thee expensive dockland flats, warehouse conversions built by thee Irish an still, now, maintained by them; only where thee used to come with picks an shovels thee now come with offshore bank accounts an bulgin investment portfolios. Waterfront property is still an investment opportunity just as it was then. The way things come around, back on themselves. As if there might *be* some order. Some pattern. As if dispensation, no, just mere fuckin acknowledgement, is passed down in the blood an sooner or later will be recognised an rewarded. Through the rise an fall of economies, whole fuckin countries, deeds are remembered an pardons are conferred. Except my grandad helped build these warehouses an died with no legs after a railcart ran over him an his descendants have done nowt but struggle all ther lives, even the short lives like me dad's. So fuck that little theory.

Fuckin bullshit. Load of bollox. Pure fuckin garbage, Kelly. Yer tryin to distract yerself from what's happening; that you are, now, here, a torturer. Yer abusin yer power.

Except Victor is no victim. See how fuckin *hard* he was. Panting. So excited. He wants it, *needs* it, as much as fuckin *I* do, the feelin, the sensation. Anythin but this moronic fuckin driftin through alleyways that lead nowhere. This fuckin timid capitulation, this fuckin accepted puppetry anythin but this, fuckin *anythin* but this.

Victor, my Victor. My lovely fuckin Victor. The beauty of you all tied up in me flat. Smile so lovely, skin so smooth an clear. Except for that on yer back, with the carvings an everythin. The words, like. Except for them.

God fuckin help me. Someone show me what to do.

I sit on a bench an spark up a ciggie, watchin the lights ripple on the water all dark like oil. A wind moves across the waters an ripples them, sets the lights squirming, a breeze almost like a breath. A whisper, a voice. All thee empty containment docks an there was a time when thee were chocka with ships, relentless activity. Loadin an unloadin. Cranes swingin an hundreds, thousands of scurryin men. So much commerce, so much success. Yeh, an so many fuckin slaves dyin to feed that growth. All the streets around here, the docks themselves are named after slavers, monsters of greed, inhuman bastards who would exploit anything if it meant more money for them an thee already had enough for them an ther descendants to live in luxury. An we remember them. More; we fuckin well *honour* them. Thee were demons, a fuckin disgrace to humanity an we christen parts of ar cities in ther names, honour them, fuckin *revere* them. An all because thee made fuckloads of money. That's all; it don't matter *how* thee made it, the massacre an torment, just as long as thee fuckin *did*. An thee certainly friggin *did*. An that's why we're supposed to love them, ther names in ar lives for always.

God fuckin help me. Someone show me what to do.

Victor.

Victor alone an unable to move. Victor alone; what have I done to him? What *will* I do to him?

—Got a spare ciggie, love?

A shape in front of me, part illuminated by a street light; beard, woolly hat, filthy sleepin bag in a roll under his arm. I take two out of me packet an hand them to him.

—Ta. Got a light?

I strike a match an he leans into the flame. He lights his fag an looks at me face an I shake the flame out.

—Ey, what's up? What's wrong? What're yer cryin for?

I shake me head. —I'm not cryin.

—Well, yer don't look too bloody happy if yer don't mind me sayin. What's happened? Someone upset yer, have thee?

He's invadin me space. I don't know him. I don't like this. Didn't fuckin ask for it an it's bein imposed on me.

—Go away, I say. —Yer've got yer fags now friggin do one.

—I'm only tryin to help, love. Hate to see people upset, I do.

—Aye, well, I'm not fuckin upset, alright? But I might be if you don't get out of me face an leave me the fuck alone.

He pulls on his cigarette; thee orange tip burns fiercer for a second or two.

—Alright, well. But look out for yerself, won't yis? There's some fuckin bad men around this time of night.

—Don't need yer advice.

—Well, yer've got it anyway. Keep yerself safe. An ta very much for the ciggies.

He wanders off, up towards James Street. In search of some little cooey to kip in, some piss-soaked dank little hole. Poor sod. I shouldn't've snapped at him like that. Seemed decent enough. Only tryin to help.

Guidance. I need some fuckin guidance. Someone to walk me through this world an never fuckin leave me alone.

I smoke the fag down to the filter then flick it away. It arcs into the dark water an dies an I walk away, down the Dock Road. I'll do a circuit; up through Chinatown, see the last throes of the party, up through thee edge of Tocky an home. Home to Victor. But as I pass a pub I hear one of me favourite songs, 'Macushla', bein sung inside an I can see faint light through the cracks in the curtains an I remember then that me dad used to drink in this pub, used to spend two or three nights a week in here an me gob's like sandpaper due to the drugs an thee approachin comedown/hangover so I go to the side door an knock on it three times. No answer so I knock three times again. It opens a crack an a pale face peers out.

—We're shut, sod off.

Thee eyes focus on me face.

—Do I know you?

—Yer used to know me dad. He drank in here all the time.

Recognition hits him. —Oh bloody hell, yeh. You're erm, you're . . . don't tell me, I'll gerrit in a minute . . .

I'm friggin chokin for a bevvy. —Kelly.

He smiles an opens the door wide. —That's right. Kelly. Haven't seen yis for ages, not since yer ahl feller died. Lovely bloke, your ahl man. Best hardwood chippy in Merseyside, an I mean that. Did me whole bar out, gantry an everythin. Come in an have a look.

I go in. Faint light in two corners, quiet groups of people at various tables, smoke hangin in grey sheets. An old man in the shadows somewhere strummin a banjo an singing:

Macushla, Macushla
Your sweet voice is calling
My blue-eyed Macushla
I may come and stay . . .

Me dad used to sing that song to me when I was little. Sat
me on his knee an sang it, thee entire thing. So sad. Such a
heartbreakin fuckin song.

—What can I get yer?

There's a lump in me throat an I have to swallow it down
before I can speak. —Pint of lager.

He pours it, hands it over to me an waves away me hand
with the coins in it.

—Put yer money away, girl. It's no good here.

—Yer sure?

—Don't be soft.

I put the money back in me purse an sip me pint. Then gulp
at it, half of it in one go cos me gob's *so* dry. The barman's
watchin me.

—See yer've inherited yer ahl man's thirst.

—Tonight I have, yeh. Bloody throat on me tonight,
tellin yis.

I gulp more. He frowns.

—Yis on yer own tonight?

—Yeh. Was with a load of mates before, like, but thee've
all gone home. Fancied another pint like, so . . .

I shrug. Oh yeh, an there's a man back at me flat, tied to
the bed. Probly gone mad by now. Screamin against his gag,
pullin at his ties. He's naked, as well. He's the best bloke I've
ever met, best shag I've ever had an he's tied to me bed right
now with no clothes on an only I can let him go. I'm burning
down below.

—Yer shouldn't be out on yer own, y'know. Not at *this*
time, like. Town's full of bleedin arseholes at this time of night.
Young girl on yer own.

—I'm alright. Can look after meself.

—Yeh, yer *say* that but . . . well, only this mornin thee
fished another body out the dock. Young girl like yerself.

334

Local girl like, probly thought she was safe, knew the city an all that. Can happen to anyone. Place's full of arseholes. Yer dad wouldn't be best pleased if he knew you were out on yer own at this time of night.

Yeh but he's dead, inny? Cold in his grave. Can't say that, tho.

—Same again?

He points to me nearly empty glass an I nod. Drugs've almost worn off now an the booze is beginnin to kick in an I can feel meself startin to sway on the stool. The man has stopped singin 'Macushla' an is now singin 'Raglan Road'. It's nice. Lovely. Soft voice in the dimly lit, murmuring pub.

The barman puts me drink down in front of me an goes off to serve someone else. Staring at the top of the bar I am, the smooth wood me dad sawed an planed an sanded an varnished an nailed into place. Me dad's hands touched this very wood I'm leanin me elbows on. Touched an made it an now it's proppin me up, drunk, hard drugs leavin me system an a man tied naked to me bed back home. How do such things happen. How do thee all come about.

—Alright.

A voice in me ear, a slurred voice. I turn me head sideways to look an oh shite it's Darren fuckin Taylor. Darren fuckin Taylor, his short tight curly hair an his square jaw. An behind him some shaven-headed shellsuited scally staring down at his feet, his crappy trainies an his shellsuit kex tucked into the white sports socks.

Last time I saw him ... goin into the toilets in Magnet after Victor ... this memory almost produces a pang of associative affection for the balloon-headed nutter but then he leers an says:

—You used to go out with Peter, didn't yis?

I shake me head. Want him to fuck off now.

—Yeh, yer did. Peter. Don't know the cunt's second name, like. Deals beak.

I nod. —Yeh.

Darren turns to his mate: —Told yer, Ally, didn't I? *Told* yer it was her, lar.

Thee Ally feller looks at me an smiles. Ugly bastard with a baghead's pallor but at least he smiles.

—Oh yeh, Darren goes on. —Told me *all* about you, Peter did.

His grin's as cold as his eyes; *ice* fuckin cold. Grin like a shark closin in for the kill.

—*Aaaaaalllllll* about you, he repeats, draggin the first word out an lickin his lips obscenely with his fat red shiny tongue. The fuckin kite on him; the fuckin *leer* on him. Aggression, harm comin off him in thick waves. Why do men hate themselves so?

—Yeh, well, Peter's *well* fuckin dumped, I say. An this is Darren Taylor but I'm drunk an sittin at a bar me dad made an Victor's tied up back at me flat so I can't help meself; I know it's dangerous but the words just pour out. —An I'm glad the fuckwit told yis all about me cos now yer've got somethin to wank about, haven't yer? Pullin yer little dobber ten times a day. Rub it fuckin raw, you do, don't yer? Wear it away to a tiny little stump, like. Not that there was much there to friggin begin with.

Ally pulls a face an starts to examine his fingernails. Darren just laughs an laps at his drink, whisky it looks like.

—Oh, you just carry on, girl. Go ed, gerrit off yer chest.

I just stare at him. At his pointed yellow teeth an his bloodshot eyes. At his fat fingers around his glass an his sovereign rings glinting.

—Cos, yer know, one dark night soon? Maybe next week, maybe next year? *You're* gunner get taught a lesson. Taught some fuckin respect, like. You *and* that skinny little no-mark yer shaggin now. All over the weedy little cunt in the Brewery you were, couple of weeks ago. Fuckin slut. Yer can't expect to diss a big fuckin beak dealer without some everafters, can yer? Gorrer have *some* kind of a sorter, like. Even a no-mark little slapper like you knows that.

This shite doesn't bother me. I'm really not friggin bothered. This thick fuckin bully an his gangster talk. Someone so devoid of a sense of humour or imagination can never be truly threatenin. It just makes me fuckin laugh.

336

—Oh aye, go on well, have a laugh. Yeh, it's all dead fuckin funny to you, innit. Fuckin laugh while yer can, slag, cos soon –

—oi!

The nice barman's leanin over the bar, the pump handles in his belly, his finger right in Taylor's face.

—No one talks to women like that in my friggin bar. Specially not no-mark scally twats like youse. See her dad? He would've made ten of youse. *She* makes ten of youse. Get some respect, yer fuckin little toerag. If I call Joey up now an tell him what I've just heard yis say, how fuckin chuffed d'yer think he'd be? Now fuck off.

Darren an Ally visibly flinch at the name 'Joey'. Darren bunches his fists but Ally puts his arms around him an shuffles him off towards the door. It's like ther dancing. Some ridiculous attempt at a waltz.

—Come ed, Daz . . . leave it eh . . .

—I'll break his fuckin nose!

—Come ed now . . . not worth it, lar, it's not fuckin worth it . . .

The barman points at Ally but stares at Darren. —Do yerself a favour an listen to yer mate there. He's obviously got a bit more fuckin sense than you. An do us *all* a favour, will yer, an fuckin do one. Gerrout. Fuck off somewhere else.

—I'll be fuckin back, you! I'll be fuckin back here!

—Yeh yeh.

—Back to fuckin torch this fuckin dump!

—Yeh yeh.

—An *you*! Darren points a sausage finger at me. —You're fuckin claimed, you, bitch! You're gettin fuckin wellied an all!

—Right!

The barman takes a pickaxe handle from somewhere an vaults the bar. Two huge fellers, one an old bloke with silver hair who looks like Big Daddy, pick up stools an stride towards Darren, who is now bein pulled through thee open door by his mate, still bellowin threats. I'm enjoyin all this. It's like watchin a film. Especially when the banjo player with a big toothless grin starts playin some fast-climbin hillbilly rhythm like in a cowboy film or somethin. It's dead friggin funny.

—I'll be fuckin back! Gerrer fuckin shooter an sort this fuckin place! Tellin youse! Yer all marked! Yer fuckin –

The door slams an cuts him off. People clap an cheer as if it was all staged for ther enjoyment an the blokes retake ther seats.

—Gorrer have a word with Joey about that cunt, Big Daddy says to the barman. —Lad's a fuckin liability. Bar the cunt.

—I know, Shirl, yeh. I will.

—Aye, well, make sure yer do. It's about time.

—I'll sort it, don't worry.

—Should've been done years ago.

—I said I'll get it sorted.

The barman smiles at me an rolls his eyes back in mock-exasperation. Climbs back over the bar. —Sorry about that, love.

—Yer alright. Not *your* fault. Didn't bother me anyway, to be honest.

I'm slurring. Me tongue's fallin over itself.

—Well, maybe it should. He's a bad lad, that Taylor one. Capable of anything.

I shrug. —Wharrabout *you*? Aren't *you* worried?

—About what?

—Him, Taylor. Tommy Maguire as well.

He makes a face an shakes his head. —Nah. Tommy's nowt. He's just a big friggin bully with a perm. Joey's the man with the clout, like, thee eldest brother. Tommy's shiters of Joey. An me an Joey go way back like, we went to school together an I know for a fact that he doesn't want *that*. He heads an invisible ball towards the door. —Fuckin associated with him. Bad for business, like. Knobhead like that's a bleedin liability. An don't *you* worry either. I'll have a word with Joey. But be careful who yer get lippy with.

I raise the glass to me mouth an lager spills over the side. Gettin really friggin drunk now. Victor. I know where Victor is.

—You should get off home, love. Get some kip, like.

—Nah. I'm alright.

—No yer not. Yer rat-arsed. An I can't let yis walk home on yer own with gobshites like *that* on the loose. Thee invisible ball gets headed again. —I'll get Shirley to run yer.

—Shirley?

—After Shirley Crabtree. Yer know, Big Daddy, the wrestler? Remember him? Before your time. But he's the fuckin spit. SHIRLEY!

The massive silver head swings up. —Hello!

—You fit to run the girl here home?

—Over the limit.

—It's not far. Where is it yer live, Kelly?

Where the fuck *do* I live? —Bedford Street South.

—Bedford Street South. Go on, lad, it's only up the friggin road.

Shirley sighs. —Aye, alright. Compo off *you* if I lose me friggin licence, tho.

—Yer a twenty-four-hour taxi service, lad. Yer shouldn't even *be* over the limit.

—Shouldn't give me doubles when I ask for singles, then, should yer?

He stands an starts puttin his coat on. I'm seein two of him an each one's massive. The barman looks intently at me.

—An you look after yerself, alright? Keep yerself safe. D'yer hear me now?

I nod.

—He was one of the soundest blokes I've ever met, your dad. Do him proud.

—I'll try, yeh.

—Tell yer mother I was askin after her. An your Adam.

Adam? At first I think he's talkin about that bloke who Victoria fisted an I look at him all puzzled. But then I remember; Adam's me brother's name. Two Adams; only just realised. But unimportant anyway.

—Alright.

Then I'm outside in the car park with Shirley an it's freezin fuckin cold an me teeth're chatterin. The door's held open for me an I stagger an stumble against it, bang me hip. A huge hand gently holds me shoulder. I feel tiny, fragile in its grip.

—Watch yerself, love. Steady there now.

I'm in the car an we're drivin through lights. Swimmin, swirlin lights. The sky is brightening an delivery trucks are parked outside shops. Shirley's tellin me something, I don't know what it is I can only register the resonance of his deep voice an we turn up Catherine Street an stop at traffic lights outside a church. A church I think I recognise cos I think it might be the one I was confirmed in altho I can never be sure, never certain, like, not with all the years an the stuff inside those years. I open the door.

—I'll gerrout here.

—No, I'll drop yis at yer door. It's alright, honest. No bother, like.

—No, it's not far now . . . I'll walk . . .

I'm stumblin over the road. A post van is honkin at me an I stick me tongue out at it. I'm inside the gloomy church, dead dark it is, only candles providin the light, some flickerin yellow points in the murk. I'm sittin in a pew an tippin powder out on to the back of me hand an spillin some of it on the floor an then I'm pressin me face to that powder, snortin an suckin at the back of me hand an almost instantaneously feelin the clouds part in me head, things clarifyin, sharpenin, the swamps of booze cut through so quick. I can hear sounds again. An I can see meself at the front of the church, seven years old in me pink frilly dress an shiny buckled shoes that me mam an dad saved up months for, starvin themselves, an all the people watchin smilin an the priest askin me if I renounced Satan an all his works an me in me small voice sayin that I did.

An I always fuckin *have* done. Always friggin *will* do. I've turned me back an sought out angels. An how fuckin hard it's been to do that, how incredibly, shatteringly, soul-wreckingly hard . . .

Victor. Oh Victor. Victor Victor Victorvictorvictorvictor-victorvictorvictorvictorrrrr . . .

A shape shifts in a pew in the gloom at the front of the church. Thought I was alone in here. The shape shifts again an I squint an see it, a slouched figure with its head in its hands. Man or woman I can't tell, it's just a slumped, defeated human figure, a shadow an as I watch its bent back rises an falls an it sighs. Just that; a deep sigh, a breath, a bone-deep body-rocking sigh in the darkness an thee eyes of Christ an Mary acknowledgin nowt, seein nothin, that one breath droppin down at ther statue feet. Surely thee'd move. Bleed or something. Shatter. But nothin. Just that one breath.

I leave. Steadier on me feet now an with an added power in me legs an a deeper boom in me chest I go home. Open the house door, go inside, close it behind me. Climb the stairs. Open me flat door, go inside. Close the door behind me. Go into the bedroom an can't see anythin, it's pitch friggin black so I turn the light on an the pale an naked stretched shape on me bed instantly begins to buck an thrash, a wild animal caught in a trap, the soft dick flappin back smackin against the taut belly which looks wet probly with pee an thee ankles an wrists rubbed raw, the skin all scraped away, blood pooled in the clawed palms. Me head is banging. Me heart is banging. I am not in myself I am outside somewhere soaring just beneath the ceiling round the lampshade observin all this strangeness goin on below.

An uncontrollable force inside.

I stand above him an place a hand gently on the thrashin chest an instantly he is calm, still. Just lyin there an breathing.

—Ssshhh . . . be still, Victor . . .

Oh the fuckin burning inside me. Swollen an bulging, this fuckin world cannot contain me.

—You'll never leave me again, Victor. Will yeh?

He shakes his head. Only his nose-tip an chin visible between the blindfold an the gag.

—No. I *know* yer won't.

Me hand leaves his chest an clasps his dick. Immediately he grows, expands. Becomin hotter as he hardens. Me throat makes words:

—The state yer in, Victor. Poor fuckin boy. Reduced to this . . . oh fuck what have I done . . .

Me hand begins to pump. Behind his gag he groans.

—I'm sorry, I'm so fuckin sorry . . . let me put yer back together again . . .

Want to suck that thing in me hand. Feel it grow inside me mouth, bulge against me tongue an tonsils, feel the hot blood an body inside me head. When he's completely hard I spit him out an reach up under me skirt an remove me panties an swing me left leg over to straddle him an then sink back on to him, guiding his hot hard dick inside. It fills me. Stuffs me. Banishes all emptiness. Thrusting. Friction.

Trance.

Me hands are around his throat. Ther up his body an around his throat an squeezin hard, *hard*. I can feel him gulpin against me palms, feel the tension of the squeezing in me shoulders, hear thee enraptured noises he's makin behind his gag an *see* the light explodin in his head, his oxygen-starved brain graspin desperately for air. Want to bring him bliss. Deliver him into a never-endin happiness. Feel him leap an burst inside me my hands clutch ever tighter an I thrust as fast as me hip joints will allow, feel somethin give an crunch in me grasp see his fingers stretched above shuddering, rigid an the blood cupped in his palms his face bulging against the wrapped cloth changing colour quickly, from white to pink to purple now dark purple his veins roped an knotted his chest ballooning to touch mine. I am gasping an panting in his ear my hands squeezin ever fuckin tighter until thee are joined at thumbtip an fingertip that neck constricted to the width of me forearm I cannot stop meself I am thrustin madly, clutchin an crushing, I feel him bulge an bloom an burst inside me hot seed cannoning through me insides tearin through membrane to settle seething in my bangin heart an as I dissolve, as I fold I hear the rattle inside his chest an I open me mouth an clamp it to the gag an taste the very last issue from his lungs. It tastes of nothin but oranges. Oranges now for ever inside me, endowed with this unique significance so sweet, so full an I rip the gag down under his chin an bare his face now nearly black an clamp me mouth to his, suckin hard, his blue protruding tongue pressin up against me teeth an I suck an suck, hard, suck all the breath out of his body an everythin that makes him an that he is, all

that he could be sucked inside to fuel me tired muscles an he
is still hard inside me his cooling come running out of me
around him an FLASH
   he is
   in red an white light
   on the stone steps in the rain
   standing at a bar
   rippled in green aquarium light
   bent between my legs his back runnin with water
   smilin through steam
   reachin for me through that steam, his hand outstretched an
reaching, reaching
   Victor Victor
   tied naked to my bed
   bleeding
   cut
   your face falling in ecstasy
   Victor
My legs suddenly give an I roll off him panting. Feel his
heartbeat through the mattress, slowing, slowing, slowing . . .
goin so fuckin slow . . . getting softer, slowing slowing. Stopped.
Such a powerful heart, to rock the mattress so. So determined
to keep the blood beating.
   When I'm able to I climb off the bed an fetch the knife
from the kitchen, the one I made my marks with, an return
to the bedroom an cut Victor's ties. Turn him gently on to
his side, push his knees up towards his chest an wrap his arms
around his knees, the position he slept in, I remember him
sleeping in. Remove his blindfold. His eyelids darkened an
closed I cannot see his eyes I do not want to see his eyes, I
am glad I cannot see his eyes, those eyes so green. I sit at his
side, cross-legged on the bed an press the knife blade to my
wrist, my left inside wrist an the big blue throbby vein there
an I sit like that for a while then I throw the knife clattering
into a corner among some small change, some coppers, don't
know how thee got there. Don't remember droppin them. Sit
like that cross-legged on the bed, Victor's bum goin cold against
me thigh an me head in me hands until it is fully light outside,

343

birds singing in the gutter above the window an I stand an turn the light off but do not open the curtains an take me new coat off an lay it over Victor, still Victor, to make him decent an presentable for the world an pull the bedclothes over him right up to his chin so just his calm head protrudes, the hair flat to his skull at the back so I ruffle it, mess it up, make it spiky an nice like it used to be under the lights, the red an white lights. Then I take all me clothes off to make meself more like him an clamber into the bed with him, under the covers an pressed against him, tryin to draw into meself the warmth that's rapidly leavin him cos I'm so cold, it's so cold, it's really so horribly fuckin cold.

ACKNOWLEDGEMENTS

Cheers to: Jasper Gibson, for a certain story, and Clive Rees, for certain others; Mark Strong and Heidi Kivekäs for silli, liquorice vodka and a stain that won't wash out; Cian, Eve and Elysia for being born; and to Gérard Houllier. Good on the Frenchman.

Ta.